THE PRESIDENT'S GOLD

DON KESTERSON

ISBN: 0998470708
ISBN 13: 9780998470702
Library of Congress Control Number: 2016920905
Amber Publishers Company, Parkersburg, WEST VIRGINIA

CHAPTER 1

Saturday, July 10, 1943
Montalban Gorge, the Philippines

Danilo Quezon checked his watch. One-forty-five. He locked his office door, then pulled the gray cord to close the heavy venetian blinds. He walked to the drafting desk and folded back blueprints that had been on the drawing board since before the Japanese Invasion. From under those blueprints, he removed maps. Adrenalin surged through his veins. This was the largest tunnel of gold yet, and he'd just finished drawing the map to it this morning. Thankfully, he would meet Father Diaz in just over an hour and pass it along. Having the maps—or any evidence—in his possession made him nervous.

Danilo folded the map, pressing the creases neatly. He placed it in a small manila envelope, shoved that in his shirt pocket, and then put on his suit jacket.

Just as he was about to open the door, a knock sounded. His heart beat pounded in his temple. He glanced at the map to be sure it was secure and out of sight. It was.

Tentatively, he opened the door.

"Danny!" Mary Catherine threw her arms around him.

He playfully released a large gasp as though she had knocked the air out of him. In reality, her unplanned arrival had.

"You're not forgetting anything, are you?" she asked, her voice husky.

Danilo pulled free and picked up three-year-old Frankie. "My Franco? I'd never forget my Franco." He twirled in a circle, bouncing the grinning boy. He looked at his wife. "Whatever could I have forgotten?"

Mary Catherine folded her arms and leaned back, a pout decorating her rosy lips. "You'd better be joking."

Danilo put Frankie on the floor. He turned to the cabinet behind his desk, twisted the lock, and opened it. A long-stemmed rose waited, a velvet ribbon flowing around the slender vase. Under it, a small box wrapped in gold foil and a red satin bow waited. He stood back so she could see the gifts, but pretended as though he didn't notice them. "Forget something? Hmmm." He turned back to her, a smile playing on his lips. "What could I have forgotten? Is it your birthday?"

Mary Catherine smacked him. "You! You know it's our anniversary!"

Danilo laughed and hugged his wife again. "I'd never forget. You know that." He kissed her pouting lips, then her cheek. His lips headed for her ear.

"No." She giggled. "Not here."

Danilo caught the wall clock. One-fifty-eight. "Hey, sweetie. Take Franco home, and I'll be there by five. How's that? Then we can have dinner by candlelight—and you can unwrap that little package." He locked the cabinet and exaggeratedly put the key in his pants pocket.

"Why can't you come home?"

"I have a meeting. I need to leave now."

"Where is it?"

"At a construction site. It won't take long. I promise." He kissed her forehead.

"Where's the site?"

"In the mountains. Look, I need to get going." He ruffled the small boy's raven hair. "Take Franco on home."

"Let us go with you."

Danilo laughed. "No. You don't want to go to one of my boring meetings."

"You said it wouldn't take long. It's a gorgeous day. I'd love to take a drive in the mountains." Mary Cat ran her hands through her wavy auburn hair, allowing the incandescent bulb to highlight the gold in it. "It is, after all, our anniversary. Don't you want to spend it with me?"

"Please, Papa?" Frankie's big blue eyes glistened.

Danilo laughed. How could he say no? Many times his "meetings" were dangerous, but the one today should be easy enough. There was no activity in the area; he just needed to make a drop of the map—no actual meeting. Five minutes, tops.

"Danny?" Mary Catherine's sultry eyes melted his resistance.

"Okay. But you and Franco must stay in the car while I have my meeting. Okay?" He glanced again at the clock. "We must go now."

Danilo led his family to the Ford Tudor Sedan. He opened the passenger door for Mary Catherine, helped her in, then closed the door after her.

"Me, Papa, me!" Frankie jumped up and down by the back door.

"Ladies first." Danilo opened the back door. "Gentlemen let ladies go first."

Frankie crawled into the sprawling backseat.

Danilo closed the door. As he did, a military vehicle filled with Japanese soldiers drove slowly by, watching.

An icy chill slithered down Danilo's spine. He dared not allow them to see his hesitation, so he met their gaze. They drove on.

He ran around the car to the driver's side. He jumped in, checked the mirrors, and turned over the motor. "Put on your scarf."

"Oh, Danilo, it's such a beautiful day—"

He turned to face his wife. "You know I love that flaming hair of yours. But you make us stand out. Franco looks like me—looks Filipino—but you don't."

"But—"

"We're in a war. Let's not draw attention to ourselves."

"You worry too much," Mary Catherine said, although she wrapped the colorful scarf around her hair. "What do we have to hide?"

If she only knew. But he did need to relax. His nervousness alone would make him appear suspicious. He started the Ford Tudor—something else

Mary Catherine had insisted on but that worried him, as few of his fellow countrymen drove at all, and the fancy American car caught everyone's attention. But at least having the family with him was a good foil. No one would think he was doing anything "unusual" with his wife and son in the car. This may be a good day after all.

And it was a beautiful drive. The cerulean sky was cloudless; the looming mountains inviting. They passed a few more Japanese patrols, but received little more than a passing glance. Even though he'd made dozens of map deliveries, he always felt tense as he drove to the drop-off. Today, with Mary Catherine's soft southern drawl tickling his ears and Frankie's exuberance bouncing in the backseat, he couldn't help but relax.

But as they climbed higher up Montalban, Danilo's gut twisted. On one trip, there had been a roadblock and he'd had to show identification. With the map in his pocket, should they stop and search, he'd be a dead man. Maybe he shouldn't have given in so easily and allowed his precious family to come along.

"Isn't this the road to Wawa Dam?" Mary Catherine asked.

"Not exactly, but we're not far from it."

"Why don't we stop there on the way home?"

Danilo shook off his apprehension. "Maybe. We'll see."

Mary Catherine laughed. "We can't stop living just because there's a war."

Danilo spotted his turn-off, not much more than an overgrown path. He backed the car up the path, fronds of tropical plants slapping the windows.

"Roll up the windows," he said, stopping the car in a well-hidden area so as not to be spotted from the road.

"It's hot out."

"I won't be long. Just a few minutes."

"This is in the middle of the wilderness." Mary Catherine shivered. "Are there wild animals around here?"

"I'm sure there are. And spiders the size of your hand." Danilo put his hands together and wiggled his fingers. That was one sure way to get her to stay in the car and keep the windows up. "I won't be long. I just need to check on the construction site and drop off some blueprints. Now, don't leave the car. Promise?"

"What kind of building is going up here in the middle of the jungle? Why can't we come with you?"

"Mary Cat, come on, now. I have business to take care of. I'll just be a few minutes. Be a good girl and we'll take the scenic drive home." He leaned over, cradled her face in his hands, and planted a kiss on her nose.

"I go with you!" Frankie bounced on the seat.

"Be good. I'll be right back."

Danilo patted his pocket to be sure the envelope was still there. It was. He quietly opened the door, slid out, squeezed past the car, and made his way up the steep path and into the dense tropical foliage. Really, they needed to find a better place to meet.

He mechanically pushed aside ferns and branches, his mind preoccupied with Mary Catherine. She'd been homesick lately, and it was only a matter of time before she'd want to return to Georgia.

When he reached the clearing with the three boulders that brought to mind the crosses on Calvary, he turned full circle, scanning the brush and trees for anything suspicious. Satisfied, he pulled the envelope from beneath his shirt and slid it between the first two rocks. Mission accomplished.

The maps he created of gold burial sites were critically important to the United States, his adopted country. It was the only hope that the gold stolen from the Chinese and several European countries could ever be returned to the rightful owners. So, even though he hated the drama of hiding the maps, it was the only way he could get them to American intelligence officials.

The rhythmic, metallic thud of a pickaxe reached his ears. He'd been told there was no activity in this area—one of the reasons they used it for the drop-off point. He stepped a few paces deeper into the woods. Besides, who would be digging this far inland? He pushed through the thickening undergrowth toward the sound.

Danilo crept into an opening in the trees, stooping down onto a prominent vista overlooking a rocky gorge. Below him, trucks moved in and out of the canyon. Men dressed in little more than rags unloaded small crates. Despite the diminutive size of the boxes, two men carried each one. To the left, more men—some Caucasian, some Asian—labored under the watchful eyes of Japanese soldiers. Other prisoners, the curves of their ribcages and bony spines visible through ragged shirts, dragged boulders tied with ropes from the tunnel they'd created. A young man struggled to push a wheelbarrow loaded with rocks the size of his head.

Danilo had documented several gold burial sites but he had never witnessed the gruesomeness of the actual operation.

A glint of sunlight reflected off something metal, catching his attention. On a facing mountain vista, a Japanese sharpshooter aimed a rifle at the workers below. Danilo scanned the mountainside. More riflemen stood guard at other positions.

And there he stood, in the open. He ducked back into the brush, praying he had not been detected.

From behind the cover of the trees and bushes, he continued to watch. Near one of the trucks, a prisoner stumbled to his knees and dropped a crate, which broke open. A guard shouted angrily and cracked a whip across the man's back, leaving a red line on his thin shirt. The prisoner, his head down, shrugged. Another soldier reared back his rifle and slammed the butt into the prisoner's head. The man crumpled.

Splattered with blood, the soldier kicked the body out of the way. Then he stepped back, shouting orders.

More prisoners fell to their knees, scooping up what had tumbled from the broken crate. Gold.

Danilo's heart pounded against his ribs. This was a site they hadn't documented, that had somehow escaped their intelligence. Someone needed to know. Right away. He searched his pockets for a notepad, but all he had was the envelope containing the maps. It would have to do. He turned it over and jotted coordinates and landmarks, wincing as the Japanese soldier's whip cracked again and again.

So, what to do? He needed to make his drop. Quickly. Then he could return to his car for—

Danilo slapped his forehead. His family. Damn. He had to get them away from here. Tomorrow, he could return with a sketch pad and get enough documentation to create a map.

He turned and hurried back the way he'd come. As he neared the three boulders, a glint of sunlight flashed across the clearing. He stopped.

A twig snapped, then another, louder sound—the unmistakable click of a bullet being cocked into a rifle chamber—clattered immediately behind him.

⚔

Father Jose Antonio Diaz checked his watch as he moved among the palmetto scrubs on Montalban Gorge's rocky knoll, just above the drop site. Quezon had proved a trustworthy cartographer; he'd never failed a mission since Lansdale had made him a part of the Army intelligence in the Philippines. But why hadn't he seen him return down the path?

Beads of sweat formed on the priest's brow. Was it possible Quezon had slipped past him? He lifted his binoculars and looked toward the road. At first he couldn't locate the car, but finally, he saw the silvery blue car. Quezon hadn't left yet. So where was he?

Father Diaz scanned the trail between the car and the clearing. No Quezon. He aimed the binoculars back to the car. The door opened—the passenger door. Mary Catherine, Quezon's American wife, stepped out. She removed the scarf from her head and shook out her wild, red mane, allowing it to whip in the stiff breeze. She then pulled the boy through the open door.

"Oh, Mother Mary, full of grace." Diaz pulled the heavy gold necklace from inside his cassock and kissed the cross it bore. "Be quiet, boy," he whispered, knowing the child couldn't hear him, but hoping the prayer hushed him. "Please, please, stay silent." Surely Mary Catherine would get the child back into the car. What was Quezon thinking, bringing his family along?

Father Diaz scanned the bushes for any sign of his *Kaibigan*. He scanned the trees, squinting as he searched for movement. *Damn him.* This could not end well. The hills were crawling with Japanese soldiers.

He hiked up the steep grade to a better vantage point. The spy network could not be compromised at any cost; it was too important.

Then, to the side, a hundred feet from where Father Diaz hid—movement. Quezon emerged from the stand of rubber trees near the edge of the cliff.

Father Diaz breathed a sigh of relief. The man would intercept his son, grab his wife and get out of there. But as Quezon hustled around the tall sori ferns, a Japanese soldier emerged from the trees only a few yards behind him, his rifle trained on Quezon's head.

"*Aking Diyos*," Father Diaz whispered. "My God, help him."

To their left, just behind a stand of mango trees and ferns, the child appeared. "Papa?"

As if in answer to Diaz's prayer, a man Diaz recognized as de la Rosa, a member of the insurgent militant group *Hukbong Bayan Laban sa mga Hapon*—the People's Army Against the Japanese—and better known as the *Huks*, stepped from the trees, scooped up the boy from behind, and placed his hand over the child's mouth.

But before they could move away from the clearing, a shot rang out.

Quezon crumpled to the ground, his outstretched arm bouncing. His gold wedding band caught the sunlight and momentary glowed. The Japanese soldier ran toward Quezon's downed body.

Frankie kicked to free himself, but he was no match for de la Rosa.

Father Diaz made the sign of the cross, then leapt from his hiding place and ran through mounds of saw palmettos toward Mary Catherine.

As he neared, she ran to meet him. "Where's Danilo? Where's Frankie?"

"Go back!" Father Diaz whispered loudly. Reaching her, he grabbed her arm and turned her back downhill.

Mary Catherine raised her fist as though to pummel Father Diaz. "I heard a shot! Where's my husband? Where's my son?"

de la Rosa burst through the trees, Frankie tucked firmly under his arm.

"Let go of my boy!" Mary Catherine jerked from Father Diaz's grasp and rushed the savage-looking man holding her son.

Father Diaz led her by the shoulders. "Quiet! Get in the car!" He said, his voice barely a stage whisper. He shoved her into the passenger seat and nodded for de la Rosa to put the boy in the back. "*Arigato*. Thank you, my friend."

de la Rosa made no reply; instead, he disappeared into the tropical foliage.

Father Diaz slid into the driver's seat, released the brake and let the car drift down the slope onto the road.

Gunshots sounded behind them.

Father Diaz made the sign of the cross. "In the name of the Father, and of the Son, and of the Holy Spirit. Lord, grant us your protection."

"What is going on?" Mary Catherine swung around to face him. "My husband is in there. We have to wait for my husband!"

"Quiet." Father Diaz started the car as it rolled.

Mary Catherine grabbed the door handle. "Stop! We can't leave him!"

Father Diaz pulled her back. "Unless you want to die—and your son as well—you will sit back and shut up."

Gunshots blasted from both behind and to their right. A shot hit the passenger side rearview mirror. Father Diaz ducked. "Get down!"

Mary Catherine stared at the priest. "What's going on?"

"Now!" Father Diaz hit the gas. He drove down the curvy mountain road as fast as the car would go. Once they were on the main highway, he checked to make sure no one was following, then drove the speed limit so as not to draw attention. As if that were possible in the obnoxious American car.

Mary Catherine cleared her throat. "Where's my husband?"

"Papa fell down," Frankie said, his voice strangely lacking emotion. He rocked, pounding his head against the back of the seat. "Papa fell down."

"Tell me right now." Mary Catherine swung to face Father Diaz. "Where is my husband?"

"I'll tell you everything when we get to the church."

"You will tell me now."

"Danilo is dead."

"He is not!"

Father Diaz straightened the car and hit the gas. "I'm sorry, Mrs. Quezon. I'm so sorry." He reached across the seat and patted the woman's hand, his voice now serene. "I'm sorry, Mary Catherine. Please, just bear with me."

Mary Catherine stared out the window. "How do you know my name?" She reached over the seat back and pulled Frankie to her. "It will be okay," she whispered to the child. "Everything will be okay."

"Papa fell down."

Twenty minutes later, Father Diaz parked in back of the parish, hiding the car the best he could under some trees.

Mary Catherine stared straight ahead, her arms wrapped around the boy, her lips pressed tight.

"Come with me. It will be safe in the church." He led Mary Catherine and Frankie through the back door to his sacristy. "Please, make yourselves comfortable." He spread his arms wide toward the armchairs facing a desk.

Father Diaz chose a gold chalice from several on a table. He opened a cabinet door, took out a bottle of wine, removed the cork and half-filled a cup, then handed the cup to Mary Catherine.

While she gulped, Father Diaz found a smaller cup and filled it from a pitcher of water. He offered the cup to the boy, but Frankie shook his head. "Papa falled down."

Mary Catherine placed her empty chalice on the priest's desk.

"Mrs. Quezon." Father Diaz leaned against the desk. He bent toward the young woman and took her hands. "I am so sorry. Your husband is dead."

Mary Catherine jerked back her hands and glared at the priest. "He can't be. It's our anniversary."

"Please listen. We need to get you and little Frankie out of the country immediately. You are not safe here."

Mary Catherine shook her head. "But Danilo—"

"Your husband was shot. It's very important that you get out of—"

The heavy wooden door creaked open. "You returned, Father?"

"Ah. Tao. Thank God you're here. Come in." Father Diaz stood. "Mrs. Quezon, this is Nguyen Tao. He's a friend of Danilo's—as well as mine."

The Vietnamese man bowed toward Mary Catherine.

Mary Catherine's hand trembled, but she held it out to Tao. "I've met you before."

Tao took out his handkerchief and handed it to Mary Catherine. He turned to Father Diaz. "Where—"

"Quezon's dead."

"Oh, no." Tao's thin chest collapsed and he bent from the waist. He then sucked in a breath, straightened, and turned to Mary Catherine, his face emotionless. "I'm so sorry. Please know that you'll be taken care of." He made the sign of the cross over his chest, then leaned over and whispered to Diaz. "Did you get the envelope?"

Father Diaz whispered back. "No, I did not. He made the drop, though. I'm not sure if it's still there."

"I can retrieve it, if necessary."

Father Diaz shook his head. "I need you to get Mrs. Quezon and the boy out of here."

Mary Catherine trembled. "America. My family. In the States."

"I know," Father Diaz said. "But it's safer to get there through Australia. We must hurry, before the Japs set up roadblocks." He looked at Tao. "I will make the arrangements once you're on the road. You know the drill."

Tao nodded. "I'll notify Lansdale when they're out and it's safe."

Father Diaz jerked his head impatiently toward the door. "A fishing trawler will meet you at the inlet MacArthur used. It should be dark by the time you get there. I'll radio so you'll be met." Softening his voice, he turned to Mary Catherine. "Mrs. Quezon, you will be safe in Tao's hands. Trust him implicitly. Do whatever he tells you, no matter how curious it may sound. Do not question his judgment."

Tao knelt down again and held out his hand, and Frankie placed his in it.

Diaz put his arms around Mary Catherine and Tao; little Frankie squeezed into the circle. "Most merciful Father, may your grace cover these children of yours. Bless their path and render their escape. Wrap them with your most Holy Spirit and send your angels to protect them. In the name of Jesus Christ, Your most Holy Son. Amen."

"Thank you, Father." Mary Catherine twisted and knotted her handkerchief. "What about D-Danilo?"

Diaz placed his hand on her shoulder. "I will take care of his rites. Please, trust me." He turned away and opened a vestment drawer. He pulled out a rosary and placed it in Mary Catherine's hand. "Take this."

"Father, I can't. It's so—it's too . . . . " She fingered the string of star sapphires linked in gold and ran her thumb over the cross of sparkling blue gemstones and diamonds.

"This rosary has been specially blessed by the Pope. It will afford you God's own protection. Keep it with you at all times." He took a deep breath. "And whatever you do, don't let it out of your sight. Ever."

Mary Catherine clutched the rosary to her chest and bowed her head.

Father Diaz kissed her forehead. "Now go. And God be with you."

Chapter 2

Somewhere over the Pacific Ocean
Tuesday July 22, 1969

The hum of the jet engines didn't offer their usual comfort. Other passengers slept, but Frank Young stared out the port window into the hazy grayness. He should've been content. After several weeks studying Thai kickboxing under the local Sensei in Bangkok, he'd been allowed to study under the grandmaster. Few were chosen for such an honor. The practices were grueling, but there was nothing he'd rather be doing. Tomorrow, he'd meet with his friend Lucky and they'd move forward with opening their dojo. He had already written his resignation from his boring engineering job, and he'd called Lucky from Taiwan.

But why had his visa been recalled? He'd never had a problem before. He'd followed the rules and obeyed the laws. The only thing he'd done other than study kickboxing was to research his birth parents. Why would anyone care that he'd done that? That is, anyone other than Mary Catherine, his mother. She'd told him his parents were both Filipino and had been killed in the war. So where did his blue eyes come from? She never had an answer for that. She said the Catholic church had brought him to an orphanage in Atlanta, and she and Richard Young had adopted him when he was three.

And then he had found the photo. A woman—obviously Mary Catherine with her flaming red hair—holding a small boy, and a Filipino man grinning broadly with his arm around her. He didn't tell her he'd found the photo. Not right away. But he did ask her if she'd ever been to the Philippines. When she denied it, he showed her the photo.

Even now, anger crawled through his veins. Why would a mother pretend she had adopted her own son? She refused to tell him anything about his birth father, saying only that Richard was his father. And even while he held the photo, she insisted it wasn't her, that she didn't know where the photo had come from. She had tried to take it from him, but he kept it, studying it for clues. At first, it was the silvery blue Ford Tudor that captured his attention and gave him an uncanny sense of déjà vu. But later, he realized a more important clue. Behind the loving couple and the car was an office building. With a magnifying glass, Frank was able to make out the name swinging from a sign: "Zapata Construction."

Frank had gone to the U.S. Embassy in Thailand and asked if they could contact the embassy in the Philippines to see if his mother had traveled there. He had also asked if he could get a visa to spend some time in the Philippines. Within an hour, he was notified his passport had been withdrawn and he was to return to the States immediately.

"We will be arriving at Los Angeles International Airport shortly." The smooth voice of the head stewardess interrupted his thoughts, although he found her British accent pleasing. "If you have not already completed your customs forms, please do so at this time. Please fasten your seat belts, make sure your trays are in the upright position, and prepare for landing."

Land—California, no doubt—grew closer. Frank stretched his legs.

Across the aisle, a couple—at least, he assumed they were a couple—had smoked home-rolled cigarettes throughout the flight. That's what he got for scheduling a last minute return—stuck in the back with the smokers. He wasn't much older than the couple, yet he seemed to be worlds apart from their way of thinking. The couple each sported waist-length, ratty-looking hair, while his dark hair was trimmed short and combed neatly. They wore dirty blue jeans and wrinkled cotton smocks, while his clothes were pressed and his dress shirt tucked neatly into his slacks. He doubted they held "real" jobs, while he'd bored himself silly making use of his engineering degree in the eight years since graduating from Duke. How had the world changed so much in just a few years?

The 707 creaked as the landing gear dropped. Within minutes, the jet bounced as it touched land, jerking as the powerful jet engines reversed.

As the plane taxied along the runway, another announcement filled the cabin. "This is your captain speaking. We will be arriving at Gate Seventeen-B. The local time is eleven-forty-five; the temperature is a balmy seventy-three degrees. Enjoy your stay in Los Angeles. Thank you for flying Pan American Airlines."

Once the plane came to a complete stop and the doors opened, Frank hung back while the other passengers crowded the plane's narrow aisle. With three hours to kill before his connecting flight to Atlanta, he was in no hurry to disembark. Hopefully, he'd get lucky and not have to dump out his luggage for customs this time.

Once the aisle cleared, Frank grabbed his leather backpack from the overhead compartment, then followed his fellow passengers to the luggage carousel. After a few long minutes, the warning lights flashed and the alarm sounded, and soon thereafter, luggage bounced along the conveyor belt. He waited for the medium-sized Samsonite bag that looked identical to dozens of other pieces—except his had been dented, scratched and torn from his many flights. A black guitar case rolled along, and the taller of the hippies leaned forward and grabbed it. Soon after, Frank's suitcase arrived, along with a brand new dent, and he nabbed it.

With luggage in hand, he joined the line for customs. As luck would have it, the hippie couple stood in front of him. Both wore sandals—sandals!—and carried no luggage except for the guitar case and the oversized denim bag they'd had on the flight.

Although the line wasn't particularly long, it moved so slowly he wondered if the customs agents had gone on break. Finally, the hippies stepped up to the booth. The agent nodded for them to step aside. Another agent dumped the contents of the bag. Cigarette papers, a sandwich baggie with herbs, and a lighter rolled on the stainless steel table. The agent then opened the guitar case, removed the guitar, and opened the compartment normally used to hold spare strings and picks. He removed another plastic bag.

Frank tried not to smile. At least that meant he should be able to walk through with just a few questions.

"Next!" the short, overweight agent in the next row yelled.

Frank handed his passport to the agent.

The agent flipped open the booklet. "Name?"

"Franklin Young."

"What was the reason for your visit to Bangkok?"

"I was studying Thai kickboxing."

"What is the total dollar amount you spent on purchases you've brought back?"

Frank handed the agent the paper he'd prepared on the airplane. He'd bought nothing this trip except a china doll for his mother's collection. Angry or not, he still loved her.

The agent glanced at the paper, took another look at his passport, then turned and shuffled through a stack of papers on his podium. His eyes grew large. He waved over a security guard.

The guard stepped next to the booth, and the agent spoke quietly to him.

The guard motioned Frank. "Come with me, sir."

Frank frowned. He'd traveled overseas many times, and he'd never been asked to do more than open his luggage. "What's the problem?"

"Come with me, please."

Frank reached for his passport. The agent handed it past Frank to the guard.

Before Frank could lift his suitcase, the guard grabbed it, too, and headed toward the sign showing baggage claim. With no other choice, Frank followed.

As soon as they exited the customs area, three men in black suits flanked them.

"We'll take over from here." The first man in a black suit grabbed Frank's elbow.

Frank jerked away.

The man clamped down on Frank's shoulder, his fingers digging into the bone.

"What's your problem?" Frank stepped back, bringing the heel of his shoe down hard on the man's instep, then snapped his elbow into the man's ribs. He fell into a defensive stance, his eyes riveting from one to the next of his captors.

The injured man dropped back, grasping his side.

The second man in a black suit stepped in front of Frank, a pistol aimed at Frank's head.

Frank froze. *You can't kung-fu a bullet.*

The third Black Suit, thinner than the others, flipped open a wallet, revealing an FBI identification card. "FBI. Special Agent Tom Warren."

"Well, Mr. Special Agent Tom Warren, I haven't done anything wrong."

"No one said you did." Agent Warren closed his wallet, waved the second agent to put away the gun, and stepped closer to Frank. "Now, please, let's not make a commotion."

The first agent straightened and took his place at Frank's left, but kept more distance than before. The group walked toward the exit.

"What do you want with me?"

"You'll find out shortly."

Frank eyed the man, confident he could take him in about two seconds. "This better not take long. I have a connecting flight to Atlanta."

"You won't be making that flight." Agent Warren pressed buttons on an elevator. "But I will personally see to it that you get to Atlanta. If I know Mary Catherine, she'll be worried sick about you."

"How do you know my mother?" Frank's fist tightened.

The elevator dinged, then the door opened and Agent Warren stepped in. Frank considered bolting. But again, he couldn't outrun a bullet.

"After you." The second agent stepped back and waited for Frank to enter.

Frank stepped in, and the remaining agents followed quickly, forming a wall behind him. Agent Warren pressed a button.

"I want to know where you're taking me."

Agent Warren sighed deeply as if bored of Franks' questions. "Mr. Young, we're simply taking you to a quiet place where we can talk about your father."

"My father has been dead for three years. What's there to talk about?"

The elevator dinged and the doors opened. The first and second FBI agents stepped out. Frank gritted his teeth but followed them, Agent Warren taking up the rear.

They walked the short distance to the automatic doors leading to outside, where a black limousine waited—as did a group of Hare Krishna followers. The bald, robed men stepped back, not even offering a flower.

Frank didn't blame them. He stepped into the limo and was immediately flanked by both agents. Agent Warren sat opposite him.

Frank squirmed for more space, but neither of his seat mates released any. He sighed loudly. "Now why do you want to talk to me about Richard Young?"

"We know all about Richard Young. Retired mayor of Roswell, Georgia. Popular man, too."

Frank scowled. "But why—"

Special Agent Tom Warren shook his head. "Mr. Young, while you were in Bangkok, you created a bit of a problem for us."

"A problem? All I did was—"

"All you did was endanger yourself, your mother, and perhaps the security of the United States of America."

Frank stared at Agent Warren. "Are you insane?"

"Mr. Young, while in Bangkok, did you not research your birth father?"

Frank's heart pounded against his ribcage. "Uh, yes, sir. At least, I tried to."

"Didn't find much, did you?"

"No, sir." Frank's voice tapered off. "I don't even know his name."

Agent Warren chuckled. "Good. Maybe we're not too late."

"Too late? Too late for what?"

"Patience, Mr. Young. You will soon know more than you ever wanted to. Trust me on that." He laughed. "I'm not authorized to tell you more until we arrive at our destination. But this will be the day you learn about your birth father." Tom nodded smugly and lowered his voice. "The day you learn about Danilo Quezon."

Danilo Quezon. Frank struggled to clear his parched throat. So many thoughts crowded his brain he couldn't make sense of any of them. He'd spent most of his life wondering about his birth parents. And soon he'd learn what his mother refused to tell him. Soon he'd know. Frank leaned back into the seat and closed his eyes. But the words continued to bang against the sides of his brain. *Danilo Quezon. My birth father.*

CHAPTER 3

San Clemente, California
July 22, 1969

After about a thirty-minute drive, the limo turned into a driveway and pulled to a stop in front of a large mansion. The men remained in the limo for several more minutes until two men dressed in black suits opened the door from the outside. Behind them stood yet another man dressed similarly. The third man flashed open a wallet showing a State Department ID. He leaned forward and shook Agent Warren's hand.

"Tim Bozeman," Agent Warren said. "Good to see you again."

"Same. Got Young?"

"Of course."

Frank's heart pounded. Was his father here? Was his father alive?

The suited men nodded at Agent Warren, but checked the credentials of the other two agents. They spoke into two-way radios, then turned to Bozeman. "They're cleared."

"Check Young," Bozeman ordered.

The men approached Frank.

"Hold up," Agent Warren called. He turned to Frank. "They're going to frisk you. Don't pull any funny stuff."

Bozeman shot a questioning glance at Agent Warren.

"Martial arts pro. Got Mason's ribs earlier."

"One wrong move, shoot him," Mason growled, still limping and nursing his ribs.

The black suits started at Frank's head, checking his ears, his eyes, his neck—and worked down. He had never been patted down with the zealousness of these two men. Nothing was off limits to their gropes. If he didn't know all the men standing around him carried guns, he'd take them all out. But finally, they finished.

Again, the black suits spoke into two-way radios, then Bozeman nodded at Frank. "Please follow me."

The original two agents slid up behind Frank, staying a step behind on either side. The new suits walked beside him, while Bozeman and Agent Warren led the group up a brick-paved path that wound around palm trees and immaculate flower beds toward a Spanish-style Mission Revival mansion.

Frank looked around. "Exactly where are we?"

"*La Casa Pacifica.*" The words slid off Bozeman's lips as if Spanish were his first language. "The Pacific House."

Frank had never heard of it, but whatever organization the mansion housed, it must've been important.

The men escorted Frank around the back of the impressive estate. They mounted stairs to a terrace with a breathtaking view of the Pacific. Massive urns overflowing with ferns and flowering plants separated intimate groupings of furniture along the length of the rambling terrace. More men wearing black suits dotted the terrace and the grounds, as if standing guard. Where in hell was he?

When they reached the building, oversized French doors swung wide, allowing Frank and the agents to enter. Most of his welcoming committee remained outside the sprawling mansion, but Bozeman, Warren, and the two men who had searched him followed them deeper into what Frank now realized was a private home. California-style furniture and breezy yellow décor gave the oversized rooms with high-arched windows a surprisingly homey feel.

They marched down a long, wide, inlaid-stone hallway and approached a set of heavy double doors, again guarded by men wearing suits. Agent Warren opened the doors. Frank followed Bozeman inside, but the other two men stayed outside and closed the doors after them.

Frank had seen his share of remarkable homes, but none as impressive as this one. To his left, floor-to-ceiling windows overlooked gardens cluttered with statuary. Inside, groupings of overstuffed plaid chairs and footstools were arranged into friendly nooks separated by shelves of books and polished tables bearing glowing lamps. A massive table with leather ornamentation graced the far end of the room, where three men sat in matching leather chairs. Two of the men wore military dress uniforms.

"Gentlemen," Bozeman said, "Meet Mr. Franklin Young."

One by one, the men shook Frank's hand and introduced themselves: Air Force General George S. Brown, Chairman Joint Chiefs; Lieutenant General Marshall S. Carter, Director of NSA; and Richard Helms, CIA.

Bozeman nodded at Agent Warren. "I think you all know Agent Tom Warren, FBI." The gentlemen shook Agent Warren's hand.

Bozeman then offered his hand to Frank—and, for the first time, a smile. "Timothy Bozeman, Ambassador to the Philippines. Pleased to meet you."

Not knowing what else to do, Frank shook the offered hand.

"Help yourself to a drink." Ambassador Bozeman nodded toward a well-stocked bar. "And then have a seat, please."

On the table sat two large pitchers of ice water with floating lemons. At this point, nothing sounded better than ice water. Frank filled a waiting tumbler, then sat in the chair offered.

Agent Warren mixed a drink at the bar before joining Frank at the table.

Bozeman sat at one of the remaining three chairs, leaving the head chair empty. The men chatted among themselves. Frank's patience hung from a rapidly unraveling thread. "Could someone please tell me what is going on?"

The men quieted. Ambassador Bozeman glanced at his watch, then at the closed door. "It's hard to tell how long we'll be waiting, so I'll go ahead and give you some background." He stood and paced while he talked. "A short while ago, you requested the U.S. Embassy in Thailand to contact the U.S. Embassy in Manila and check the passport of your mother, using her maiden name, Mary Catherine James, for travel in the Philippines in 1939 or the early 1940s." He looked at Frank with a raised eyebrow.

Frank simply stared at him. How could they possibly know all of this? And more importantly, why would they care?

Bozeman stopped pacing and stood near Frank. "This set off red flags all over the State Department, who notified the Central Intelligence Agency."

"But why?"

"After you and your mother left the Philippines, your passports were tagged."

Frank shook his head. "I've never been in the Philippines."

Bozeman smiled. "Oh, yes, you were." He resumed pacing. "Regardless, your inquiry caused quite a problem for us."

Helms's fist tapped the table. "You just about blew our entire mission before it could begin." He leaned back and glanced quickly at the other men. "I'm sorry. Mr. Ambassador, please continue."

Bozeman nodded. "Let me back up and give you a little history." He stopped behind his chair and leaned his elbows on its back, his eyes aimed at Frank. "Have you heard of General Yamashita's gold, Mr. Young?"

"Of course. You can't travel throughout Asia and not hear the stories. But it's my understanding the war loot taken from the Chinese and others never belonged to Yamashita."

"Correct—to a point."

"And, according to some, it's all a legend."

"The gold exists." A tight smile formed on Bozeman's lips. "During the second war, many tons of gold were transported—some of it by Yamashita and his men—to the Philippine Islands. Some of that gold lies at the bottom of the ocean in ships that were purposely sunk when the U.S. found out about the transport. As for the rest, the Japanese used forced labor, including that provided by POWs, to dig massive burial sites in which much of the stolen gold was buried." He paused and leaned toward Frank. "Danilo Quezon—your father—drew maps of where those burial sites were located."

Not knowing what else to do, Frank nodded.

General Brown cleared his throat. "Your father was part of an OSS network. Uh, the OSS—Office of Strategic Services—was the precursor to today's CIA." He lit a cigar. "Through his work, your father prevented communism from infecting much of our world. His contribution strengthened our country and will continue to support this country for decades to come."

"I thought my birth father was Filipino."

Helms snarled. "He was. When he married your mother, he became a U.S. citizen as well. Because of his dual citizenship, he was able to do a top-notch job for the U.S. Government."

"So you're telling me he was a *spy?*"

Helms nodded. "One of our best."

Smoke wafted through the room, filling up the silence. Frank rubbed his forehead. "Is my father alive?"

Bozeman shook his head. "No. I'm sorry. He was killed in the line of duty in 1943."

Frank thought for a moment he'd be ill. It was too much to take in. He'd just learned about his father—and within minutes, his father was again taken from him.

"Your father was important to our intelligence." Helms tapped an unlit cigarette on the table. "As I said before, much of the strength of this country is directly due to his efforts. He has bequeathed you a great legacy."

But he is dead.

Frank stood, walked to the bar behind him and poured a straight bourbon. Standing with his back to the men, he took a long drink. The whiskey burned his throat, his esophagus, and then his stomach. He lifted the glass to his lips again, and emptied the drink. He poured himself a second drink, this one diluted with ice, then returned to his chair, placing the drink in front of him.

"How did my father die?"

Again, CIA head Helms answered. "He was transferring information about burial locations from the top of Montalban Gorge. He was discovered and shot."

Three large boulders nestled together. A loud bang. Like an explosion. From behind the largest boulder, a man's hand hit the ground. Bounced. A gold wedding band glinted in the sunlight. Frank squeezed his eyes shut.

Helms's voice softened. "Your mother and you were with him at the time."

Frank's stomach churned. Since a small child, he'd had dreams about a strange place, a mountain road, tropical foliage. About a man. And a priest. About boulders—and about a bouncing hand. Involuntarily, Frank shuddered.

"Your father was an honorable man," Carter stated in a low voice. "Who gave his life serving this country."

An honorable man. My father.

"After your father was killed," Helms continued, "all of his files were destroyed to protect you and your mother—as well as everyone else involved in the spy ring. And you, of course, were issued a new birth certificate showing you as a war orphan. Mary Catherine and Richard Young adopted you."

"Mary Catherine is my *birth* mother."

"According to all official records, Mary Catherine is your adoptive mother. You will do well to refer to her as such."

Frank stared at him. He had questions, lots of questions. But there were so many of them they clattered around inside his head, unable to form a coherent thread.

Helms finally lit the cigarette he'd been playing with. "Rumor has it that maps of the burial sites are circulating, and we believe President Marcos may have at least some of them."

Frank couldn't stop his hand from straying to his temple, rubbing the throb that grew there.

Helms sucked smoke deep into his lungs, then released it slowly. Bozeman again paced. "Mr. Young, the first thing we need you to do is to get close to Marcos. Once you've done that, you'll be in a much better position to help us find the gold."

"And how can I do that?"

"A couple of ways. First, find out if Marcos has any maps and get those maps to us. Second, find out how much gold Marcos has already recovered and where it is. And third, find out where the remaining burial sites are."

A half-laugh escaped Frank's lips. "Why me? Why not one of your trained people?"

"We could send a CIA agent in there, but Marcos would spot him in a moment; he's worked with them for a number of years. We think you can get closer than anyone because you're an unknown. You don't look or act CIA. Plus, being Filipino, you'd blend right in."

"I don't know where the gold is!" Frank clenched his teeth until his jaw ached. He swallowed hard. "And I don't even remember my father."

"It was a long time ago," Helms said, his gruff voice suddenly smooth with patronization. "Much has happened to cloud your memory. Perhaps going to the place where you lived with him will help clear those clouds."

"I'm an engineer. I don't have any training to spy on people."

"And that's why you're perfect for this. We'll give you a quick debriefing, provide you with a few tools and instructions, but mostly, we don't want you trained. Marcos can smell CIA a hundred feet away."

Frank set down his drink and stared into it. Yes, he'd been bored silly with his engineering career. But he wanted to return to Atlanta and open a dojo with Lucky, his college roommate. "No. I don't want to do it."

The French doors opened. President Richard M. Nixon strode in.

Everybody—except for Frank—stood; the military officers saluted.

Frank realized his mouth hung open. He closed it and clumsily clamored to his feet.

President Nixon walked close and shook Frank's hand. "Good afternoon, Mr. Young."

"Pres—President Nixon."

"Gentlemen, my last meeting ran a little long." President Nixon dropped into the chair at the end of the table. "Mr. Young, welcome to my home." He looked around the table. "Please continue."

Helms's steely gaze settled back on Frank. "We want you to go into the Philippines posing as an international marketing agent for Triangle Tobacco."

He nodded as though it were a done deal. "They're planning to launch cigarettes in the Philippines. Since you're an alumnus of Duke University and familiar with tobacco country, you'll be a natural fit for Triangle." He puffed on a cigarette. "Ferdinand Marcos is extremely interested in the industry. This will give you a means to get close to him."

Frank's mouth fell open. "Me?" He grabbed the goblet and took another drink of water. "You want *me* to get close to President Marcos?" He shook his head. "Why on earth would I want to do that?"

"Do you know who Edward Lansdale is?" President Nixon asked.

"He runs the Saigon CIA, right?"

Nixon nodded. "And Santa Romana? Do you know who Severino Santa Romana is?"

Frank shook his head. "No, Mr. President."

"Your father worked closely with Lansdale and Santa Romana. But Santa Romana has become powerful, and we no longer know whose side he is on."

Frank stared at him dumbly.

Nixon nodded, jowls shaking. "Let me back up a bit. Many years ago, after the war, Lansdale and Santa Romana reserved some of that gold your father located for the CIA to fight communism. We created a special trust fund to develop a worldwide anti-communist network. The CIA has used the trust to distribute gold bullion certificates to influential parties throughout the world—thus, ensuring loyalty to our cause." He exchanged glances with Helms. "We're afraid that, if Marcos is digging up more gold, he'll claim it as his own, and not only will that de-value the gold, but Marcos will gain ultimate power."

"We've got to stop him." Helms snuffed out his cigarette.

Nixon clasped his hands together and leaned forward. "Whoever holds the gold holds the power."

Frank's head pounded.

Bozeman's shoulders straightened. "My office and my staff in the Philippines will be open to you at all times."

"I'm an engineer. I'm not a spy."

"You are the best shot we have," Nixon said.

"I don't want to get involved in this."

Nixon shot a disapproving look at Frank. "You'll do it because the survival of this country depends on you. If that much gold falls into the wrong hands, it could finance wars unlike any we can possibly imagine." The President's jowls shook. "Whoever has possession of that gold will quite literally rule the world."

Frank tapped on the table.

President Nixon glared at Frank. "Are you a communist?"

"No, sir."

"Good. Then I expect you'll want to cooperate and help your country."

"If he doesn't," Helms said, "We can confiscate his passport."

Bozeman glared at Frank. "I really thought you'd want to learn about your birth father. I assumed that's why you were doing research in Bangkok."

Nixon leaned forward. "I will be meeting with President Marcos in a few days, but I'll only be staying overnight. I'd like you to be in the Philippines before I leave there."

The room was silent. No one spoke. Frank was pretty sure his voice wouldn't work anyway.

Director Helms cleared his throat. "We'll finance your mission and offer you our full support and as much protection as we can. Your connection to the CIA and the U.S. Government will be top secret. Only the men here in this room and one other agent will know anything about it. We will be a part of your team."

Frank swallowed hard. His life had been decided for him—perhaps by the father he didn't even remember. He couldn't think of any way he could say no.

President Nixon cleared his throat. "Mr. Young, two days ago I spoke to Neil Armstrong and Edwin Aldrin from Apollo 11—while they were *on the moon*. I'm sure these brave men had doubts about their mission, but that didn't stop them from serving their country." He placed his loosely clasped hands back on the table and leaned forward, locking eyes with Frank. "And if these men can go to the moon, then surely, you can go to the Philippines."

CHAPTER 4

The phone rang a third time, then a fourth. Mary Catherine Young folded her magazine and stood. "Caretta?" Where was that woman? Was it so hard to answer the phone before it rang off the hook?

Mary Catherine stalked over to the phone and snatched up the receiver. "Young residence."

A few heartbeats of silence answered her, then an accented male voice spoke. "Mary Catherine Quezon?"

Quezon? Mary Catherine's heart stopped beating. "Who is this?"

"My apologies. It's Mary Catherine *Young*, isn't it?"

She opened her mouth to speak, then closed it. Finally, she found her voice—and her temper. "Who is this, I said!"

"Are you aware your son is in the Philippines?" the voice asked softly.

The room tilted on an invisible axis. Mary Catherine grabbed the arm of the wingback next to her and sank into the chair. Her hand, with a mind of its own, found the sapphire rosary on the table beside the chair and worked it with her fingers. "Franklin?"

"Yes, Franklin." The voice turned heavy. "I can no longer protect him."

Mary Catherine struggled to place the voice. The accent was European, perhaps Italian, although his English was flawless. She shivered. She'd heard the distinctive voice before—a long time ago.

"Use whatever influence you have to get your son out of here. It isn't safe."

Puddles formed in Mary Catherine's eyes, and she blinked hard. "Why? Why did he go there?"

"To finish what was started."

"I don't know what you mean. What was—"

A dial tone answered her.

Mary Catherine stared at the receiver, then gingerly placed it on the hook. A hot tear trickled down her cheek, and it angered her. She stood, swiped at her eyes, and stomped over to the antique buffet, where she poured Smirnoff Vodka from the decanter into a crystal highball.

"Mrs. Young? You called for me?" Caretta stood in the doorway, wiping her hands on her apron.

Mary Catherine threw back the drink and slammed the highball onto the buffet. "Answer the phone before the third ring, damn it!"

CHAPTER 5

Malacañang Palace, The Philippines
August 2, 1969

Frank stood outside Malacañang Palace watching the Pasig River lazily roll by. He'd anticipated meeting Ferdinand Marcos, but he never dreamed it would be at the president's personal residence. *Amazing what money can buy.* He tapped the parchment envelope against the gold-plated box he carried.

"Mr. Young, President Marcos will see you now." The stocky colonel's eyes were like black ice.

Frank fought the shiver that snaked its way up his spine when he looked at the man. Bozeman had warned him that if Colonel Ver ever discovered he was Danilo's son and he was there undercover, he'd slit his throat without thinking twice. Now that he had met him in person, Frank had no doubt the man was a cold-blooded killer.

Still, Frank gave a respectful nod and followed the colonel into the entrance hall of the palace. Despite its warm beige color, the marble walls and floors radiated coolness, which Frank welcomed after standing so long in the summer sun. He was led through a large set of doors depicting Malakas and Maganda, the first Filipino man and woman, and up a sweeping staircase to the second floor, then into the presidential study, where Ferdinand Marcos sat at his desk. A uniformed guard stood nearby.

"President Marcos, may I present Mr. Franklin Young." The colonel stepped aside, but he didn't leave the room.

President Marcos wore a white *barong tagalong,* a formal embroidered shirt worn untucked. Frank had expected to see him dressed in a suit, like Nixon. The room, though, was furnished much like photos he'd seen of the Oval Office in The White House.

Marcos stood and extended his hand. "Mr. Young, it is my pleasure to welcome you to Malacañang Palace."

Frank's stomach twisted as he shook the president's hand and bowed respectfully. "Thank you for meeting with me, Mr. President." He straightened and smiled, then quickly looked away; Bozeman had talked to him about protocol—too much direct eye contact might be considered offensive. "On behalf of Triangle Tobacco, it is an honor to be here."

President Marcos pursed his lips in the direction of one of the chairs facing his desk—a sign Frank should sit there—then resumed his seat. "We are pleased to have you here, Mr. Young. I have met with two of the tobacco companies in the United States, but you are the first representative of Triangle Tobacco to speak with me, and the first ever to visit me in my own country. How may I help you?"

"Mr. President, it is I who am honored to help you. Triangle Tobacco would like to present you with a small token of appreciation." He offered the box and envelope to Marcos, finding it easier to part with the two million dollar check than he'd expected. Something in him suddenly wanted to please this man, even though guilt for that thought quickly followed. "It is a small contribution to your political fund. We want you to know that we are behind you in your effort to keep the Philippines a strong democracy."

"That is very kind, but I cannot accept your gracious gift."

Frank expected as much. It would be considered pretentious and greedy for a Filipino to accept a gift without first putting up a fuss. "Please, Mr. President, you would do Triangle Tobacco a great honor by acknowledging this token of our support." He slightly bowed in deference.

"If you insist, Mr. Young. I am pleased that your company shares the same beliefs and values I do." President Marcos opened the envelope, and with a look of childlike expectation, peered at the check it contained. "This is very generous, Mr. Young. Very generous, indeed." He smiled at Frank.

"It is our pleasure, I assure you. I only wish it could be more." Frank wanted to believe the words, even as he heard himself saying them.

"Are you Filipino?"

"Yes. I lived in America while attending university, but it is good to be home. Part of the reason I accepted my position with Triangle Tobacco was so I could return to the Philippines. It was a perfect marriage, Mr. President. They wanted someone to market their product in Asia, and I wanted to come home." Since when did lies fall so smoothly from his lips?

"We welcome you back, then." Marcos lifted the lid on the golden box. "*Pure Gold.*" He chuckled softly as he picked up one of the packs of cigarettes the box held. "That is an interesting name for tobacco."

Frank smiled. "Yes, Mr. President. The tobacco leaves are harvested early, and they dry to a light golden color. I believe you will find the taste quite smooth."

President Marcos opened the pack and tapped out a cigarette.

Frank jumped up. In one motion, he produced a gold Zippo lighter and flicked it open. In his zest to light the president's cigarette, he failed to realize that Colonel Ver already held a flaming lighter.

Marcos ignored Ver's offer and allowed Frank to have the honor. "Thank you, Mr. Young."

Ver glared at Frank, his dark eyes raw with hatred.

Frank shook off the icy fingers of dread that crawled over his spine. "Please, Mr. President." He struggled to keep the tremble out of his voice. "I would be honored if you would call me Frank."

"Frank." Marcos leaned back. "I don't know many Filipinos named *Frank.*"

The room grew quiet. After a few more long seconds of silence, he held his left hand within his right.

"Ahhh." Marcos drew on the cigarette, held the smoke in his lungs for a moment, then leaned his head back and blew a steady stream into the air. "Smooth, yes. I like Pure Gold." He took another drag and repeated the action of holding, then blowing. "Mr. Young, we may have to do business together."

Frank hadn't realized he'd been holding his breath. He wasn't cut out for this undercover stuff. "It would be my pleasure, Mr. President. Triangle Tobacco will be honored to supply the Philippines with tobacco."

Ver opened the door and held it for Frank. Again, his narrow eyes bore into Frank, his hatred tangible.

This time, Frank couldn't contain the shiver. He'd just scored a great victory, had just accomplished his first assignment, yet instead of joy, trepidation filled his veins. He wondered if it were just his mother's phone calls imploring him to come home. No. It was more than that. His martial arts training had taught him to be aware of his intuition, to trust his senses. And every fiber of his body screamed *danger.*

▲

Ferdinand Marcos waited until the footsteps died away outside his office door, signaling that Franklin Young had left the second floor of the palace. He turned his attention to the soulless man in front of him. "Well, Fabian, what's your take?"

Colonel Ver's eyes constricted. "Don't trust him."

"I thought as much. Keep your eye on him."

"It will be my honor, sir." A sneer fractured the colonel's scarred face. "My honor."

CHAPTER 6

Malacañang Palace, The Philippines
September 9, 1969

Rosalita Laurel smoothed wisps of dark hair back into the bun at the nape of her neck as she climbed the red-carpeted hardwood of the Grand Staircase. At the top, she paused in the vestibule to admire one of her favorites in Imelda's vast art collection, the painting of Nereids. Imelda had done a remarkable job of updating the palace since Rosalita had last visited. It wasn't exactly to her taste, though she did like the new sawali-look panels—so much nicer than the old stucco. But then, Imelda's sense of style had always run toward the pretentious. It was her duty to show the poor how they, too, could reach grand heights and wealth, she'd often told Rosalita. She was their representative of success.

Rosalita continued her stroll down the hallway. She no longer questioned her friend's ambition. She pushed through the heavy double doors on the left that opened into the presidential family's living quarters. "Imelda? Imelda, darling, I'm here!"

Imelda's head housekeeper—she didn't like the word *servant*—swept out her hand, indicating that Rosalita should follow her into Imelda's suite. "The Queen's Room," Imelda called it.

Rosalita entered the room for the first time since the renovations. "Oh, Imelda, it's lovely." She swung around full circle. "I can't believe what you've done with it!"

"I knew you'd like it." Imelda beamed. "And your gown is stunning, my friend. That shade of green makes your eyes sparkle." She motioned for Rosalita to follow her and her latest dressing assistant. "Let's pick out our jewelry."

Rosalita trailed Imelda past an enormous canopied bed and into the dressing room that was larger than some Filipino homes.

Several trays of jewelry were stacked on a marble table. "I have a hair comb that will match your gown perfectly. You must wear it!" She clapped her hands at the young assistant, one of her "blue ladies," so named because of the blue uniforms they wore. "Sofia! Take these trays in there." Imelda turned back to Rosalita and her face softened. "Let me find the comb. I know you'll love it."

Sofia lugged the trays into the bedroom, then returned for four additional trays.

"Just lay them there on the bed."

Sofia did as she was told, then backed against the wall to await her next command.

Imelda turned her attention to the trays. Each one held a heavily jeweled necklace, matching earrings, one or two rings, and sometimes a bracelet. She spread them about on the bed. "Which do you like best?"

Rosalita lifted a heavy gold choker set with rubies and emerald-cut diamonds. "This will set off both your dress and your eyes, Imelda." She clasped the choker on her friend's neck, then held up the mirror for her to see.

"It's pretty, yes." Imelda pointed to another tray. "But what about this one, with nothing but diamonds?" She unclasped the fastener on the choker she wore, while Rosalita carefully lifted out the necklace.

Rosalita placed the necklace on Imelda's neck, then turned her around. "Oh, yes. This one is definitely better." She picked up the mirror and held it to Imelda's face.

Imelda nodded and preened. "I haven't worn this one yet. It's from Bulgari. I picked it up in America."

Rosalita smiled. "Now where is that hair comb you promised?"

Imelda lifted a blue velvet drape from another of the cherry wood trays, displaying three gold hair combs, each inlaid with jewels.

Rosalita gasped. "They're dazzling." She picked the one with pear-shaped white diamonds arranged to create daisy petals around a central yellow diamond. The three daisies were set in platinum, supported by a gold stem and leaves. "Here, help me put it on." She turned around, and Imelda slid the comb just above the bun on the nape of her neck.

"It is only made lovelier by your flawless skin, sweet Rosalita." Imelda stepped back. "I should be jealous of your beauty. You remind me of a younger me."

Rosalita touched the comb, turned, and kissed Imelda on the cheek. "You are so kind to me."

"And you to me. Of all my friends, you're the one I trust the most."

"Speaking of your friends, you'd better finish getting dressed. I'm sure the guests have been waiting at the Cultural Center for hours, and it'll take you three times as long to pick out your shoes as it did to select your jewels."

"You won't believe it, but I already know which ones I'm wearing. I had a pair specially made for today."

Rosalita chuckled and shook her head. "And what's not to believe about *that?*"

While Imelda went to her shoe room, Sofia cleared the jewelry trays from the bed.

Rosalita checked her hair and make-up in the antique gilt-framed mirror, then stepped through the glass pocket-doors onto the balcony overlooking the Pasig River.

"What do you think?" Imelda said from behind her. She slowly turned in a circle, her hands held out at her sides.

"Breathtaking. Did Christian make it?"

"Of course. He makes nearly all my gowns now. He does the finest embroidery and beadwork in the world."

"He has outdone himself again, my friend." Rosalita fluffed one of the butterfly sleeves on Imelda's rose-colored gown. "We should be going. We don't want fashionably late to turn into *too* late."

"Of course." Imelda picked up the gold compact with her name emblazoned on the outside in diamonds and tucked it inside a crystal-covered white clutch. "Rosalita." She touched her friend's arm. "Would you please do me a favor?"

"Certainly."

"There's a man—a very handsome man, single, too—who I'd like you to meet and—"

"Imelda! You sound like my mother. I've told you, I don't need a man in my life. I have much to accomplish before I marry."

"Please listen, Rosalita. This is not about finding a husband for you. This man . . . he has delivered a generous donation to Ferdinand's political campaign. He is a representative of an American tobacco company, and he wants to bring his cigarettes into the Philippines."

"So?"

"I believe he may be wealthy. Perhaps powerful, I don't know. His name is Frank Young. I'd like you to get to know him. Keep an eye on him. See what you can find out."

"You want me to *spy?* Imelda, I—"

"It is for the security of our country." Imelda grasped both of Rosalita's hands in hers. "And for the safety of Ferdinand and me . . . and our children. Please."

Rosalita smiled and squeezed Imelda's hands. "Of course."

"And who knows? He is an attractive man. If he turns out to be legitimate, perhaps you will fall in love with him." Imelda threw back her head and laughed.

Chapter 7

The Cultural Center of the Philippines
September 9, 1969

Frank sipped the brandy flavored with iced-tea powder, again missing the taste of sweet tea from home. At least the brandy dulled the bitterness and helped the drink go down. He inhaled deeply, welcoming the scent of the *lechón* cooking over pits of coals stationed around the Cultural Center. Usually one or two of the whole suckling pigs would be cooked for a celebration, but the Marcoses had at least a dozen, each surrounded by huge dishes of fresh lumpia, *ukoy* shrimp patties, jumping salad filled with tiny live shrimp, and platters of purple yams, jicama and fresh fruit. Still more tables were loaded with a variety of pastries and sweet rice cakes, and one even served *halo-halo,* a shaved ice dessert that caused a crowd to gather in the evening's humid weather.

Frank helped himself to a slice of *kesong puti*, his favorite white cheese.

"It'll make you fat," a velvety voice scolded.

Frank turned. He almost gasped aloud. He'd seen many beautiful women, but this one—he caught his breath. Her smoldering green eyes were like jade, decorating her flawless, creamy skin. Raven hair swept into a French braid framed her delicate features. The braided hair ended in a bun at her neck, held in place by a glittering hairpin. The diamonds in the pin sparkled no greater than the glint in her eyes. Words escaped Frank.

The woman giggled, almost child-like. She proffered a hand. "Rosalita Laurel."

Frank rested his cocktail glass on the table. He took the offered hand, swept down from the waist, and kissed it. *Soft, fragrant.* She smelled of coconut milk. *Breathe, Frank. Breathe.* "Frank," he said. "Frank Young. I'm honored to meet you." "Pleased to meet you, Frank. You must be a friend of the Marcoses, as well?" She tilted her head to one side.

"New acquaintance, I would say. My company is opening a business here, with President Marcos's blessings." He looked over to where the president stood with his wife by his side on a slightly raised platform, greeting guests.

Imelda eyes caught Rosalita's and seemed to light up. She nodded slightly. *Perhaps that was just her way of saying hello.* Frank cleared his constricting throat. "I represent Triangle Tobacco."

"You're American, aren't you?"

Frank bowed slightly. "Yes. How did—"

"I went to school at Wellesley."

"Ah. In Massachusetts."

"Yes. And you're from . . . ?"

"Atlanta."

She lowered her head slightly and looked up at Frank, her long lashes covering sparkling green eyes. "I thought I detected a hint of a southern drawl."

Frank's voice left him. A tuxedoed server stopped by him, offering a tray of embellished drinks. Frank grabbed one and took a long drink.

"So, Mr. Tobacco Representative," she said, her voice soft and sultry. She turned her face to the side and looked at Frank from that angle. "You wouldn't happen to have a cigarette, would you?"

Relax. Frank hadn't felt this way in front of a woman since seventh grade. And neither had he had problems controlling his voice since that same year. Was it possible for a pretty woman to turn a twenty-nine year-old man into an adolescent? Obviously, it was. Frank fumbled with pulling the gold cigarette case from his jacket pocket. He'd planned to save these particular cigarettes for President Marcos, but knew an opportunity when he saw one. "Of course," he finally said, his voice higher than normal. He bowed slightly as he offered the cigarette.

"Thank you." Rosalita examined the long, thin cigarette, but made no comment before she placed it between her lips, leaning forward for him to light it. As he did, she met his eyes.

Again, his breath caught. Only now, he didn't feel like a thirteen-year-old. He felt very much like a grown, red-blooded man. Heat flushed his cheeks. Rosalita drew a long drag on the cigarette, held the smoke, then released it slowly. "Smooth." She linked her arm through his and nodded toward a man who stood with his back to them at a table across the way. "Come, let me introduce you to my Uncle Fernando. Have you met him?"

"Vice President Lopez is your uncle?" Perhaps he should spend some time with Rosalita, after all.

Rosalita giggled. "Yes and no. It's an honorary title. He and my father were close friends for decades, and he's always been an important part of my family. But I don't think of him as the vice president. To me, he is the man who kept sweet treats for me in his pocket. In fact, I'll bet he has some there now."

As they strolled through the crowd, the eyes of many male guests followed Rosalita, and those same eyes pried him curiously. Maybe he shouldn't be seen with her—he'd be too high-profile. Then again, if Rosalita considered him good company, wouldn't doors open for him? He looked around, wondering how many of these men were armed. Most seemed amiable enough. They were celebrating, after all. But the two armed soldiers he'd seen perched atop the Cultural Center told him he was never far away from danger when in the presence of Marcos.

"*Tiyo* Fernando." Rosalita leaned on her toes to kiss the man on the cheek.

"Ahhh, my Rosalita." The vice president kissed his pseudo-niece on the forehead.

"Uncle, I'd like you to meet my friend, Frank Young."

Frank shook the man's hand and bowed his head. "It is my pleasure, sir."

"You have something for me, Uncle?" Rosalita held up what was left of her cigarette, and immediately a waiter appeared at her side to take it from her slender fingers and dispose of it.

Vice President Fernando chuckled, then reached into his pocket and pulled out his fist. He dropped a piece of candy into Rosalita's hand, then held out his fist to Frank. "And for your friend, too."

Frank sheepishly held his hand, and the vice president dropped a candy into his open palm. "You're welcome, my dear." Vice President Fernando Lopez's voice brought Frank back to the present.

"Yes, thank you, sir." Frank's mouth felt dry, and he desperately craved a drink. *A stiff one, not the fruity concoctions presented.*

"Fernando," President Marcos said as he walked up and clapped the vice president on back. "I see you've met my new friend, Frank Young." As usual, he was flanked by Colonel Ver.

Lopez's face remained placid, but his eyes revealed new interest in Frank. "Yes, my darling Rosalita introduced us."

Rosalita held out her hand, and Marcos kissed it. "You look lovely, Rosalita, as always." He turned to Frank. "You have excellent taste in the ladies, Frank. I'm glad you and Rosalita have made acquaintance."

Marcos winked at Rosalita. "My dear, would you please excuse us?"

Rosalita waved her hand. "Business, Ferdinand? You men should learn how to relax and enjoy a great party." She kissed her uncle's cheek, then Marcos's, then turned to Frank. "We will talk again later, yes? I will save a dance for you." She waltzed toward Imelda.

Frank opened his mouth to speak, then closed it, realizing hers wasn't a request, but a statement. To his left, Marcos laughed softly.

"Frank, you said you have some exciting news for me. What is it?"

Frank straightened his shoulders and smiled. *Game on.* "Triangle Tobacco has officially announced the name of an exciting new product we'd like to introduce solely in the Philippines. It's specially designed to appeal to the fairer sex." He grinned broadly. "We have an underserved Filipina population where tobacco is concerned, wouldn't you agree?" Frank nodded in agreement with himself, encouraging Marcos and Lopez to do the same.

They did, but Frank knew this meant nothing, because in the Philippines, a nod didn't necessarily signify agreement, only that the speaker was heard.

"How can you market a cigarette specifically to women?" Vice President Lopez asked.

"It's longer and slimmer than the traditional cigarette. Its slender styling looks quite attractive between the fingers of a lady."

Lopez's eyes lit up.

"Plus, it's a faint shade of blue."

"Blue?" Marcos frowned.

"Bear with me, please, Mr. President." Frank smiled and reached inside his jacket pocket, producing a slim, gold cigarette case. He opened it, revealing dark blue velvet lining that cradled seven slim, pale blue cigarettes. "Gentlemen, may I present Blue Lady Slims."

Marcos's reached into the case, pulled one out and held it up to admire. He threw back his head and laughed. "My friends, we are going to make a fortune."

CHAPTER 8

"Mother, I'm not going to argue with you." Frank shook his head, even though Mary Catherine couldn't see him across the phone lines.

"It's too dangerous for you there, Frankie. Come home. I insist."

"You insist? Don't be ridiculous. Besides, the Philippines *are* my home. I was born here, remember? Or is that something else you've conveniently forgotten?"

"Don't be thorny, Frankie. I didn't raise you to speak to me that way."

"I simply want to know why you've kept this from me all these years. You led me to believe you didn't know my father. Now I've learned that I knew him, too. All those times I asked you about things I remembered . . . you told me they were dreams. Sometimes I thought I was going crazy."

"I did what I thought was best for you. Richard was so good to me—to *us*—I didn't want to, uh, *confuse* things."

"Don't you think I deserved to know you were my birth mother? That you not only knew my real father, but *was married* to him?"

"I told you what I thought you needed to know."

"You *lied* to me, Mother!"

"I did what I had to do."

Frank sighed. He needed to lighten up on her. After his visit with President Nixon and all his men, he knew his mother had also been caught up in something bigger than her. "I know, Ma. I know." Even though

Frank stood in Bozeman's office using Bozeman's personal phone at the American embassy—the only place he was told was safe to make phone calls—he lowered his voice. "You had to because my father was a spy. I know that."

"A *spy!* What are you talking about? Your father wasn't a spy. Where did you hear such foolishness? Your father worked in construction. He was a very respectable man."

"If he was so respectable, why on earth would you act like you never knew him? Why would you dishonor him so?"

"You have no idea how horrible that day was. I don't want to think about it, and you shouldn't either."

Frank's head ached. She was right. He needed to quit thinking so much.

Mary Catherine sniffed on the other end of the line. "Let's discuss something nicer. The echo on overseas phone calls makes conversation difficult enough as it is. How do you like your new job? You're working for a tobacco company. If that isn't the pot calling the kettle black."

Frank sighed. It would be futile to push for more answers unless he could catch her off guard. When Mary Catherine shut down, she may as well be Fort Knox. "I like my job. I especially like that it's put me in the Philippines. It's nice to experience a new facet of my own cultural history."

Mary Catherine said nothing.

"Can you send me some of those green legal pads I like?" Frank asked. "I can't find them here."

"Of course, dear. I'll have Caretta pick up some when she does the grocery shopping tomorrow afternoon. Is there anything else you need?"

"Yes, actually. Mother, do you recall my father ever mentioning any maps? Or anything about gold bars or buried treasure?"

"Treasure? Richard wouldn't have known anything about buried treasure. Skeletons in people's closets, now that might be something he would've known about, but not buried treasure."

"I'm talking about Danilo, my birth father. Don't make this so complicated. Please, answer the question."

"I have a bridge club meeting in half an hour. I really don't have time for this."

"Mother, answer the question. You know a lot more than you're telling me."

The phone was silent for a moment. "Frankie," she finally said, "sometimes when you dig for buried treasure, you find nothing but a pile of bones. Now let it be, before those bones become yours."

Chapter 9

Montalban Gorge, The Philippines
October 16, 1969

Frank pulled his car to the rocky area on the side of the road, consulted his notes, then hung binoculars and a canteen around his neck and stepped out of the car. He backtracked a few hundred feet down the road until he came to the footpath he'd seen. Though branches hung low over the pathway, it wasn't overgrown, and the packed soil proved the path had regular foot traffic.

He walked through the thickening foliage for a few minutes, then came upon a clearing with rough-hewn tables and benches, surrounded by tree stumps. Not exactly a great spot for burying—or digging for—treasure. It was the third such roadside spot he'd found today.

He pulled a swig from the canteen, recapped it, and headed back toward his car. It had been three months since President Nixon had recruited him to discover how much gold Marcos was hiding from the U.S. and where that gold was. Getting close to Marcos was actually much easier than he'd expected—money really did talk. But finding out where was the gold—or treasure maps to the gold—had proved much more difficult. So far, he had discovered exactly nothing.

It couldn't be but three or four hours until nightfall, and he didn't want to be traveling the mountain's treacherous curves after dark. As he neared the end of the path, a rustling sound caught his attention. Immediately, his body tensed. Was he being followed? Was someone else on the trail? Or off the trail? After standing still for a few seconds, he continued. *I'm getting tired. That's it. One more stop, and I'm calling it a day.*

Just as he reached the edge of the woods, a stocky man stepped in front of him.

"Hello," said the stranger in English. "See anything?"

"Like what?" Frank took a step back.

The stranger motioned toward Frank's binoculars. "I assumed you were bird watching."

"Uhhh, sightseeing, yes. I mean, no, I didn't see any birds." He took another half-step backward. There was something familiar about the man. Again, the feeling of déjà vu washed over him, but before he could identify what, exactly, his subconscious knew, the thought was gone.

"I don't think I've seen you around here before." The stranger turned his head to study Frank. "Why are you here?" The question wasn't rude, just inquisitive.

Yet, Frank couldn't shake a feeling of wariness. The man didn't appear to be Filipino. His English, although excellent, suggested a European accent. With his dark hair and eyes, he must've been Spanish or—yes! Italian.

The stranger again tilted his head, and as he did, the sun, dipping in the sky, reflected something metallic around the man's neck. A crucifix. A large, gold crucifix.

Again, sharp white light stabbed Frank's consciousness. He'd seen that crucifix before. He'd seen this man before. "Is there something you need?"

"No, no. I'm sorry for holding you up. You just remind me of someone I once knew. Many, many years ago. The light is fading. My aging eyes sometimes play tricks on me."

Frank smiled, but found it hard to believe that eyes so piercing could have trouble seeing. Besides, dusk was still an hour away. *Did he know my father?* "I'd better get going before it gets any later."

"I like to come out here and pray a few times a week," the man continued. "Commune with both God and nature, if you will. This area takes me back to my youth." The stranger ducked his head and disappeared into the woods without looking back.

The late afternoon sky was streaked with darkening clouds as Frank returned to his car and headed on up the mountain. He rolled up the driver's side window as the air grew damp and forbidding. The incoming weather matched his mood as he brooded over the other situation what had never left his mind since he'd discovered the yellowed photograph. Who was his birth father? Who was Danilo Quezon?

Frank navigated the switchback turn and started down the other side of the mountain. This would be the perfect location to bury gold; he was sure of it.

After half an hour of navigating hairpin curves, Frank reached the base of the mountain just as the sky opened and rain poured. The road ahead of him disappeared into the mist, so he pulled over. He sat thinking in his car, his mind wandering with the pounding of the rain. Within minutes, his fingers, still gripping the wheel, ached from the cold. The rental car had no heater, and the windows had fogged.

Frank rubbed his sleeve against the window, but it did little to improve his visibility in the torrential downpour. He might be stuck here for hours.

An old church sat just off the road. Through blinding sheets of white rain, he stared at it for a long moment, then shook off the feeling of familiarity. The rain showed no signs of ending and he didn't intend to sit in his car all night. He jumped out of the car, but before he even took a step, he was soaked to the skin. Regardless, he sprinted to the church. It would be just his luck to find the doors locked or the inside as wet as the outside. Surprisingly, when he grabbed the doorknob, the door swung open easily. And it was warm and dry inside. He had found refuge.

Frank moistened two fingers in the small fount just inside the door and made the sign of the cross. He walked to the front of the church and genuflected before the altar. Tapestries depicting the stations of the cross decorated the walls, and in the fading light, he studied them. It had been a long time since he'd been in a church, but growing up, he'd regularly attended Mass. Perhaps that accounted for his sense of familiarity.

A door stood open. Frank walked through it into a hallway, where. a large oil portrait of a priest hung. "Father Jose Antonio Diaz" was inscribed on the ornate frame. He stared at the picture. His scalp tingled as though from pin pricks. The man he had just seen in the jungle looked uncannily like this man.

Frank went over and sat in one of the pews and pulled out the ancient tourist map he'd found in the stacks at Philippine Christian College and tucked into his pocket. It showed that the road he traveled continued across the mountain and came out on the other side of the island. He traced the main road with a finger from the bottom of the gorge to the top of the mountain, then all the way down the other side. He turned over the map to check for a date. Printed in 1956.

The rain began to slacken, so Frank headed back out to his car. He was still soaked to the bone from his run to the church. But before he turned the ignition key, he thought again about the picture of Father Jose Antonio Diaz. Something about it haunted him. With a grunt, he jumped from the car and ran back into the church.

As he opened the front door, another door at the opposite end of the church shut. Was he hearing things? He crept toward the rear door, ready for a confrontation. Moving quietly, quickly, his back against the wall, he kept one hand drawn back, ready to drop whoever was there. Puddles of water dotted the floor, and a large puddle had formed in front of the rear door. Someone had likely been in the church while he'd been there moments before. He eased open the back door, but saw no evidence of where the person had gone. He turned back into the church.

What if someone took his car? The skin on the back of his neck prickled as his eyes bored into the shadows. Without another thought, Frank lifted the picture of Father Diaz off the wall, turned and ran out the front door toward his car. Yes, it was still there. He stuffed the picture in the back seat, then started the car and drove off.

Just ahead was a side road he didn't recall seeing on the old map. The main road rimmed the gorge in places and was mostly traveled for the views it offered and the peaceful quiet of the woods. But why would a side road exist here? Probably a logging trail. Still, Frank thought he might as well have a look before he ran out of daylight.

He put the car back into gear and drove about a hundred yards; the side road turned into muddy ruts. Grass grew between what now looked like parallel footpaths. He thought about backing out of the road and continuing down the mountain. A freshly broken tree branch protruded from the side of a tall pine beside the road just ahead. Someone had recently driven a very large vehicle out here.

Again, Frank pulled out the map, and this time he traced the mountain road onto an engineer's pad. He drew in the approximate location of the dirt road and made a small asterisk where he'd just parked his car. He shouldered the binoculars but left the canteen behind. He'd only be gone a few minutes. Probably another dead end anyway.

Something in his gut told him differently. Sure enough, he'd only walked a few dozen yards when he saw more broken branches and grass that had been flattened by wide tires.

He made his way down the path, heeding his instinct to proceed quietly. The farther he walked, the more tension worked its way into his neck and shoulders. By the time he heard the sound of the engine, the hair on the back of his neck stood erect.

Frank moved off the rutted road into the palmetto-canopied area on the right, edging closer to the sound of heavy equipment. He glanced at the late-afternoon sky, realizing that soon whoever was out here would be calling it quits for the day. Within less than an hour it would be too dark to work.

As he came within sight of the activity, a deep yellow John Deere scraper backed up several hundred yards ahead of him. *Excavation. Using American equipment?* They were digging for something. Gold? *Of course, gold.*

Frank's suspicions were confirmed when he looked through his binoculars and recognized Colonel Fabian Ver commanding a small group of men. Ver wasn't dressed in his usual military uniform, but was wearing coveralls. The way he barked orders, however, left no doubt that he ruled the dozen or so men the same way he'd command his soldiers. Frank shifted in the thick patch of saw palmettos, adjusting his position so he could check out the faces of the other men. He recognized one of the men, Oscar Jimenez, a senior employee of Rodolfo Cuenca, one of President Marcos's cronies who not only owned the largest construction company in the Philippines, but was also a major contributor to Marcos's political campaign. *Like me.* Frank couldn't stop the tremor that ran through his body.

Frank scanned the rest of the faces, but recognized none of the other men. The one who stood conversing with Ver looked distinctly American, and another off to the side appeared to be Latino. Jimenez walked up to the Latino and started shouting, but Frank couldn't make out the words. The man shouted back. At first, Frank thought they were just trying to be heard over the earth-moving equipment, but when Jimenez began gesticulating wildly, Frank realized they were arguing.

The Latino puffed out his chest and shoved his finger into Jimenez's face.

Frank held his breath. You didn't point fingers in the Philippines—not even when indicating directions.

Jimenez drew back a fist, but his chest exploded. He looked down wide-eyed, as if surprised to see the red stain blooming on his shirt. Before he hit the ground, the Latino suffered the same fate.

Ver looked around the work site at all of the workers, then calmly re-holstered his pistol, bent over Jimenez and, with a finger, scooped out both of his eyeballs, leaving them hanging from the sockets by their stalks. Ver stood and motioned for the mess to be cleaned up.

Frank felt lightheaded. He gulped in a long, shuddering drink of air and swallowed hard, then retched into the palmettos, thankful the roar of the heavy equipment covered the sound.

The man driving the scraper stepped down off the machine without turning it off, and hooked his hands into Jimenez's armpits. Another Filipino grabbed the Latino by the feet. The two men dragged the bodies to the edge of the cliff, then kicked them like footballs off the high ledge into the ravine below.

Without ceremony, the scraper-driver returned to his machine and continued working. Ver walked back to the mouth of the shaft they were digging and resumed barking orders.

Frank dropped the binoculars and rubbed his sweaty palms on his trousers. *Murderer.* He'd just seen Ver kill two men, one of whom he'd met at the Cultural Center's grand opening.

This time, he didn't worry about making noise as he scrambled out of the prickly palmetto patch and hustled back to his car. He wouldn't be heard over the rumbling of the heavy equipment anyway, and he damned sure didn't want to be on this mountain—or anywhere near Ver—come nightfall.

Sleep that night came fitfully, punctuated by the intermittent storms raging outside Frank's bedroom window. Ver had found at least one more of the sites where the gold was buried; he was certain of it. And Ver worked for Marcos. *Did Marcos have these maps he had heard so much about? What was his father's involvement? What had he gotten himself into? Whatever it was, it was getting dangerous. Who was the stranger he had met in the jungle? Why was the Father's picture and that old church so compelling?* Frank wanted to find those maps so badly he could taste the bitterness of angst in his mouth.

Construction. Jimenez and Cuenca worked in construction. The old photo of his mother and Danilo Quezon was taken in front of Zapata Construction. What, exactly, had his father been involved in? Was he truly an honorable man? Or was he Ver's crony?

The next morning, the cloudless sky gleamed brilliant blue and reflected in the puddled water on the walkway in front of Frank's bungalow. The men Ver had killed last night would never see a sky like this again. Frank shook his head in an effort to clear the morbid thought from his mind.

He tossed his gym bag full of legal pads into the passenger seat and headed toward the library in hope of finding records on construction companies in Manila and its surrounding communities. It would be much quicker and easier to go straight to the city offices, but he couldn't risk being seen by the mayor or any of President Marcos's other acquaintances.

Frank smiled at the thin-faced man working at the circulation desk. The man grinned, nodded and opened the hinged countertop so Frank could come behind the desk and do his own research. After over a month of regular visits, the librarians now treated Frank as if he belonged there.

He slid behind the desk and pulled a fresh legal pad from his bag. As was his habit, he flipped the first few clean sheets over the binding so he later could turn them back to cover and hide his research notes.

Instead of asking for municipal records, Frank scrolled through the catalogue and the microfilm database in search of any articles mentioning new construction or requests for construction bids. Forty-five minutes later, he found what he wanted. Zapata Construction Company had been the front-runner in the bid for the new construction that instead had been awarded to Cuenca's company. Oscar Jimenez—the man he'd just seen murdered—worked for Cuenca Construction.

But what he really wanted to know was about the Zapata Construction. Five more minutes into his microfilm research, Frank discovered that Zapata Construction may or may not have been affiliated with Zapata Oil and Zapata Off-Shore, originally owned by U.S. House of Representatives member George H. W. Bush.

Frank dug deeper. His breath caught in his throat when he uncovered an article tying Zapata to the CIA. It all made sense. He quickly checked his notes to make sure he'd written down the address to Zapata Construction. He replaced the microfilm and the article clips he'd strewn about the study table, then packed his notepads and headed out the door.

"See you *bakas*," the librarian called after him.

"Tomorrow, yeah, sure." Frank jogged to his car and looked around to see if anyone was watching him. A man across the street looked away and quickly walked off. Paranoia in full swing, Frank started his car, dropped it into drive and sped away in the same direction, but the man was gone.

Chapter 10

Malacañang Palace, The Philippines
November 14, 1969

Rosalita tapped her leather-bound note pad and glanced up at Imelda. "We still have some holes in the agenda for our tea this afternoon."

Imelda ran a manicured finger around the rim of her crystal water glass. "Yes. After we finish discussing the Cultural Center and the Arts Gala, we need to remind our ladies it's their job to encourage their husbands to make the right decisions."

"And what 'right' decisions are we encouraging today, my friend?" Rosalita couldn't stop her smile. Most of the ladies coming to this "tea" were married to congressmen, senators, judges or other influential citizens. With Imelda's "encouragement," they often swayed their husband's votes or attitudes on issues important to Marcos's agendas.

"Foremost," Imelda said, her dark eyes lowering, "it's important to do whatever we can to keep those horrid election-tampering accusations off the front page of the newspapers." She shook her head.

"Ahhh. So Evelina LaMarr will be here today?" Evelina's husband was the editor of the largest newspaper in the Philippines.

"Yes. But it's also important that we come up with suggestions for other news-worthy items to keep the attention away from the accusations." Imelda shook her head. "I just don't understand why these people make these accusations. Don't they know we're doing everything we can for our country?"

"Oh my!" Rosalita jumped up. "Speaking of Evelina, I forgot to bring my gift for her and Sonny's new baby boy. I should run back and get it before tea begins."

"Okay, but hurry. I want to make sure you're here when the other ladies arrive. You have a way of setting the tone of our meetings, Rosalita."

Rosalita kissed her friend's cheeks, then stepped out of Imelda's office and closed the door behind her. When she turned, she was startled to see Severino Santa Romana standing just outside of Ferdinand's office.

Though Santa Romana and Marcos had been friends since before Ferdinand became president, usually they met in more discreet places.

Rosalita stood motionless as Santa Romana made the sign of the cross, pulled out a gold chain from inside his barong, kissed the large cross it bore and then replaced it inside his neckline. Only then did the handsome older man step inside Ferdinand's office.

Rosalita walked softly down the hall, taking care that her heels didn't clack on the hardwood floor. She stopped in pretended admiration of Imelda's new piece of artwork—a knock-off, she was certain of it—so she could eavesdrop outside Ferdinand's office. At first, she could only hear murmuring, but then Santa Romana's voice grew louder, more agitated.

"I know you must be aware of the accusation that you've stolen millions of U.S. dollars sent for medical supplies, housing improvements, and nutrition for the very poor."

Marcos chuckled. "Calm down, Santy. I've accounted for every dollar. Besides, Nixon will continue to support the Philippines—financially and otherwise—because the U.S. needs access to Clark Air Base. And if the CIA believes we can recover more gold, they'll back us, because they'll want their share."

"There's no way the U.S. is going to back off of the Tripartite Gold Commission."

"We are repatriating the gold." Marcos chuckled again. "That is, any gold that has a readable source imprint." His voice lowered, and Rosalita had to step closer to hear him. "But I still need your help."

Santa Romana cleared his throat. "In what manner?"

"If one of the groups under your umbrella can accompany the bullion to its location, these transfers could become quite lucrative for you. I can guarantee you a percentage of each account's net asset in return for gate-keeping. Plus, we'll want to place some of the gold in the names of your aliases."

"Of course. And what part will Lansdale play in these transfers?"

"Little, if any. He's assured me that you've even surpassed his own ability to handle the setup of account names, transfers, bank codes and passwords." Marcos laughed. "He called you 'The Man with No Name.'"

"I'd like to keep it that way. I want no one else outside the Philippines to know I exist. If you agree, then we dig next at Camp Aguinaldo, yes?"

"Agreed. We think we've cracked the code on the maps, so we can move from location to location without wasting as much time." Marcos huffed. "Of course, if we're off by even an inch, it can throw off the search by weeks. I'm putting together a team who can help us navigate not only the maps, but the terrain, especially underground. Over time, some of the landmarks on the maps have shifted. Trees have fallen, rivers have re-routed themselves through the mountains, other such things. The searches require men with experience."

"We can move the men who are digging at Fort Boniface to Aguinaldo."

"Actually," said Marcos, "I'd like to leave them at Boniface. They've been digging for a very long time—"

"Years. Without results."

"So I think it will make a good show for the Japanese and the press to see us digging there without success. As far as I'm concerned, we'll let the men dig there through the next decade. They won't recover anything. It'll throw off any other treasure hunters to the true existence of the treasure. They'll think we are fools in pursuit of a foolish dream."

Rosalita's heart pounded. Ver had recently recovered thousands of tons of gold and jewels near the Montalban Gorge. Imelda had told her about the room Marcos was reinforcing to store it in the palace, as soon as the gold bars returned from being re-smelted to remove their source markings. But to know there was so much more left to be discovered, uncovered and fed into the coffers of these men made her feel weak. *If that gold falls into the wrong hands* . . . Rosalita shuddered.

"I also want to begin recovery at Fort Santiago right away."

Fort Santiago? Imelda had mentioned that she wanted to start historical restoration there.

"How will you pull that off, Ferdinand? It's a protected site."

"Of course it is. What better place for the Japanese to bury gold, than where the U.S. would never have bombed? Fort Santiago is a sixteenth-century Spanish fort. You know my wife's penchant for beautification and preservation of such places. Restoration of Fort Santiago will provide the perfect guise for our excavation in the area." Marcos coughed. "That's why I wanted to bring Frank Young on board. I'd like to have his hand in that particular project."

"Frank Young?"

"The cigarette seller."

"I know who he is." Santa Ramona's voice dropped even lower, and Rosalita moved right next to the slightly opened door, her heart pounding at the mention of Frank's name. "Why him?"

"I had him checked out. He has a degree in engineering. That could come in handy."

"You have your pick of engineers. Why involve an American?"

"He's an interesting young man," Marcos said. "And I want to get to know him better."

"Leave him alone! He has nothing to do with—"

"My, my. A bit touchy, aren't we? Is there something you know about him I don't?"

"The only thing I know about him is that he appears to be an amiable young man. I don't know why you'd want to involve him in your—"

"My what?"

"Look, I will help you in whatever way I can. I will give you my assistance, I will give you my loyalty, I will give you my identity. I will even give you my very soul . . ." He paused, and his voice grew heavier. "But leave Frank Young out of this. I don't trust new people."

Marcos chuckled, and this time, something in his tone caused shivers to run up Rosalita's arms.

The room grew quiet; their meeting had reached its end. Rosalita had heard enough. If she were caught eavesdropping, she'd compromise more than just her friendship with the Marcoses. She slipped off her heels, grabbed them by the straps, and scurried down the hallway and through the doors that led to the Grand Staircase.

CHAPTER 11

Manila, The Philippines
January 23, 1970

The early morning sun slanted through the window, illuminating dust motes as Frank stretched into the cool-down phase of his martial arts practice. He'd awoken before dawn in a panic, remembering that, while he'd changed the license plate on his car back to the one he used when driving around town as a rep for Triangle Tobacco, he'd forgotten to remove the Philippine flag sticker from the back bumper. He hustled outside in the dark, peeled off the removable sticker, double-checked the license plate, and threw a Pure Gold baseball cap into the rear window. He might not be good at disguises, but his car certainly had to be.

Frank tried to return to bed, but it was no use. He felt anxious about his trip to the Marcoses' palace later today. Though prayer usually calmed his mind, it did nothing for him this morning, and his pocket rosary felt more like a trinket than the holy talisman he'd always considered it to be. Instead, he launched into an hour of Thai kickboxing, followed by several Kung Fu katas and now Tai Chi. He finished with the meditation practices he'd learned from the Buddhists in Thailand. Something told him he'd need to be at the top of his game today.

The closer he became to President Marcos, the more he flirted with danger. Bozeman had warned him of this, but now he *felt it*. Ver always watched him with suspicious eyes, and he'd seen first-hand the man's lack of moral principles. Ver's promotion from colonel to general evidenced Marcos's appreciation for the man's fierce loyalty. Frank had also learned through his research that Marcos and Ver were related.

Frank felt other eyes on him as well, but some of it was to be expected. Since Marcos's inauguration at the end of last month, the streets of Manila were daily flooded with protesters—as many as fifty thousand. Police ended some of the protests with bloodshed, but demonstrators, albeit in smaller numbers, still persisted.

"Osmeña and Magsaysay are full of *bulla bulla*," General Ver had said after the inauguration. "They paid out a small fortune to the poor just to get them to demonstrate."

Frank didn't believe that to be true for a moment. The Filipinos didn't have to be bought; they had opinions of their own. Common word on the street was that Malacañang Palace was full of gold bars, though the Filipinos were divided on whether they were legitimately obtained or otherwise confiscated. Some even said the U.S. had given Marcos gold bullion, but Frank knew better.

As to the truth about the presence of gold bars in the palace, Frank decided tonight was the night he'd find out.

The thought made his stomach clench. He'd hoped to secure another private meeting with Marcos, but he knew he'd done much better than most—especially during such a tumultuous time—to receive an invitation to the palace at all. Frank didn't think it would be that hard to figure out where in the palace the gold was located, if that's where it was indeed stored, because Marcos loved bragging about his wealth. But actually getting close enough to see it and prove its existence was a different story. Marcos had surrounded himself with the Philippine Constabulary, as well as a group of military officers put together by General Ver. And if Ver caught him looking for the gold . . . .

A tremor raced through Frank's torso. The thought of what Ver might do sickened him.

He grabbed a pair of latex gloves and sprinkled baby powder in them so they'd come off easily. He couldn't risk leaving fingerprints behind. He stuffed the gloves in his pocket and brushed off the residue. The two tiny tools the CIA had given him to pick locks slipped easily into the hidden fold of his wallet. He hoped he would remember the instructions Howard Hunt had so patiently gone over with him.

Frank glanced at his rosary he'd earlier tossed on his desk. At this point, he could use any help he could get. He snatched the string of beads and shoved them in his pocket as well, and then, for good measure, crossed himself. "Father, Son and Holy Spirit. Be with me."

⅄

Later that night, Frank pushed his way through the crowd of protesters near Malacañang Palace. It surprised him to see not only grown men and women, but even young children, bearing placards. Some looked too young to read the signs they held.

Moments later in the palace courtyard, Frank was frisked and asked to hand over his car keys. Odd, he thought, but he supposed he could understand the necessity of surrendering anything that could be used as a weapon. He took a deep, calming breath. *My body is strong. It is the only weapon I need.*

Rosalita waited for him inside the palace doors. She grabbed his arm. "I hoped you'd be here tonight," she said, her voice thick.

As always when he saw Rosalita, words escaped him. In fact, his senses went numb, overwhelmed by the teasing hint of her perfume, the satiny softness of her skin, the melodious rhythm of her slightly-accented English, and the flawless beauty of every square inch of her.

"Are you okay?"

Frank filled his lungs with oxygen, which helped clear his head. "Yes. Sorry. It's so good to see you."

"I'm afraid I'm a bit too forward. I just assumed you'd want to see me. Perhaps I assume too much?"

"Oh, no. No, no, no." He smiled, then, remembering his manners, bent at the waist and dramatically kissed her hand. "I am quite honored, milady."

Rosalita giggled. "Now you're just being silly. Come on. Let's head upstairs."

Finally relaxed, Frank nodded and linked arms with her. He'd need to break free from her to look for the gold and the maps, but for now her presence was comforting. Ver wouldn't touch him while she was present—or so he hoped.

The thought of Ver sent a new wave of panic over him. His legs weakened and almost betrayed him.

Get a grip, man. Frank willed his heart to calm. As long as he kept his true purpose from Ver, he had no reason to feel panicked. *Except that you're hoping to break into a treasure vault tonight, right under the nose of the president and all his men.*

"Are you even listening to me?" Rosalita admonished. "Honestly, I don't think you've heard a word I've said. I thought you'd be pleased that so many of the women here are smoking Blue Lady Slims."

"I'm sorry, Rosalita. I'm pleased, yes. I guess I'm amazed at the heavy security here tonight. I've never seen this many armed men on my previous visits. It's like the whole Philippine Army is here."

"Well, not the *whole* army. Some of them are Marines." She chuckled. "But there are enough of them to keep Osmeña's thugs from getting any bright ideas. Poor Ferdinand has had four assassination threats in the past two days alone. I'm really frightened for him and Imelda during the upcoming State of the Nation address." She shook her head. "They aren't sleeping well." "Hey, hey. It's okay. I'm sure they'll both be fine. Look around you, Rosalita. The palace is a fortress. Even if they have to stay put until the rioting calms down, this is not such a bad place to hibernate, is it?" He lifted Rosalita's chin with a finger, surprised to see puddles in her eyes. This woman really cared for the Marcoses.

Rosalita smiled bravely. "Not if you have any appreciation for fine art, it isn't."

Frank laughed, relieved the tension had passed. "That's right! You were an art major at Wellesley." He looked around the second floor at the plethora of paintings and artwork. "Have you ever seen so much fine art in one place? Other than a museum, of course."

"Not everything is as it appears."

"Excuse me? What do you—"

"I don't mean to sound petty. Imelda has some incredible pieces in her collection."

Rosalita offered a coy look from beneath her lashes. "It's just that, well, let's just say a few so-called collectors have taken advantage of her and sold her fakes."

"You're kidding me! And she hasn't sued them?"

"You can't convince her they aren't originals, or that they haven't been painted by an up-and-coming Rembrandt. Believe me, I've tried. I only made her angry."

"I can't imagine seeing Imelda angry. She always wears that charming smile of hers, like a Filipina Mona Lisa."

Rosalita laughed and patted Frank's arm. "Trust me. She may be a beauty queen on the surface, but there's a raging fire beneath. She's merely learned to keep her anger controlled in the public eye. It serves her well." She tilted her head. "I would do well to learn from her."

"Oh?"

"Let's just say I spent enough time in America to express what I'm thinking—sometimes *without* thinking."

Frank smiled and glanced around, imagining what might lie behind every closed door. He wondered if he could get Rosalita to divulge some of the Marcoses' secrets—without thinking. "This is quite an impressive home. So many rooms."

"Yes, and Imelda has recently renovated much of it. Wait until you see the discotheque." She guided Frank through another set of double doors, which led to yet another broad staircase. "It takes up most of the third floor."

"I have to admit, when I received the invitation to the disco party I was surprised, but when I heard the palace had its own discotheque, I figured it was a rumor—just a ballroom decorated for a dance. So it's really true."

"Absolutely, it's true! You won't believe it. I introduced Imelda to David Mancuso when we were shopping in Manhattan in the spring. David was building his own private discotheque in his house, and Imelda simply had to have one of her own. In fact, David's private club probably isn't even finished yet, because Imelda coaxed his interior designer to fly back with us to the Philippines. The man lived here in the palace for two months while he redesigned the top floor."

"How big is the palace, anyway?"

"Square footage? I have no idea. It has three floors, plus the basement makes four. There are other buildings on the grounds, of course, but I only come here."

"What's in the basement?"

Rosalita shrugged. "I'm not really sure. Housekeepers' quarters? No, that can't be right; most of Imelda's staff has rooms on the first floor. I have no idea. It must not be anything remarkable, or I'm sure Imelda would have redesigned it and thrown a party there as well."

Nothing remarkable. Would Rosalita find crates of gold remarkable?

As they reached the top of the stairs, Sly and the Family Stone's "Everyday People" blasted from the four-foot-high speakers that perched on the sides of a stage at the back of the discotheque. A huge mirrored ball hung from the center of the ceiling, splashing a kaleidoscope of electric colors across the polished floor. Frank felt as if he'd walked into a nightclub instead of a room in Malacañang Palace. "Unbelievable."

"Isn't it?" Rosalita grabbed his arm and pulled him toward the dance floor. "Come on, Frank. I love this song."

Frank turned his head and grimaced but knew it was useless. Maybe if he went ahead and got a dance out of the way, he could avoid it the rest of the night.

No such luck.

Three songs later, he insisted that Rosalita needed a cocktail, and he was just the man to retrieve it. "Allow me. Please"

She laughed. "You're a good sport, Frank. I suppose you deserve a drink."

"Besides, I haven't even said hello to our host and hostess. Have you seen them?"

"Imelda will be fashionably late, of course, even to her own party. I'm guessing Ferdinand is in his office. Both will be on the second floor." Rosalita linked her arm through his again. "Want to see if we can find them?"

Despite her charms, Frank suddenly felt smothered, trapped. He'd have to break away from her if he wanted to search the palace. But he hadn't seen the entire second floor either, so he may as well accompany her.

This time when they reached the Grand Staircase, Rosalita bore left instead of right, where the Marcoses' offices were located. A uniformed soldier nodded and stepped aside from the double doors he guarded. As if she belonged there, Rosalita entered without knocking. The soldier cut Frank a stern look, but Frank only nodded and walked through the doors, close on Rosalita's heels.

"Imelda? Imelda, dear, where are you?"

A housekeeper appeared and slightly bowed. "I'm sorry, Miss Laurel. The first lady went upstairs to dance."

Rosalita turned on her heel and pulled Frank along with her. "Funny, I didn't see her, did you? I guess she went up the backstairs."

Backstairs. Frank glanced around, trying to figure out where those would be located. He should have known the palace would have private stairways and exits to provide safe passage for the president during an emergency.

Rosalita pulled a Blue Lady Slim from her clutch and held it to her lips. Frank lit it for her, trying to ignore the sensual look she sent his way as he did so. He didn't want a relationship with this woman—at least, nothing more than friendship. She seemed insistent on taking things up a notch, however, and Frank knew most men would consider him a fool for not taking her as a lover. Rosalita had it all—wealth, political connections, intelligence and smoldering beauty. But getting involved with her could be the death of him—quite literally.

"Ready for another dance? I've caught my breath, now." Frank dreaded another dance, but offered his elbow, and Rosalita smiled as she linked her arm with his.

As they walked the hallway, President Marcos, flanked by Fabian Ver, Minister of Defense Juan Ponce Enrile, a few men Frank recognized as chiefs of the Philippine Constabulary, and at least half a dozen men he didn't know walked toward them.

Marcos cocked his head sideways and smiled. "Miss Rosalita and Mr. Young, what a pleasure it is to have you." He kissed Rosalita's hand and then extended a handshake to Frank. "I'm so glad you came, Frank."

"Thank you so much for having me, Mr. President." Frank bowed his head as he spoke.

"Rosalita, will you forgive me if I steal away your escort? We'll only be gone a little while."

Surprised, Frank looked up. Ver glared at him with narrow eyes.

"Really, Ferdinand, you *must* learn to have a good time." Rosalita reached up and kissed Frank's cheek before she turned loose of his arm and walked past the group of men. One of the men toward the back of the group turned to watch as she walked away, then met Frank's eyes with a mischievous smile.

"Thank you for parting with her, Frank. We were just about to open a celebratory bottle of scotch sent to me by your President Nixon. Won't you join us for a drink in my study?"

Frank's mouth moved, but it was a moment before his tongue worked. "Yes. Yes, of course. Thank you."

Frank fell in alongside Marcos, inadvertently forcing Ver to walk behind him. He imagined the man burning holes in his skull with his beady eyes as they rounded the corner into Marcos's well-appointed study.

Marcos motioned toward a bar-cart, and Juan Ponce Enrile, the Secretary of Justice, took crystal glasses from the shelf and filled them with ice from the ice bucket.

"I'm sorry, Frank." Marcos opened his arms and gestured toward the group of men. "Where are my manners? Let me introduce you to my friends." He opened a small gold box on his desk, retrieved a cigarette, and motioned toward each of the men in turn, his hand held flat.

Don't ever point, Frank reminded himself.

"This is Major General Fidel Ramos, Commander of the Philippine Constabulary; Army Major General Rafael Zagala; AFP Chief of Staff General Romeo Espino; Air Force Chief Major General Jose Rancudo; Navy Admiral Hilario Ruiz; Colonel Ignacio Paz—Paz is Chief of Intelligence of the Joint General Staff—and Eduardo Cojaungco. We call Eduardo 'Danding.' Danding is Chairman of the San Miguel Corporation."

Marcos smiled, then continued. "Colonel Romeo Gatan is PC Commander of the Rizal province, and Colonel Alfredo Montoya is the PC Metropolitan Command Chief. You've already met Brigadier General Tomas Diaz of the First PC Zone, Juan Ponce Enrile, and Fabian Ver. Ver has recently been promoted to general."

Ver forced a smile, revealing a row of small, even teeth. His eyes, however, remained icy.

"These men are my twelve apostles," Marcos said.

Chuckles broke out among the group as Enrile handed out the scotch on the rocks. *Why am I here then*, Frank wondered. It struck him as odd that all the men were members of the Philippine military, with the exception of Danding. The San Miguel Corporation was at one time strictly a brewery, but now also distributed Coca-Cola and other food products throughout the Philippines.

Marcos beckoned toward Frank. "And gentlemen, please meet my friend Franklin Young, whom we call 'Frank.' Frank is with Triangle Tobacco in America. Triangle is not only my campaign supporter, but the manufacturer of Pure Gold cigarettes, as well as the popular new Blue Lady Slims, created especially for our Filipinas." He again opened the gold box on his desk and pushed it toward the men. "You must try them, but first we toast." Marcos held up his glass. "To loyalty."

"To loyalty," the men echoed.

"To loyalty," Frank said a heartbeat later. Marcos locked eyes with him over his glass. As Frank raised his glass, he felt his soul being sucked into a vortex of evil.

Enrile made the rounds, adding another shot to each man's glass, but this time the men sipped of their own accord as they talked amongst themselves. Frank thanked Enrile as the man poured a few fingers into his glass.

"Gentlemen," Marcos said, and those gathered immediately quieted. "Let's take care of business so we can join the party upstairs." He turned to

Frank. "If you'll please excuse us, Frank. I should let you return to Rosalita's side before she comes after me."

A few of the men laughed, but Ver's face remained stern. Admiral Ruiz opened the door for Frank and shook his hand on the way out the door. "Pleased to meet you, Frank. We'll talk again, I'm sure."

Frank nodded. Ruiz shut the door, closing him out of the meeting.

⚔

Rosalita accepted a glass of champagne from the server's tray and made her way through the crowd to the lounge sofa by the side of the stage where Imelda sat. "Brilliant party, Imelda. The band is excellent."

"They're from New York, of course. I knew you'd like them."

"Do you have it? Have they finished with it yet?"

Imelda smiled and held out her fist.

Rosalita opened her hand, and Imelda dropped an object into it. A shiny brass key. She clenched a fist around the treasure, snaked her hand into her satin clutch, and deposited the key to Franklin Young's bungalow. A smile curled her lips.

Imelda laughed. "I believe you have a penchant for this sort of work, my dear Rosalita. Maybe you can replace Sean Connery in the spy business. You can wear a wig and be the new James Bondetta."

Rosalita shook her head, but had to laugh at the mischievous twinkle in her friend's eye. "I haven't done anything. Yet."

"Ahhh, but you will. Now that you have the key to his home, you will." Imelda placed her hand alongside Rosalita's cheek and smiled. "Who knows? Perhaps by the time we learn all there is to know about Franklin Young, you'll have the key to his heart as well."

CHAPTER 12

Stunned by how easily he was dismissed from the group in Marcos's office, Frank stood in the hallway, unsure of his next step. What was that all about anyway? Why would Marcos want to introduce him to all those men? Had he really grown close enough to the president for the man to invite him to meet his inner circle? *No. If so, he'd have wanted me to stay. Marcos wants the men to know who I am so they can watch me.*

As he reached the Grand Stairway, Frank looked around. Other than a few late-arriving guests he didn't know, he was alone. He slipped down the stairway, nodding to a couple he passed. A man in a powder-blue leisure suit stood at the bottom of the stairs, his hand in his pocket. As Frank passed him, the man glanced at Frank, then ran up the stairs. When Frank reached the palace's reception hall, he avoided the multiple gatherings of guests and ducked into a door near the back of the large room, which led to a wide hallway. At the end of the hall, another closed door beckoned him. Frank looked over his shoulder. Not another soul around. He reached into his pocket and slipped on the latex gloves, then pushed through the door and found another, narrower hall with several doors along both sides. He opened the first door to find a small, sparsely furnished bedroom. Same with the next four doors. When he reached the fifth door, he opened it to find an older woman sitting on the edge of a low bed, sewing what looked to be an apron.

"Oh!" She gripped the material to her chest in surprise.

"I'm sorry! Ummm, *paumanhin. Kailangan ko ng banyo.* Where is the toilet?"

The woman visibly relaxed and pointed upstairs, her smile revealing missing front teeth.

"*Salamat.* Thank you." Frank stepped backward and closed the door. Hopefully, she didn't realize he wore suspicious rubber gloves. He took a deep breath and moved to the next door. Again, a bedroom. He was getting nowhere. Then he noticed the last door in the hallway was painted black, whereas the others were stained wood. He stood outside it, listening, before he slowly turned the knob.

Locked. It was the first locked doorway he'd found. Even the staff bedrooms didn't have privacy locks on the door. Frank fished out his lock-picking tools.

Looking around, he quietly slipped the tools in the lock. Within seconds, he heard the telltale click. He grabbed the doorknob with his gloved hands, and with one last glance over his shoulder, Frank shot through the door.

This hall was short. Two yards long, at most, dimly lit by a bare bulb overhead, its pull-chain dangling within reach. When his eyes adjusted, he saw that the hall turned right, and he slid against the wall until he reached the corner. He peeked around the corner, surprised to see concrete stairs leading down. *The basement!* Frank quickly retraced his steps, locked the black door, then headed down the stairs.

The lower he descended, the darker and danker the still air grew. He remained pressed against the wall as he moved down the steps. Midway down, his fingers found another corner and he peered around the edge of it, thinking he'd found another hallway. He stepped inside, hands outstretched in the inky darkness. His lighter always handy, he snatched it and flicked the flint, illuminating the immediate area. A low passageway ran under the palace, filled with pipes and conduits. He stepped out onto the stairs again and continued downward.

When he reached the bottom of the stairs, another door awaited. This one bore a small, square window, and through it he saw a longer, wider hallway lit by wire-covered hanging lights. The hallway was empty, but with better lighting and finished walls, he assumed it was used more often. He tested the knob. The door opened.

He skulked down the hallway, trying to keep his hard-soled shoes from making a sound on the wet, unfinished concrete floor. The still air hung heavy; the stench of copper and ammonia assaulted his nose. The passage had six steel doors down the left side and another door at the end with a sliver of light glowing from under the door. A rubber water hose lay coiled midway down the hall, one end attached to a leaking spigot protruding from the wall.

Frank reached the first door, which sported a large metal plate with a lock above the doorknob. He put his hand on the knob, but just as he started to twist, a shuffling sound came from inside the room.

He froze.

The blood rushing through his ears made it hard to know if he'd imagined the sound.

Then he heard it again. Rats, perhaps?

He gripped the knob tighter, started to turn it, but before it moved a centimeter, another sound, like scratching, came from behind the door. With as much patience as he could muster, Frank turned the knob with his gloved hand. It wasn't locked. He'd only opened it a few inches when something skittered across his foot, causing his heart to lurch in his chest. A huge rat ran down the hallway and disappeared into a hole in the concrete wall.

Except for a dripping sound from the spigot several yards away, the passageway again grew silent. Frank pushed the door open enough to let in scant light from the hallway. The stench of feces, urine and vomit took his breath. He gagged and buried his nose in the crook of his arm. As his eyes adjusted to the darkness, horror crawled through his veins. Oh, God, what had he stumbled upon?

Iron shackles, attached to the wall with thick chains, lay on the floor. A straight-backed metal chair and a heavy-looking metal desk with an empty wine bottle and a jar half-full of eggs sat in the corner. In the opposite corner lay what was left of a human head, still covered with dark hair but little tissue.

The rat had feasted well.

Frank averted his eyes and focused on the jar of eggs. Something wasn't as it seemed. The murky liquid didn't hold eggs, but grayish balls, like ping-pong balls, except with strings attached. Some of the balls had dark spots in the middle.

Eyeballs.

Ver. The dig site on Montalban Gorge. Frank's stomach lurched. He jumped from the room like he'd caught fire, closing the door to the torture chamber. Suddenly claustrophobic and dizzy despite the width and length of the hallway, he bowed his head, forcing himself to take slow, steady breaths. When he opened his eyes, he saw bloodstains on the floor. His eyes followed the spatter across the floor and up the wall. He stepped away from the wall, noticing for the first time that a thick spray of old, dark blood discolored the area where he'd stood. The coppery smell—blood.

Undoubtedly, Ver used this place to imprison, torture and kill anyone who went against him or Marcos.

What could he do? Who could he tell? There was no one here he could trust. Frank had never felt so alone—and trapped—in his life.

Frank hurried toward the door with the peeking light at the end of the hall.

He turned the knob, but the door was locked. He retrieved his lock pick and again picked the lock and entered the room. Here the floor was dry and made of smooth stones, and a thick red carpet runner ran down the center and around the corner. Evenly spaced wall sconces cast warm light, a stark contrast to the passageway he'd just left. Two larger sconces flanked a large wooden door with intricately carved panels, reminding Frank of the doors he'd seen in some of the fine hotels and restaurants in Thailand. *Malacañang Palace—like heaven and hell in one place.*

Of course, the door was locked. With shaking hands, Frank quickly picked the lock. Despite the coolness of the air underground, a bead of sweat dripped from his nose.

The door was heavier than any of the others, and it swung outward instead of inward. A key fell from above the doorframe, making a tingling sound as it hit the floor. Frank's mouth fell open. Someone had put the key above the door. *How strange!* Air sucked in as he pulled open the door to darkness. He felt alongside the wall until his fingers found a switch.

Nothing could have prepared Frank for what the brilliant light illuminated. Overhead a huge crystal chandelier sent prisms of light to every corner and crevice of the huge room that contained—Frank gasped—wall-to-wall bars of gold. Every bar gleamed as if it had been polished to a shine. And actually, it had. No doubt the gold had been re-smelt to remove the country of origin imprint that would have allowed it to be returned to its rightful owners as per the Tripartite Gold Commission.

Gold bars were stacked like bricks into rectangular columns that reached above Frank's head. Only a few inches lay between each stack, and the stacks ran along all four walls. More stacks filled the center of the room, these only about chest-high, leaving just enough room to walk between them like grocery store aisles. Before he could stop himself, Frank let out a long, low whistle. Why hadn't he brought a camera?

He immediately bit his lip and pulled the door closed behind him. He turned, still unable to process the wealth he saw. Tons and tons and tons of gold. Thousands of tons of gold. *Thousands.* Frank shivered.

How many burial sites of hidden gold had been harvested? And the maps! Did Marcos have the maps? If Marcos felt safe in keeping the gold here, wouldn't he keep the maps here as well?

Frank moved between the stacks, looking for any place where maps could be stored. It didn't help that he had no clue what he was looking for. Rolls of parchment? Packets folded like roadmaps? A legal pad like the ones he carried?

Near the back of the large room stood a desk. It was not as grand as the desk in Marcos's office, but instead appeared utilitarian and out of place among the room's opulence. He drew closer. A set of scales rested on one end, surrounded by lead weights, reminding him of the scales of justice. *What justice is there in holding men prisoner, in killing and torturing for the sake of wealth?* Frank's jaws ached, and he realized he'd been clenching his teeth.

An ornate door stood to the left of the desk. It, too, was locked. Frank reached for his tools, but a nagging voice in the back of his mind told him he'd been gone too long. He needed to get back before he was missed. He'd explore this door another day—a day when he brought his camera along.

He moved to the desk, opening and closing drawers as quickly and quietly as possible. He found a pocket-sized ledger. He rifled through it, but it contained only short strings of numbers and dates. Bank accounts, maybe? He placed it back in the drawer, exactly where it was before, and moved on. A bottom drawer held four crystal highballs and a bottle half full of rum. No maps.

Frank moved around the room's perimeter, checking for any hidden shelves or doors, but found nothing. When he made his way back to the door, he took one last look around, trying to memorize everything he saw and shook his head. He eased the door open, glancing around, then stepped out into the dank hallway.

He replaced the key over the doorframe and headed back through the dark, putrid hallway. He turned his head from the torture chamber as he passed, not allowing his mind to think of what terrors had happened in that space.

He was mostly up the first section of the stairs when the door above swung open, spilling light from upstairs into the short hallway. Frank leapt up the final three stairs and ducked inside the space where the water pipes ran. He moved several feet back. Cobwebs and spider webs wrapped around his head.

"I can't imagine he'd be down here," said a deep voice Frank didn't recognize. "How would he know this place even exists?"

"He shouldn't. He's somewhere in this palace, though, isn't he? He wouldn't have left without saying goodbye to Rosalita, and the men at the door haven't seen him." Ver's voice caused every muscle in Frank's body to tense for battle. He drew up his hands and stiffened his fingers, ready to attack before he was attacked.

Two sets of booted footsteps came down the stairs. From the darkness, Frank recognized Colonel Villacrusis as the man who accompanied Ver. He'd met the amicable Villacrusis at the Cultural Center grand opening gala and knew the man was an intelligence officer. If Villacrusis also knew of the torture chamber . . . how far had the roots of corruption grown?

The door at the bottom of the stairs opened, but Frank didn't hear it close. The men's muddled voices echoed against the concrete walls so that Frank couldn't make out what they were saying.

Frank focused on his breathing in order to slow his galloping heart. Soon the footsteps returned.

"Could Takeda have made copies of the maps?" Ver asked.

"According to Valmores, no. But we have no way of knowing."

Maps! The word shot through Frank's brain like a bullet.

"Perhaps Chichibu gave him two satchels, and Valmores kept one for himself."

"Relax." Villacrusis clapped Ver on the back as the two men passed Frank's hiding spot again. "He's a very poor man. He has nothing. If he'd known he had maps at his disposal, don't you think he'd have already uncovered some of the gold?"

"You're right, Vill. It's just that treasure hunting has become a weekend sport in the Philippines. Treasure maps are everywhere, but they all lead to nowhere. I don't want any valid maps to fall into the hands of anyone outside the Rebel Group."

When the door slammed and the lock clicked above, Frank waited for a few moments, then cautiously tiptoed from his hiding place and shook off the spider webs. One step at a time, he hugged the wall until he reached the door. He pressed his ear against it.

Ver's voice boomed from the other side. "Do not let anyone in or out of this door. Got it?"

"Yes, sir," a man's voice answered.

Frank considered his odds. He could wait in the dank hallway a while longer, then hope the guard wouldn't hear him unlocking the door and wouldn't have a gun pointed at him when he opened it.

Or, he could go back to the room of gold and see where that locked ornate door led. Frank bounded down the stairs, ran pell-mell through the dank hall of the torture chamber, and again used his pick tools to open the door to the room of gold. He quickly relocked the door and ran back to the ornate door by the desk. The lock was actually easier to pick than the other doors, and, once opened, led to a carpeted stairway. He jogged up the spiral stairs for what felt like at least two stories. It stopped at a heavy door. He pushed. *Damn it!* Another lock. Frantically, Frank picked it. He opened the door an inch, then two. When he saw a high-canopied bed, he realized he'd found the bedroom of one of the Marcoses. He slipped through the door and turned the lock, then dove behind the bed.

Grateful his years of martial arts training had paid off, Frank slunk through the house as quietly and gracefully as a ninja, working his way past two housekeepers who never set eyes on him. He reached the main doorway to the Presidential Residence. *Shit.* He'd forgotten the guard outside the door.

Hastily, Frank retraced his steps back to the bedroom. If stairs went down to the first floor and basement, then stairs must also go up to the third floor. And Rosalita had mentioned that Imelda may have gone to the ballroom from the backstairs. He opened a door to find only a closet with no exit.

Another bedroom, perhaps. Frank slipped through a short hallway he'd missed before and found himself in another bedroom, this one more feminine. Did Marcos and Imelda have separate bedrooms? How odd.

Sure enough, in the exact same place where the door to the stairwell leading down was located in the first bedroom, Frank found a door leading to a stairwell going up, this one carpeted in deep purple. Of course; Imelda's back stairway to her discotheque. Quickly, he stuffed his picking tools back in his wallet and his latex gloves in his jacket pocket. He'd hardly made it a few steps before he heard the thumping rhythm of the band overhead.

When he reached the door at the top of the stairs, he opened it a crack and peered out, realizing he was behind the stage, hidden from view by shimmery curtains. For the first time in what seemed like hours, Frank breathed a sigh of relief.

Then he noticed his hands.

They were covered with baby powder. He parted the curtains, happy to see a packed dance floor with Rosalita and Imelda in its center, drinking up the spotlight. Frank slipped along the perimeter of the crowd until he made it to a restroom door. Thank God, no one was inside.

He locked the door behind him, took off his jacket and hung it on the knob. After scrubbing his hands and splashing cold water on his face, he noticed a half-drunk glass of amber liquid over melting ice perched on the corner of a small dressing table. He picked it up, sniffed it, and tossed back the double-shot of tequila. *Someone else's drink. The alcohol would be strong enough to kill germs. As if that were his greatest worry.*

Fortified, his hands barely shaking, he again shook off the remaining cobwebs, then put on his jacket, smoothed back his hair and stepped outside the lavatory.

Only to come face-to-face with Fabian Ver. Villacrusis stood right on the man's heels.

Ver's eyes narrowed and he drew within an inch of Frank's face, snarling. "We've missed you. Where have you been?"

Frank breathed out heavily. "I think I had a little . . . too much to drink."

Ver's nostrils flared and his upper lip curled as Frank's tequila breath hit his nose. Then he laughed, catching Frank completely off-guard. The man was a mercurial time bomb.

Ver turned to the colonel. "It seems that Frank here can't handle his liquor. Let's hope he can handle his ladies better." The general clapped Frank on the back, harder than Frank thought necessary, then strolled into the discotheque laughing heartily.

Chapter 13

Manila, The Philippines
February 7, 1970

Frank leaned back in the comfortable guest chair in Timothy Bozeman's office. He'd spent twenty minutes on the telephone with CIA Director Richard Helms, and now Bozeman was cross-examining him.

"Think, Frank. Think. This is important." Bozeman rubbed his forehead.

Frank shook his head. "All I was thinking about was getting out of there with my eyeballs intact. It was dark, spiders were crawling over my shoulders, rats were playing with my shoelaces, and Ver was steps away."

"Stop with the drama."

"You weren't there."

"Okay, okay. Maps. What did Ver say about the maps?"

Frank rubbed his temples. "Ver asked Villacrusis if some Japanese guy could've made copies of the maps."

Bozeman sighed. "You're not a very good spy."

"No shit. Can I go home now?"

Bozeman laughed. "Not until you get the maps. Now, the name. Was it Murakusi?"

"Murakusi," Frank muttered, running the name through his memory drives. "I don't think so. Doesn't sound familiar."

"Chichibu?"

"Yeah. Yes! That was one of the names."

"There were multiple names?"

"Yes. Ver said, are you sure these are the only maps Valmores had? Somebody could've given him two satchels and kept one for himself."

Bozeman expelled a sharp laugh. "Takeda General, Takeda."

"Yes. Takeda."

"Great. Okay. I'll call Helms back and give him the names."

"Is it okay if I go grab a coffee?"

"Sure. Go ahead." Bozeman turned his back to Frank and dialed the phone.

Frank walked down the hallway to the stairwell, then ambled down the stairs. He wasn't sure why the names of the people were important or what it had to do with finding the gold. He just hoped it meant he was a step closer to going home.

He found his way to the break room. Thankfully, it was empty and he didn't have to make small talk with anyone. But the coffee pot was empty. Frank sighed. He opened drawers and cabinets until he found the pre-measured coffee packets, then filled the carafe with cold water and started the American-made machine. While the coffee pot wheezed and gurgled, Frank opened more drawers until he found a stash of cheese crackers. He opened a package and nibbled until the coffee machine finally quieted.

He filled two Styrofoam cups with the steaming liquid, then meandered back up the stairs to Bozeman's office.

Tim Bozeman was off the phone and busy writing on a legal pad. He didn't look up, not even when Frank placed one of the coffees in front of him.

"Thanks." Bozeman finished a paragraph, then lifted his eyes. "We need to get you ready to leave for Tokyo."

Images of pagodas and kimonos filled Frank's imagination. "Tokyo? Why?"

"You might be the one who can get Takeda to talk."

"Why me?"

"You don't have 'C-I-A' written all over you."

Frank grimaced.

"Hey, look. It's a free vacation."

Frank grunted. "Yeah. Right. Nothing comes free in this job."

"Except the coffee." Bozeman lifted his coffee cup and took a sip. "Do you know what the Golden Lily is?"

"Isn't that just the name used for the treasure burials?"

"Yes. There were some key figures in Operation Golden Lily." Bozeman ripped off the top sheet of his legal pad and drew a rough flowchart with two large bubbles on the top. In the left bubble he wrote the name *Emperor Hirohito*, then looked at Frank. "Hirohito was the emperor, but—." He drew a line under Hirohito's name and another circle. In it, he wrote *Prince Yasuhito Chichibu*. "Chichibu is Hirohito's brother and right hand man. Hirohito assigned Chichibu the job of heading *Kin no yuri*—or *Golden Lily*—and Chichibu had two generals working with him." Bozeman drew two lines and connecting circles under Chichibu's name. In the left circle, he printed *General Tomoyuki Yamashita*. "Yamashita, who led Japanese forces here on the Islands against America, is credited with masterminding Operation Golden Lily."

"Wasn't he executed after the war?"

"Yes. Hung. Right here in Manila." Bozeman moved to the circle just to the right. "Also working under Chichibu was Takeda Tsuneyoshi. Takeda had been a prince and a cousin of Emperor Hirohito before MacArthur and Truman forced the Japanese to reduce their royal family." He jabbed his pen at Takeda name. "We think Takeda may be the weak link—the one who will talk."

Frank nodded.

"He's the one you'll go see."

"And how will he decide to talk to me?"

"Well, Takeda had a faithful Filipino servant." Bozeman drew a line beneath Takeda's bubble and connected it to yet another bubble, this one with the name *Benjamin Valmores*.

Frank leaned in. "Valmores! He's the one Ver told Villacrusis may have kept a copy of the maps."

"Right. But we doubt that. Valmores was faithful to Takeda, although he still lives here." Bozeman circled the name again. "Benjamin Valmores remains tight-lipped, especially since—are you ready for it?"

Frank nodded.

"Valmores is now friends with Villacrusis."

Frank's mouth dropped open. "So . . . that would be why Villacrusis defended Valmores? Said that he was a poor man, and if he had possession of any maps, he wouldn't be poor."

"Exactly. And, because Valmores is pals with Villacrusis now, you can't approach him. However, you can use his name to gain an audience with Takeda." Bozeman rubbed his lip to hide his sly smile. He leaned toward Frank. "A reliable source has told us that Valmores was given *red maps*—original wax-coated treasure maps—by Takeda, which Takeda had told him he'd return for one day. Which means Valmores is either playing it cool, biding his time, or he's still loyal to Takeda. The man lives quite humbly in the San Fernando area, and, we've been told, he's been seen searching for gold with Villacrusis, going deep into the jungle."

"Without finding anything?"

Bozeman shrugged. "Not as far as we know." The sly smile returned. "You'll have a couple of weeks before you leave the Philippines. If I were you, I'd spend that time keeping an eye on Valmores—from a distance, of course."

"For what purpose?"

"Just to get to know him a bit before talking to Takeda. And, if you can do so without seeming like you're fishing, try to talk to the man. You have some common friends, so it shouldn't be too hard to get to meet the man and chat with him."

Frank nodded.

Bozeman returned to the top of his flowchart, to the empty circle on the top right. In it, he wrote *Yakuza*. He tapped the paper with his pen, drawing Frank's attention to the circle. "The Yakuza are an organized crime element in Japan. You must constantly be vigilant. They have been involved with the gold—either in the looting of it or the hiding of it—we're just not sure to what extent. We do know they are always on the lookout for anyone asking questions or searching. If they get wind that someone is talking to Takeda about it, they will intervene."

Frank frowned. "What do you mean, *intervene*?"

"Let's just say they don't play nice. But you're smart. Keep your mouth shut and don't let anyone see you with Takeda."

Frank sighed. Although he really wasn't looking forward to pulling information out of a Japanese prince—or plying keep-away from a violent organized crime mob—it would be good to get away from the Philippines for a while. He stood. "When do I leave?"

Chapter 14

Tokyo, Japan
March 24, 1970

Frank stepped out of the hot springs bath onto the bamboo mat and allowed the slight, dark woman to dry him. She dabbed at his skin with a soft white towel, taking care never to meet his eyes, and then she helped him slip into a cotton *yukata*. He slid his feet into a pair of *geta*, walking less awkwardly in the elevated wooden sandals now than when he first arrived weeks ago. "*Domo arigato*, Michiko." It was the first time he'd addressed her since they'd lain together last night.

Michiko bowed, then offered a shy smile, though she still didn't look him in the eye. "Tomorrow, *Furanku-sama*?"

Frank lifted her chin, insisting she meet his gaze. "*Hai, dozo.* Tomorrow." He kissed her lightly on the tip of her nose, eliciting a giggle. She glided across the room and made herself busy with tea. Frank watched her graceful movements for several moments, then turned away.

After he'd dressed in khakis, a comfortable shirt and a pair of sneakers, Frank shouldered his gym bag and headed uptown. He thought of Rosalita and the night they'd spent together before he left for Japan. He much preferred arranged sex with Michiko—not that she was a better lover. That wasn't the case. But he'd had enough complications in his life already.

He chewed his lip. Rosalita had insisted she didn't want a relationship. Friendship. Romance. And yes, intimacy. But no ties. She liked him, and he had to admit he'd grown to like her, but there was something about her that made him want to keep her at arm's length. That is, unless he was wrapped in those arms. They'd created spectacular fireworks his last night in Manila. But the morning he'd left, Rosalita bid him goodbye with a peck on the cheek instead of the passionate farewell kiss one would expect from a part-time lover.

And he hadn't minded. Not one bit. What he minded was thinking of Rosalita while lying with Michiko.

Enough. Frank pushed both women from his mind. He had more important things to focus on, like his upcoming meeting with Takeda Tsuneyoshi.

While still in the Philippines, he'd tracked down the man named *Valmores.* Even though Bozeman seemed to think he'd be able to chat with Valmores, it hadn't been that easy. Valmores was with Villacrusis almost constantly, and, with no parties or programs at the palace, there was never a good time to just bump into the man. But that hadn't stopped Frank from following the man and doing a little research. He'd learned Valmores' habits—quite an easy routine to follow—and knew that he did not search on his own for the gold. In fact, he seemed to want nothing to do with it, even though word was he'd been an eyewitness, watching as the tunnels were dug and the gold was transported into the caves. Valmores accompanied Villacrusis on occasional hikes through the rainforests where foliage grew so thick Valmores had to use a *bolo* to cut a trail for them to walk. Even from a distance, it appeared to be tedious work that always led nowhere, as far as Frank could tell. If they did find anything, Villacrusis must have been marking the trails for digging at a later date, because Frank had yet to see any earth moved. It made him wonder if the maps Valmores had given Colonel Villacrusis were some of the fake ones that floated around the Philippines.

No, Villacrusis would know they were fakes. Ver planted most of those to throw off the weekend treasure hunters anyway.

Frank sighed. It was time to visit Prince Takeda. Instead of taking a taxi, he walked to the prince's up-scale home in a mostly retired military residential district. Frank hiked with one eye constantly on the lookout for the unsavory Yakuza. Even as he pounded on the door and spoke to Takeda's servant,

Frank kept a wary eye. He had hoped the servant would allow him in, but instead, left him on the stoop.

After what seemed like a long time, the house servant returned. "He does not wish to speak with you, sir. I am sorry." He bowed to Frank, only intermittently glancing at his face, but never making eye contact.

"Please. Tell General Takeda he would do me great honor by speaking with me. I have news from the Philippines."

The man bowed again and re-entered the house. Frank paced in front of the gated residence. Perhaps he hadn't thought this through. Who would he tell Takeda he was? He'd need a different name, so he couldn't be traced back to Marcos. Surely the general wouldn't speak with him if he thought he was helping Marcos uncover loot that the Japanese felt still belonged to them.

The house servant reappeared. "General Takeda wishes you a good day, but he does not wish to see you."

"Please. I've come a very long way just to speak with him. I only need five minutes of his time."

"The general says he does not wish to answer any more questions for Ramos, or Villacrusis, or any of President Marcos's men."

What? Villacrusis had already been here? And which Ramos did he mean? Brigadier General Onofer T. Ramos? He was a comptroller, for goodness sakes. Certainly not Fidel Ramos? Frank shook his head, searching for words. "No. No, I'm not—President Marcos did not send me. Tell him . . . tell him I'm here with news from Benjamin Valmores."

The house servant's shoulders sagged. "I do not—"

"Please? *Please.* Just tell him that. If he doesn't want to see me after you tell him that, I'll go away. I promise."

With a look of resignation, the man again turned and trudged up the walkway to the big house. Frank dropped his gym bag and rolled his head from side to side, flexing the tight muscles in his neck and shoulders. What did he really expect Takeda to say, anyway? "Sure, come in! Here are copies of the maps I gave Valmores. I kept these just in case you came calling."

Frank figured he'd wasted the trip to Japan. *Nah.* He'd spent the past three weeks studying the language and Japanese writing, browsing the impressive libraries in Tokyo and brushing up on martial arts techniques specific to the Tokyo region of Japan. Plus, he'd met and become friends with Okubu Eusebio, a treasure hunter who'd helped him gain understanding of many Japanese map symbols and the Kung dialect. Okubu claimed to have been General Yamashita's interpreter. As a young boy, Okubu had seen many crates of gold buried in Baguio, and now he regularly traveled to the Philippines to work with a man named Roxas, who headed the Treasure Hunters Association of the Philippines. Okubu had provided Frank with a valuable piece of information he felt sure Ver didn't have; most authentic treasure maps were inscribed backward. They were meant to be read in a mirror.

"Mister! Hey, mister!" The house servant called from the doorway, grinning and waving. "General Takeda will see you now."

Frank opened the gate, then remembered his gym bag, backtracked, shouldered it, and hustled up the sidewalk.

"This way, mister."

Frank followed the man down a short, wide hallway and through a sliding pocket door, where he found himself in a courtyard. Cherry trees, sculpted bonsai trees, and jade plants in ornate containers surrounded a koi pond with a small fountain in its center.

Takeda Tsuneyoshi sat courtside on a padded bench. He smiled and stood as Frank neared him, then the two men exchanged bows.

"Thank you for meeting with me, Prince Takeda. I won't take up much of your time." He resisted the urge to extend his hand for a shake. "I'm Frank Young."

"Mr. Young, you bring news of Ben-ha-meen Valmores?"

So that was my golden ticket. "Uhhh, yes. Yes, sir. Mr. Valmores sends you his greetings."

The general's smile broadened. "Please, sit. Tsutomu will bring us tea."

The servant bowed and disappeared into the house.

"You come all the way from the Philippines with a message from Ben-ha-meen?"

"Yes, sir. No, I came on other business, but my friend Benjamin asked me to see you and to let you know he is well."

Takeda nodded and grinned. "Ben-ha-meen was my favorite. He was very loyal to me and Prince Chichibu."

And you rewarded him with maps to the buried treasure? "Yes, he spoke highly of you." *How could he broach the subject of the maps?*

"Is he working with President Marcos's men? Are they hard on him? I've been worried about him ever since those men came here. They did not want to take 'no' for an answer."

What had he stumbled into? "Benjamin appears to be well. He's not in any distress. In fact, I believe he is friends with Colonel Villacrusis. The two seem to be working together."

Takeda's eyebrows shot skyward.

Tsutomo appeared with a small porcelain teapot and two cups, filling each to the rim with pale green, steaming brew. After each man had taken a cup from the tray and the house servant had padded away, Takeda leaned forward.

"Ben-ha-meen is working with President Marcos to find the treasure?"

Frank choked on his tea and sent hot droplets coursing down his chin. He swiped at his mouth, then reached for the napkin Takeda offered. "Please, pardon me. I think I got strangled."

A wise smile curled the general's mouth. "I believe I startled you."

Frank's face grew hot. "Yes, sir. I must admit I didn't expect that."

Takeda chuckled. "I am an old man, Mr. Young. I will not be long on this earth. I have no time for games."

Frank nodded.

"If you are a friend of Ben-ha-meen, and he sent you here, then you already know of the buried treasure and of the maps I gave him to keep for me."

"To keep for you, yes."

Takeda shrugged. "I told him when I gave him the satchel to keep them until I came back for them in twenty years. If I did not return, the satchel and its contents were his." The man grew quiet, then spoke softly. "Twenty years have come and gone. I will never return to the Philippines."

"Why? Don't you want the gold?"

"I have everything I need."

Frank glanced around. Takeda's home was simple, yet elegant and beautifully furnished. It evoked a feeling of peacefulness and calm. Frank could see why the man would be happy here. "But you worked so hard for so many years to hide the gold. It seems you'd want to reclaim some of it, or, at least, see it again."

The former prince stared off in the distance, looking into years past. "Buddha teaches us to avoid taking the lives of living beings. But Emperor Hirohito laid down strict rules for me to follow. Once the site map was finalized, the men took inventory, and I walked the site for a final inspection. The prisoners of war and the Filipino laborers were sent inside the tunnel. I gave the ultimate order. The vault was sealed with the laborers inside, guaranteeing secrecy until the Imperial family could reclaim the treasure." His voice remained constant, showing no emotion. "The emperor believed the men's spirits would guard his treasure." He paused. "My duty was to obey my emperor."

A shiver chilled Frank's spine.

Puddles formed in Tanaka's eyes. "I wish to put that part of my life behind me."

"I understand. Thank you for telling me."

A brief, sad smile crossed the man's face. "A burden shared is less than one carried alone." He took a deep breath and straightened his shoulders. "Ben-ha-meen and his family were very poor when I met him. If he uncovers some of the treasure, they will have more wealth than imaginable. He deserves the gold more than anyone I know. Perhaps Villacrusis and Ramos have the resources to help Ben-ha-meen open some of the tunnels."

"There are a hundred and seventy-two burial sites, right?" Frank had heard from multiple sources—including his eavesdropping on Ver—there were one hundred seventy-two maps.

Tanaka's rheumy eyes met Frank's. He studied him for a moment as though sizing him up, then said, "There are one hundred and seventy-five sites."

A hundred seventy-five? Had Valmores kept the other three maps for himself?

Frank cleared his throat. "Benjamin only mentioned a hundred seventy-two maps."

The old man's head tilted to one side. "No, there were one hundred seventy-five. The satchel held the maps, inventory lists, my compass, a magnifying glass, and my drawing tools. I took out the inventory lists and accounted for all the maps myself. They were all there when I gave the satchel to Ben-ha-meen for safekeeping."

"Do you have copies?"

"No. The Americans were coming, and we had to leave or be killed. I knew Ben-ha-meen would be safe, because he was Filipino. I put the maps in his care. There were no copies." He leaned back. "Sometimes I traveled under the name Kimsu Murakusi. I am the grandson of Emperor Meiji. I was second in command to Prince Chichibu during Operation Golden Lily." He waved his hands in the air. "Golden Lily is the name we used for the treasure burial operation."

Frank recalled Golden Lily from his research. Prince Chichibu had taken command of all Manila during Golden Lily Operation, and Prince Takeda had overseen the operations in San Fernando. He thought of the gold he'd seen in Marcos's basement. The thought that so much more gold existed made him lightheaded.

"Mr. Young? Are you okay?"

"Yes. Forgive me. I believe my travels are catching up with me."

"Perhaps you should rest." Takeda raised his hand in the air, and immediately Tsutomu appeared. "Please see Mr. Young out."

Tsutomu bowed.

What had he done wrong? Why had the visit ended so abruptly? "Before you go, Mr. Young, do you have any other message from Ben-ha-meen?"

"No, sir. He simply asked me to see if you were well and to deliver his wishes for your continued good health." A thought occurred to Frank. "He seems very fond of you."

Takeda's face lit up. "This pleases me. I am fond of Ben-ha-meen as well. Mr. Young, would you please deliver a small gift from me to Ben-ha-meen when you return to the Philippines?"

Frank's mind raced with a litany of possible gifts. "Of course."

The former prince motioned to Tsutomu and whispered something in the man's ear. Tsutomu bowed and scurried into the house, then returned a moment later and placed something in Takeda's hand.

Takeda handed a gold sovereign to Frank. "Once I scolded Ben-ha-meen for opening a large jar full of these coins. It was purely by accident, as he was looking for salt. I told him that if he ever touched another of his gold coins, I'd cut off his hands.

"That night, while Ben-ha-meen slept, I poured a tall jar of these coins in the bed alongside him. When he woke up the next morning, he called to me, panicked. He was afraid to move, afraid of touching the coins." Takeda chuckled. "I laughed and laughed over my prank. The coins were my own, but he didn't know that. Please, give him the coin. He will then know you have found me safe and well."

Frank felt the heft of the gold coin in his hand. The one coin alone could pay for his trip back to the Philippines, and yet Takeda parted with it as if it were nothing. *He had jars of these coins.* Takeda was right about one thing. He didn't need the gold in the tunnels.

CHAPTER 15

On his way home, Frank felt the heavy coin in his pants pocket bouncing against his leg. His stomach growled, reminding him he'd missed lunch. He turned down the side street toward restaurant row. As the train trundled over the bridge above him, drowning the other city sounds beneath its noise, he hunched his shoulders toward his ears. He walked a few blocks, and from one of the rooms somewhere above him, the smell of opium wafted on the breeze. He sidestepped bicycles and dodged pedestrians until, tired of the crowded streets, he took a shortcut through a trash-strewn alley.

Big mistake. He'd not reached the halfway point when he realized he was being followed. He stole a glance over his shoulder, sickened to see the two men who'd seemed to crop up nearly every place he'd been this past week, though he'd never seen them together. *Yakuza*. Bozeman had warned him this criminal faction of Japan's infamous Black Curtain would hunt him down if they got wind he searched for the gold.

The Black Curtain manipulated Japanese policy and government to increase their personal wealth and power. They were made up of several different branches, but the Yakuza proved the most feared—criminals and outlaws who weren't afraid to torture, maim or kill to accomplish the Black Curtain's goals.

Frank picked up his pace, refusing to run, despite his gut telling him to sprint. Had the men followed him to Takeda's house? Or were they working for Takeda?

A refrigerator-sized man stepped into the other end of the alley, arms crossed. Even in the shadow of the tall buildings, Frank could see that the big man held nunchucks. He had nowhere to run.

Despite his fear, Frank found himself mesmerized by the man's technique; rolling the nunchucks over the back of his hand as he swung them was easy enough, but the figure eights, strikes and freestyle moves he displayed in his *kata* told Frank the man knew his weapon well.

Frank knew his weapon well, too. His body. Training in judo, kung fu, Jeet Kun Do, Hapkido, Aikido, and Thai kickboxing since he was young, he knew that, with concentration, he could move with enough coordination and assurance to control his opponent's rhythm. And rhythm would be the only thing to get him out of this mess. He noticed the man was right-handed, so he'd have to strike left to throw him off-kilter.

He dropped his gym bag and kicked it to the side, out of his way. *Take on the weapon first.* Not wasting any time, he rushed the man standing in front of him, glad to see his eyes grow wide as he drew near him. Frank feinted right. As he was sliding out of the way, the man brought the nunchucks down on Frank's left calf. Before the attacker could recoil his nunchucks, numbing pain seared through Frank's leg and down into his foot.

Frank brought his left arm up, catching his attacker on the shoulder. He drove a hard right-hand punch into the man's ribcage. As the man moved off to Frank's left, Frank drove a side kick hard into the man's knee.

His knee shattered, the man fell. Yet, on his way to the ground, he swung the nunchucks. Shooting pain scorched Frank's side.

Frank lunged and delivered a spinning wheel kick to the man's head. The giant went out cold.

Frank grabbed the nunchucks and swung around. It was always the guy coming from behind who could do the most damage, and he had two of them. He spun the nunchucks like a windmill and flung it a foot lower than the head of the second attacker. The man ducked, and as he did, the nunchucks caught him across the bridge of his nose. The man stumbled backward from the blow as blood poured onto his chest. He was stunned but not out.

Frank reverse-kicked at the third man, who quickly stepped back, out of range of the kick. He tried to sweep Frank but missed, which gave Frank the advantage.

Frank scooped up the nunchucks from the ground and brought them down on the man's head. "Two down, one to go."

The bloody man with the broken nose drove a kick into the back of Frank's knee, taking him to the ground. The man then threw a punch toward Frank's head.

Frank tried to absorb the punch in an arm bar, but missed, only deflecting the punch, but it pushed the man off-balance. Frank jumped to his feet. He swung a figure eight with the nunchucks, this time landing them on top of the attacker's head, splitting open his skull.

Too easy. Frank chuckled, limped over, shook out the pain in his knee, picked up his gym bag and straightened his clothes. As he turned and stepped over the first man he'd crippled, he stopped. "Next time, you'd better bring more friends."

He dropped the nunchucks on the man's oversized head and hobbled out of the alley, catering to the throbbing pain in his leg.

CHAPTER 16

Mary Catherine tapped on the closed menu. It was times like this she wished she still smoked. Twenty years ago, smoking was acceptable. Classy, even. She'd had one of those long cigarette holders—a gift from Danilo. He'd told her it was 24 karat gold. It was long and slim and felt so smooth. She loved to hold it, smoke from it, show it off.

And right now, the act of smoking would help pass the time and soothe her growing impatience. Perhaps high society in other areas of the world believed in being "fashionably late," but this was the South. Polite, proper people were respectful enough of others to be on time.

Her tap grew louder. Maybe the woman wouldn't show. Wouldn't that be the dive? After calling right out of the blue and introducing herself as Frank's friend, saying she'd be coming through Atlanta and asking if she could stop by.

Mary Catherine wasn't about to invite a stranger to her home. Not even a woman. You just never knew these days. So she'd suggested Ledmann's, a traditional Southern restaurant near her home.

"Would you like another drink while you wait, ma'am?"

Mary Catherine started. She hadn't seen the waiter approach. She glanced at the empty tumbler of sweet tea and vodka. "Yes. Please."

Five more minutes. If the woman wasn't here in five minutes, she was leaving.

"Ma'am?"

Mary Catherine eyed the maître d'. "What is it?"

"A Miss Laurel has asked to join your table."

"A Miss who?" Mary Catherine scowled. She already didn't like this "friend." Rosalita was the only name she'd left. It was undoubtedly her. Finally. "Yes. It's about time." She sat with her back to the entrance and kept her eyes pointed ahead, not even looking out the window next to her.

"Excuse me, ma'am." The waiter placed her drink in front of her.

"Thank you."

Before she could take a drink, the maître d' returned and pulled out the chair opposite her.

A young woman smiled sheepishly. "I'm so sorry I'm late." She sat and allowed the maître d' to scoot in her chair. "I'm Rosalita."

Mary Catherine's mouth dropped open. She'd expected to see a . . . an *American*. Instead, the woman was definitely Filipina. Her raven hair draped her shoulders, framing her flawless café au lait skin. But her eyes. Instead of the expected shades of brown or black, Rosalita's almond-shaped eyes were green. Almost olive green.

Warm, humid nights on the beach drinking cocktails, laughter bubbling all around them. Danilo. Danilo's grin, the way it filled his entire face. Mary Catherine shivered.

Rosalita's smile dropped.

Get it together. Mary Catherine pasted on a pleasant expression. "I'm sorry. Forgive me."

Rosalita's polite smile returned. "That's okay." Sunlight caught the rhinestones in her hair clasp, throwing prisms of light across the room.

They aren't rhinestones. Mary Catherine caught her breath. *They're diamonds.*

"I'm so sorry for showing up out of the blue like this." Rosalita's voice, velvety soft and melodic, cascaded over the table.

Despite her irritation, Mary Catherine couldn't help but smile—genuinely smile—at this lovely young woman. "How do you know my son?"

"Oh, Franklin! I do love him, you know." She giggled and shyly looked at Mary Catherine through long lashes.

Mary Catherine wasn't sure if she meant *love* in the romantic sense or *love* as a friend. But she could easily see how Frankie could be enamored of such an adorable woman. *She* was charmed by her.

"We met at a fundraiser at the palace. Imelda and I have been friends for a long time, so when Ferdinand introduced me to Franklin—"

Mary Catherine felt her heart skip a beat, she took a sip of spiked sweet tea to calm herself. *Imelda? Ferdinand? The Marcoses?* Who was this woman? And what was her Frankie doing carousing around with Marcos? That Filipino scumbag was not someone her son should be rubbing elbows with. Mary Catherine pressed her napkin over her mouth. "I'm sorry."

Rosalita's laugh covered the awkwardness. "It's quite all right. I'm so clumsy myself."

The waiter stepped up to the table, his tablet open. "Are you ready to order, ma'am?"

"Can't you see—" Mary Catherine stopped. Rosalita would never speak sharply to anyone. She was sure of it. "I'm sorry," she said to the waiter. "Yes. I'll have the crab salad on rye, no lettuce. With a side of tomato, but only if they are fresh and homegrown."

"Yes, ma'am. Of course." He looked at Rosalita.

"I'll have the same," she replied. "And whatever Mrs. Young is drinking is fine, too."

"Oh, please. Call me Mary Catherine."

Rosalita beamed. "Yes. Of course, Mary Catherine. Thank you."

Throughout lunch, they chatted. Mary Catherine felt so at ease with this young lady, and confided in her things she'd not told anyone, such as her fear that Frank would leave the States permanently and she'd rarely see her son. Not that she saw him often now.

"Oh, Mary Catherine. Frank would never forget his mama. I can't imagine how anyone could." Her eyes moistened. "I could never move far from my mama. When I was at Wellesley, I had such a phone bill. I called Mama almost every night. And I still do. I think when you're an only child, you have an especially close relationship with your mama. Don't you think?"

With every fiber of her being, Mary Catherine wanted to agree. But she feared Franklin would forget she existed if she didn't remind him frequently. But now that she had met Rosalita, maybe she had yet another way to keep up with her son's comings and goings.

"What about Frank's papa?" Rosalita covered her mouth. "Oh, I'm sorry. Sometimes I say things I shouldn't."

Mary Catherine took a long drink of spiked tea. "I don't mind. Richard, my late husband, and I adopted him when he was five."

"Oh, Mrs. Young. I'm so sorry. I didn't mean to dredge up unpleasant memories. Please, forgive me. I speak before I should." She reached across the table and patted Mary Catherine's hand. "I shouldn't have asked such a personal question." Her face brightened. "What do you suggest for dessert?"

Mary Catherine relaxed. "The peach cobbler. Oh, heavenly!"

The ladies chatted throughout dessert, careful to avoid further difficult topics. By the time the cobbler was picked at and the à la mode melted, Mary Catherine was sure she'd like to have this young woman as her daughter-in-law. She placed her napkin over her plate. "Rosalita, we must stay in touch."

"Oh, yes. I'd love that."

"Are you going to be in town long? Why don't you stop over at the house for tea tomorrow? It's just up in Roswell, not far."

Rosalita again showed her perfect teeth. "That would be lovely. I'll look forward to finishing our conversation then."

⅄

"So, you just wanted to hear my voice? Frank, if I didn't know better, I'd think you had a crush on me." Rosalita's soft laugh warmed Frank.

"Don't be silly. I wanted to talk to a friend. Someone who speaks plain English and doesn't think I'm a 'roco American.'"

"A *what?*"

"Roco. You know, *loco*. Crazy American."

Rosalita giggled. "I get it. But you're only *half*-American. At least they got the other part right."

"Hey, I didn't call to get harassed."

"Sure you did. If you'd wanted kind and loving words, you'd have called your mother."

Frank laughed. "Obviously, you don't know my mother."

"Your mother is a very sweet lady."

"It's obvious you've never met my mother."

"We had lunch together a few weeks ago."

"What are you talking about?" Blood pulsed through Frank's head.

"Imelda and I were shopping in New York while she had business there, and she returned to the Philippines early. I'd made plans to visit my friend from Wellesley, who lives in Atlanta. So, while I was there, I figured it would only be polite to give your mother a ring."

Frank struggled to keep the irritation out of his voice. "Go on."

"Your mother was thrilled to learn that you and I are friends. Ecstatic, in fact. She said she felt as if a tiny piece of her son's life in the Philippines dropped into her lap. She actually blinked back tears."

Frank huffed. "I'll bet she did."

"Really, Frank." Rosalita's voice turned sour. "I found your mother to be quite charming. A real Southern belle. She invited me to tea the next evening, and we had a wonderful visit. I learned so much about her Little Frankie. You never told me they called you 'Frankie.' I should have guessed it, of course. Everyone in the South has a nickname, don't they?"

"Yeah. Uh-huh."

"It's obvious your mother loves you very much. I don't know why you speak so bitterly of her."

"That's right, Rosalita. You *don't know*. There's plenty you don't know, and I don't care to get into it with you." The line grew silent, and after a moment Frank wondered if he'd lost the connection. "You still there?"

"Yes. Though I'm not sure why."

"I'm sorry. I didn't call to snap at you. It's just that—well, I never expected you to have tea parties with my mother in my absence."

Rosalita sniffed. "I enjoyed talking with Mary Catherine. She's an entertaining hostess. I'm sorry if it upset you, Frank. I thought you'd be pleased."

Frank doodled on the green engineering pad as he spoke. "No, I'm not upset. Yes. Yes, I am. But not with you." He sighed. "Not with my mother, either. Not really. I'm not sure why it bothers me. I guess I just figured—well, I don't know what."

Rosalita laughed softly. "Ahhh, I get it now. You thought you'd be the one to introduce us someday. You wanted to be there."

Frank dropped his pencil and stood up, pacing. Hell, no. Not only had he never planned on introducing the two women, he'd never, ever intended for their paths to cross. "Actually—"

"I knew it! Oh, Frank, I'm sorry to have spoiled it for you. But rest assured, your mother and I got along famously. I had a very pleasant visit with her, and we even had cocktails before I left."

Imagine that.

"By the way, she asked me to tell you she'd mailed a package to you on Thursday of last week, so you should probably get it soon. Tell me, Little Frankie, does your mommy send you cookies in the mail?"

Rosalita's raucous laugh made Frank pull the phone from his ear and wonder, yet again, why he'd really called this woman.

CHAPTER 17

Tokyo, Japan
December 8, 1970

"I need to meet with you as soon as possible." Okubu Eusebio's voice trembled. Why would the treasure hunter be calling him? Frank rubbed his forehead. "Is everything okay?"

"Yes, yes. Better than okay. I have exciting news. We must talk in person. Can you meet me at the library this afternoon?"

Frank had planned to go to the University of Tokyo's library again, anyway. He'd been studying Japanese history books and diaries from the World War II period, and because he didn't have student status, the librarians wouldn't let him check out the books. He had to read onsite. No matter; he loved browsing the stacks and poring over piles of books, especially now that his Japanese language skills had improved.

As he mounted the steps of the library, Frank glanced around. Sure enough, his usual tails stood nearby, having predicted his destination when he'd turned down the avenue toward the university. Frank smiled and nodded, obviously infuriating the man wearing dark sunglasses, who jerked his head and spat on the sidewalk.

Though he'd been followed almost daily since his visit with Takeda, he hadn't been confronted since the encounter in the alley. He'd like to think that his prowess and skill had caused the Yakuza to fear him, but he knew better. The men were ruthless. The next time they would show up with guns.

Okubu claimed that if they'd wanted Frank dead, he'd have been moldering in his own gore by now. They were watching him, following him, even checking out the same books behind him in the library. He had sat at a library table and read a couple of children's picture books, as well as Shakespeare written in English, just to further provoke the men. They must know by now he was following the trail to the treasure, and once he'd found it, they'd make him suffer until he confessed all he knew.

All the more reason to continue his research.

Okubu waited in a glass-partitioned room, three books on the table in front of him. His eyes twinkled when Frank walked through the door. "Sit, sit! I have much to tell you."

Frank chuckled. Most of the Japanese he'd encountered were calm and re-served, but Okubu's dramatic animation proved a stark contrast to his coun-trymen. Most people thought the old man suffered from a mental imbalance. Frank knew he simply had true zest for life.

"I received an important phone call last night." Okubu leaned toward Frank, and his eyes grew to huge orbs behind the thick, convex lenses of his eyeglasses. "Do you remember me speaking of my friend Roger Roxas?"

Roxas. Roxas. "He's the guy from the Treasure Hunters Association of the Philippines?"

"Exactly!"

"So?"

"So he found a tunnel." Okubu lowered his voice. "It's the tunnel from the map I drew when I interpreted for General Yamashita."

Frank leaned forward. "Go on."

"Actually, my map wasn't a very good one. I was young then, and I knew nothing about map-making. But I knew enough to know the burial sites were located in the mountain behind where Baguio Hospital now sits. I also knew they were burying treasure there, because I once saw them carry in a gold Buddha on a litter. It was only about two feet high, but it took six men to carry it. It must have weighed a ton.

"Anyway, a man named Albert Fuchigami joined Roger's treasure-hunt-ing group. Albert's father owned a produce shop at the base of that mountain.

When Albert was a boy, his father took him into a hidden tunnel behind the hospital. The tunnel had rail tracks in it, and he and his father followed the tracks a long way into the tunnel. Off the main tunnel, there were side tunnels full of wooden crates. Albert said his father cracked open one of the crates to show him gold 'biscuits.'

"He was a little boy at the time, so he didn't understand that the biscuits were valuable, though he remembers thinking they looked like candy bars wrapped in shiny paper. He hadn't thought of it much in his later years, until his father died two years ago. On his deathbed, Mr. Fuchigami gave Albert a map of the tunnel.

"Albert spent over a year digging around on his own, to no avail. He got angry and burned the map, thinking his father had played a trick on him."

Realization dawned on Frank. "The map was written backward."

Okubu nodded with his entire upper body, reminding Frank of the bobbing, drinking toy bird he'd had as a child. "When Albert told Roger his story, Roger remembered what I'd told him about General Yamashita's headquarters being located on the mountain behind Baguio Hospital, and he started digging there. After a few months, he found what he thought to be a sealed entrance to a tunnel. He's been digging for several months since then, but this weekend, he broke through to a tunnel." Okubu shivered with excitement.

"The tunnel had metal tracks for a hand cart," he continued, "just as Albert remembered, and some kind of rudimentary electrical wiring. Inside the sealed area, they found some bayonets, a two-way radio, and a skeleton wearing a Japanese uniform. The skeleton cradled a rifle in his arms.

"Roger followed the tunnel almost two hundred meters, and he found another short side-tunnel that appeared to be a first-aid station. It held old boxes of bandages and syringes, but nothing else. From there, he made it another forty meters or so, but the tunnel ended in a roof collapse."

"Collapse? Or had they blasted it shut in multiple places?"

"My guess is that he reached an area they'd sealed by blasting. I told him so. I watched it happen many times." Okubu stared at his hands, his eyes shrinking with memory. "Sometimes there were men left inside." When he looked up, his eyes brimmed. He sniffed hard. "Roger is getting a few more men together, and they're going back in this weekend. He said he'd covered his tracks with a minor explosion of his own to seal off what he'd found. Once he has the equipment he needs, he'll resume exploration."

Frank could hardly believe it. For nearly two years he'd been searching for the maps and the treasure buried in the Philippines. Several times he had contemplated calling Nixon and giving up, and now an old man in Japan provided him his first huge break. "Tell me what you know about Roger Roxas. Who is he working with?"

"Working with? Oh, you mean President Marcos's men." Okubu shook his head. "No, Rogelio—Roger—is his own man. Some of Marcos's men have joined the Treasure Hunters Association, but they've never stuck around more than a few months. Treasure hunting is laborious and expensive. Most men run out of money or steam after several weeks, and they give up. Plus, there are so many fake maps out there; the men end up running in circles to find nothing but their own tails."

"Do you think Marcos's men are watching Roxas, then?"

"I'm certain of it. But he's of no more concern to them than the other dozens of treasure hunters. Roxas is a class act, as you say it. He insists that all the treasure hunters in his group follow the law, and he always applies for government permits before he begins digging."

"So Marcos actually gave him permission to dig?"

"In a sense, yes. The Philippine Government requires that treasure hunters surrender thirty percent of anything they find; it's part of their permit agreement. Roger told me that his permit was signed by President Marcos's uncle, Judge Pio Marcos. He presides over the Baguio court, and that's the region where this particular tunnel is located."

Frank wondered if he should call Bozeman now, or wait until he'd verified the tunnel for himself. "Are you invested in the treasure hunt? Are you going back to the Philippines?"

Okubu wilted. "No. I am an old man, my friend. My heart is weak, and I don't think I could stand the travel." He shrugged and held up his palms. "My only investment is the information I've given Roger. I've never been with him on the digs."

"Did he pay you for the information? Perhaps you have rights to some of the gold."

"Rogelio Roxas is a fair man. If he finds the gold, he will see that I am rewarded." He laughed and his eyes grew large again. "Believe me, even after Marcos takes his thirty percent, there still will be enough gold in that tunnel to make a hundred men wealthy beyond belief."

Frank ran his fingers along the edge of his notepad. "How much do think is in there?"

"Keep this in mind. I translated Allied soldiers' English for Yamashita, and back again. An American soldier usually did the initial tally of the crates they buried, then a Japanese soldier would follow behind him, to make certain the inventory proved accurate. Any discrepancy would cost both soldiers their lives.

"I was young, but I could count. I remember that one of the tunnels—and I believe the one behind the Baguio Hospital is the one I'm recalling—held one thousand crates of gold bars, plus twenty-five crates of jewels and a gold Buddha."

"Any idea how many of the gold bars each crate contained?"

Okubu shook his head. "No, but it took four men to carry each box. The boxes were about the size of a case of Coca-Cola, and moved on litters."

Frank let out a long, low whistle, provoking a face-splitting grin from Okubu. "You're sure you don't want to go see this for yourself? You've spent much of your life following the progress on those searches."

"No, Frank." He placed his hands flat on the table between them. "But I would like you to go."

"Me?" Frank couldn't wait to set his eyes on the dig, but he couldn't imagine why Okubu would want him there.

"You are my friend, Frank. I trust you. You have searched for answers. I only want to know that it's for real. If Roger really finds the gold, I know he will do the right thing, and eventually some of the gold will come my way. But what I want more than that is verification. I want to know that I was right. That alone will mean a lot to an old man." A smile curved his thin lips.

Frank nodded, trying to keep down his excitement. "I will do that for you. Of course."

"Can you leave tomorrow?"

Frank laughed and held up his hands. "Whoa! What's the rush? You've already said your friend Rogelio has to get equipment together, and he'll have to dig through the collapsed portion of the tunnel. Besides, it's not like I can just walk up to him and ask him if he's found any gold."

"No, but I can tell him you're my friend, and that you'd like to help."

Frank thought of Fabian Ver, of the way he'd killed the two men at Montalban Gorge, of the jar of eyeballs in the torture chamber. He shuddered. "I don't want to get involved with your friend's dig. My goal has always been to find the maps. Do you understand?"

Okubu's mouth drew downward. "I think so." Then his face brightened. "But, Frank, if you see the site—actually see the gold coming out of the burial sites—you'll know Yamashita's gold is more than a legend. You'll know I'm telling the truth, and you'll know for a fact that there's more gold to be found. I hope you will reconsider."

"If there were a way that I could watch them from a safe distance without—"

"Oh, but there is! The hospital. Baguio Hospital overlooks the mountainside where the tunnel is located. In fact, I'll bet that the staff and patients there have been watching Rogelio dig all year. You know how the Filipinos are about the gold and treasure hunting. They've probably been taking bets all along whether or not he finds anything."

"So this isn't exactly a covert operation?" Frank rubbed the back of his neck.

Okubu chuckled. "Of course not. It would be nearly impossible to hide recovery of treasure from that particular location. Besides, once Roger finds anything, he must immediately report it to Judge Pio Marcos. I expect the tunnel will be flooded with the Philippine military when that happens."

Frank nodded.

"So, when can you leave?"

Frank couldn't help but laugh. The man's excitement proved contagious. "I absolutely *must* spend Christmas with my mother in America. But I can return to the Philippines after the holidays. It's time I get back there, anyway."

Okubu clapped his hands like a child, then extended a handshake to Frank. He clasped Frank's hand in both of his and squeezed. "Now let's celebrate over a cup of sake, shall we?"

CHAPTER 18

Roswell, Georgia
January 10, 1971

Frank sighed, walked over to the television set and turned up the volume. He'd missed watching *Ironside* while in Japan and the Philippines, and now his mother insisted on talking over his favorite show.

"Don't you think it will affect your job?" Mary Catherine paced the den as she ranted. "I mean, since the government outlawed tobacco advertising on television, who's going to know anything about Pure Gold and the other cigarettes Triangle makes? Magazine ads will probably go next. And all this negative press! Emphysema, lung cancer, heart attacks . . . maybe you should talk to your father's friends about getting into politics, or perhaps you can go back into engineering. People will simply *stop smoking* now, and then where will you be?"

Frank settled on the words *your father*. Even though Richard Young had been a good father and a decent man, he couldn't have held a candle to Danilo Quezon and the risks he took each day.

"I've never felt good about you working in tobacco anyway. It's becoming so, oh, *lower class*." Mary Catherine dropped ice cubes into a crystal highball. "I should have known if you got involved with those Dukes, they'd drag you into tobacco."

Frank took a deep breath. "Mother, I'm not involved with the Dukes. Just because I went to Duke University doesn't mean I'm on a first-name basis with Doris Duke and the family."

Mary Catherine took a swallow of Smirnoff and swirled the rest in her glass. "Do you know that sweet little Rosalita smoked? Of course you do. She said you're the one who brought those things to the Philippines. Blue Skinnies? Is that what they're called?"

"Blue Lady Slims, Mother. Blue Lady Slims." He'd told her at least a dozen times, already.

"I really like that girl, Frankie. Have you thought of marrying her? She obviously comes from money. Those were real diamonds on her hair pin."

"I'm not marrying Rosalita, Mother. We're friends. That's all."

"Don't be a fool, Frankie. She's absolutely gorgeous, and she's smart, too. She went to Wellesley, and that's not an easy school to seduce."

"I know where she went to school," Frank muttered.

"And since you *insist* on spending time in the Philippines—against your mother's wishes, let it be said—her connections over there could help keep you safe."

Frank whipped around in the La-Z-Boy. "Keep me safe from *what*, Mother? Why should I need protection in the Philippines?"

Mary Catherine's eyes flared over the rim of her glass as she took a long sip. "Don't be silly, Frankie. Everyone knows those islands are full of heroin addicts and criminals. All I'm saying is that it would comfort me to know that my son has connections in high places."

Mary Catherine poured another drink, and her voice lilted. "Rosalita told me she's friends with the First Lady. What's her name? Imelda? Yes, Imelda Marcos. They go shopping together in New York City! Can you imagine? Jetting about the world with a president's wife." She waved in Frank's general direction. "Now *that's* the kind of connection this family could use. Can you imagine what a marriage to someone connected with the president of the Philippines could have done for your father's career? And the ladies in the garden club would turn as green as kudzu if Rosalita were my daughter-in-law. I can't begin—"

"Stop it, Mother!" Frank jumped to his feet. "Richard wasn't my father, and Rosalita isn't my wife. The only reason you want me to have connections in the Philippines is because you believe I'm in danger there. Danger that has something to do with my real father. What is it you're not telling me? Why have you kept this from me all these years? Leading me to believe I was adopted. How can you say you love me when you tell me such lies?"

Mary Catherine reached inside the pocket of her sweater and fondled the sapphire rosary. She glared at her son, and minutes ticked by before she spoke, her voice low and chillingly calm. "Richard *was* your father, God rest his soul. And he *did* adopt you. I have never lied about that. As to keeping Danilo's identity from you, it was for your own good. It would be of no use for you to learn that he'd been murdered in the Philippines by some Japanese man who probably mistook him for someone else. There wasn't even a trial, and as far as I know, there wasn't an investigation, either. The Philippines were wild in those days. The best thing I could do was to get us out of there and put those years behind us.

"Richard was a generous man, and you've lacked nothing, even though you never attempted to show an interest in the things he enjoyed. He was good to you, Frankie. You should show more respect for his memory."

Frank blinked hard. His mother had flipped from Rosalita, to Richard's career, to her own social status, to the dangers of the Philippines, to his perceived disrespect of his late adoptive father—all in a matter of a few minutes. He felt like he'd been strapped into a rollercoaster from hell he never wanted to ride.

He threw up his hands. "I need to finish packing. I think I'm going to drive on to Durham tonight, instead of fighting the morning traffic, so I'll be rested for my business meeting tomorrow afternoon."

"But—"

"I'm meeting a friend for drinks tomorrow night, and then I'm flying out to the Philippines first thing Tuesday morning." He turned and headed up the stairs.

"The Philippines." Mary Catherine reached for her rosary, pressed it to her bosom, then tossed back the rest of her drink. She set the highball on the bar and looked up the empty stairway. "Marry that girl!" she yelled.

Chapter 19

Durham, North Carolina
January 11, 1971

In the swirling smoke of the bar, Nguyen Luc watched the entrance as he sipped on his Pabst Blue Ribbon. He hadn't seen his college roommate for over two years, although his father had updated him a few times on Frank's whereabouts.

Frank Young finally walked through the doorway, shook off the rain and slipped out of his wet parka.

Luc stood and waved him toward the high-top table. "Hey, man!" He stood and stretched out his hand to shake hands with his friend, then smacked him on the stomach. "Put on a few pounds, Frankie?"

Frank landed a soft punch in Luc's gut. "Must be catching, huh, Lucky?" The two embraced with slaps on the back, falling into their old routine like never a day had passed.

Lucky pushed an empty mug toward his friend, and Frank picked up the pitcher of beer and poured. "So what's been going on, old man?" Lucky waited for a full mug. "The last time we talked, you were in the Philippines pushing cigarettes."

Frank grinned. "Among other things."

Lucky lifted his beer mug and Frank clinked his against it. The two gulped down the entire contents of their mugs, then slammed down their mugs simultaneously.

Frank chuckled. "Some things never change."

Lucky shook his head, grinning. "You like your new job? Momma Young told me you'd jaunted off to Japan, trying to outrun a pretty Filipina who has the hots for you."

"You've got to be kidding me." Frank shook his head. "Nothing could be further from the truth. It's my job, man. I'm an international rep for Triangle. That means multiple countries."

Lucky poured them each another beer. "You wanted to find out about your father," he prompted. "So, did you find anything?"

Frank shrugged. "Yes and no." He took another long swig from his mug and wiped his mouth. "I'll have to admit, when I see certain things, I get an overwhelming sense that I've seen them before, that I've walked in these steps before."

"What did your mother say, when you asked her about it?"

"Pffft. What do you think she said?" Frank shook his head. "She pretty much denied everything and changed the subject, per usual." He readjusted himself on the stool. "No. No, that's not fair. She told me she thought some really bad people had killed my father, perhaps mistaking him for someone else. Since she was an American without the protection of her Filipino husband in a country involved in a war, she didn't feel safe, so she took me and fled the country. I guess it wasn't long thereafter when she met my step-dad." He shrugged. "You know the rest."

Lucky nodded. "You say you're going back tomorrow?"

"Yeah. I fly out early in the morning."

"Going to see your fine Filipina?" Lucky grinned.

Frank laughed. "Actually, yes. She's picking me up at the airport. Well, her driver is picking me up, but I'm sure she'll be along for the ride."

Lucky's eyebrows shot skyward. "Her *driver?* Man, sounds like you've got it made. Do I hear wedding bells?"

"Did Mom put you up to that?" Frank guzzled the rest of his beer. "We're really good friends, that's all. Rosalita has a lot of connections, and she can help me do my job a lot better. She opens doors I couldn't open otherwise."

"Oh? What kind of doors?"

Frank leaned conspiratorially toward his old friend, the effects of the alcohol relaxing his normally reserved manner. "Her best friend is Imelda Marcos."

"What! You're double-dating with the president of the Philippines? Get outta here!"

Frank chuckled. "I think that's stretching things, but yes, I've been inside the Malacañang Palace a few times."

Lucky laughed hard and loud, drawing stares from other patrons. But when he spoke, his voice was modulated so only Frank could hear. "Seriously, who'd have believed that Frankie Young would be sipping tea with President Marcos?"

Frank grinned. "We don't sip tea together, but I confess we've had drinks in his office."

Lucky shook his head. "So, what do you talk about with the prez? Does he ask your opinion on political matters? I've been watching some of the up-roar over there on TV and reading about it in the papers, and it sounds like he could use some advice."

"Not exactly." Frank lifted a shoulder. "I don't know; we talk about the tobacco business. Marcos is really interested in tobacco. Actually, I think he's interested in anything that can make him another peso richer."

"While the rest of the country starves."

Frank's lips twisted to one side. "Pretty much, yes."

"Tell me about this woman. Rosie, your mother said?"

"Rosalita." Frank laughed. "I'm not sure she'd appreciate being called *Rosie*, though I might have to give it a try."

"Nothing serious going on with her? Besides her connections, I mean?"

Frank shrugged. "She's easy on the eyes."

"The way your mom talked, I was checking my schedule to make sure I could pencil in time to get fitted for a tux. I will be the best man in your wedding, right?"

Frank shot a scathing look Lucky's way. "Very funny. See, that's the thing. Rosalita just happened to be in Atlanta and looked up Mom and met her for lunch. We were talking long distance—I was in Japan, so it could have been a bad connection—but I keep getting the feeling that there's more going on with her than meets the eye. It feels like she's keeping tabs on me."

Lucky stared hard at his friend. "Maybe she's the jealous type?"

"Could be. You know how territorial women can be. But that's the other thing; she swears she doesn't want a commitment—which suits me fine—and I'm pretty sure she dates other men when I'm out of town. It's not like we're exclusive."

"Speaking of exclusive—when are you planning on coming home for good? I'm more than ready to open that dojo we've been talking about since our freshman year."

Frank took a deep breath and held it. He released it slowly. "Yeah. About that . . . ."

"What? Change your mind?"

"No, no, no. Not at all. If anything, I'm more ready than ever. I just don't know when I'll be able to get out of my, uh, position."

"Money, huh? Well, keep putting some away." Lucky pointed to the nearly empty beer pitcher. "Ready for another?"

"Nah, I'd love to, but I've got an early flight in the morning." Frank stood and slid his bar stool beneath the high-top. He reached for his wallet, but Lucky threw up a hand to stop him.

"I got this. Bro, it's been great. We gotta do this again. It's been too long. When will you be back in the States?"

"I usually get back here every four to six months. I'll probably be spending less and less time in the Philippines, as the brand gets established over there. Not sure where they'll send me next, though."

After Frank had said his goodbyes, Luc watched him until he was out of sight. Still, he waited a few more minutes. Finally, he motioned to the bartender and headed to the back of the pub, into the restaurant office, closing the door behind him. He picked up the phone and made a call.

"He's gone."

"Did he say anything about the operation?" Nguyen Tao asked.

"Not a word."

"Did he mention his father?"

"Only when I asked, but even then he didn't give much information. He didn't even mention his name."

"And Marcos?"

"Yes, he told me that he'd had drinks with the president in his office."

"We knew about that. Did he mention anything they've talked about?"

"Nothing other than the tobacco business."

"Good. Anything else I should know?"

"Actually, I'm concerned about this woman he's dating. Rosalita."

"We know about her."

"Doesn't sound like he fully trusts her. She checks up on him. Could be just a jealous sort, but I wonder if maybe she's trying to get information for Marcos. She's best friends with Imelda, after all."

"It's possible. We'll keep an eye on things. Anything else?"

"That's it."

"Thank you, son. I appreciate your help."

Luc hesitated a moment. "Uhhh, Dad?"

"Yes?"

"Take care of him, will you?"

Tao's pause mirrored that of his son. "I always have."

Chapter 20

Frank paced the small, second-floor waiting room in Baguio General Hospital, sipping a cup of bitter coffee. From his vantage point, he watched the foggy mountainside as General Fabian Ver and two soldiers he didn't recognize traipse through the tall pines toward the area where Rogelio Roxas had been digging for the past year. He half-expected bodies to come rolling down the mountainside, but instead, Ver and his men trundled down, Ver looking none too happy. Had they killed Rogelio and his crew?

Frank had spent countless hours over the past several days watching them, always aware of the difference between their equipment and that he'd seen at Montalban Gorge. Rogelio's crew bore pickaxes, shovels, wheelbarrows, scythes and rope—the stuff of back-breaking labor. At last count yesterday, Frank noted twenty-eight men, in addition to Roxas, working the site. They came early and left late.

This morning, the crew had acted differently. The men appeared more animated, and they hauled more rope, a wooden crate and a metal cart up the mountain with them. Ver's appearance convinced Frank they'd found something. But who would have told Ver of any discovery?

Okubu had said that Roxas followed the law implicitly. He'd report anything he found, despite having to share a portion. But Ver left empty-handed, scowling. The drive from Manila to Baguio City took a while, and Frank knew Ver wouldn't have come this far without reason. That is, unless Marcos visited The Mansion. The Mansion had been built for U.S. generals in the early 1900s, then was destroyed during the Philippine battle for liberation in 1945. Rebuilding took place a few years later—complete with a gate to rival that of Buckingham Palace—and now Marcos used it for special meetings or when he visited the Baguio area.

Surely Roxas wouldn't carry out any treasures he'd found while Marcos stayed nearby—if indeed he visited The Mansion. That would mean a certain death sentence.

Frank couldn't stand it. He tossed back the last dregs of his coffee, grimaced at the taste, crushed the paper cup and headed out the door. Downstairs, he paused on the hospital's portico, careful that Ver and his men were nowhere in sight. Okubu's answer when Frank had asked if Marcos was having Rogelio Roxas watched echoed in Frank's mind: *"I am certain of it."*

Curiosity drove Frank onward. He hustled toward visitor parking, grabbed his car with the "not Frank Young's car" license plate and drove up Kennon Road to the backside of the mountain. He parked on the side of the road near an overlook, about a quarter kilometer past where the Lion's Club workers were carving a giant lion's head into the limestone. Camp John Hay, a U.S. military recreation area that General Yamashita had used as his headquarters, lay just ahead, where Frank's car would blend with the dozens of other tourists' cars lining the area.

Frank walked alongside the road, avoiding the rocky outcrops that bore little vegetation. He came to a heavily forested area and began his ascent up the mountain. After he'd climbed a few meters, he stopped and turned his rust-colored windbreaker wrong-side-out, figuring the dark green lining would provide better camouflage. The climb proved treacherous at times, and Frank wished he'd worn boots that provided better traction on the steep areas of damp moss. Hand over hand, he used scrub pines and jutting rocks to hoist upward, until the road below him looked like a long, slate-colored snake. When he reached an area not quite as steep, he stood, stretched his spine, and began the hike around the side of the mountain, back toward Baguio General Hospital.

Along the way, he found three separate dig sites, each with soil hard-packed from the summer's heavy rains, proving they were old and likely unproductive. Soon he reached earshot of voices, and he backtracked about a hundred meters and again climbed upward. When he felt he'd reached a height where the men wouldn't see him, he picked his way through the thick underbrush until he reached a precipitous ledge protruding over the side of the mountain.

Despite the temptation, he didn't climb out on the rock, though he knew he could lie flat there without being seen by Roxas and his men below. But he'd seen the rock from the waiting room of the hospital, and if anyone near the hospital were watching, they couldn't miss him. So, instead, he hugged his body against the massive rock, shimmying between it and another boulder until he found a place where he could sink low behind a short, scraggly pine and—hopefully—watch unnoticed.

Frank hadn't counted on the wind being so strong and cold this high up on the mountainside, and it beat against his windbreaker, at times nearly deafening him. He pulled his jacket tight around his body in an effort to prevent the noisy flapping, and he cupped a hand against his ear to funnel in the voices from below. It didn't work.

Still, he had a bird's-eye view, and he watched the men exit from and disappear into the tunnel entrance, though he never saw Roxas. After what felt like an hour of crouching, Frank backed out from his spot behind the pine, stood behind the boulder and stretched his screaming legs. Overhead, the sky had paled to dull chrome as the sun sank behind the other side of the mountain. Though the wind gusts had died, the evening air chilled him, and he shivered. Frank rocked backward on his heels, feeling the burn in his hamstrings, then returned to his position behind the pine. He'd give it another half hour—he needed to begin the descent down the mountainside before darkness set in.

As he peered down on the operation, a reflection of light, like that from a mirror, caught his attention on the hill opposite. Someone else was watching from a distance. Was it Ver or one of his men? No, they would have stayed in the tunnel. Frank ducked out of the line of sight—or so he hoped.

The thought of nightfall sickened him. He'd decided during his sleepless twilight hours that if nothing happened today he'd call Bozeman tonight and insist he was going home. Bozeman remained miffed and somewhat cold since Frank had left for Japan. Frank felt sure the man had tried to get Nixon to call him off the case, but after explaining to the President what had happened with Ver at Marcos's residence, Nixon thought Frank's "vacation" in Japan would provide a measure of safety and distance until things cooled down.

No sooner did Frank settle in his hiding spot than four men emerged from the tunnel entrance and walked into the tree line, where they tossed uprooted shrubs and pine boughs aside. They uncovered the metal cart he'd seen lugged up the mountainside that morning. Had they hidden it from Ver?

The four tugged the cart free from its hiding place and half-dragged, half-shoved it into the tunnel. Minutes that seemed like hours passed before the men returned, led by Roxas, who carried a dirty bag that appeared to be heavy despite its small size. Gold coins? Jewels? Frank could only speculate.

Two more men emerged toting what appeared to be a heavy, intricate model of a cathedral or church—made of gold. Behind them, two men with ropes strapped across their chests like plow mules pulled at the metal cart, while four more men flanked the cart, two on each side, and another two pushed from behind. The wooden crate they'd carried up the mountain that morning sat on the cart, but the lid could no longer rest on its top.

And then he saw the gold Buddha. It appeared to be at least three feet tall, and judging by the effort exerted by the men bearing it, the Buddha must weigh a good metric ton.

So the rumors were true. There was a golden Buddha. And it was here.

Frank forced himself to breathe slowly and deeply. Now was not the time to let his excitement take over. Finally, his heart rate slowed and he resumed watching.

Roxas set down the bag, ran toward an area piled with large rocks, and yanked up a burlap sack. Grinning broadly, he threw the sack over the Buddha's head, pulled it back off, kissed the statue, and then replaced the sack.

Though Frank couldn't hear a word over the wind howling in his ears, he could easily read Roxas's lips as he pumped a fist into the air. "Eureka!"

Frank scrambled down the mountain and returned to his room at a local inn. He immediately called President Nixon, although his secretary said the President was unavailable. Frank pulled stretched the phone cord as far as it would go and put the clunky phone next to him as he bathed. Afterwards, he tried to sleep, but his mind wouldn't stop.

The phone rang. The ring itself startled Frank, out of a twilight sleep

"Give me good news, son." Nixon didn't mince words.

Frank's heart drummed a cadence in his chest. "The Treasure Hunter's Association has found something. In a tunnel in the mountain across the road from Baguio Hospital, on the backside of the same mountain where Camp John Hay is located. I saw them carry out a gold Buddha." His voice cracked with nerves and elation. "It took eight men to move the cart that carried it."

"A Buddha, you say. Interesting. Anything else?"

"Yes, sir. They carried out several swords, old guns, and a leather bag that looked to hold something quite heavy. Coins, I'm guessing, though it could've held jewels."

"Were any of Marcos's men a part of the group?"

"No, I don't believe so, sir. Rogelio Roxas is the man who secured permits for the treasure hunt, through Judge Pio Marcos. General Ver visited the site four or five hours earlier, but I believe the men hid what they'd found from him."

"If this Roxas pulled permits, he'll have to turn over a portion of his find to Marcos."

"That's right, sir. Thirty percent, I'm told. I've also been told that Roger Roxas plays by the rules, so I expect he'll report his finding to Judge Marcos soon."

"I see. He probably hid it from Ver to keep him from confiscating the find before Roxas had a chance to report it." Nixon cleared his throat. "Well, unless he plays the role of King Solomon, he'll have to sell the Buddha, because you can't lop off thirty percent of a statue and hand it over to Marcos."

"Yes, Mr. President. If the statue comes up for sale or auction, should I put a bid on it for you?"

"No, absolutely not. You'll show no more interest over this thing than any other local with your same means. If word gets to the U.S. about the find—and I'm sure it'll make international headlines soon—we'll take it from there."

"Yes, sir."

"That Buddha may be just the tip of the iceberg."

"My source told me he believes there was one Buddha buried in that mountain, along with at least a thousand crates of gold biscuits."

The line grew silent, and Frank though he might have lost the connection. "Are you there, sir?"

"I'm still here. Keep an eye on that dig site, and don't hesitate to call me."

"Of course, sir."

"And, son?"

"Yes, sir?"

"Watch your back."

◢

The next day, Roxas and six of his crew members returned to the site, but this time, they blasted shut the tunnel, transplanted scrub pines and papaya bushes in front of the entrance, then swept the area with rakes, taking care to reposition the pile of rocks they'd made during the dig. Did that mean gold remained in the tunnel, but they didn't want to retrieve it yet? Or had they emptied the site and merely wanted to cover their tracks? Frank didn't dare check the tunnel to find out.

The following morning, Frank decided to return to Manila, as he expected he'd learn from Rosalita or her ties to the palace whether or not Marcos knew of Roxas's discovery.

Since the bungalow he'd rented before he left for Japan had a new occupant, he'd made himself quite comfortable in a three-room suite in the Manila Hotel. The hotel had come highly recommended by Rosalita, and despite its high room rate, Bozeman never blinked when Frank requested reimbursement.

When he arrived in Manila and stepped into his suite, Frank felt icy fingers strumming his nerves. Something was wrong. He set his gym bag at his feet, but left the door open a crack, in case he needed an easy out. He cocked his head, listening for the slightest sound. When the refrigerator in the kitchenette hummed to life, Frank tensed, then puffed his cheeks and released pent-up breath. He walked stealthily toward his bedroom, peering first in the closet—empty except for his clothes, stacks of books and a half-box of green engineer's notepads—then in the bathroom. He stood a few steps away from the shower and yanked back the curtain, relieved to find an empty stall.

Still, something wasn't right. Confident now, he returned to the living area, closed and locked the door. He looked around, visually scouring the room top to bottom. His eyes returned twice to the small desk, so he trusted his instincts. Frank allowed his eyes to roam the desk, but he never touched it. Instead, he knelt on the floor and looked underneath it, then ran his hands along its underside, checking for bugs. Repeating the action in the drawers but finding nothing but take-out food menus, copies of the Holy Bible written in English and Tagalog, and a phone directory, he finally touched the items on top of the desk.

A ceramic teacup he'd carried from the kitchenette held pens, pencils, paperclips and stamps. Nothing unusual there. Then he realized what was different. The pad he'd last been writing on—the one on which he'd doodled dozens of Japanese map symbols while trying to break their codes—held a blank page. He ran his fingers over it as if reading Braille, his sensitive fingertips picking up on the indentions his pen had made in the pages below. The page of symbols had been torn out.

Someone has been in my room! Frank ran a hand through his hair, then stepped around the desk. He picked up and replaced each item as if the energy of the last person who'd touched it would transfer an identity. No such luck.

Think. Think. He'd seen Ver at the dig site just two days ago, but he'd left, likely to return here to Manila. Regardless, Ver could have sent his men, instead of searching the room himself. Frank looked around. No, if Ver had been here, he'd have trashed the room or somehow left his mark so Frank would know he meant business.

Who then? Rosalita? Impossible. Sure, she'd recommended the hotel, but he'd had the feeling it was her subtle way of testing his finances; see if he'd balk at paying the hotel's exorbitant fees for a month in the suite. Still, her close relationship to the Marcoses might prompt her to spy on him.

What about the maids? That idea held merit. Frank checked the kitchen garbage can—empty. Ditto the wastebasket beside the writing desk and the one in the bathroom. But why would they tear off a page on his notepad? *The symbols.* That had to be it. To a layman's eye, they'd look like doodles scribbled while chatting on the telephone. Some well-meaning housekeeper had torn off the "dirty" page, providing him with a fresh, clean sheet of paper for note-taking.

Frank breathed easier, but he couldn't shake the feeling that Rosalita may have had something to do with the missing page of symbols.

The phone rang. Frank sucked in his breath. His trembling hand hovered over the receiver a moment before he picked it up.

"Hello?"

"Franklin! I'm so glad you're back." Rosalita's voice sounded half an octave too high.

"Hey, there," Frank said. "I was just thinking about you."

Chapter 21

April 5, 1971
Baguio, Luzon, the Philippines

Rogelio Roxas struggled to shake off the heavy sleep weighing down his eyelids as he peered at the clock. *2:18 a.m.* He rubbed his face with his hands and confirmed the time. When the pounding on the door convinced him he wasn't dreaming, he threw back the covers and stumbled toward the door, cursing as he tripped over the large box of keys that had been mistakenly delivered to his house instead of to his locksmith shop in town.

"Who is it?" he asked, his voice thick with slumber. He pushed aside the curtains and peered out the window nearest the front door.

A rifle butt smashed through window. Shards of glass exploded over his face and chest. "Open up! Now, or we shoot!"

Hands shaking, Rogelio unlocked the multiple locks on the door, including the new slide latch he'd installed after finding the Buddha statue, the gold biscuits and the diamonds that had been stored in the Buddha's removable head. As soon as he released the chain latch, the door burst inward, knocking him to the floor.

Within seconds, a sub-machine gun pointed at his head. When he finally forced himself to look away from the gun's barrel, he saw eight men, one of whom was Joe Oihara, the Japanese man who'd came to inspect the Buddha only four days ago. Oihara claimed to be a close friend of the Marcoses—indeed, had said he was staying with Ferdinand's mother. He wanted to buy the Buddha and promised to return with a down payment of a million pesos in a week.

"Who are you?" he asked the officer who stood above him, the barrel of his gun now resting against Rogelio's temple.

"Criminal Investigation Services, of the National Bureau of Investigations."

Rogelio tried to cringe away from the gun barrel, but the pressure against his temple was renewed. "But, I've done nothing—"

The man held up a search warrant. "You're in violation of Central Bank regulations for possession of illegal firearms." The man nodded toward the rusty bayonets, rifle and dirty samurai swords piled in the corner—the ones Rogelio and his men had recovered in the tunnel.

Judge Pio Marcos's name was on the search warrant. Rogelio's stomach turned. "They don't work. They're old. I found them in a tunnel. I've tried four times to report them to Judge Marcos, but he won't return my calls."

"Rogelio?" The sleep-muffled voice of Rogelio's wife came from the bedroom.

The man standing above him jerked his head toward the door.

Rogelio's bladder voided.

Two armed men rushed the short hallway leading to Rogelio and his children's bedrooms. Rogelio had hired two friends as bodyguards. They slept on the floor of his children's bedroom, but neither was armed. He didn't want loaded guns where the kids could get them.

"Nooo," he whimpered. "Please, *please,* don't hurt my family."

From the guest room on the other side of the house, Rogelio's brother Dan burst through the door. "What is this? Who are you? Let go of my brother!" He charged one of the officers, knocked him to the floor, pounced atop him and punched him in the face.

Instantly, two more officers pulled Dan off the man, each twisting one of Dan's arms behind his back until he yelped. The bloody-nosed man stood, wiped his nose on his sleeve, glared at Dan, then plunged his fist into Dan's crotch, causing him to fall to his knees and vomit in agony.

"Please," Rogelio cried. "Take me. Do whatever you want to me. Just please don't hurt my wife, my babies."

Something smashed into his temple; bright light seared his brain. Someone lifted him from behind, tied his hands behind his back, and dragged him backward, sitting him against the wall. The room faded in and out of blackness, and he realized some of the men were laughing at the wet streak he'd left behind as they dragged him across the floor.

Despite the scorching pain of opening his eyes, Rogelio tried to focus on the hallway door, hoping to see his wife and children again before they killed him. The stench of vomit burned his nose. Dan lay several feet away, curled into a fetal position while an officer stood above him, his boot resting firmly on Dan's head.

Six of the officers emerged from the hallway, grunting with effort as they dragged the gold Buddha on a blanket.

The bitch is heavy, isn't it? The unprompted thought made Rogelio smile, and he felt as if only half of his mouth worked. The room grew dark again.

When he resurfaced into reality, Oihara was pawing through the small leather bag of diamonds, picking up handfuls, letting them drip through his fingers back into the bag. His eyes blazed and a wicked grin split his face. The Buddha was gone.

A man clad in the uniform of the Philippine Army carried out a rusted, broken .22 caliber rifle, Rogelio's daughter's pink piggy bank tucked under his arm. Another man hauled the heavy wooden box that held seventeen of the gold biscuits they'd found. The samurai swords, bayonets, and antique rifles had disappeared.

The eight men congregated in Rogelio's living room, surrounding Rogelio's bodyguards and his brother. They took turns kicking them and beating them with rifle butts. Before he succumbed to the blackness encroaching on his periphery, a fine mist of blood sprayed the new wallpaper his wife had hung on the other side of the living room.

Soft slaps on the face brought Rogelio back to consciousness. His wife hunched over him, the side of her face red and swollen, her lips split and bleeding. "Rogelio, please. Please wake up!"

Despite the pain they caused, fresh tears stung his eyes, and Rogelio hauled himself to one elbow, pulling his wife to his chest. A sob choked his words. "The children—"

"They're okay. The men didn't touch them. Dan is with them in the bedroom."

As if on cue, Dan emerged from the hallway, Rogelio's sons and daughter under his arms. The kids broke free and ran to their parents, rivulets coursing from their terrified eyes.

"Daddy! Oh, Daddy, we thought you were dead." His daughter collapsed on top of him, while his wife pulled their sons into an embrace. The five sat huddled on the floor as emotion washed through Rogelio's heart.

Quickly, thankfulness for his family's lives turned to anger. These men had broken into his home, beaten his wife, his brother, his friends. He'd have given Judge Marcos the damned Buddha, rather than put his family through this nightmare.

"What time is it?" he asked.

Dan shrugged, holding up his left wrist to show that his watch had also been stolen. He limped toward the guest bedroom, then returned. "Nearly 4:30."

Rogelio's wife, accompanied by both bodyguards, stepped out the door to their outside kitchen and put on water for tea. Rogelio hobbled to the bathroom and cleaned the dried blood from his face as best as he could with the vision from one eye. The other had long since swollen shut.

He twisted the handle on his safety razor, opening the butterfly wings to expose the blade within. He shook out the blade and lifted it to his swollen eye, wincing as pain burned his shoulder with the movement. Rogelio held his breath to steady himself as he sliced across the swollen lid. He dropped the blade and grabbed a wet washcloth, pressing it to his eye until most of the bleeding subsided.

From the medicine cabinet, he took out a can of salve and smeared it across the cut. He squinted and blinked a few times. Pressure relieved, the eye began to open.

Rogelio rejoined his family and friends in the living room, where his wife filled cups with hot tea. The children were curled on a pallet against the wall, their eyes already heavy with sleep. Rogelio yearned for their peaceful innocence.

"What now?" Dan asked quietly.

Rogelio sipped from his cup of steaming tea, wincing as the hot liquid met his cut lip. "Now we contact the authorities."

"The authorities?" His wife's eyes blazed from her battered face. "Those men *were the authorities!*"

Rogelio shook his head. "I don't think so. I'm betting that Buddha and the gold never make it to the clerk of courts. I'm going to do what anyone should do after being robbed and beaten. As soon as they open, I'm going to the newspapers. I'm going to get as much press on this as possible, and I'm going to ask them to accompany me to the police station. If the press is with me, the police won't be able to sweep this under the rug. Then I'm going straight to Judge Pio Marcos's court, and I'm going to ask him why he didn't return my calls when I tried to report the treasure, and why he signed that search warrant."

"Why *would* Judge Marcos sign the search warrant?" Rogelio's wife asked. "He gave you permission to dig for the gold."

"I can think of only one reason." Dan locked eyes with his brother.

Rogelio nodded. "President Marcos ordered him to do it."

CHAPTER 22

Manila Hotel, Philippines
January 22, 1972

Frank sat in the Ilang-Ilang Café of the Manila Hotel, reading the breakfast menu he already knew by heart. The thought of *champorado* with *danggit*—the chocolate sticky rice pudding served with a side of crisped, sun-dried fish—nearly gagged him. What he would give this morning for some good ol' Southern biscuits, gravy and grits!

His waitress poured a cup of hot *barako* coffee. Frank thanked her, then pushed it aside. The brew proved so strong and bitter as to make his throat clench, and he'd yet to develop a taste for it. "It'll put steel in your manhood," Rosalita had once told him, laughing.

He opened a copy of *The Philippines Free Press* to see yet another front-page article about the Constitutional Convention. The "Con-Con," as the locals called it, was the event on which the poor had pinned all their hopes. The Convention promised that rewriting the 1935 Constitution would provide a roadmap to prosperity and fairness for all Filipinos. The new constitution would be more than simply the country's fundamental law; it would be a sacred document that would lift nearly forty million Filipinos from poverty.

That is, until Ferdinand Marcos dipped his finger in the inkwell.

Of course, Marcos had neither right nor reason to be a part of the Con-Con, but that didn't stop him from interfering where he could affect change to benefit himself. A few weeks prior to the convention date, Marcos invited more and more delegates to Malacañang, where he wined, dined, gifted and otherwise did his best to influence them to see things his way. *Wouldn't it be grand if the Constitution allowed him to be President indefinitely? Or what about Prime Minister? Yes, a parliamentarian government might be in order, and Prime Minister Marcos would be the perfect man to run it!*

Independent delegates blasted Malacañang in the press for meddling in the convention, but that didn't slow Marcos.

On the eve of Con-con, Rosalita invited Frank to accompany her to a birthday party for Marcos's dog, held in the hotel where Frank resided.

Frank shook his head even now, thinking about it. Marcos's dog gave "party favors" of checks to each of the guests—the majority of whom were Convention delegates—in consideration for their "canine" support. His own check was written for a thousand pesos, but Rosalita hinted that the delegates now had "ten thousand new reasons" to support the Marcos' family pets.

Frank shoveled down the last bite of his rice and eggs, wiped his mouth and signed for his meal. As he headed back to his room to pick up his gym bag before heading out, the concierge stopped him.

"Mr. Young? I have an important message for you." The man held out a small, sealed envelope.

Frank accepted the envelope and tipped the man, then headed to his room. By now, the elevator attendants knew his routine, and the man pushed the number to his floor without asking. "Lovely day, Mr. Young."

"Yes. Yes, it is. Thank you," Frank mumbled as he ripped open the envelope. He instantly recognized Rosalita's looping script.

I have a special surprise for you.
Pick you up at noon.

                    Rosalita

Frank sighed, refolded the note and stuffed it and the envelope in his pocket. Nice of her to ask if he had plans.

Regardless of his annoyance, Frank forced a smile when Rosalita's driver Tony met him in the hotel lobby four hours later. The man opened the rear passenger door of Rosalita's new Mercedes-Benz—she had a new one delivered the first of each year—and Frank slid inside.

"Hello, Frank." Rosalita kissed him on the cheek. "Curious about your surprise?"

Frank didn't answer right away. His first instinct was to scold her for assuming he'd drop everything and do as she wished, but he needed her to get him back into Malacañang Palace later in the week. Better keep her happy. "Of course. I can't believe you planned a surprise for me." Yikes. His voice sounded too flat. He quickly kissed Rosalita's neck and smiled.

"Calm down, frisky man. The surprise isn't all *that* grand. Besides, I actually have two surprises." A mischievous grin crossed her pink-glossy lips. "Tony?"

The driver met Rosalita's eyes in the rearview mirror and lifted a cardboard U.S. Air Mail box.

"Take it," Rosalita instructed.

Frank took the box, noting that the packing tape had been cut. Glancing at Rosalita, he opened the cardboard flaps. He lifted out a large glass jar of Tang Instant Breakfast Drink, another glass jar of Sanka Coffee. "What? Thank you! What I wouldn't have given for this a few hours ago." He replaced them and picked up one of the dozen metal Snack Pack pudding cans the box held. "Chocolate and vanilla pudding! Real American food." He laughed out loud. "Rosalita, this is wonderful!"

Rosalita giggled. "My college roomie sent it for you. She's always sending me care packages, and when she asked what I needed, I remembered you talking about how you missed these things."

"You did this for me?" Frank couldn't believe how much her thoughtfulness touched him. He quickly turned his head and composed himself. "Thank you." Frank cupped Rosalita's head in his hand and pulled her toward him, kissing her soft mouth. She was driving him crazy; he wanted her, he didn't want her. He didn't want to get serious with her, but he missed her when they were apart. He cared for her, but his gut told him not to trust her.

Rosalita's eyes twinkled as she stared at him. "You're too easy, Franklin. Who knew all it took was a Snack Pack to melt your heart?"

Frank laughed.

"I hope I haven't made a huge mistake." Rosalita's brow wrinkled.

"What do you mean?"

"Well, if a box of American treats blew your mind, then my other surprise might ruin you for life."

Frank rubbed his hands together. "Tell me more."

Rosalita shook her head and graced him with a teasing smile. "Oh, no. You'll have to wait and see. Now let's change the subject before you get too carried away."

Frank grinned. "Okay. So, how are the plans coming for that dance event you're planning?"

Rosalita's jade green eyes grew round. "Oh, Frank, the girls have worked so hard, and they've come so far; I can't wait for everyone to see them. I'm telling you, this will rival anything you've seen in New York City."

Frank chuckled. "I haven't seen many dances in New York City."

Rosalita playfully smacked his leg. "Don't tell Imelda. She's under the impression you're an extremely cultured Filipino-American. If she learns you aren't up to speed, she'll have you on one of her cultural committees so she can coach you to better represent the Philippines each time you visit the States."

A cultural committee. Ugh. That wasn't exactly the way Frank wanted to spend time with the Marcoses. "Well, we'll have to make certain she sees me at your dance performance so she'll remain under the impression that I'm extremely cultured. You'll help with that, of course."

"Oh, of course." Rosalita held her head erect and looked down her nose. They laughed.

Rosalita's smile faded. "Actually, Imelda is driving me a bit bonkers."

"Why's that?"

She shook her head. "Oh, I don't know. She's always been—well, *odd*— she and Ferdinand both. Lately, though, she's been showing me these little doodles of things God has revealed to her. Nearly every time I'm with her,

I have to sit through an hour of her sketches, while she points out the day's latest revelation."

"What do you mean?"

Rosalita waved her hand. "It starts with a heart, or a cross, or a circle. Then she'll add another, or draw one on top of the other, all the while explaining the mysteries of the universe. God is love. We're all connected. That sort of thing. Honestly, I think she's convinced she should be canonized."

"You're kidding me, right?"

"I'm not sure. She's always talking about how generous she and Ferdinand are with the poor, how they've given up everything for their people—all this while they're hoarding money and buying expensive jewels and 'their people' are starving." Rosalita's fingers tapped on her knee. "Honestly, Frank, she hints around that she should be made a saint. Can you imagine?"

"Saint Imelda." Frank shook his head.

Rosalita laughed dryly. "Saint Imelda and Ferdinand the Psychic. They're quite a pair."

"Ferdinand the Psychic? What now?"

Rosalita's eyebrows rose and her lips pulled to one side. "Oh, yes. He's quite convinced he has psychic powers. You know how he's into numerology. The number of the day, plus the month, plus the year; it all has meaning. Well, now he thinks he can sometimes predict the future."

"No kidding?"

"No kidding. He's been using his skills to find buried treasure."

Frank's jaw muscles twitched. "Buried treasure?"

"Yes. You know about the treasure Ferdinand found a year or so ago. Well, there's a lot more of it."

"So the rumors are true?"

Rosalita touched Frank's leg with her fingertips. "Honey, they aren't rumors. Even though Marcos insists on making the media look foolish when they bring up the treasure, there's more gold in these islands than anyone will ever find. Villacrusis got his hand on a big stack of old maps. Marcos has had him digging all over the islands for buried treasure for over a year now.

"For the longest time, he had no success. The landmarks used on the maps have changed over the years; rockslides have occurred, trees have died or fallen, weather has altered the landscape. If their measurements are off by a foot, months of excavation are wasted." She shook her head.

"So?" Frank turned up his palms.

"So while you were in America, Marcos hit pay-dirt."

Frank's throat constricted. "Really?"

Rosalita nodded and smoothed a stray hair back into her ponytail. "They carried out a huge gold Buddha and some other treasure. Ferdinand already has bank vaults full of gold bars, so it's not as if he needs more."

"A gold Buddha? Is it anything like the one the press said that guy found in Baguio City?"

Rosalita cut a sharp look toward Frank. "It's the same one, Frank. Ferdinand employed Rogelio Roxas. The man tried to steal the Buddha out from under him."

Frank knew better, but felt his head slowly nodding, anyway. "Oh."

Rosalita huffed, and her voice took on a sharp edge. "Judge Pio Marcos arranged the job for Roxas. He provided the permits and heavy equipment for Roxas and his team to excavate. Marcos even paid the man a salary in addition to offering him a large percentage of anything he found. You know, you cannot trust anyone these days."

Boy, you can say that again. Frank stared out the window, acutely aware of the change in Rosalita's eyes as she spoke, as if she'd scoured her mind for the exact words, words she repeated by rote, complete with Tagalog accent. As Frank's stepfather would have said, Rosalita usually talked like a damn Yankee. Though fluent in Tagalog, she rarely spoke the language, and when she did, she spoke it with a polish the locals would never use. But not just now. Now she sounded like Imelda.

Rosalita leaned forward and touched her driver's shoulder. "Just ahead, Tony, on the left."

Frank leaned forward to peer at what lay ahead, wishing they hadn't reached their destination just when the conversation was getting interesting. Could Rosalita really believe that Rogelio Roxas had been hired by Marcos to find buried treasure? *Of course she could.* She wasn't there to see what he had seen. Frank wondered what other lies and false impressions Ferdinand and Imelda had made on his girlfr—

Frank put the brakes on his thought. *She's* not *my girlfriend.*

The car pulled to a stop and Rosalita grabbed his hand in both of hers. "You're going to be so surprised!"

When Tony opened the door, Frank stepped out and looked around at the row of food stalls lining the streets. Surely she didn't expect them to have lunch here. The vendors hawked things he couldn't bear to eat, despite his years of international travel. Sure, he enjoyed the tangy adobo pork, the varied rice dishes, even the barbequed pigs' ears called *walkman,* but he couldn't bear the thought of *balut*—partially developed duck eggs—or the skewers of fried chicken feet or barbecued chicken intestines. No amount of dipping sauce could get him past the thought of eating these things that many Filipinos considered delicacies.

"We're not eating here, are we?" Frank's stomach had already begun to churn.

Rosalita's lips parted in a wicked smile. "Yes, we are. Trust me." She took Frank's hand and pulled him down the street to a stall surrounded by patrons, many of them American. Frank glanced up at the sign. In simple block letters, it read "Tom's. Since 1958."

Tom's. Sounded American enough. He stepped closer to read the menu, and his eyes bulged in their sockets. "Man, this is so cool!" Frank resisted the urge to clap his hands like a schoolboy. There, on the faded menu board, he read the list of foods he'd never seen in the Philippines. Lexington-style barbecue. Fried fish with hush puppies. Pintos with cornbread and slaw. Fried chicken with potato salad and a biscuit. Shrimp and grits. Red beans and rice. Sweet tea.

"Sweet tea! Biscuits! Grits!" Frank burst out laughing, and several of the people in line turned around, smiling. "Not just American food. *Southern* food!"

"First time you've been here, huh?" A middle-aged man wearing a faded University of New Orleans baseball cap smiled.

"I didn't know this place existed!"

Chuckles erupted from some of the patrons, most of whom Frank figured had felt the same way when they'd discovered the food stall.

"Baby, you're the best!" Frank picked up Rosalita and spun her around, then sat her down and kissed her hard.

Mr. New Orleans grinned. "You know what they say: best way to a man's heart is through his stomach!"

CHAPTER 23

When Tony and Rosalita dropped off Frank at the Manila Hotel toting his box of goodies, his stomach still bulged from the food he'd eaten at the food stall. And the tea! He practically sloshed when he walked. The afternoon air refreshed him, and he needed to walk off some of his overindulgence, so he left his box for the concierge. After the disappearance of his notes, his paranoia hardly allowed even the maids into his room. He set out to stroll the block a few times.

As he walked, he mulled over Rosalita's news about Marcos and the maps. Everything he'd learned proved true; Villacrusis did get the maps from Valmores, and now Marcos had paid Villacrusis and Ver to locate the treasure. But where were the maps?

Frank rounded the corner to the back of the hotel. He glanced up. An older gentleman, stooped over but still taller than most Filipinos, walked toward him. The wool coat he wore was torn at the shoulder, exposing the gray lining, and the pocket of the coat had been torn on two sides and swung as he walked. And, even from a distance, Frank could see that the sole of one of his shoes had separated from the leather and flopped with each step the man took.

There was something very familiar about him. Frank's brain went into overdrive, searching his memory banks for the name that went with the face.

As he neared, the man looked up. His eyes met Frank's, then widened, and his mouth dropped open as if he'd seen a ghost. And in that second,

Frank knew who he was. The man he'd seen on Montalban Gorge what? Three years ago? He'd looked so different that day on the mountain, clean and well-dressed. The gold cross he'd worn that day could have bought a whole new wardrobe to replace the meager threads he wore today. But it was him.

The man turned and, as quickly as he could, tried to disappear back into the alley.

Frank ran after him. He cut into the alley and saw the man just a few yards in front of him.

"Hey!" Frank yelled.

The man didn't turn. Instead, he disappeared into the steam that curled over the sidewalk from several laundry vents.

"Hey. Come back. Wait up." Frank jogged blindly into the moist, white cloud.

Two large hands gripped Frank's arms from behind, twisted them behind his back and shoved him face-first against the brick wall of the hotel. "Quiet!" the deep voice said.

Steel pressed into Frank's side.

Instinctively, Frank squirmed to free himself, but the steel pressed harder.

"Don't make me do something I'd rather not do," the man hissed. "Now stand down or be taken down. One way or the other, it's your choice." The stranger slammed Frank's head against the brick wall. "Do I have your attention now?"

Frank grunted.

"You will walk with me," the stranger said. "Slowly. And I am going to keep this gun in your ribcage all the way. Yes, Franco Quezon, I know who you are."

Frank's heart picked up speed. "What did you just call me?" He struggled to turn around, but the click of a gun cocking stopped him. "Who are you?"

The man jiggled the gun. "You are in no position to ask questions. Walk."

Frank's mind raced. What had he gotten into? Was this familiar face one of Marcos' men? How was he going to get out of this with his body intact?

The man walked Frank through and past the billowing steam, then produced a key and entered the hotel through a back door, into a noisy room with several people busily . . . cooking. They were in the prep kitchen.

One by one, the workers looked up and met his captor's eyes. Some gave him a slight nod, then looked away as if they'd seen nothing at all. Others smiled. One shrugged. Not a soul looked at Frank.

"Through that door," the gunman ordered.

Frank walked through the kitchen, out a door, and down a side hallway into a dimly lit corridor.

Once alone, the man turned and stared hard into Frank's eyes, the gun still pointed at his heart.

"Who are you?"

"I am Severino Santa Romana." The man waited for his revelation to sink in.

Frank felt as if he'd been slapped. "You're . . . ." He couldn't finish the sentence.

"Yes. I work with your pals, Lansdale and Nixon." One eyebrow lifted. "And your other friend, Marcos."

Nixon said they didn't know whose side Santa Romana was on. Frank racked his brain to think of everything he'd heard about the man, then realized he knew very little.

A wry smile flitted across Santa Romana's lips, but disappeared as quickly as it had come. "The picture you took from the old church—yes, that was me. I was the parish priest—Father Jose Antonio Diaz. I served the Roman Catholic Church before and during World War II." As if waiting for a question not spoken, he shrugged. "Yes. I took my vows quite seriously."

Frank stared at the man. It was too much to take in.

"Now, may I put my gun away, or should I just shoot you? I would prefer not to, but I will if I must." The priest's English was excellent, but his words carried a heavy European accent.

"I like breathing, so please put it away." Frank paused for a second. "But if you worked—work—for Lansdale and Nixon, then how—"

"I don't work *for* them. I work *with* them. We have mutual interests and concerns—serious agendas set before us that we believe will benefit our countries. Our world, even."

"And Marcos?"

Santa Romana nodded slowly. "Marcos and I have had a ... *relationship* for many, many years."

"Keep your friends close and your enemies closer?"

This time, Santa Romana allowed a real smile. "Something like that. Advice you should learn to follow as well."

Frank jutted his chin. "What do you mean?"

"Stop searching for buried treasure. I can't protect you forever."

"Protect me? *Protect* me? How have you ever protected me?"

Santa Romana sighed, turned his head and stared into the past. "I've protected you since you were a small boy, Franco Quezon."

Frank searched the man's eyes. *How does he know my birth name?*

The man allowed himself a small smile. "I know; only your father called you Franco. You told me."

Frank thought of the day he'd met this man on the mountain. He'd said no such thing. "No, I never told you that."

"Yes, you did." The man held his hand low and parallel to the ground. "You were only this high. Three, maybe four years old. It was on the very same mountain where I saw you a few years ago, near Montalban Gorge." His dark eyes softened. "Your father had just been murdered by a Japanese soldier. I took you and your mama back to the parish church. I didn't know what to do. I was heartbroken. Danilo was my dear, dear friend. But first, we had to get you and your mama out of the country—alive."

Frank closed his eyes. *Murder. Took me, took Mother away.* Then, clearer than ever before, he remembered a man's hand. It protruded from behind a big rock, hit the ground, bounced, a gold wedding band glinting in the sunlight.

"Behind a big rock. His hand—"

Santa Romana hung his head. When he looked up, his eyes were puddled. "You saw it. I have wondered for many, many years if you had seen your father's . . . fate." He placed a hand on Frank's shoulder. "I'm sorry. It must have been difficult for you."

Frank swallowed the lump of fire burning his throat. "I didn't know—I didn't know it was my—the man I saw—I only saw his hand . . . ."

Santa Romana nodded and offered a weak smile. "God is merciful."

Frank's voice cracked. "Merciful? My father was murdered by a Japanese soldier. Why? Why was he murdered? What did he do?"

"Your father accepted the risks he took." Santa Romana locked eyes with Frank. "Just as you have accepted the risks you are taking." His voice softened. "Danilo was my good friend, Frankie. He and I worked together for several years. He retrieved information, passed it through me to Edward Lansdale. He even drew some of the maps. He was a brave man, and he loved you and your mother very much."

Frank turned his head and stared down the corridor, unseeing.

"You must return to the States. Stop hunting for buried treasure." The old priest slowly shook his head. "If you know what's good for you."

Frank whipped around and shoved his finger under Santa Romana's nose. "You have no idea what's good for me." He took a deep breath. "Besides, I'm not looking for buried treasure."

"No? Then what were you doing at Montalban Gorge? What were you doing on the mountain in Baguio City?"

Frank's heart paused. "How did you know I was on the mountain in Baguio?"

"I told you, Frankie, I've been taking care of you." He shook his head. "At least, I've been trying to. I even tried to get Marcos to send you packing. You need to get out of here. Go back to your life in the States."

Frank studied the old man.

"Don't you know General Ver would pluck out your eyes if he knew you'd seen a treasure vault site?"

"Look, I don't want any of that damned buried treasure. I haven't been searching for treasure. Have you seen me touch a shovel or pick since I've been here? No, you haven't."

Santa Romana's eyes narrowed. "Then what do you want?"

"I'm here as a representative of Triangle Cigarettes."

The old man chuckled. "Maybe Marcos believes that—at least, right now—but I don't. Now, why are you here?"

"I told you."

"Don't lie to me."

Frank's brain shot into overdrive. He lowered his voice, but not his eyes. "I'd like to learn more about my father."

"I'm sure you do, but that's still not why you're here."

"Seems like you know more about me than I do. Why don't you tell me why I'm here?"

"I figure the CIA has sent you to find out if Marcos is abiding by his agreement."

"What agreement?"

"Don't play dumb." Santa Romana leaned closer. "And they probably want to know how much gold has been recovered and where it is, and they probably want to know where the remaining gold is buried. Did I miss anything?"

"I don't know what you're talking about."

"Then I guess you don't need my help."

Hope crowded Frank's confusion. "How can you help me?"

"Franco!" Santa Romana geared back, and for a moment, Frank thought he might slap him. "Didn't they give you any training at all? Nothing?" He shook his head. "Damn them!"

Confusion regained its stronghold.

Santa Romana stepped closer to Frank, crowding him, so their faces were almost touching. "Listen to me. Ferdinand has all the original maps in his office. They are under lock and key, and there's no way to get them without adding your eyeballs to Ver's collection." Spittle sprinkled over Frank's face. "Is he playing by his agreement? Of course not. Where is the gold buried? Everywhere. There are over one hundred official locations—and a couple more that haven't been documented. Ferdinand has already cleaned out four locations. He has re-smelt the gold and hidden it in various locations, including the basement of the palace, the summer palace, a hidden cellar behind the Baguio City Mansion, and a bunker behind the Cultural Center."

Santa Romana had used up all the oxygen. Frank struggled to breathe. "What about copies of the maps?"

"Most are garbage. You know that already. There are some good ones around, but, other than Villacrusis, who seems to have found some from somewhere, I don't know where they are or who has them." Santa Romana moved even closer until their noses practically touched, and when he spoke, Frank had to struggle to hear. "Now, your job is done. Report what you know to Nixon and get out of here. Immediately."

Was he telling the truth? Whose side was he on?

"Don't trust anyone except Bozeman. He's a good guy. Everyone else has hands in someone's pockets."

Rosalita? Frank was sure he hadn't spoken aloud.

"Your Rosalita is an investor in Villacrusis's digs. Can she be trusted?" Santa Romana shrugged. "I don't know. Maybe. If you can get her off these islands and away from the Marcoses." He smiled, one gold tooth decorating his yellowed teeth. "Of course, you'll have to take her mother too—she won't go without her mama."

The oxygen in the hall seemed used up. Frank sucked for air.

"I can no longer protect you." Santa Romana stepped back, finally, but his voice dripped with disappointment. "You must leave here now." He turned and walked back the way they had come. He paused with one hand on the door and looked over his shoulder at Frank. "Should you see me again, don't follow me." He swung the gun and raised his chin. "By the way, you have not seen me. You do not know me. In your world, Severino Santa Romana does not exist."

CHAPTER 24

Atlanta, Georgia
September 30, 1972

Frank folded *The Atlanta Constitution* and laid it atop his mother's bed tray. Above her hospital bed, monitors clicked and whirred in mind-numbing rhythm. Frank leaned forward and propped his elbows on his knees, dropping his head into his hands, as if in prayer. He sucked in a shallow breath, feeling as if the wind had been knocked from his lungs.

The newspaper reported that Nixon's Attorney General, John Mitchell, controlled a secret fund for the Republican Party to finance spy missions against the Democrats, thereby gathering intelligence that would assure Nixon's re-election. On the heels of the news that Ferdinand Marcos had declared martial law last week, he'd learned that Howard Hunt of the CIA, whom he'd met several times in Nixon's office, had been indicted in the Democratic National Committee's office break-in. Frank felt sick enough to crawl into bed beside his mother.

How much more can I take? He ran his fingers through his hair, then stood and paced the floor, his emotions ranging from grief to anger to fear to trepidation. Without thinking, he found himself poised above his mother, gently stroking her hennaed curls. In a fateful way, her near-death sickness had likely saved his life.

In President Marcos's proclamation of martial law, he'd declared that his national defense team could arrest and hold anyone they deemed suspect of committing crimes against Marcos or his New Society Movement. It unnerved Frank to think of it, even though he was thousands of miles away. Marcos had given Ver open and legal license to kill. Sooner rather than later, if Frank had stayed in the Philippines, he'd have come up on Ver's to-do list.

As thinly veiled as Marcos's crony capitalism had become, Frank couldn't help but wonder if its continued success had been what had spurred on President Nixon. After all, both had acted in violation of their own country's laws to achieve re-election and advance their own wealth and power. When would it end?

Frank traced his fingers along his mother's yellowed arm, taking care not to touch the dark, bruised areas from the many needle-sticks she'd suffered at the hands of the nurses and doctors. His eyes rested on her enormously distended stomach; the ascites caused her to look as if she were ready to deliver a baby any day now.

He unwrapped the sapphire rosary from her fingers and studied it. For as long as he could remember, his mother had cherished that rosary. When his father—his stepfather—died, she sat for hours, rocking in her chair, her hands clasped around the rosary. A few times she had shown it to him. Beads of star sapphires formed a circle; a gold bead closed that circle and joined a short chain of more star sapphires that ended with a gold cross. On one side of the cross were diamonds; on the other, an inscription too small to read with the naked eye. The gold bead was inscribed as well. After close study, he figured out what the inscription was: the symbol for the Greek letter *Alpha.*

Frank shrugged. The jewels were real—beads of star sapphires, diamonds on the cross—and she'd told him once it had been blessed by the Pope.

He took a step backward, feeling his face grow hot as the sound of urine flowing into the container beneath the bed reached his ears. Such an intimate act; Frank wanted to turn his head, but the dark, purple-gray color of his mother's voiding held him captive, like watching a traffic accident in slow motion.

Of course, he'd done his research. His mother's alcoholic cirrhosis had reached advanced stages, and nothing short of a liver transplant would save her life. If that. The surgery remained in experimental stages, and his mother's hepatologist told him that even if she could afford the surgery—and she damned well could—she'd only have a twenty-five percent chance of living a full year.

He should have been a better son. Years ago the doctors had warned that another drink could kill her, yet he'd watched her down glass after glass, just to avoid the argument. He should have been more insistent. He should have stayed with her, instead of globe-hopping, searching for buried treasure.

Frank thought of the day last August when he'd gone to Manila to watch Roxas speak at a rally organized by Senator Sergio Osmeña, Jr. The press had published "vile rumors" that Roxas had been robbed by President Marcos's men and was later arrested and even tortured for failing to appear at a criminal hearing for which he'd not received notification. Senator Osmeña, leader of the opposition Liberal Party, had bailed Roxas out of jail and now heralded the man as an example of President Marcos's corruption.

Frank had watched while mingling near the back of the huge crowd gathered at Plaza Miranda as the more prominent opposition leaders took their places on the platform. Where was Roxas? Frank's eyes followed the trail of security, and he realized Roxas sat in a truck near the stage. Smart move. He could always hastily be driven away should anything go wrong.

And boy, did something go wrong.

Frank felt the explosion before he heard it. He watched in disbelief as General Ver, dressed in full uniform, sidled up to the far edge of the crowd and casually lofted the grenade in an arc over his head and body into the center of the throng of people. Within a split-second, another grenade was lobbed into the crowd, but Frank couldn't tell from which direction it had come; he'd already planted his face on the concrete.

Now, he deflated as he thought of it. Roxas survived the carnage, though ten people were killed and over sixty wounded. The last he heard, though, Roxas had fled Manila; someone had exposed his hiding place. He'd been arrested and held in a stockade in Zambales. Frank also heard that Marcos had given the order to his Presidential Security Command to bomb the rally in order to blame the attack on communist terrorists and arrest some of the more prominent opposition leaders, calling them leftists and taking the first steps toward declaring martial law, which Frank had thought impossible.

But, Marcos had succeeded.

Mary Catherine stirred, although she did not awake. Frank gave the rosary one last squeeze, then put it in her hand and closed her fist around it. He'd begged her to leave it at home and bring another one. Several nurses had commented on the piece, and Frank worried it would disappear. Mary Catherine had rasped a laugh, told him anyone who'd steal a rosary would be shot into hell on a rocket.

Along with all those who sold their souls for gold.

Chapter 25

December 10, 1972
Boston, Massachusetts

Rosalita wrapped the draping cashmere scarf around her neck and linked arms with Caroline, one of her friends at Wellesley, to prevent slipping on the snow-dusted cobblestones. "Aren't you chilly?"

Caroline shot a glance at her friend from beneath thick lashes. "Your Filipina blood is thin." She waved a gloved hand toward the window boxes stuffed with evergreen branches on the brick apartments they passed. "I'll bet Christmas isn't this beautiful over there, is it? I can't imagine Christmas without snow."

Rosalita had to agree. There was something magical about strolling down Acorn Street in the early evening. They timed their walk perfectly each time so they'd reach Beacon Street just as the gaslights were lit and the historic homes on Beacon Hill began to glow from within. She couldn't imagine a better place to spend the holidays. A long sigh escaped her.

"What's that all about?" Caroline stopped walking and studied her friend.

"What?"

"That sigh. Tell me what's wrong."

"Oh, nothing. It's just good to be here."

Caroline patted her friend's arm. "Have you even called him to let him know you were here?"

Rosalita rolled her eyes. "Called who?"

Caroline chuckled. "You know, when you phoned and said you wanted to visit, I figured you just wanted to be in the same country—"

"Oh, come on, Caroline! I came to visit *you*." The cold night air caused her nose to run, and she sniffed loudly.

But her friend's words continued to haunt her. That night as Rosalita sat in front of her bedroom mirror brushing her hair, all she could think about was Frank. He was in Georgia—had been for more than a month. And yes, she had phoned him. Before she'd left the Philippines. She told him where she'd be and left the number.

She glanced at the clock, wondering if he'd call tonight. But who was she fooling? He hadn't called since she'd arrived—almost a week ago. Was it possible he had a lady friend there? A high school sweetheart, perhaps? "Damn it!" She stood and paced the bedroom, feeling like a schoolgirl who hoped her crush would call. "I'm not waiting for him!"

She twisted her hair into a ponytail holder at the nape of her neck, picked up the phone and dialed Mary Catherine's phone number. In a moment, the housekeeper answered.

"Is Franklin Young available?" Rosalita asked.

"Who's calling, please?"

"Rosalita Laurel."

"Just a moment, please."

Rosalita pursed her lips and blew out pent-up frustration and nervousness. Finally, the phone clicked and Frank's deep voice spoke.

She didn't want him to think she was pursuing him—but she should've thought of that before she'd made the call. "How's your mother?" she blurted. "I've been worried about her."

"Oh, Rosalita, I'm so glad you called." His voice sounded heavy with exhaustion. "She's not well, Rosalita. Not well at all."

Guilt swathed Rosalita. "I'm so sorry, Frank. Is there anything I can do?"

"No. Yeah, actually. Well . . . maybe." A soft, tired laugh escaped Frank's mouth. "I'm sorry. I'm not thinking straight."

"What is it? What do you need?"

Frank sighed, and Rosalita ached to hold him, pull his head to her bosom and stroke his hair.

"Would it be too much to ask you to come and visit me? Mom and me, I mean? I know you're in the States to visit your friend, and it's a holiday—"

"Of course I'll come." Relief flowed through Rosalita's chest like warm water. "I'll call the airlines first thing in the morning." Could Frank hear the smile in her voice? She didn't want to sound overly joyous. "Do you need me to bring anything? I mean, is there anything your mother needs?"

"No, nothing I can think of. It's just that, well, it might lift Mom's spirits to see you. And I sure could use a friendly face right now."

Rosalita wound a strand of hair around her finger. "Is she getting any better at all?"

"It's her third hospitalization in two months. But you know," he said, and his voice lifted a bit, "I think she's starting to get better. The doctors said her liver is starting to improve, but her face still looks like a puffy dandelion. Honestly, Rosalita, I've never seen anyone so yellow. Even the whites of her eyes are yellow."

"I once saw Ferdinand like that. It's a strange sight, indeed."

"Ferdinand? Marcos, you mean?"

"Oh. Uh, yes. But don't tell anyone I said that. Ferdinand has had liver problems for a long time. It's nothing as serious as your mother's condition—"

"That's because Ferdinand isn't an *alcoholic,* right?"

Rosalita held her breath. Frank rarely snapped at her. An uncomfortable silence stretched across the phone lines between them. She spoke softly, hoping she didn't misstep again. "I only meant to say that Ferdinand had a yellow pallor like your mother, but he was released from the doctor's care after only a few days. He didn't need hospitalization."

"I'm sorry, Rosalita. I'm just tired. A little touchy, I guess." Frank sighed again. "To be honest, I've grown tired of fighting with my mother about her drinking, but I feel guilty about it, because I can't help but wonder if she'd stop if I were here with her." *Whoever wrote about the sins of our fathers must never have experienced the guilt of our mothers.*

"Frank, I don't know your mother very well, but I do know she's a grown woman, and you are not responsible for any of her actions—including her drinking. It's a choice she makes every time she takes a sip, and just as you can't make her drink, you can't make her stop." Rosalita desperately wanted to wrap Frank in her arms, feel his around her.

"I know you're right." Frank sniffed. "Rosalita?"

"Yes?"

"Thank you. And thank you for promising to come."

Rosalita's eyes filled and she felt the warm trickle slide down her cheek. "There's nowhere else I'd rather be."

Chapter 26

Washington, DC
September 5, 1973

"Mr. President." Frank offered his hand.

Nixon accepted his shake. "Frank, it's good to see you." His tight smile revealed deep lines at the corners of the man's eyes and mouth. Nixon glanced around the room. "Gentlemen, please sit."

Frank did a silent roll call of the men as they sat; Nixon, Bozeman, and a man with heavily oiled hair whom Frank had never met. Behind Nixon stood two Secret Service guards, complete with hissing walkie-talkies; another stood just inside the door. At least a few more were posted in the hallway outside the door. In the center of the table waited a carafe of coffee and a pitcher of water.

"I expect you're wondering why I called you here earlier than our typical annual meeting, Frank."

Nixon never wasted time, and Frank admired him for that. It proved a refreshing change from the small talk he felt forced to make with Ferdinand Marcos. Still, Nixon always found a way to insert a splinter under Frank's skin, something to irritate and fester long after the meeting had ended.

"I have a feeling I know why I'm here." The air felt shallow in his lungs, and Frank sucked in a deep breath, resisted the urge to blow it out long and hard.

"Oh?" Nixon pursed his lips.

"Yes, sir. I expect you'd like to call an end to my work in the Philippines. Am I correct?"

One of Nixon's eyebrows lifted. "You've nearly done that already, haven't you, son?"

The question caught Frank off guard. He opened his mouth, but Nixon spoke again.

"I understand all that business with your mother. Family must come first, right? You're all she has left." He waved a hand in the air. "Cirrhosis of the liver. Ugly, ugly disease."

There was the splinter. Frank felt heat flooding his chest, crawling up his neck, choking life from the words he wanted to say.

Nixon's intense dark eyes penetrated through Frank's defenses. "The short answer is *no.*"

Frank struggled to wrap his mind around the word. "Excuse me, sir?" He'd already called Lucky and they had looked for a place to open a dojo in Atlanta. Then he'd be nearby while he kept an eye on his mother.

"No. I'm not ending your work in the Philippines. I brought you here for another reason."

Somewhere in the room, the secondhand on a clock ticked loudly. "And what is that, Mr. President?"

Nixon motioned to the man sitting on his right, the oily-haired man Frank had forgotten was in the room. "I'd like to introduce you to Mr. William Colby."

Frank had heard the name plenty of times, though he'd never seen the man's face. Colby served as head of covert operations in the Far East. He'd earned a nasty reputation for being responsible for the deaths of thousands during the Vietnam War.

"Mr. Colby is replacing Schlesinger as Director of the CIA."

Frank blinked hard. He knew Schlesinger had made a few condescending statements about President Nixon, but he never dreamed the man would be fired for expressing an opinion. *Don't forget who you're working for, Frankie-Boy. The power is not your own.*

Frank turned his attention to Colby. "Congratulations, Mr. Colby." *Colby. Colby.* Something else niggled Frank's brain about the man. Ahhh, yes. He'd learned during research that Colby sometimes served as legal counsel for Nugan-Hand Bank in Australia, a bank Frank believed Marcos had used to launder gold and money. *Interesting choice.*

A thin smile parted the man's lips, and his cheeks raised his glasses upward on his face. "Mr. Young." He nodded.

Nixon interlaced his fingers and rested his hands on the table. "I'd like for Colby here to have a relationship with you similar to what Lansdale had with your father."

An acidic taste flooded Frank's mouth. "Go on, please."

Nixon lowered his head and looked at Frank through bushy black eyebrows. "I realize you must be frustrated about not finding the maps to the buried gold, but I also know that Marcos is recovering gold on a regular basis now, and sooner or later, he'll get sloppy." His right eyebrow raised. "The man is greedy. He's digging gold faster than he can sell it, and yet he still wants more."

Bozeman nodded, his expression grim.

"Marcos is opening bank accounts all over the world," Nixon said, "stashing money and gold. He's becoming one of the most powerful people in the world, all because of gold." Nixon shook his head, his jowls jiggling. "Japan holds all the cards right now; they have one of the largest economies in the world, and Singapore is right on their heels. Meanwhile, communism is creeping across the globe like a vile mold."

He locked eyes with Frank. "We need to intercept that gold, before Marcos lets it slide into the hands of the wrong people."

Frank sucked in a long, deep breath. If he didn't speak now, he'd never sleep through another night. "I know Marcos is funneling some of the money into the U.S." He sat for a moment, allowing his words to register. When Nixon opened his mouth to speak, Frank continued. "Not only is some of the gold being deposited into U.S. banks, the Black Eagle Trust is funding your CIA." He locked eyes with William Colby, who slicked back a strand of oiled hair, returning it to its home of neat furrows. Frank resisted the urge to wipe his own hands on his trousers.

"Now hold on a minute." Nixon's eyes narrowed. "Of course some of the gold is funding the CIA. Where else would we get the kind of money we need to stamp out communism? The U.S. has protected the Philippines since the war. We've kept them out of the Vietnam drama, too. Practically rebuilt their country for them. We've supported Marcos as he's reorganized his country—"

"Declared martial law on them, you mean." Frank had brought along a few splinters of his own.

Nixon's face reddened and his cheeks puffed. He leaned across the table. "Marcos stopped a civil war with his declaration." He sat back and smoothed his tie. "You're young, Franklin, but I presume you studied history. You know about the bloodshed here in our own country, north against south. Marcos stopped that from happening in the Philippines. A divided country cannot stand." He paused for a moment, taking an audible breath. "The Black Eagle Trust empowers the U.S. to coax other governments into cooperation. Money can help those who are confused to see things more clearly. If we can help another country or its leaders in a time of crisis, not only can they avert disaster, but so can we. We remain allied, stronger. That gold gives us an asset base for their patronage."

Frank's stomach ached. "And the China Mandate?"

Colby choked on his coffee.

Nixon's eyes shot over to Colby and watched as he dabbed at his chin with a napkin, finally regaining composure. "We've been over this, Frank. If you know your history, we never went through with it. We discussed it, and we, the United States of America, decided it was not in our best interest."

Colby's eyes grew wide behind his eyeglasses. Was this the first the man had heard of the secret agreement which was never finalized by Nixon and Chairman Mao, or did his surprise stem from Frank's knowledge of the pact?

Frank quietly cleared his throat. "I'm guessing Marcos made his own deal with the Chinese." If he thought he wanted out of the project before, he certainly wanted no part of it now. He swallowed hard. "I want out."

Nixon's eyes grew dark and cold. "Excuse me?"

"You've made it clear the U.S. is getting a share of the gold from Marcos, and doing so without my help. You don't need me."

Nixon closed his eyes. When he opened them, they were clearer, colder. "Marcos has been sending a small share of his recoveries to us. A *very* small share. A drop in the bucket, while he has a bottomless well at his disposal. We need those maps. We need that gold. You can help us obtain what we need."

"Help your campaign remain strong, right, sir?"

"What?"

Frank shrugged. He'd come this far; he might as well see it through. *Insert the splinter.* "I read the *Post*, sir. I keep my ear to the ground." *Shove it deeper.* "Accusations of dirty money funneled into your campaign fund. Wiretaps at the Watergate Complex. Spying on the Democratic Party." He leaned forward and lowered his voice. "The House is calling you a thief. Congress is whispering 'impeachment.' Why should I stay involved—"

Nixon slammed his fist onto the table, causing Bozeman's water glass to jump. "I am not a crook!" He stood, tipping his chair over backward in the process. His eyes filled with disgust, even hate, as he locked them with Frank's. "You are hereby relieved from your duties with the U.S. Government." He leveled his heated gaze at Bozeman, then Colby. "Franklin Young is on his own."

CHAPTER 27

Atlanta, Georgia
November 19, 1973

Frank stood on the sidewalk along Roswell Road and examined the glass-fronted building. Sure, it needed a little more work, especially the upstairs, but the upper floors could wait on renovations to become his apartment home. Right now, the ground floor needed his full attention, especially if he planned to meet his new dojo's grand opening date, scheduled just after the new year.

He checked his watch. Where in the hell was Lucky? He should be here by now.

Frank and Lucky had planned this venture since they were freshmen at Duke. Fifteen years. When Lucky was ready to move forward, Frank had been tied up in the Philippines. And now that Frank was ready, Lucky wasn't able to leave his job in Durham. When Frank suggested he be a silent partner, Lucky asked no questions. He only said, "Absolutely!"

Frank should've had plenty of money without Lucky's financial backing, but even with income from both Triangle Tobacco and the U.S. Government, international travel wasn't cheap.

Frank pulled on the hem of his t-shirt, rubbed away a streak on the glass door he'd just cleaned. Who was he kidding? His money hadn't disappeared on travel. He hadn't even thrown it away entertaining Rosalita, whose tastes often ran to the extremely expensive. No, he'd had money when he returned to the U.S.

He'd wasted it—yes, *wasted* was the appropriate word—on every common and experimental treatment known for his mother's cirrhosis. And this morning when the trash bag broke as he carried it to the curb, out fell an empty Smirnoff bottle, its neck sticking out from the sheet of newspaper in which Mary Catherine had carefully wrapped it.

"Hey, you bum! Get away from my store!"

Frank whirled around to see Lucky strutting down the street, his eyes cloaked in a pair of dark-lensed aviators.

Frank grinned. "Hey, man! Can't you afford a watch?" He opened his arms, embraced his old friend and clapped him on the back.

"Hey, hey, not too close." Lucky waved a hand in front of his nose. "You need a shower."

"Awww, man. One of us has to do the grunt work around here if we're gonna get this place off the ground. You sure haven't broken a sweat."

"You should have read the fine print in our contract."

"What fine print?"

"The part that said 'Silent partners don't sweat.'" Lucky grinned and draped his arm around Frank's shoulder.

Frank took a feign shot at Lucky's gut. He stepped back and swept his arm dramatically toward the storefront of their business. "Whaddya think?" He sniffed deeply. "You smell that, Lucky?"

Lucky sniffed the air once, twice. "What?"

"That's the smell of success."

Lucky laughed. "All I can smell is you."

"Come on, man. Let me give you the grand tour." Frank held open the door as Lucky stepped in ahead of him. The scent of the freshly waxed floor greeted them, and Frank motioned toward a twelve-foot Formica counter along the left wall. "Just had that delivered this morning. That's where we'll check in the students, handle class registration, take payments, that sort of thing." Above the counter hung a huge framed portrait of Bruce Lee, shirtless, wearing a black belt tied around his head.

Lucky twirled his sunglasses by the earpiece. "Nice! It looks . . . I don't know . . . modern, kinda classy."

Frank waved his hand toward the opposite wall, where he'd hung framed photos of himself and Lucky receiving various martial arts awards, the most prominent being Frank's induction into the United States Tae Kwon Do Union.

Lucky let out a long, low whistle. "Wow. This will get 'em talking. Impressive." He looked around, nodding, then smiled. "I've gotta say, Frankie, you've done an incredible job." Warm relief spread through Frank's chest. "There's more to be done, of course. I still need to order mats, have some of the tiles replaced in the corner over there, replace the old plumbing and fixtures in the restrooms. If the contractor shows up this week to fix the tiles, I think we'll be ready for press photos."

"Great!" Lucky hooked a thumb toward the ceiling. "What about the upstairs?"

Frank shook his head. "See for yourself. It's an eyesore." He led Lucky through the door at the back of the dojo marked *Employees Only*, then through another marked *Private* and up the back stairs of the building. "Watch your step. A few of these treads are loose."

"Smells old up here," Lucky said when they'd reached the second floor landing. "Needs to be aired out."

"Yeah, the windows had been painted shut for who knows how long. I broke them loose, but it'll need a few weeks of fresh air to get the musty odor out of here." Frank unlocked the deadbolt and opened the door to what would soon be his new home.

"Man, what an exercise in 1950s décor!" Lucky laughed and rubbed his hand over the peeling wallpaper. "Velvet-flocked. Nice."

Frank grinned. "Told you it needs work. That's a little further down on the checklist, though. One thing at a time."

"I'm sure Mary Catherine will be sad to see you move out of her house again, but at least you'll only be a few miles away." Lucky strolled toward the kitchen. "How's she doing, by the way?"

Frank shook his head. "Not a good day to ask."

"Oh? She's not sick again, is she?"

"Matter of time. I found an empty bottle this morning."

"Damn. I'm sorry to hear that, Frank. She can't turn the devil loose, can she?"

"Probably not a good time for me to be leaving her, but if she'll drink while I'm living in the house, she'll drink while I'm not there. Only so much I can do."

Lucky shifted from one foot to the other and back a few times, causing the board beneath his feet to creak. "What about that other item on your checklist?"

"Other item?"

"Yeah. The pretty little Filipina item." Lucky grinned.

Frank felt a flicker of anger, but it quickly dissipated. "Ahhh, you know how those long-distance relationships go."

Lucky's eyebrows lifted. "You're no longer seeing her? I thought she spent a lot of time in the States."

Frank shrugged. "Shopping with Imelda. Say, you think I should call the newspaper, stage a little fake grand opening, so you can be in the ribbon-cutting photos?" He forced a smile. "We can have them hold the article until our real grand opening. I've already taken out a month's worth of ads, so they promised me a nice piece about the business."

"So, you don't want to talk about the Filipina?"

Frank met his friend's dark eyes, then shook his head. "Short version: I refuse to return to the Philippines and she refuses to leave her mama to live here."

"Ahhh, Frankie. I'm sorry, man." He cast a sideways glance. "You sure you don't want to return to the islands?"

"No." Frank grunted. "Absolutely not. I'm done there."

Lucky laughed. "You sure about that?"

"I've never been surer about anything else in my life. I will never again step foot on the Philippines."

Chapter 28

August 24, 1974
Manila, the Philippines

As Frank stepped off the plane, humid air wrapped around him and dampened his clothes. The last few days had felt more like the force of a hurricane than a whirlwind of activity. The call from President Gerald Ford had caught him off guard. He didn't recognize the man's voice; at first he thought himself the butt of a practical joke. After all, Nixon usually placed his calls through a third party. But not Gerald Ford.

Ford had him on a plane to Washington in less than four hours, and when Frank walked into The Oval Office, he felt respected, appreciated, instead of used and disposable.

President Ford even allowed him the option of a "no," a word Nixon would not accept. At first, Frank had used that alternative. Ford's face had sagged, but his eyes revealed something Frank had never seen in Nixon's or Marcos's. It took Frank a moment to recognize it as compassion.

"I understand, Mr. Young. I didn't sign up for this position either," President Ford had said. "But here I am, and I'm not going to dodge my responsibilities." He'd smiled at Frank, and his smile was genuine, if somewhat sad. "From everything I've read," he placed his hand on a huge file as he spoke, "you've served the United States very well, sometimes at great personal risk. Please allow me to thank you on behalf of the American people, who may never know what you've done to protect and help them, and to keep our country strong."

President Ford stood and reached out to shake Frank's hand, and Frank accepted. Frank turned and made it all the way to the door, flanked by men of the Secret Service, before he whirled around.

"Wait. Mr. President, if you can give me a few days to tie up some loose ends in Georgia, I'll do it. I'll go to the Philippines and try again to get the maps."

President Ford walked around his desk, met Frank halfway across the office and, standing over that great seal etched into the carpet, shook Frank's hand. Frank would remember that moment forever.

When Frank returned to Atlanta to prepare for his trip, Lucky was there.

"Hey, man! I thought I'd hang out here for a while, see how business is doing." Lucky patted the paunch of his stomach. "Getting a little soft around the middle. Figured I could use some time in the dojo to get back into shape. You got space for another instructor?"

Frank could hardly believe it. Everything was falling into place, almost as if it were preordained. Or pre-arranged. One phone call later to his mother's doctor, and nurses were scheduled to keep check on his mother. Two days later, he stood sweating in the Philippines.

President Ford hadn't wasted any time either. Frank still didn't know who at Triangle Tobacco had ties to the White House, but Frank's former position—if such a thing really existed—was instantly reinstated. Frank carried a fresh check made out to Ferdinand Marcos, supposedly a profit-sharing bonus from Triangle's tobacco sales in the Philippines.

"It ought to get your foot in the door," President Ford had said.

Indeed. The check totaled one million U.S. dollars—which was probably more than Triangle Tobacco had cleared in the past year in their Philippines operations.

Frank walked to where the car arranged by Triangle should be waiting. Despite the heat, icy fingers of dread stoked the back of his neck. He glanced over his shoulder, feeling eyes dancing all over him. No one was there. Under the canopied walkway, a man in a *barong tagalong* held a sign in front of a small sedan: "Frank Young." Parked just in front of the sedan was a sleek, black Mercedes. Rosalita Laurel sat erect on its hood, her legs languidly draped over the side, while her driver Tony stood by the rear passenger door.

Frank grinned as he stood partway between the two cars, holding out his hands, but a flash of military uniform in the throng of people across the way caught his eye. General Cannu. He *was* being watched! Frank rubbed his chin, wondering how long before he saw the unseeable Santa Romana.

Rosalita sat up straight and looked over her shoulder in the direction Frank had stared. "What is it, baby? You look like you've seen a ghost."

The man holding a sign with Frank's name turned as well. "Sir? Is everything okay?"

Frank licked his lips and nodded. "Yeah. I think I just got a little lightheaded from the quick change in altitude."

Tony nodded and opened the door. "That happens sometimes, sir." Tony motioned to the man wearing the *barong tagalong*. "Please, sir, won't you follow us? Mr. Young will be riding with Miss Laurel."

The man grinned at Frank and bobbed his head. "*Mawari*. I understand. I would rather ride with her too."

Frank slid into the seat beside Rosalita while Tony took care of his luggage. He inhaled, breathing her scent deep into his lungs, his brain. "This is quite a pleasant surprise. I never expected to see you here, especially since I just told you I was coming two days ago."

She leaned forward, her mouth only centimeters from his. "I knew you couldn't stay away, Frank."

He watched her full, glistening lips move, couldn't wait another moment to taste them.

"Oh, my," she said, her cheeks flushing when the two finally pulled their mouths apart. A throaty laugh escaped her. "I take it you missed me."

Frank slid his hand into her hair, pulled her face back to him, and kissed her with all his pent-up passion.

Rosalita crawled onto his lap. Her heat traveled over his stomach and thighs. Too soon, Tony rounded the car. Frank slid Rosalita off his legs and into the seat, always careful to preserve her necessary virginal Filipina reputation.

She grinned at him, her smile both sinuous and innocent, her lips swollen from his chastising kiss. Her smoldering eyes made him wonder why he'd stayed away so long. Rosalita smoothed her skirt as Tony entered the car and glanced at her in the rearview mirror.

"The Manila Hotel, Miss Laurel?" Tony asked.

"Yes, please, Tony. I think Frank would like to freshen up and rest a bit before dinner tonight."

"Dinner?" Frank rubbed his chin.

Rosalita turned back to him, her eyes twinkling. "Do you have other plans? Surely you must eat something." Her gaze traced a line down his jaw, his neck, his chest.

Frank grinned. "Dinner it is."

"Great. Imelda is having something special prepared for us."

Frank's breath seized in his lungs. "Imelda?"

Rosalita nodded. "Ferdinand stopped in to say hello during our ladies' tea yesterday. Imelda told him you were returning to the Philippines, and he suggested a small dinner party to welcome you home."

Home. Frank glanced out the window at the passing rows of ramshackle homes made of bamboo and iron and straw. *This was my father's home.* He couldn't make sense of it all. *Dinner with Ferdinand. Welcome home. Cannu is watching. Find the maps.* He felt like a pawn on a chessboard from hell.

"Frank? Is that okay with you? You look confused. Are you disappointed? I thought you'd like—"

Frank squeezed Rosalita's hand. "Of course I'm not disappointed. I'd love to say hello to the Marcoses again. In fact, I have something for Ferdinand, though it's business-related. I should probably save it for another time."

Rosalita lowered her head, then looked up through a fringe of lashes, her eyes full of concern. "Are you sure you're okay?"

Frank forced a smile. "Yes, I'm fine. I'm sure it's just jet lag. I'll be back to normal after that short rest you suggested."

Rosalita softly kissed him, then sat up straight and folded her hands in her lap. "Perfect," she said as Tony pulled the car in front of the Manila Hotel. "We'll pick you up in two hours."

Chapter 29

Ferdinand Marcos sat at the head of the long table, and even though Frank could feel his eyes sometimes boring into him, when he'd look toward the man, his gaze would be elsewhere. *Don't be paranoid.*

"Frank," Marcos said just as Frank took a mouthful of the sweet dessert wine. "I'm sorry I didn't ask you earlier; is your mother doing better?"

Frank swallowed hard. "Yes, thank you. She is quite comfortable at home, and seems to have made a strong recovery."

He pursed his lips toward Rosalita. "We've often inquired about you to our dear Rosalita. I'm glad you're back home in the Philippines."

Home. There's that word again. "It's good to be back, sir."

Marcos forced a thin-lipped smile, then looked around the table at his guests. "Ladies, would you please excuse us men for a brief moment?" He scooted out his chair as he spoke, evidence he didn't expect complaints.

Rosalita turned to Frank with a disappointed pout. "Don't let him keep you long," she whispered, lightly brushing his thigh with her fingertips under the table.

Frank nodded, smiled and followed Marcos and his cronies out of the room. He had to wonder if Marcos had any real friends. It seemed he was always flanked by those who worked for him or gave him money.

As they exited the room, a twitter of feminine laughter came from the dining table behind them. Frank turned to see that Rosalita had moved to the empty seat beside Imelda, and she and several of the ladies stared at Frank with knowing gleams in their eyes. Another burst of giggles assured him he was the subject of their conversation. Heat rose up his neck, and he quick-stepped to catch up with the men.

Like baby ducks, the men walked single-file behind Marcos toward his office, with Frank taking up the rear. As soon as they arrived, Marcos poured a round of drinks. When everyone had glass in hand, Marcos raised his skyward. "To allegiance."

"To allegiance," the men answered in unison.

"Anyone know what time it is?" General Tomas Diaz carefully enunciated his words around intoxication.

Several men looked at their watches, then the whole group broke into laughter. Frank didn't get the joke.

Sten Larsson, a tall Swede introduced to Frank as a friend of Marcos, elbowed him. "They all have matching watches. A gift from the president."

"Ohhh." Frank nodded and sipped from his glass.

"They call them the Rolex Twelve." Sten chuckled and shook his head.

Marcos refilled his glass for the third time since they'd stepped into the room, then handed the bottle to Danding, who served refills around the room. Frank couldn't help but notice Marcos appeared to be drinking heavier these days. Were his liver problems related to cirrhosis, like his mother's? If so, the man was sprinting toward disaster.

"So, you're with American Tobacco?" Sten leaned closer to Frank in order to be heard over boisterous conversation in the room.

"No, no. I'm with an American tobacco company, Triangle Tobacco. American Tobacco is a competitor." Frank grinned.

Sten held up a hand. "I'm sorry. I am a naturalized American citizen, but I don't know a thing about tobacco. I'm from Chicago, not the South, like you."

"It's okay." He laughed. "Tell me, how do you know President Marcos?"

"I'm his psychic." A wry smile twisted the man's mouth. "Too bad I wasn't intuitive enough to get the name of your company right."

Frank laughed. "Hey, we all have our days." He sipped his drink. "Does Marcos use your services for political decisions?"

Sten shook his head. "I'm helping him with the hunt."

Frank tried not to look shocked. "Oh, yes. The hunt. I've been out of the country for a while, so I'm a bit out of touch with where they're looking now."

Sten's face clouded. He probably feared he'd said too much to Frank.

"He's had some great successes in the past," Frank continued, "but this dry spell has really tried his patience." He lifted his glass toward Sten. "I hope you can help rectify that."

Relief washed over Sten's face like a wave, and he smiled. "Yes, I believe I can." He nodded toward a large safe sitting on the floor behind the president's ornate desk. "Those maps are so cryptic. I believe we'll do better without them."

Frank followed Sten's gaze to a brass—or was that gold?—safe. His pulse pounded in his ears, drowning out Sten's words. That safe must weigh a ton. How many people knew the combination? Marcos, for sure. Ver, probably. Anyone else?

Frank realized Sten was still talking.

"But Villacrusis stopped me," Sten continued. "He told me I wasn't allowed to dig on Clark Air Base, even with permission from the U.S. Air Force. When he told me I could be of service to President Marcos, that I could help the Filipino people emerge from poverty, I jumped at the chance."

Frank had heard that one before. "Yes, the Filipino people need all the help they can get." Even a novice mind reader could tell Frank meant his words. "Have you had any success yet?"

"No, not here. President Marcos already knows where most of the burial sites are, but he needs my help to pinpoint exactly where they should start digging." The Swede lifted his glass for emphasis. "However, I've had success off the Florida Keys. Have you heard of Mel Fisher?"

Frank shrugged.

"I helped him find a Spanish galleon filled with New World gold." Sten's eyes sparkled. "It was such an exciting day. I'm looking forward to that kind of success here in the Philippines."

Frank raised his glass. "To success!"

The door opened. Before Frank saw who it was, he knew. The fine hairs on the nape of his neck rose to attention to salute the general. Fabian Ver never failed to cause Frank's hackles to rise. Frank excused himself from Sten and made his way toward Marcos at the front of the room.

"Mr. President, thank you so much for your kind hospitality. Your warmth has made me feel honored to be back in the Philippines." The two shook hands.

"It is good to have you back." Marcos's words had a mild slur.

"Sir, would you be offended if I took an early leave? Forgive me, but between jet lag and time changes . . . ."

Marcos smiled, even as his eyes hardened. "Of course not, Frank. Go home, rest. We will meet again soon."

"I'd like that very much, sir. In fact, I have something for you from Triangle Tobacco."

Marcos's face lifted. "Oh? In that case, let's meet tomorrow afternoon. I have a busy schedule, but I will always make time for you, my friend."

The alcohol made its own grand speech; Marcos merely made time for the check he expected to receive. Frank bowed toward the man. "Thank you, Mr. President. I am honored. And thank you for such a grand evening." He turned to walk away, but found himself nose-to-nose with General Ver.

"Pardon me." Frank thrust his hand between himself and the general, his fingertips brushing Ver's uniform. *Always in uniform. Always asserting his position, his power.* When Ver didn't look down, Frank stared at his own hand, pursed his lips and waited, until Ver had no choice but to accept the handshake. "General, what a pleasant surprise. I've missed you. I hope you've been well." Frank's lips twisted into a wry smile, and he half-hoped Ver interpreted it as mocking.

The man's beady eyes narrowed. He gripped Frank's hands and squeezed until the bones rubbed together. "Back in the Philippines to ply your cigarettes? I suppose you haven't heard that President Marcos is fighting black market tobacco now?"

Frank felt his chest grow warm, but kept his gaze and his grip steady. "Actually, that's why I'm here. If I help the president flood the country with legal tobacco, there will be no need for the substandard black market prod-ucts, and the Filipino Government can make a tidy profit in the process."

A hard smile slashed across Ver's face. "Who said it was substandard?"

The two locked eyes for a moment, then Ver broke out in a harsh laugh, spewing foul breath brimming with the stench of stale alcohol. Frank held the man's eyes and laughed along with him. "I'll be sure to have a case of Pure Gold delivered to your house, general, so we can raise your standards of good taste."

Frank returned to President Marcos's office the next day. It showed no signs of the revelry that had taken place the previous night, but Marcos's bleary eyes couldn't say the same. The skin around the president's eyes puffed, and his face bore lines that hadn't been prominent the night before.

While they spoke, Frank struggled to keep his eyes from flitting to the large safe behind Marcos's desk. At times, it seemed the safe zoomed into his field of vision, larger than life, as Marcos's face blurred out of focus. Frank slipped his hand into his coat pocket, fondled the small bottle. He'd replaced the eye drops with ipecac syrup, but he knew the drug would take at least fifteen minutes to work. He'd never been in Marcos's office longer than that.

"Things seem much more peaceful here in the Philippines than when I left, Mr. President." *Not even a glass of water on his desk. This isn't going to work.*

Marcos's watery eyes brightened. "Many criticized my declaration of mar-tial law, but it restored security to our islands. I know what is best for my country, for my people. I am glad to see you recognize the difference, Frank." Marcos allowed a tired smile. "Perhaps I should have you share what you've noticed with Aquino's people."

Frank laughed, then choked on it. He coughed softly, then allowed the cough to grow, forcing himself to make strangling noises, squinting his eyes with a prayer that they'd water.

"Are you okay?" Marcos asked.

Frank shook his head and coughed harder, gasping for breath.

Marcos pointed with his lips to a water pitcher on the credenza near his desk, told Frank he should pour a glass.

Frank did, while making a gagging sound in his throat, then swallowed a mouthful of water. He cleared his throat a few times, sipped again, then sat the glass on the coaster Marcos had provided. "Thank you, sir," he said hoarsely. "My apologies. I'm so sorry. I don't know what happened there." Frank wiped imaginary sweat from his brow and rubbed his hand on his slacks.

"Are you okay?"

Marcos's smile showed genuine concern, and a pang of guilt stabbed Frank in the gut. Again the box containing the maps zoomed into his periphery, and Frank looked at the lone water glass on Marcos's desk. *How in the hell can I pull this off?*

"Something stronger, perhaps?" Marcos picked up two highballs in one hand and lifted the half-full decanter in his other.

Frank worried for a moment that he'd voiced his question out loud. "Yes, please. Thank you."

Though noon hadn't arrived, Marcos poured two fingers into both glasses and passed one to Frank as he returned to his chair.

Frank took a long, slow sip, but when he realized Marcos had drained his glass in one drink, he downed his own. "Thank you, sir." He nodded toward the bottle and cleared his throat again. "Is it too early for one more?"

Marcos smiled and started to stand.

"Please," Frank said, holding up a hand as he rose from the chair. "Allow me." He retrieved Marcos's glass and turned toward the credenza. "Mr. President, if I can ever be of service to you, whether that means talking to Aquino or parading down the street with a banner, please let me know. It is my honor to support you and the Filipino people. As you have said, this is my home." He slipped the eye-drop bottle Bozeman had provided from his pocket, gave a healthy squeeze into Marcos's glass, then slid the empty bottle back into his pocket. He looked back over his shoulder. "Ice?"

Marcos nodded. "I wasn't serious about Aquino, but I appreciate your willingness to be of assistance."

Frank dropped two cubes into each glass, poured the liquor, swirled both glasses. He placed Marcos's glass in front of him. "Perhaps I can be of help in other ways." He reached into the front of his suit, pulled out the envelope from Triangle Tobacco and handed it to Marcos.

Marcos's eyebrows lifted and a childlike smile flitted across his face. He slid his finger into the corner, broke the seal, pulled out the check. "This is quite a large check, Frank. Another donation?"

Frank smiled. "No, sir. At least not all of it. Most is actually your portion of the profit from the sale of Pure Gold and Blue Lady Slims here in the Philippines. Triangle simply rounded up the figure to make a nice, even amount. There should be one million ways to thank you for allowing us into the Islands."

Marcos couldn't contain his grin. "This is amazing. I never expected this kind of profit. Are you really selling this many cigarettes here? I had no idea."

"Pure Gold is definitely a good seller, but Blue Lady Slims have far exceeded our expectations." Frank smiled and pulled out his own cigarette case, opened it and offered one to Marcos, hoping the nicotine would speed the nausea process. He held a light while Marcos took a draw.

Marcos opened his mouth and allowed the smoke to curl lazily for a moment before exhaling. He licked his lips. "I must admit, this is one of the smoothest smokes I've ever tasted." He held up his glass. "To a long and profitable business relationship. And to our friendship. It is good to have you back, Frank."

The two downed their glasses.

"Miss Laurel seems quite happy to have you back as well." A twinkle lit Marcos's eyes.

Heat tiptoed up Frank's neck. He'd never had a woman twist and tear at his emotions the way Rosalita did. "I enjoy her company, as well."

Marcos turned his cigarette in a crystal dish, shaving off the ash until it resembled a sharpened pencil. "You have been seeing her for quite some time, yes?"

Here it comes. Frank cleared his throat. "I met Rosalita around the same time I made your acquaintance, Mr. President."

Marcos waved his cigarette in the air, a trail of smoke following it. "Please. When we are alone, you would do me great honor by calling me Ferdinand." He smiled. "Of course, when we are in the company of others, I must request that you refer to me in formal terms."

"Of course, Mr. President—er, Ferdinand. This great honor is all mine. I am humbled, sir."

An unattractive burp escaped Marcos's lips, and he quickly covered his mouth. "Excuse me."

Frank smiled. *Finally.* "Of course."

"Where were we? Oh, yes." A sly grin bent Marcos's lips. "The rumors about you."

"Rumors?" Frank heart rate quickened.

"Many people have questions about your return to the Philippines after such a long absence." Marcos again took a long drag from his cigarette.

"Well, my absence could hardly be helped. My mother's illness, and all."

Marcos's forehead creased. "It isn't the absence that has people talking, Frank." He paused and his pupils constricted. "It's your sudden return."

Rosalita. She's been talking to Imelda about me.

Marcos leaned back against his chair and pressed the heel of his hand to his stomach. A low rumble stirred in his gut.

"Well, sir, I must admit, I've been a little homesick for the Philippines." He stared at his hands in his lap for a moment. "I'd hoped my mother would return with me, but she is set in her ways and comfortable in her own home." He looked up to see a pale-faced Marcos wiping at one watering eye. "I understand how she feels, as the Philippines feel like home to me."

Marcos leaned forward, and his smile appeared forced. "Is it the Philippines that feel like home to you, or something *in* the Philippines?"

Is he talking about his pursuit of the gold? Had Santa Romana—or Nixon—given him up to Marcos? "I'm sorry, sir. I don't follow your train of thought."

"Did you not return to propose marriage to Rosalita? Hmmm?" Marcos smiled, but his lips quickly curled into a grimace and he stood.

"Mr. Pres—Ferdinand, are you okay?"

Marcos took a step from behind his desk, then quickly turned and grabbed his trash can and vomited into it.

"Sir! Are you all right?" Frank rushed around the desk, pulling out his handkerchief to press into Marcos's hand.

"I'm sorry, Frank. Please forgive me. I don't know what has made me so suddenly ill."

Frank hustled to the credenza, poured a glass of water and offered it to Marcos. "Here you go. Sip on this."

Marcos tried to smile. "I am embarrassed." He sipped from the glass, then wiped his mouth on Frank's handkerchief. "I'm feeling better, now. If you'll excuse me for just a moment." Marcos picked up the trash can and carried it out the door, calling out to his housekeeper as he did so.

Well, Frank, you didn't think that one through very well. He stared at the safe on the floor, fearing he'd blown his chance to get into it.

Then Ferdinand retched again, and his footsteps echoed down the hall.

Frank hurriedly closed the door to the office, went to the safe, slipped on the latex glove he'd brought just for this purpose, and worked on the large numbered dial. It didn't open. As Frank slid back toward his chair, he noticed two maps lying on the cadenza behind the desk. He pulled out his camera and snapped pictures of both maps.

He knew not to take any greater chances, so he quickly restacked the maps, making sure he'd gotten them in the correct order, and slipped the glove back into his pocket. He rounded the desk, re-opened the door, and had just returned to his chair when one of Marcos's bodyguards came in.

Frank whirled around. "Is President Marcos okay?"

The man scowled at Frank. "President Marcos will not be returning to your meeting today. He has asked me to convey his regret." He stood with his feet spread apart, as if ready for battle.

Frank stood, his heart still racing. "I am so sorry to hear that. Is there anything I can do?"

A muscle twitched in the man's jaw. "You can leave."

Chapter 30

Manila, The Philippines
August 2, 1974

Santa Romana rubbed his face with both hands. If only he could go back in time and do things differently. If only he'd known then what he knew now. But he hadn't, and he couldn't, so now he had to make the best out of the convoluted mess that remained. And do his best to keep any more innocent people from dying. It was too late to save himself—but then, he wasn't entirely innocent, was he?

Ver had nothing on him. Good men had died because of his role in the acquisition of gold. And for what? Money had lost its mean to him personally. And initially, he'd participated for what he'd felt was the greater good of mankind—so the Vatican would have its gold returned and the Catholic Church would have money for all its programs. Later, he'd dedicated himself to the American OSS/CIA, believing they would make the world a better place to live.

But at what cost? Many had blamed him for the death of his good friend, Emilio Jorgé Laurel, who happened to be in the wrong place at the wrong time and learned too much. While he had nothing to do with his death, in hindsight, he might have prevented it. Especially knowing it left his beautiful but overly-dependent wife alone with a young daughter to raise. Guilt had made Santa Romana keep an eye on young Rosalita, but even from the time she was in grammar school, she was strong and independent like her father.

Seeing her fall in love with the son of his good friend Danilo gave him some relief, some sense that this mess had created something good.

Danilo. Santa Romana sighed. He had promised Danilo that he'd see to it that his son would be taken care of. Shortly, after Danilo's death, he had decided the best way to fulfill his promise was to give Franklin his own gold burial site. But how? It was so dangerous now. He should've realized sooner that Marcos valued nothing more than gold—not friendship, not ethics, not even life. And Ver was nothing more than a madman with a mission.

Santa Romana sighed from deep within. He had Danilo's map, the map to the only tunnel of gold Marcos was oblivious to, the one map he had drawn himself. Now he was running out of time. He had to get the map to Danilo's son before it was too late.

Santa Romana grasped the golden cross that hung around his neck. He had never intended to sell his soul to the devil. But somehow, that seemed to have happened. He closed his eyes. "Hail Mary, full of grace, the Lord is with thee. Blessed art thou among women and blessed is the fruit of thy womb, Jesus. Holy Mary, mother of God, pray for us sinners now and at the hour of our death. Amen." He squeezed the cross until it cut into his hands, then repeated hoarsely, "Pray for us sinners now." He struggled to keep his voice steady. "And at the hour of our death."

⟁

Frank tried to disentangle his arm from Rosalita without waking her. Instead of getting out of bed as he'd planned, he lay on his side, watching her sleep. Even in slumber, her body had fluidity he could compare only to the sea. With each breath she took, he felt the ebb and flow of the tide, in and out, in and out. Her face glowed soft, succulent. He lifted her hair from her neck, held it to his nose, breathed the scent of coconut and jasmine.

"What are you doing?" Her full lips parted in a sleepy smile.

"I'm trying to figure out how you ended up here."

She languorously rose onto one elbow. "In your bed?"

"In my life."

"Oh, that. You're just lucky, I guess."

Frank grinned. "That's what I was going to say."

Rosalita squinted and looked at him from one eye. She shook her finger at him, a warning, then flipped back the covers and climbed out of bed. "What time is it?"

"Seven-thirty or so, I think."

She smoothed back her hair and twisted it into a knot high on the back of her head. "I've got to run."

"Do you want to shower here? I can help you. Get it done faster."

A throaty laugh escaped her lips. "I'm sure you could, but I can't imagine it would get me out the door any more quickly." She slipped into a satin robe, tied the belt around her waist, then picked up Frank's boxers and tossed them at his head. "Get dressed. I need you to drive me home."

When he returned to the hotel, the concierge flagged him with a message. "For you, Mr. Young. It is urgent."

Frank breathed a prayer that it wasn't from his mother's nurse. As he headed toward the elevator, he tore open the envelope.

Meet me at my old church at noon.
It will be worth your time.

Frank checked his watch. He had over two hours to burn before time to meet Santa Romana, or whatever he called himself these days, and the drive to Montalban Gorge would only take about half an hour. He had enough time to develop the film in his camera before leaving. He wanted to take the map photos to the Embassy and have Bozeman send them to President Ford as soon as possible; let him know he took the job seriously and prove himself capable. He stuffed the camera in his gym bag. As he packed it, he did something he rarely did. He packed the handgun he'd bought before he'd returned to the Philippines.

He still couldn't believe he'd found the maps. So what if he didn't have all of them? If he turned in copies of all the maps, they wouldn't have any use for him. Not that he wanted to work for the U.S. Government forever, but he didn't want to become unnecessary either. *Disposable.* Frank wiped the word from his mind, but the chill it created stuck with him a moment. Ford might bear out to be a trustworthy man, but Frank didn't have a shred of trust for William Colby. The new CIA director was on the same level as men like General Ver. A real greaser. He knew in his gut Colby wouldn't hesitate to wipe out his existence, if it would eradicate every trace of his involvement with the gold.

Frank slid the small camera into his trouser pocket, hoisted his gym bag onto his shoulder and headed downstairs to his car. Six miles outside of Manila, he pulled over at a small roadside market and backed his car up against some bushes. Frank briefly milled around the market and selected bananas, a young coconut and ripe mangoes. He carried his booty to the back of the car and lifted the trunk lid. While the lid was up, he quickly switched out license plates, then, munching on a banana, Frank closed the trunk and got into his car.

When he reached Quezon City, Frank found a place to have his film developed. Even though he inquired about a rush job, the photos wouldn't be ready for at least two days. No matter; he'd rather make the drive again than risk processing the film in Manila. Marcos had eyes and ears everywhere.

Frank filled out the form using the name *Nguyen Manuel.* He smiled. Lucky would be so proud of him. He pulled out the Nikon camera and opened the back to retrieve the film. But the camera was empty. His heart thudded to a near-stop and then raced ahead at double speed. For several seconds, Frank stared at the space that should have held film. Finally, the gears in his mind started to turn again. He had put the film in, hadn't he? Yes. He was sure of it. He'd put in a fresh roll right before he went to the palace. He remembered inserting the film. Besides, he reasoned, he'd had to advance the film between each photo he shot of the maps.

Someone had stolen the film!

"Sir? You need help?" the old man behind the counter said in stiff English. Frank stared at the man.

After a long minute, the man backed away from the counter, his eyes never leaving Frank.

Frank sighed. "No. No, I'm fine. Thank you. I must have left my film at home."

The man's shoulders relaxed, though his gaze was still wary. "So sorry. You get film, you come back, yes?"

"Yes. Uh, yes." Frank picked up the form, folded it and stuck it in his pocket. "I'll come back."

He left the shop and got into his car. Who could have taken the film? Frank met his own eyes in the rearview mirror, and they scared him. He looked around before he pulled out on the highway and drove off toward the old church.

"Damn!" He slammed his fist against the dashboard. "Damn, damn, damn!" He'd left the camera in his room when he'd driven Rosalita home. How could he have made the same mistake twice?

Then a sick feeling pierced his gut. Did Rosalita take it? She'd had every opportunity. While he slept. While he showered. While he answered the door for room service. *Oh, God, don't let it be her.*

His eyesight blurred and he blinked hard to keep his focus on the twisting road to Montalban Gorge. Why did this always happen? Just when he felt closest to Rosalita, when he let down his guard, when he planned to let her in—all the way in—his trust in her crumbled around his feet.

A dog ran across the road in front of Frank. He swerved, headed for the ditch, cut the wheel hard in the other direction, and nearly sideswiped a vegetable truck. Trembling, he slowed the car and wiped his sweaty palms on his trousers.

Who had that film? If Rosalita had taken it, what would she have done with it? Given it to Imelda?

His gut flipped. If she had, Ver would be after him. Right now.

But if not Rosalita, then who? Santa Romana kept a residence in the Manila Hotel. He could have someone watching Frank's suite, searching it.

I'll ask him. He'd be face-to-face with the man in a matter of minutes. He'd know if Santa Romana tried to lie about it.

Frank pulled over in the wide spot on the side of the road where he'd stopped before during the hard rain. He practiced deep breathing for a moment, centering himself before his meeting. He got out of the car and picked up his gym bag, then stuck the gun in the waistband in back of his pants. Surely he could take down an old man like Santa Romana with his bare hands. He could even handle a couple of men. But soldiers or Ver with a gun, that was another matter.

Santa Romana emerged from the church dressed head to toe in black. Something gleamed in the sunlight. A chain with a gold cross. A memory floated through Frank's mind, but he couldn't capture it.

"Santa Romana?"

The man's eyes darted back and forth and he glanced over his shoulder. "Get back in your car—*now.*" He spun Frank around and walked behind him, so close on his heels that Frank felt the man's breath on his neck.

Frank did as he was told, shutting the door behind him. Santa Romana slid into the passenger seat. Frank dared a look at him.

"Drive."

Frank pulled onto the road and headed higher up the mountain. "What's going on?"

Santa Romana looked over his shoulder, obviously concerned about being seen.

"Tell me what this is about, or I stop right here in the middle of the road." Frank lifted his foot from the accelerator to punctuate his point.

"That could mean your death, along with mine."

Frank glanced at the man, saw pleading in his eyes. Fear, even. He drove onward, concerned that Santa Romana would want him to stop at the place where he'd seen General Ver kill the two men. The place where Ver'd been digging for gold. His nerves thrummed until they passed that spot, and then he felt himself relax a little.

"Just ahead," Santa Romana said, "around this curve." He waved his hand to a weedy area. "Pull over there."

Frank drove his car into the tall weeds. Santa Romana encouraged him to drive farther into the brush until they were several yards into the woods. When he stopped the car, Santa Romana got out and roughed up the pressed-down grasses with his feet, erasing any sign that a car was in the woods.

Either the man truly felt afraid, or he suffered paranoid delusions. Neither scenario calmed Frank's raw nerves.

Santa Romana hustled toward him. "I apologize for my cryptic note and for my erratic behavior, but we must be watchful and careful."

Frank didn't have to guess who Santa Romana worried might catch them together.

"Please, follow me." Santa Romana turned without waiting and walked deeper into the woods. When they'd walked a dozen yards, Santa Romana slowed and half-turned as he walked, often making eye contact with Frank. "When you saw me at the hotel over two years ago, you asked many questions I couldn't answer at the time. I promised you I'd tell you what you need to know before I die." He paused and locked eyes with Frank. "That time has come." Santa Romana turned and walked onward, pushing his way past palmetto fronds and pine boughs.

"What do you mean? What time has come?"

Santa Romana didn't answer, but kept walking until they reached a sandy outcrop. The old man could still move. There he stopped and turned to Frank. "Here is where it happened." He waved his arm toward an area of scrubby weeds and boulders.

Frank opened his mouth to ask what he meant, but his eyes settled on three large boulders nestled together, reminding him of an altar. The air around him grew thin. Frank saw it again; the man's hand hitting the ground. Bouncing. Lying still. Protruding from behind the third boulder. Wedding band glinting in the sunlight.

He fell to his knees.

Santa Romana placed a hand on his shoulder. "You recognize this place?"

Frank nodded, but couldn't speak.

"This is where your father was killed."

Another memory surfaced. Someone held his hand. A man grabbed his mother. A man wearing a priest's cassock, a gold cross necklace. *Father Diaz.*

Frank turned, the world around him moving in slow motion. "You were there. *Here.* You saw it, too! Why didn't you save him?" Frank stepped close to Santa Romana.

Santa Romana flinched, but then his face relaxed. "I could not save him. I couldn't get to him in time." His eyes searched Frank's. "I did what Danilo would want me to do. I saved you."

Frank stared at Santa Romana, then walked past him out onto the vista. He drew a deep breath while overlooking the area below. After a few minutes to compose himself, he returned to the boulders where Santa Romana remained.

"I have much to tell you, and little time to share."

Frank looked at Santa Romana's old, strong face, "You—you saved me?" He nodded, answering his own question. "You saved me. Why? I don't understand all this." Frank paced the dry ground. "I've researched you. You've got more aliases than, I don't know who. Father Jose Diaz, Severino Santa Romana, Jose Santa Romana, Jose Garcia—who knows how many I'm missing? I've found records. Ferdinand Marcos used to be your attorney. You've been involved in the search for some of the hidden gold." He paused, his eyes penetrating into the old man's. "How much of this is true? You told me at the hotel that you moved gold. Are you in charge of moving gold through the Catholic Church?"

"Are you in cahoots with Marcos? Some of that gold belongs to the European royal families, doesn't it? That's why you've traveled to Europe, isn't it? Is that what you're doing? Trying to return it to them?"

A tired smile creased Santa Romana's face. "So many questions, Franco." He placed his hand on Frank's shoulder. "Let's take it slowly, okay? I've already told you that I worked as a go-between for Danilo and Lansdale. The United States, specifically the CIA, needs incredible amounts of money to fund covert operations. This money must come from sources outside the U.S. Government coffers in order to maintain secrecy. If the American people or the Filipinos or the Russians or the Chinese or the Japanese knew every move made by the CIA, it would be rendered ineffective, yes? If Americans were taxed to fund operations outside of the military, they'd want an accounting of their money, and rightfully so.

"Each time Marcos recovers gold, he must re-smelt it to remove the markings that would otherwise prove it belongs to the Chinese or the Burmese or the Vietnamese or whoever. Else, he could never trade or sell it. He couldn't move it outside of the Philippines; it would be worthless to him.

"When it's re-smelted, some of it is funneled into the coffers of the CIA as a fee for smelting, transport out of the country, and so on."

Frank held up a hand. "How can the U.S. transport gold out of the Philippines? I don't understand."

"Clark Air Base." Santa Romana paused for a moment while Frank digested his answer. "Yes, Franco. The rolling blackouts? Each time one occurs, flights leave the airbase. Those flights carry precious cargo, and I'm not talking about U.S. soldiers." He leaned forward until his face was centimeters from Frank's. "Those planes are loaded with gold."

Frank shuffled this new information around in his head, tried to make the pieces of the puzzle fit. "Where—where are they taking it?"

Santa Romana shrugged and licked blood from his cut lip. "Different places. Some of it actually makes it into legal bank accounts in the U.S. Of course, some of those accounts are opened in fictitious names, but it's quite legal to have an alias in the United States. Authors and actors do that all the time."

"And the rest of it?"

"Hard to say. Of course, some of it goes into the Black Eagle Trust. Some of it goes directly into Marcos's accounts in other countries."

"But why would the U.S. help Marcos shuttle gold to other countries? It makes sense that they'd want it in their own U.S. banks; strengthen the economy, shore up their reserves, that sort of thing. Why other countries?"

Santa Romana cocked his head to one side. "Some of it is stored there as a form of bribery. Buying votes against Communism, you might say." Santa Romana's eyes sparkled. "As for other shipments, let's just say Marcos isn't the only one with bank accounts in other countries under alias names. Powerful Americans have been opening such accounts for decades."

"Who? Lansdale? Kissinger? Nixon?" Frank's head buzzed with new realization.

"You've heard of the M Fund?"

Frank nodded. "Yes, the fund that MacArthur established during the Japanese occupation, run by General Marquat."

Santa Romana lifted one shoulder. "It goes even deeper than that."

Frank stared deep into Santa Romana's eyes. "Is Ford involved?"

Santa Romana laughed harshly. "You must be joking. Gerald Ford is a puppet. When have you ever heard of a man being named Vice President of the United States without being elected? And when have you ever heard of that same man becoming President, also without an election?" He shook his head. "Even Ford has no real understanding of how he got where he is today."

"Did Nixon make that happen?"

"Of course not. Nixon didn't have that kind of power. If he did, he'd still be in charge."

"So, who's really running the country?"

Santa Romana leaned forward. Even though they were miles from anyone who could overhear, he whispered. "The same people who have always run America. The CIA."

Frank sucked in a deep, shuddering breath, then heaved it out. He looked again at the three boulders, again saw his father's hand hit the ground. "What about you and Yamashita? If you talked with him, you must have known for where the gold was hidden. Why didn't you just point it out to Lansdale yourself? Why involve my father?"

"I wasn't the one who involved your father, Franco. Vice President Wallace moved him into the OSS, the organization that later became the CIA. He did the same thing to Lansdale. Danilo answered to Lansdale, just as I did. I must tell you, though, I felt fortunate to work with your father. He was an honest man, devoted to our cause." Santa Romana stared at the gorge, into years long since past. He turned back and looked into Frank's eyes. "You remind me of your father in many ways."

Frank's throat constricted and his jaws ached.

"As to Yamashita . . . ." A long, tired sigh wheezed out of Santa Romana's chest. "I questioned General Yamashita briefly." He stared at the ground as he spoke. "His driver eventually led me to thirteen of the Golden Lily treasure vaults." When he looked at Frank again, his eyes glistened with the pain of shame and regret. "Four are right here on this mountain."

Santa Romana pointed down the gorge. "One was right down there. Your father stumbled upon the Japanese burying gold there, and that's why he was killed. We never found out who shot him."

Frank let out pent-up breath.

"Your father was my friend."

Frank felt a sob building in his chest and quickly changed the subject. "You said there were four burial sites on this mountain. Where are the other three?"

"General Ver has already cleaned out one of them."

Frank nodded. He knew all about Ver opening one of the burial sites. He'd seen it with his own eyes.

"I expect they'll open the other one soon. Yet, there is one that will remain untouched, as they don't know it exists. The map leading to this dig site belongs to the man who delivered you into my arms the day your father was killed."

"And the fourth one?"

Santa Romana reached inside his jacket, pulled out a wax-covered map and handed it to Frank. "Marcos and Ver don't know about the fourth one, either."

Frank opened the map. Enigmatic symbols sketched across its surface, some of which he recognized from his research. He looked at Santa Romana with raised eyebrows.

"Yes. This is your tunnel, Franco. I have now fulfilled my promise to your father and my friend."

Frank stared at the map, ran his trembling fingers across it as if reading Braille.

Santa Romana pointed higher up on the mountain. "It's up there."

Frank stared toward the mountain's peak.

"I know you said you where not interested in the gold, but shortly after your father died, I decided this was something I must do for him. I always believed he would have done the same for me." He lowered his voice as though someone might be listening and he was about to impart a great secret. "You must read the map in a mirror. The symbols for rocks and trees have been switched." A wry smile curved Santa Romana's lips. "Franco, it's important that you do not try to recover the treasure right now. Even if you hire a team and use a false identity, it's much too dangerous for you to be here right now. People are watching you."

"Who? Who is watching me?" Frank shook his head. "Ver? I know he keeps an eye on me."

"Ver watches everyone, as he should. He is hated almost as much as he is feared. But he's not the only one. Marcos has other men watching you. Your frequent comings and goings have raised eyebrows. As has your relationship with Rosalita Laurel." He allowed a slight smile to play at his lips. "You're being watched in the U.S. as well, but you are more protected there than here."

"I'm protected in the U.S.? By whom?"

"Nguyen Tao and his son, Nguyen Luc."

"Nguyen Luc?" Frank's vision blurred "Lucky? My friend Lucky?"

"Yes. Your friend."

"What does Lucky have to do with this? I've known Lucky since—"

"Since you were college roommates. I know. Tao arranged for that."

"What? Why would—" Frank raised his hands above his head and shook them. "Who in the hell is Tao?"

"Tao is the man who ushered you and your mother out of the Philippines the day your father was killed. He is part of our spy network. Both of us were very close to your father." Santa Romana's eyes softened. "He is Lucky's father."

Frank turned and paced a few steps into the woods, turned, paced again. Had his whole world been a sham? His chest ached with the heaviness of stone. "I thought Lucky was my friend."

"Franco, he *is* your friend. He didn't know his father was CIA. He wasn't aware of the manipulation—had no clue being assigned as your roommate was anything other than chance." Santa Romana laughed. "In fact, Lucky was distraught that his father seemed more interested in your well-being than his own."

There were too many things to think about. All through college, he and Lucky had been the best of friends. Hadn't they? He'd never met Lucky's dad. He was always traveling, always away on business.

Frank dropped to the ground and covered his head. Lucky had been the one constant in his life. The one friend he could depend on, the one friend who understood him better than he understood himself. And it had all been a sham?

Santa Romana touched Frank's shoulder. "Lucky wasn't aware of the situation any more than you were." He dropped down to his knees to be level with Frank.

"When you met with Nixon, Tao informed Lucky that he was CIA and brought him into the picture. Up until that time, Lucky didn't know his father's role."

Frank picked up a fallen pine branch and snapped it in half. "He went into business with me not because he trusted me, but because he was told to do it."

"I don't think that's true. No one instructed Lucky to do that."

"He showed up to run the dojo when I came back from meeting with President Ford. Is that a coincidence, too?"

Santa Romana shook his head. "I believe Tao may have arranged that. But just as you had the option to decline your assignment, so did Lucky." His voice softened. "Lucky did what he did because he wanted to do it."

Frank stared at the map. He wiped a hand over his face, an effort to clear the fog clouding his mind. *Lucky is a part of this. Santa Romana has had my back all along. Nixon is corrupt. The U.S. has been getting gold from the Philippines for decades.*

"What part does Rosalita play in all this?" Frank's tongue felt thick as he spoke.

Santa Romana shrugged. "Only the part you've allowed her to play." He stood and offered his hand to help Frank to his feet. "Rosalita has invested money with Villacrusis in his search for gold, but so have dozens of other people. Many Filipinos search for the treasure, but the saying about a needle in a haystack doesn't begin to compare to the difficulty in finding the burial sites. Even with the maps, most of the sites remain elusive." He shrugged.

"It's possible Rosalita is watching you, but if so, she is doing it at Ferdinand's behest, or perhaps Imelda's. I have heard nothing of it, however."

"Would they have told you? If she were watching me, I mean?"

"Perhaps. Perhaps not." He held out his hands. "I have long believed that Ferdinand and I should remain in each other's trust. Recently, I have discovered that I've been a fool. I trusted him too much."

"What do you mean?"

Santa Romana motioned to two boulders. He sat down on one of them and rested his elbows on his knees. "Because I traveled to Europe so often, I made Marcos my power of attorney. He made it possible for me to transfer much of the bullion out of the country and into the hands of the Church.

"I have learned that now he has abused that power and trust. Many of my accounts now operate under new names, aliases. I can't touch my own money. Marcos stole it from me."

Frank took a seat on the rock opposite Santa Romana. "Can't you get it back? If you have ties to the U.S., can't William Colby or President Ford force Marcos to give you back your money? The U.S. still has some say-so over what happens in the Philippines, right? I mean, we could stop travel from Clark Air Base, and then Marcos couldn't get the gold out of the country."

"I am on my own, Franco. My usefulness has reached an end where Marcos is concerned." Santa Romana shook his head. "I have reached my expiration date."

"So? You've got maps. You start over. Uncover your own sites. You don't need Marcos, right?"

Santa Romana took both Frank's hands into his own and looked hard into his eyes. "I need to tell you something. It's very important."

Frank squirmed uncomfortably.

"Listen. If you don't remember anything else I've ever told you, remember this. Many years ago, I gave your mother a very special rosary. One made of sapphires and diamonds."

Frank nodded. "She still has it. She said it was blessed by the Pope. But I—"

"It *was* blessed by the Pope. Personally. But that's not why it's important." He scooted closer to Frank. "Listen. There were two rosaries. I gave one to your mother. The other one was stolen, although I know where it is. Someday, I suspect it will resurface." He released Frank's hands and intertwined his fingers. "Frank. Make sure nothing happens to that rosary. And when the day comes—and it will—when you have a puzzle to solve, remember this: the answers are on those rosaries."

"What are you talking about?"

"Until you have both of them, it is irrelevant. The knowledge I have given you could get you killed."

"But—"

"Quiet, now. We must hurry. Just know this: the inscriptions on the rosaries are much more valuable than that which you hold." He tapped the map clutched in Frank's hand. "Like this map, the rosary is simply a vessel. Its value is not from the jewels decorating it. Its value is the knowledge it contains."

Frank remembered his worry that one of the nurses would take his mother's rosary.

Santa Romana stared out into the gorge. "My days are numbered, Franco."

"What do you mean?"

Santa Romana looked at Frank with eyes that displayed what? Fear? No. Wisdom? Maybe. "I will be dead in a matter of weeks, if not days."

Breath squeezed from Frank's lungs. "Are you ill?"

Santa Romana slowly shook his head. "I'll be murdered. It may look like an accident—no, it *will* look like an accident. Or, perhaps, as though I died from an illness."

"An illness?"

"Don't be surprised by anything. When they want me gone, I'll be gone." He held out his palms. "Despite hundreds of accounts and foundations in almost as many names, my family will be left with nothing. The umbrella has spread too wide. What used to fund peace and goodwill now provides for hit men and henchmen, for Mafia and drugs. I've lost control. I've lost power. My time is at an end."

"Can't you—"

"It is out of my control, Franco. There is nowhere I can run, nowhere to hide." He looked skyward. "God has protected me far beyond what I have deserved. If He allows it, Marcos or whoever will see that it comes to pass. If it is God's will that it's my time to go, I will go peacefully. The CIA thinks I am too powerful; the Chinese and the Japanese just want their gold. And Fabian Ver has wanted me dead for decades. Soon, he will have his wish."

He met Frank's stare. "Remember this. Ver will always get what he wants. That's why I urge you to let this go for now. Marcos won't always be in power. The Filipino people won't tolerate him forever. Wait until another president is at the helm. Then you can return for your birthright."

My birthright. Frank stared at the three-boulder altar until he lost track of time.

Santa Romana grabbed Frank by the shoulders. "One more thing. When the time comes, study Revelation 22:13. Got it?"

"Revelation 22:13," Frank mumbled.

"Don't forget that. I can't write it down for you, as you'll later realize. But when you are missing a piece to a puzzle, this verse will be your answer. So don't forget it."

"Revelation 22:13." Frank said, this time putting the scripture in his memory.

"Yes." He released Frank. "Now, go."

Frank paused, waiting to follow Santa Romana down the mountain.

"You go on. I'm going this way. You should never be seen with me. Never."

Frank nodded.

Santa Romana wrapped his arms around him. "Take care of yourself, my friend." He held him at arm's length. "Danilo would be so proud." The man's eyes puddled and he nodded. "I will tell him about the fine man you became." He turned and walked across the overgrown boulder-strewn area, then disappeared into the trees.

Frank stood at the edge of the gorge. He walked over to the boulders where he'd last seen his father. The nightmare that had plagued his life had been explained. Now, if only his real life could be made so clear.

CHAPTER 31

Ferdinand linked his wife's arm and the two walked together up the stairway of Malacañang Palace. A few steps behind them were Frank and Rosalita, followed by Florentino Villacrusis and his wife. Tonight, Ferdinand wanted to draw his friends closer, so he led the group into his and Imelda's personal wing of the palace. He dismissed the house manager as soon as they entered, and he motioned for everyone to take a seat while he poured drinks.

"It is distressing to lose one so close to us. But he wouldn't want us to mourn." Ferdinand handed the last glass to Frank, then raised his in the air. "To Santy!"

"To Santy," the party chorused.

He gulped down his drink and turned to refill his glass, then met Frank's eyes. "It's a shame you did not know him, Frank. Our friend Santy only kept a few close friends. He was a very private man."

Frank nodded, his eyes on his hands.

Ferdinand tossed back his drink. The funeral was over, they'd paid their respects, and now it was time to move forward. They'd already spent more time on Santa Romana than the man deserved. Damned fool. He turned his back to the group and allowed himself a smile. Ver was right. He did feel better after wiping out his main competitor. Santy had gained too much wealth and power. Fortunately, the man didn't realize the power of attorney form he signed would give Ferdinand full power over the Santa Romana estate. Well, once he'd pressured Santy's wife to turn it over to him, that is.

He poured another drink, avoiding the look of displeasure in Imelda's eyes. She thought he drank too much, but he reasoned that if she wouldn't flash their wealth across the nations, he wouldn't drink.

"We should enjoy the friendships we have, while we still have them." Ferdinand bent and kissed his wife on the cheek. "Show love to those whom we love."

Imelda eyed him with a critical sideways glance, but he noticed the smile teasing the corners of her lips, and he believed she'd forgiven him.

"Speaking of friendships—Frank, Florentino, would you accompany me to my study?"

Rosalita dabbed at her eyes and touched Frank's hand before he stood. "I guess we're on our own again, ladies."

Imelda chuckled. "Please, Rosalita, do not let them know we enjoy it so much."

The two men followed Ferdinand, and once they were in his study, he motioned for Florentino to close the door. He'd kept Frank Young at arm's length long enough. Rosalita had been watching the man at Imelda's request for years, and she trusted him enough to fall in love with him, whether she'd confessed it or not. With Santy gone, Ferdinand no longer had reason not to use Frank's engineering background, plus his obvious connections to U.S. money, to help him in his quest for more gold.

"Drink, gentlemen?" Ferdinand poured without waiting for answers.

"Thank you." Frank leaned forward and accepted the offered glass.

"Cheers," Florentino said, tossing back his drink immediately.

Ferdinand watched the two men for a moment. When he caught Florentino's eyes, he lifted an eyebrow.

Florentino gave an almost imperceptible nod and sipped from his glass.

"Frank." Animated, Ferdinand swung his drink through air. "Frank, my friend, I have a business proposition for you."

"Excellent. What can Triangle Tobacco and I do for you, sir?"

Ferdinand shook his head and smiled. "Actually, this has nothing to do with the tobacco industry."

"Oh?"

Ferdinand liked the way Frank shifted in his seat, eyed him with a blend of respect, curiosity and caution. Perhaps even fear. *One could hope.* Men respected those they feared. One more reason he kept Ver close at hand. He'd seen Ver make men piss themselves.

"You have heard stories of buried treasure in the Philippines, yes? You read the newspapers, have heard the rumors?"

Frank's Adam's apple bobbed. "Of course. Even as a child, I heard people talk of gold in these islands." He held out a hand. "I've yet to find any though." His laugh was hoarse, and he swallowed quickly from his glass.

"Would you believe me if I told you that I have?"

The smooth-faced man's brow creased. "You have what?"

"Found gold." Ferdinand couldn't stifle the laugh that burbled in his throat. "Lots and lots and lots of gold."

Villacrusis joined in his laughter.

"Really?" Frank sat forward, his stocky, muscled body straining at the thin fabric of the *barong tagalong* he'd worn under his suit jacket. "You found it here in the Philippines? Oh, wait, of course you did. The gold mines." He grinned. "You almost had me there for a moment, sir. I thought you were talking about buried war loot."

Villacrusis laughed again, and Ferdinand joined him. They laughed until Ferdinand had to wipe his eyes. Frank chuckled, but his look was one of puzzlement, which Ferdinand found even funnier.

"Oh, Frankie, Frankie! You do bring me joy." Ferdinand's side ached, and he rubbed it with one hand. He set down his glass and leaned toward Frank. "I *am* talking about war loot. Gold bullion, barrels and copper boxes filled with diamonds, rubies, emeralds and all kinds of coins and jewelry. Tons and tons and tons of gold, Frankie. More than you have ever seen in your life."

Frank's eyes bulged and he blinked rapidly. "You have found some of this treasure? The stuff General Yamashita buried during World War II?"

Ferdinand sat back and crossed his legs. He loved the warm satisfaction that flooded his chest when he bragged about his treasures. "Oh, yes. I've found entire rooms full of gold, Frankie. More than you could ever imagine." He smiled. "More than Yamashita and all of his men could have buried alone."

"I thought Yamashita was the only one who buried gold in the Philippines."

Ferdinand grinned. "Other generals, princes even, buried vaults of treasure all over these islands, Frankie. And now . . ." He paused for dramatic effect. "I have the maps to show me where all of it is hidden."

Frank fidgeted with the hem on his shirt. "That's amazing." He glanced at Ferdinand, then at Villacrusis, then back again. "But, well, why are you telling me this, sir? Shouldn't you keep news like that a secret?"

Ferdinand looked at Villacrusis. "See, I told you he was bright." He leaned forward and rested an elbow on his knee. "Frankie understands the need for secrecy."

"Yes, sir." Villacrusis nodded.

"Frank, I am telling you because this is the offer I want to make to you." He stood and walked around the room as he spoke. "I've watched you since the day you arrived in the Philippines with your cigarettes and your marketing plan. You're trustworthy, you're savvy and you are intelligent." He raised his eyebrows and nodded at Frank. "Yes, I know you graduated from the American Duke University at the top of your class. I've done my research." He smiled. "You're an engineer by training. Someone with your education and understanding can help in the recovery of these treasure vaults. Tell me, are you familiar with reverse engineering?"

"Of course."

"That's how we plan to locate more of the treasure. Some of the vaults are booby-trapped, so our group believes reverse engineering will be the safest way to get to the gold."

Frank cocked his head to one side. "Your group? What group, sir?"

"The Rebel Group," said Villacrusis.

"Rebels?" Frank frowned. "What are you rebelling against?"

Ferdinand waved an arm in the air. "We aren't rebelling. That's the name Florentino and Fabian gave the group. We're a group of treasure hunters."

Villacrusis cleared his throat. "Maybe we should change the name. It does have a negative ring to it."

Marcos nodded. "That's a good idea. Let's think of a new name. If Frankie agrees, we'll add a new member to our group and come up with a new name." He walked over and stood in front of Frank, who wiped a fine bead of sweat from his forehead. "What do you think, Frankie?"

"About the name, or about the group?"

Ferdinand threw back his head and laughed. "Perfect! Perfect. You will bring more than intelligence to our group, Frankie. You make me smile." He never should have listened to Santy. The man's paranoia had kept him from bringing Frank on board for far too long. He sat down in the chair beside Frank and clapped a hand on the man's arm. "You will join?" He didn't care if it sounded like a question or a command. He always got what he wanted, and tonight, he wanted Franklin Young.

Frank nodded. "I . . ." He cleared his throat and threw back the rest of his drink. "I am honored to join your group."

Chapter 32

February 22, 1975
Reno, Nevada

Gary Morgan rifled through the stack of mail and shook his head when he found yet another letter from the Philippines. Gerhart Krueger was driving him crazy. Why wouldn't the man take *no* for an answer? He threw the envelope in the trashcan by his desk, then thought better of it, retrieved it, and slid the letter opener along its seam.

"Good grief. Write much?" Gary flipped through the pages; there must have been a dozen or more. He'd never received such a long letter from Krueger. And to beat all, this one was handwritten.

He poured another cup of coffee, added a shot of whiskey from the bottle in his bottom desk drawer, then propped his feet on his desk and started reading. He skimmed the first few paragraphs—niceties he couldn't waste time on. He anticipated skimming the rest of the letter, too. He'd already done the math; Krueger had told him Marcos wanted three hundred metric tons per year of gold processed, and that didn't match up with the twenty-two metric tons per year the Philippine mines produced. Krueger had to be crazy.

But on the second page of the letter, he found information that grabbed him by the throat and wouldn't let go.

Buried treasure on U.S. bases, Clark Air Base and Subic Naval Base .... 172 sites with 34 major locations .... Retrieval of those 34 sites will make everyone involved rich beyond their wildest dreams …. Marcos will take you to these sites, let you see for yourself … show you the original Japanese treasure maps … gold bullion buried in Mosler vaults in tunnels … 999 billion Yen … kegs of gemstones, gold Buddhas ….

The phrase *gold Buddhas* caught his eye. He remembered news headlines about a man named Roxas and how he'd been arrested and beaten after finding a gold Buddha worth millions.

Gary read on, learning that President Marcos himself now requested his presence in the Philippines. Before, Krueger had hinted that might be the case, but now he spelled it out. Marcos wanted Gary to not only help them locate the gold, he wanted him to re-smelt it and change the purity and markings of the gold, so that it appeared to have been harvested from the gold mines in the Philippines. He wanted Philippine stamps pressed into the gold, so there could be no question of its origin when Marcos sold it.

"A hundred seventy-two vaults of World War II treasure." Speaking the words aloud somehow made them more truthful. Twenty minutes and three shots of liquor later, Gary phoned Gerhart Krueger.

"Morgan!" Gerhart Krueger yelled into the phone. "I hoped you'd call. You got my letter, I presume?"

"Have it in my hand, Krueger."

"What do you think? Marcos wants you here, man. He wants you bad. I've told him you're the best metallurgist in the States, if not the world. Now I don't think he believed me at first, but I've convinced him. I need you to prove me right, buddy. What say you?"

Gary's gut told him this man was a little too energetic, too pushy.

But Gary was no fool. He could be as slick and greasy as a snake oil salesman if necessary. He read the figures in the letter again. *Three hundred metric tons each year.* His vision grew foggy as he saw his future of leisure and fortune—and freedom from the huge financial debt he owed the John Birch Society.

"Morgan? You there? Gary?"

"Yeah, I'm here. Sorry. Overseas static. You know."

"Right. Sooo, what do you say? Can you meet with President Marcos? Once in a lifetime opportunity, man. I think you should jump on it."

Gary nodded, even though Krueger couldn't see him. "I'll come for about three days; see what you've got going on. I could use a little vacation anyway. Meet the president—yeah, that'd be cool."

"Great!"

Despite the connection, Krueger's shout caused Gary to pull the phone from his ear. He laughed. "I'll make some calls first thing Monday morning; tie up a few loose ends here. I can be there before the end of the month. I'll call you when I have an itinerary."

"Sounds good, buddy. I look forward to seeing you."

Gary hung up the phone and sneered. *And I look forward to seeing that gold.*

CHAPTER 33

March 1, 1975
Malacañang Palace, The Philippines

Frank zipped his windbreaker and shoved his hands in his pockets, then turned to face the palace, his back against the chilly evening breeze.

"Gentlemen, tonight you will go on your first treasure hunt together." President Marcos beamed as he waved his arm toward the Pasig River. "General Ver will take you on that Navy vessel . . ." He pointed to the small military ship. ". . . and take you out to Manila Bay."

Frank set his jaw. The last thing he wanted was to be on a boat with Fabian Ver. He looked at Sten Larsson, Gerhart Krueger, and Gary Morgan, wondering if Marcos planned to have Ver take the four of them out to the sea to be disposed. *No, Marcos had worked hard to pull this team together, and his hero-worship for Larsson wouldn't allow his murder.* Yet.

Larsson rubbed his hands together. "I have a good feeling about this."

Marcos smiled and clapped him on the back. "That's what I wanted to hear, Sten. Your intuitiveness will help direct Ver to the appropriate dive spot."

"We're diving?" Gary Morgan asked.

"No," Marcos said. "*You're* diving." He laughed. "Everything you men should need is on the boat." He turned back to Morgan. "You won't be diving alone, my friend. Ver has selected a few of his best-trained divers to assist you. But I know you enjoy going below, and I thought that, since you'll be refining our catch of the day, you should be one of the first to see it."

Morgan's eyes lit. "That's wonderful!" He smacked Krueger on the back. "Let's get going! Time is wasting."

Frank had to admit the contagious excitement buoyed his mood. Even Ver wore a pleasant face instead of the stern, hard eyes that constantly searched for flaws in everyone. Since they'd all signed the Leber Group contract Marcos had drawn up, Ver treated him differently. Frank couldn't exactly call it *trust*, but the man at least now offered him grudging respect.

Sten lifted an imaginary drink. "Here's to the Leber Group."

Marcos chuckled. "Leber Group. Much better than *Rebel Group*, don't you think, Frankie?"

Frank grinned and nodded. The new name had been Villacrusis's. *Rebel* spelled backward was *Leber*. Ver's men were reverse engineering the already-excavated sites to better learn how to approach the next ones, so why not reverse the name? It fit.

Marcos turned and walked back toward the palace.

"Sir?" Frank called. "Aren't you coming with us?"

Marcos shook his head. "How I wish!" He motioned for Frank to step closer, and when he did, Marcos spoke quietly. "I have business to attend, but I want Ver to go on with today's search to see if Sten is all he says he is. We have a good idea where a sunken ship filled with treasure is located, thanks to a map, but we've yet to pinpoint the exact position." He placed a hand on Frank's shoulder. "I'd like you to keep an eye on Gary Morgan. He's new to us, and though Krueger recommends him, Krueger is lazy and foolish." He dropped his hand and straightened, watching the men board the Philippine Navy boat. "Before we let these men any closer into our circle, I want to have your and Ver's opinion about them." He leveled his gaze at Frank. "I'm relying on you, Frankie. I trust you."

Frank's throat clogged around the words he wanted to speak. Finally, he choked out a strangled, "Thank you. I will keep an eye on things."

As he headed down the dock toward the boat, Frank watched the way Krueger and Morgan huddled together, staring at Ver and Sten. Marcos had a knack for these things; Frank had to give him credit. *Why, then, does he trust me?*

Frank knew the answer. *He doesn't.* Marcos didn't rise to his position by putting trust in anyone, with perhaps the exception of his wife. Rosalita had told him that Imelda shared with her that Ferdinand drew up a secret presidential decree, leaving Imelda in full power in the event of his death. Other than Imelda, Marcos fully trusted no one. Not even Ver.

When Frank boarded the vessel, it surprised him to see a man he'd met last week named Leopold Giga conversing with Ben Valmores. Frank thought of what Santa Romana had told him about Valmores having kept a few maps for himself. He looked at the man and smiled warmly.

Valmores returned his smile, his eyes crinkling.

Within minutes, the boat was at sea. Ver and the boat's captain studied the map and, after an hour had passed, Ver announced they'd found the place. Then Sten Larsson took center stage.

Frank watched the man, part out of curiosity, part out of absurdity.

Larsson walked starboard and held out his arms over the water. He closed his eyes and rocked back and forth, and Frank wondered that he didn't topple overboard. After a moment, he turned to face the group of men who'd gathered to watch him divine the waters. "It's not here."

Ver's face darkened. "What do you mean, it's not here? These are the coordinates on the map." He waved the map in the air. "There has to be a ship down there."

"This is not the place." Sten closed his eyes again for a moment, and when he opened them, he pointed ahead of them. "It's over there."

Ver shot the man a hateful look, but then his face relaxed, and he turned to the captain. "Go where he says."

Nearly a thousand yards away, Sten held up his hands. "This is it!" he shouted. He turned to Ver. "She's below us. Anchor here."

Frank stepped back, trying to keep out of the way of the beehive of activity that suddenly erupted around him. Navy divers emerged from a lower deck, already dressed in full gear, and flipped backward off the boat. Morgan grabbed his suit and started to undress, but Ver stopped him.

"Not yet." He eyed Sten from the corner of his eye. "Wait and see what they find."

Valmores, Giga, Krueger and Morgan paced the deck for nearly twenty minutes. Frank looked out over the edge of the boat, watching the bubbles as they surfaced.

Ver walked up behind him. "This had better not be a hoax, or Sten Larsson will be sorry."

Just then, the surface of the water broke before them. One of the Navy divers plunged his fist skyward and tore off his mask. "We've found her, general! The *Nachi* is directly below us!"

Frank and Ver locked eyes, and Frank had to wonder whose grew the largest. *A sunken treasure ship! And they'd found it!* The chill of excitement crawled across his skin, and a giggle burbled from his throat.

Ver laughed, too, and Frank had to quell the urge to hug him. He knew the man was a monster, and no matter what kind of victory they shared, Frank refused to like him.

Ver turned to Morgan and jerked a thumb toward the sea. "Diver down."

Morgan grinned and yanked on his dive suit. Several around him cheered.

In less than half an hour, Morgan and the Navy divers resurfaced with the ship's bell. They'd also dropped markers suspended from ropes attached to small buoys so that they could return with more equipment later to remove the heavy treasure.

"It's incredible," Morgan said. "I've never seen so much gold in my entire life. And let me tell you, as a metallurgist, I've seen a lot." He waved his hands as he spoke. "Crates and crates and crates of gold biscuits. Barrels of coins and gemstones. Who knows what all is on that ship. Hell, it's no wonder she sunk! It'll take multiple ships bigger than this boat to tote that load back to shore."

The next day, the same team, minus Sten, who'd eaten some bad shrimp and fell ill, boarded the Navy boat and headed back to Sten's spot. When Frank found a moment to speak with Ver without the others nearby, he asked the question that had plagued him since he'd stepped onto the dock that morning. "Excuse me, general."

"Yes?" Ver's eyes narrowed, as if in anticipation of what Frank planned to ask.

Frank wished Villacrusis had joined him. Ver always seemed calmer, almost sociable when amiable Villacrusis was around. "I see that we've brought quite a bit of equipment on board, but I'm wondering why we didn't bring a larger vessel? The way Morgan talked last night, there's hundreds of metric tons down there. There's no way we can carry more than a pittance of that on this boat."

Ver studied Frank's face.

And then Frank realized why: they had no intention of bringing up any gold today.

Ver finally spoke. "This is the only vessel I have available right now. The Philippine Navy has other priorities, and the skeleton crew we have here are the only people I want to trust with the knowledge of this discovery for now."

Frank nodded and shoved his hands in his pockets. "That makes sense." He turned and let the ocean breeze blow across his face as Ver went to consult again with the captain.

Hours later, Morgan came up to Frank. "What do you think's going on?"

Frank lifted a shoulder. "What do you mean?"

"We've been going in circles for at least a couple of hours now. Where are the markers?"

Frank checked his watch. He'd been lost in thought of what he'd report back to Bozeman and Ford for so long that he'd lost track of the time. Over three hours had slipped away.

Ver cocked an ear in Morgan's direction and stomped across the deck to join them. He waved his arms in the air. "The markers are gone!"

"What?" Morgan said. "You're kidding me!"

Ver glared at the man. "I kid no one. The divers said we should have used wires." He stood with his fists on his hips and stared at Valmores and Giga. Then he turned back to Morgan. "I say we go back. Tomorrow we'll bring Sten with us, and we'll drop the markers with wire."

Morgan looked at Frank and then turned back to General Ver. "What if someone cut the ropes?"

A flustered look briefly crossed Ver's face, and Frank knew Morgan had nailed it. *But who would have cut the ropes?* It had to have been Ver. That's why he hadn't brought a bigger boat. Then again, Morgan and Krueger could have sent someone out early this morning to cut the ropes and buy them time to score some of the gold for themselves. *Sten was ill.* Or was he? Could Sten have done it? *No.* When Frank had last seen him, the man looked positively green. He'd blamed it on shrimp, but Frank wondered if he hadn't been seasick.

"It is possible someone cut the ropes," Ver said. "But unlikely. The diver is right. We should have used wire." He glanced over his shoulder. "Once Sten locates the *Nachi* again, we'll mark the spot, and I'll send out a patrol boat to monitor the area."

Two days later, however, they still hadn't returned to the *Nachi*. Ver had called Frank to tell him the vessel they'd borrowed from the Philippine Navy had been commandeered by President Marcos to escort him and Imelda to the summer palace.

The following week, when Frank called in his report to Bozeman, he reported that Sten had located the *Nachi* a second time. "The man's abilities are eerie, I'll admit," he said.

"So how much gold was recovered?" Bozeman asked.

Frank cleared his throat. "None."

"What do you mean—*none*? I thought you'd said that Gary Morgan saw tons of gold and diamonds."

"Gemstones. I said 'gemstones.' But it doesn't matter. The first time we went out to recover the gold, the markers were gone. The second time, wire markers were left, and Ver put an armed patrol in the area. But when we went back with a dive team, the markers had disappeared again."

"What happened to the patrol?"

Frank huffed into the phone. "Marcos happened to them, that's what. He called them in to escort his presidential yacht back into the bay. While they were away, the markers disappeared."

"But they're going back out again, yes? Marcos wouldn't leave the gold resting at the bottom of the ocean. Not once General Ver verified its location."

"I suspect the gold is being recovered as we speak. But with the exception of Ver and probably a few others, the Leber Group is not privy to that information. Marcos has already assigned Morgan, Krueger, Valmores, Giga and me to work with Villacrusis on one of the underground burial sites. He's moved on."

"So the gold won't be split among the Leber Group partners, then?"

"How can something that has never been recovered be shared with anyone?"

CHAPTER 34

March 11, 1975
Mariveles, The Philippines

Frank eased into the deck chair on the presidential yacht and took a long sip from his drink. In a matter of moments, his tension seeped away. "Ahhh."

Marcos chuckled.

Frank leaned forward and clinked his glass against Marcos's.

"So." Morgan looked at Marcos. "You're serious about leaving that gold down there?" He shook his head. "That's a lot to leave behind."

Marcos gave a thin-lipped smile. "The Japanese prime minister visited me last week. Do you find it a mere coincidence that he brought Captain Enpei's widow with him? Enpei was the commander of the *Nachi*. The prime minister requested permission to search the waters for Enpei's body, so his wife can give him a proper burial." Marcos grimaced. "Of course, I had to refuse. I told them the water was too murky and frigid, and that it would put a diver at great risk to dive there."

Frank emptied his drink. Before he could set it down, a waiter appeared and replaced it with a fresh one. "Do you think the Japanese could have cut the ropes on the markers?"

Marcos nodded. "Yes, I do. That's why I feel we shouldn't draw attention to the area with our presence out there. Without the markers, anyone who searches without the aid of you or Sten will have no chance of finding the

Nachi. We searched for years in that same grid, and yet we never saw her, until you brought us there.

"Besides, there is plenty of gold in these islands, and much of it will be easier to recover than what is buried under the sea."

Morgan leaned toward Frank and spoke quietly out of the side of his mouth. "I think Ver cut those ropes."

Frank glanced at him, but focused his attention on Marcos. He didn't like Morgan, and everything the man did seemed to scrape Frank's nerves. "Where do you propose we dig, sir?"

Marcos tossed back his drink and leaned forward. "There are so many places! Sites at the military bases, the Baguio mountains, Rizal and Metro Manila."

"The U.S. military bases?" Morgan said. "Can you dig there?"

Marcos smiled. "I can do anything. I'm the president." He threw back his head and laughed.

Frank swallowed his morals and held up his glass. "To President Marcos!"

"To President Marcos!" the men chorused.

"It's the truth, you know." Marcos' eyes glinted. "My summer palace is filled with gold we found at Camp Aguinaldo in Quezon City. It's a Philippine base, of course, but as the national headquarters for our army, we had to take every precaution to keep the recovery a secret." He sipped from his glass. "But we did it."

"The summer palace?" Kruger asked. "That's where we're headed tonight?"

Marcos nodded and smiled.

"Can we see it?" Morgan asked. "The gold, I mean? Will you show us?"

Marcos shook his head. "No, no. It is protected, guarded at all times. Hidden in a secret location. I can't show anyone."

Morgan looked at Frank and winked, then turned back to Marcos. "What good is it, if you can't show it off?" He smiled. "Besides, you can trust us. After all, we're all on your team. The Leber Group!" He held up his glass, and again the men all followed suit and drained their drinks.

Again, the waiter immediately refilled their glasses. Frank felt like royalty.

"Yes, we are all on the same team," Marcos said, his voice patronizing.

"Then will you show us the gold?" Morgan asked.

"You have seen gold at the bottom of the ocean, yes? What more proof do you need?"

Morgan coughed out a harsh laugh. "Gold we can't recover." He shook his head and gave Krueger a mocking glance. "I have a feeling that we're on a wild goose chase." He turned to Marcos, whose eyes had narrowed. "No disrespect meant by that, Mr. President. You must understand that I can't help but have doubts, having come all this way only to be told the gold I've actually found, if indeed it is real gold—I haven't touched or tested it—can't be brought out. I mean, forgive me, but if I had a dollar for every man who wanted me to invest in a treasure hunt . . ." He held out his hands. "I guess it comes with the territory, though. When you're a metallurgist, everyone thinks you can perform alchemy." He laughed at his own joke.

Frank heard ticking inside his head, like the secondhand on a clock. Was it the liquor? Or the ticking of death? Marcos would probably have Morgan snuffed before daybreak.

Fury blazed in Marcos's eyes, and Frank held his breath. If Ver had been in the group, Morgan would be sightless by now.

Marcos glared at Krueger. "This is the man you bring to me?" He glared at Morgan and pursed his lips. "I have brought you here, treated you like a prince, and you dare to speak this way to me?"

Morgan's face burned red even in the semi-darkness. He held up both hands. "Mr. President, sir. I'm sorry, sir. I didn't mean—forgive me. It's just—well, I'm frustrated over the *Nachi*. I came a long way, sir. I wouldn't be here if I didn't trust you. Again, please forgive me. My tongue is loosened by this fine drink, and I'm speaking like a fool."

Marcos's face thawed.

"If you say there's gold, then there's gold. I guess—well, I'd only hoped to see a bar or two." Morgan's smile was strained and cautious.

Marcos tossed back his head and broke into raucous laughter. Frank didn't know how to react, but soon he and the others joined in, if somewhat uncomfortably.

"Oh, Morgan. Gary Morgan," Marcos said, again swiping at his eyes. "A bar or two." He took a long gulp from his glass, then leaned forward and placed his elbows on his knees, his eyes glittering. "I have already recovered more gold bars and biscuits than there are stars in this sky." He waved his hand toward the heavens. "And you are right. You should see them. When we arrive at the summer palace, I will show you one or two." He again roared with laughter.

By the time they disembarked in the inlet in front of the sprawling Spanish hacienda at Mariveles, Marcos's speech was slurred and his feet shuffled. A crowd of servants met them, standing in lines on both sides of the dock and bowing their heads as the group walked toward the palace. Frank could hardly believe the respect Marcos commanded. Or demanded.

Inside, each was shown to his room, where their bags were already waiting on them. Frank felt a little nervous to see his gym bag sitting at the foot of his canopied bed, but when he opened it, it looked as if no one had tampered with it. He quickly changed and slipped into a fresh *barong tagalong* and returned to the main hall where the others soon joined him one-by-one. Marcos was the last to arrive, but he looked surprisingly fresh, and he spoke with well-enunciated words. "Gentlemen, the staff has prepared a feast, but before we eat, I have something to show you."

Frank fell in behind Krueger and Morgan, and Sten walked beside him. Marcos led them down a long hallway decorated with hand-painted Spanish tiles spaced at equal intervals. Huge terracotta vases filled with fresh flowers decorated the corridor. When they reached the end and turned the corner, Marcos removed a key from around his neck and opened a doorway. Frank glanced over his shoulder to see two armed palace guards behind him. He offered a weak smile, then turned to follow the group.

As Marcos led them down the stairs, Frank's stomach fluttered. He wanted to blame it on the liquor and the ocean waves, but he knew the feeling was reminiscent of his visit to the basement level of Malacañang Palace. He saw no black-painted hallways or doors, however, so by the time they reached the warmly-lit basement, his stomach calmed.

Marcos stopped in front of a set of inlaid-wood double doors, then turned to face them. "You cannot speak of what you've seen here, except among those present." He unlocked the doors and opened them wide.

"*Mon Dieu,*" Sten whispered.

Morgan was not so subtle, and his whistle reverberated off the stacks of gold bullion. "This is a whole damn football field of gold!"

Frank followed the troop inside the room where gold was stacked in similar formation to that in Malacañang Palace. Except this room was larger. Much, much larger. He looked above him, trying to estimate the length and width of the room, since he couldn't see its end because of the high stacks of bullion that nearly reached the ceiling.

Morgan ran his fingers along a row of gold bars, then turned to Marcos, his eyes wild. "May I?"

"Sure." Marcos offered an indulgent smile.

Morgan picked up a small bar, his hands sinking low as he hefted it. The bars were obviously heavier than they looked.

Morgan held the bar toward the light, turned it over and over in his hands, and then rubbed his fingers over the imprint.

Frank peered at the stamp; it looked like a Chinese marking, but he couldn't interpret the words.

"I can't believe all this gold." Krueger looked around in awe. "I'm seeing it, but I can't believe my eyes."

Morgan's face changed from one of wonder to one of suspicion. "Why is it here? On your property, I mean? Wouldn't it be safer in a bank? I mean, I've heard of stuffing money in your mattress, but this beats all."

Marcos didn't appear perturbed by the question. "If I were to inject even half the gold in the Philippines into the world market, the world's economic structure would crumble. This gold would be worthless."

Frank nodded. Marcos was right. The man was much smarter than Nixon had credited him.

Marcos touched his finger to the marking on the gold bar Morgan still held. "This is why I need your help. These markings make this gold traceable to the countries from which they were taken decades, perhaps even centuries ago. We have no way of knowing how long ago the Japanese stole this gold, or if the countries they stole it from had previously taken it from someone else."

"Then what's the problem?" Morgan asked.

"International law requires that any World War II treasure bearing identifiable marks be returned to the country of origin." He swept his arm around the room. "This is a small amount, compared to what is still buried in these islands. Unless you can help me alter the gold, it will all be forfeited." He locked eyes with Morgan. "Neither of us will have any of it."

"But these are national treasures!" Sten's fist tightened. "What you found is not only the property of other nations, it's part of that country's history. How can you ignore that fact?"

As Marcos stared at Sten Larsson, his eyes brimmed with curiosity. "You've seen the impoverished areas of my country, yes? You would have me deliver all this gold into the hands of a communist regime while my own people starve?" He shook his head in disgust. "No. I won't let that happen. This gold will be the salvation of my people."

Morgan looked from Marcos to Sten and back again. "I'll have to think about it. You both have good points."

On the cruise back to Malacañang Palace two days later, Morgan agreed to change the markings when he re-smelted the gold.

"I'd like to use my own refinery," Morgan said. "If you want me to alter the gold, I would prefer to re-smelt it myself."

"Can you bring the equipment here?" Marcos asked.

"Of course. It'll take a little time to tear it down, ship it here, then reassemble, but I'd be more comfortable that way. Plus, I've developed a way to remove more impurities so the gold will be of higher value."

Sten stood. "Mr. President, gentlemen, if you'll excuse me, I'm going to call it a night. It's been a whirlwind trip, and I'm exhausted."

"If you don't mind, I'll join him. Our festivities these past two days have taken their toll on me." Krueger chuckled. "Guess I'm getting old."

Marcos nodded and smiled. "I bid each of you a night of healthful rest."

Frank and Morgan said their goodnights to the two men as well, then turned back to Marcos.

Marcos smiled and lit a cigarette. He looked at Morgan. "Then you'll return to Nevada and ship your equipment here."

"Of course. That'll cost quite a bit of money, you understand."

Marcos's face turned stormy. "That is your problem, Mr. Morgan. I won't finance any part of these operations. As President of the Philippines, I cannot."

Morgan held up his hands. "Whoa, now. Wait a minute." He waved toward Frank. "You expect us to spend our own money to dig out the gold for you?" He snorted a laugh.

"That's exactly what I expect. If you spend your own money, then you're personally invested in the project. I'm not a fool, Mr. Morgan. I could pay to have your equipment shipped out here, I could throw money at the excavation crews, I could pay each of you to stand over the dig sites and watch the men like hawks. But since I can't personally be there, you could steal from me and I'd never know it." He shook his head. "No. I have never financed any of the recoveries, and I won't pay for these either."

"You mean General Ver and Colonel Villacrusis used their own money for the excavations?" Morgan's mouth continued to work after he'd finished speaking.

"That's what I mean, yes. And you see they were fairly compensated, which is why they are anxious to begin yet another project. Believe me, Morgan, there will be plenty of money to go around, and then some, once we have recovered even one tunnel of gold."

Marcos sat back and waved his hand around the stateroom. "Have I not treated you well? Have you not been on helicopter rides around the islands like tourists? Have you not partaken in the finest food and drink? Have your accommodations not been the most luxurious we have to offer?" A line creased the man's forehead and he held out his palms. "If you do not wish to participate, please, say so now, and we will not waste each other's time."

Frank heard the ticking in his ears again. *Say so now, and Ver will add your eyes to the little jar he keeps in the palace basement.* He shivered.

"I'm sorry, Mr. President. I didn't mean to upset you. When you put it that way, I understand. I'll handle my end of the bargain, don't worry. I can access the funds I need to move the equipment."

Frank breathed a tremulous sigh of relief.

Marcos sat back and pursed his lips. "Then it is settled. Now the only remaining problem is how to sell the gold."

Morgan looked at Frank and raised his eyebrows. He turned to Marcos. "I don't understand. Why is it a problem to sell it, once I've changed the markings? I thought that was the only problem."

Frank knew the answer to this one. "If too much gold comes out of the Philippines too soon, the Japanese, the Chinese, the Burmese, the Indians, the Americans—everyone will believe the so-called rumors of Yamashita's gold are true. The Japanese will want it back, and the Chinese will claim rightful ownership."

Marcos nodded with a satisfied smile, so Frank continued. "The Philippines could be caught in the middle of a tug-of-war between those two Asian powerhouses. With America still housing military bases here, things could quickly escalate into another world war."

Morgan's eyes widened. "Wow. I hadn't considered what we have at stake here."

"Frank is right," Marcos said. "Selling the gold must be done a little at a time, unless we can come up with a way to move it under a different pretense."

The three remained quiet a moment, studying the problem. Morgan leaned back. "What about oil?"

"What do you mean?" Marcos asked.

"Trade it for oil. The Arabs have too much oil, you have too much gold. Make a swap. Then you can sell the oil, and they can sell the gold, and no one will know any difference."

Frank stared at the man, realizing that, while he might be a snake, he was an intelligent snake.

Marcos clapped his hands. "An excellent idea. I'll start to work on that right away, so by the time you have re-smelted the gold and given it Philippine markings, I'll be ready to make the trade." He stroked his chin. "I'll set up a few more accounts in the U.S. and Europe in the meantime, so I'll have a place to keep the money."

"Why wouldn't you keep it here in the Philippines?" Frank asked.

"Yeah," Morgan said. "You should open your own bank. You could keep the gold and make loans, so you'd acquire even more money on interest."

"Spoken like a former banker, Gary." Marcos laughed. "I have no interest in banking. I'll leave that to others."

Still, Frank watched as the idea took root in Marcos's eyes, and he wondered how long it would be before Marcos established his own bank in the Philippines. He leaned forward to light another cigarette for the president. "So, what's next then?"

Marcos took a long drag from his cigarette, leaned his head back, and blew the smoke heavenward. "Next," he said and grinned at Frank, "we dig."

CHAPTER 35

June 2, 1975
Manila, The Philippines

Frank mopped sweat from his brow, again scolding himself for not getting up earlier to do his martial arts practice before the sun burned off the morning haze. His new bungalow offered the perfect place to work out between the main house and the small outdoor kitchen, where curious neighbors wouldn't stare while he practiced. *Well, most of them.*

"Good morning, Mista Young!" The stooped, balding woman called from across the low fence that separated their properties.

"Hello, Mrs. Yow. Pleasant morning, isn't it?"

"Always a pleasure, yes." She smiled broadly, proud of her few remaining teeth.

Mrs. Yow was hard of hearing, and most of their conversations ended in frustration for Frank, with Mrs. Yow smiling and nodding at any nonsensical thing he might say.

Frank threw up a hand and self-consciously tugged on his shirt despite the heat and went inside for a shower. As he entered the house, the phone rang. He hoped the afternoon trip to Teresa-2, the site where Marcos proposed they should dig, hadn't been cancelled.

"Franklin Young?" The man's gruff voice was distinctly American, and the echo on the line told Frank that was likely the origin of the call as well.

"Who is calling?"

The voice chuckled. "This is Robert F. Welch. You don't know me, but I received your name from a friend of yours."

Frank didn't like that the man automatically assumed he was the one speaking, nor did he like that someone had passed along his name and contact number without asking.

"Which friend?"

"*Ex*-President Richard Nixon. Your friend, not mine."

Frank held the phone out, ready to hang up, then thought better of it. "What do you want?"

"Nixon said you were the suspicious type. I don't mind that. If that son-of-a-bitch had been more suspicious, he wouldn't have ended up tossed out on his keister. Not that I mind. He lost me when he recognized Red China.

"Anyway, that's okay. He don't like me either. But sometimes business requires us to deal with people we don't like, isn't that right?"

Frank remained silent.

"Like you have to deal with all those damn flips. I'm sure if you had a choice, you'd be elsewhere. We've wasted more than enough money through that phony bunch in the U.N."

Frank gritted his teeth. Obviously, the man had no idea he was part-Filipino. "What do you want, Mr. Welch?"

"I want you to keep an eye on Gary Morgan. Morgan tells me you're buddies in the gold business over there."

Frank dug his nails into his palms, then winced. Why was Morgan talking about the gold to outsiders? Did Marcos know he had a loose-lipped metallurgist? "I know who Morgan is, yes."

Again the man chuckled. "I like you more and more," he said. "Let me put us on an even playing field; I'll tell you something about me, since I know something about you. Then maybe you'll feel like talking to me.

"I met Gary Morgan through some of my business associates. See, I'm the founder of the John Birch Society. We're a group of God-fearing, red-blooded American men who don't want to see our fair country fall into the hands of the Communists. In fact, that's the only thing I have in common with your friend Nixon. That's why we crossed paths.

"The John Birch Society also moves a lot of gold and silver. That's how I came to know Morgan. My associates and I have used Morgan's metal-refining skills for a while now. Morgan called us a while back, says he needs a loan. He's got some kind of treasure hunt going with you and some other guys in the Philippines, and he needs money to finance his part in the operation. That true? He needs more money to dig for treasure?"

"Mr. Welch, you should be asking Gary Morgan these questions."

"Uh-huh. I gave him the money. Morgan has quite a salvage operation here in the States, and if he doesn't pay me back in cash, I can take it out of his business. I'd rather not do that, see? Nixon trusts you, and Marcos trusts you, so I guess you can't be all bad. Now, I'm not asking you to do anything except keep an eye on Gary Morgan. He's in debt to me for about half a million already, and I expect he'll be wanting more before I see a dime from him. I just want you to call me if you see any funny business going on. Got it?"

"What makes you think I'd do that?"

"If you find all this gold Morgan says you're going to dig up, you'll need some place to put it, won't you? Just so happens, the John Birch Society has ways and means of sneaking gold into America without anyone knowing a thing. Been doing it for decades." He paused a moment. "Now you know how your buddy Nixon and I came to discuss you."

Frank grabbed the back of a chair and sat down hard. He leaned his head back and stared at the ceiling, gulping in deep breaths to remain calm. How far had the web of deceit been spun? He swallowed past the knot in his throat. "I'll keep an eye on him." *You can bet on it.*

Welch laughed. "I knew you would."

Later that evening, Frank stood at the Teresa-2 mining site with General Ver and Ben Valmores, studying the Golden Lily treasure map. Frank made sketches on a green engineer's pad, marking his interpretation of the map onto the page. "If what I'm interpreting is correct, Teresa-2 is only one level of a multi-tier tunnel. That means once we clear out this one, we can dig down to the others beneath it."

"Yes, yes. That's right," Ben said. "One level has the trucks, another has a gold Buddha and barrels with diamonds."

Frank furrowed his brow. "Trucks? What kind of trucks?"

Ben spread his arms wide. "Big trucks. Trucks that carried the dirt and rocks out of the burial sites. They filled the trucks with gold bars, then drove them into the tunnel, but they couldn't unload them and get them out, so they just let the air out of the tires and left them there."

"Why did they let the air out of the tires?" Ver asked.

"The weight of the truck would sink it into the ground down to the axles. But they didn't waste any extra room. They even emptied out the gas tanks and filled them with jade and emeralds and other gemstones."

Frank shook his head. "Unbelievable."

Ben smiled. "You can believe it."

Frank looked at Ver, surprised to see the man smiling as he shook his head. Then Ver's head snapped up. Frank turned, surprised to see the presidential convoy coming up the dusty road toward them.

Soldiers and the excavation crew stopped what they were doing and saluted as Marcos stepped out of car. Marcos returned the salute and waved, and the men returned to their duties. Frank squinted into the sun, cursing under his breath as Marcos walked toward them. He'd become so used to talking casually with the man that at times he nearly forgot to execute the formalities that were required of the president's subordinates while in public. One minor infraction that Ver considered disrespectful could get him thrown off the site, if not into jail. Martial law allowed Marcos to do anything he wanted to anyone, at any time. Frank couldn't risk forgetting that.

"Mr. President, it is a pleasure to have you here." Ver offered his hand.

"I wanted to see how you're progressing." Marcos shook hands with Frank and Ben. "Mr. Valmores, would you please excuse us for a moment?"

"Yes, Mr. President." Valmores bowed his head and avoided Marcos's eyes.

Marcos pursed his lips toward an area of scrub brush, and Frank and Ver accompanied him in that direction. When they were safely out of earshot of the other men, Marcos turned. "How close are we?"

Ver's icy eyes glittered in the setting sun. "Close, Mr. President. After repeating the measurements this afternoon, Frank has confirmed what Ben Valmores told us. Teresa-2 has multiple tiers. We should break through to the first in a matter of days."

"Excellent." Marcos smiled. "Morgan should be ready to start smelting as soon as the gold comes out of the tunnel. Once we've stamped it with our new seal, it'll be ready to move."

Frank glanced at Ver, whose face registered the confusion Frank felt. "Where are we moving it, sir?"

Marcos's smile grew. "That is what I came all the way out here to tell you. I've decided to open a bank."

A smile crept across Frank's face before he could stop it. "Congratulations, Mr. President."

"I'm thinking of opening a branch of Nugen Hand Bank here in Manila. Imelda has already acquired the building."

Frank knew the name well. "They're based in Sydney, Australia. Right, sir?"

Marcos beamed. "That's right, Frankie. Nugen Hand's Cayman bank has moved some gold for me in the past, so I trust them. If we get it opened, then we'll move the gold from the Manila branch into Nugen Hand's Australia branch in Sydney, which will give us a clean paper trail for clean gold. Otherwise, we will use the branch in Hong Kong. At the moment, I'm just waiting on the blessing from the United States to move forward with a branch here in the Philippines."

The CIA? That didn't make sense. "The U.S.? Why would you need the U.S. to give approval for you to open a branch of an Australian bank?"

Marcos stared hard at Frank. "I don't need their approval. I don't need anyone's approval, Mr. Young. I will get their *blessing.* William Colby is the new CIA Director in America. Colby encouraged Mr. Hand to extend his bank's reach into the Philippines. Michael Hand worked for Colby in the CIA before he got into banking." Marcos's frozen countenance melted as if a pleasant thought occurred to him. "In fact, I'm certain Mr. Colby hopes to wash some of his own money here in the Philippines, just like he launders it in Australia and the Caymans." He grinned.

William Colby. Frank's blood pressure pounded through his veins and sweat formed on the back of his neck. He straightened—imperceptibly, he hoped—creating a strong stance in case he needed to physically defend himself.

He looked around. There were at least twenty-five men at the dig site, a half-dozen or more in Marcos's convoy, and Marcos and Ver stood here by his side. Yet he'd never felt the enormity of his aloneness until now.

Santa Romana was right. He could trust no one.

Chapter 36

Frank opened the note and read it again. "Franklin Young: Use pay phone at U.S. Embassy. Call 001-702-555-0545."

Frank stared at the message. It was a U.S. number. Should he call? Or was it a prank? Or worse, a trap?

He glanced up at the U.S. flag, the stars and stripes flapping in the breeze, the cloudless cyan sky an apt backdrop to the Embassy. He checked his watch. Nine-ten a.m. Which meant it would be what? About nine p.m. on the East Coast, six p.m. on the West Coast. So, regardless of where he was calling, it would be a decent hour.

As had become his habit, he looked around him to see if anyone was following or watching. Would he ever be able to simply go about his business without worrying someone was out to get him? What a privilege few appreciated.

Let's do it. Frank took a deep breath and walked across the street, through the black posts that served as a not-very-subtle vehicle barrier, and to the glass doors of the white stone building. Once inside, he turned in a full circle, getting his bearings. He'd always jogged up the stairs to Tim Bozeman's office. But this time, he followed a hallway to his right. Just past the men's room, a set of pay phones waited. Frank went to the first, then glanced around. No. Too easy. He went back into the lobby and looked around. The women's room was to the left. And yes, sure enough, a pay phone was right outside. He went to it and dropped in coins. It took a while, but finally the phone rang.

"Yeah?"

Frank hesitated. What decent person answered his phone that way? "I have a message to call—"

"Young?"

"Yes."

"Glad you called. Gary Morgan here. Thought you might want to know what went down."

"I heard you'd left."

"Damn straight I left. Short version: the bastards planned to assassinate me, but they couldn't find the maps. I thought I'd give you the heads up. They're gone."

"Gone? What do you mean?"

"I destroyed the damn things."

Frank's mouth quit working. Finally, he stuttered, "The maps? The maps are gone?"

"Hell, yeah. If they found the maps, they'd have no reason to keep me alive."

"Why did you have—"

"Okay, let's just say I got my hands on the maps. Okay? Let's call it a life insurance policy. As long as they thought I had the maps, they had to keep me alive. So, I destroyed them."

"But why—"

"Just get out of there. Now. And sleep with a pistol under your pillow. Forever."

"But—"

The line went dead. Frank stared at it. Had Morgan hung up on him? Or had someone disconnected them?

His hands trembled as he hung up the receiver. More likely, his three minutes were up. Now what? His brain flashed through all the possible scenarios. No doubt Ver would be out to punish anyone and everyone he could associate with Morgan.

And then it hit him. His job here was over. He truly was no longer needed. Laughter squeezed through his chattering teeth. He was free! He could go home now. There was nothing more he could do.

He tested his wobbly legs before walking. Not sure they wouldn't still give out on him, he walked next to the wall, ready to grab hold. What should he do next? He blinked away thoughts of Rosalita. She'd have to wait. Next? See Bozeman. Frank was already at the Embassy, so all he had to do was go to Bozeman's office.

Third floor, second door. His legs protested the stairs, but he forced them up. By the time he reached the third floor, he could breathe.

Bozeman, of course, was not in his office. Frank sat and waited.

Two hours later, Bozeman walked in. "Frank? What are you—"

"Sit down and listen up." Frank had made good use of his wait by figuring out exactly what he needed. "There are no longer any maps. That jerk Morgan, Gary Morgan, burnt them. He said if anyone found them, Marcos would have him killed. So, he burnt them." Frank tossed the phone number on Bozeman's desk. "Call him yourself and ask him."

Bozeman glanced at the paper and looked back to Frank. "Go on."

"So my job here is done. If there are no maps, there's no reason for me to be here. So, I want to go home."

"Well, I, uh—"

"Listen up. I want you to pick up that phone, call President Ford, and tell him my mission here is complete. There are no maps to recover now." Frank leaned back in his chair.

Bozeman simply stared at him.

"Go on. Make the call."

"Hold on. Surely there are other copies. There must be."

"In Japan. Chichibu has them. But he died in 1957, so who knows where they ended up."

Bozeman's eyebrow raised.

"No. I'm not going to Japan. I'm going home. Make the call."

"But—"

"It's too dangerous for me in Japan. You know that. I've done everything I can do. I've done more than most people would do. Please, I want to go home. Make the call."

Bozeman nodded. "Okay, but it's almost midnight at the White House. I can't get through to the President right now."

Frank swallowed a curse. He exhaled loudly. "Okay. Tonight, you'll call?"

"Yes. I'll call tonight."

"And I need a plane out of here. First flight you can get for me." He thought again of Rosalita. "No, make that the second flight."

Bozeman picked up his pen and made some notes. "To Atlanta?"

"Yes. Please."

Bozeman wrote Frank's information on his notepad, then leaned back in his chair. "It's been nice working with you, Frank."

Frank stood. He hadn't expected this to be so easy. He started to say something, then shut his mouth. "Yes." He offered Bozeman his hand.

Bozeman also stood and shook Frank's extended hand. "Stop in tomorrow, and I'll have your flight info."

"Thank you." Frank backed out of the office, wondering if his luck had finally changed.

Chapter 37

September 6, 1975
Manila, The Philippines

Elation filled Frank's soul. He was done. He was going home, and he was staying home.

Rosalita. Frank pounded his fist on the steering wheel. He couldn't leave her behind. Not this time. He jaw set in determination, he swung around the block. Every parking place in the busy shopping district was filled. He drove up the street. He drove around the block. He drove down the street. Finally, a place opened in front of him. He zipped into it, then jogged the three blocks back to the GOLD AND GEMS store.

He glanced over the pre-made diamond rings. None had that special "something" he wanted.

"May I help you, sir?" The clerk wore a formal barong tagalog under an Italian silk suit.

"I need something special."

"Do you have an occasion in mind?"

"Engagement. To a very special woman."

The clerk eyed Frank, then nodded. "Follow me."

Frank followed him into a back room. Only one display case was in the room. The clerk turned on the light above the case. It held seven diamond rings, each well over two carats. The center one was a solitaire, simple, yet elegant. Classy. "I'll take that one."

"Would you like to have it resized now or later?"

"Later. Yes, later is fine."

"Cash or charge?"

Frank tossed his American Express on the counter, and within a few moments, he had the ring in his pocket and he was back in his car.

He didn't stop until he pulled in front of Rosalita's house. Her Mercedes waited next to a hibiscus tree with hand-sized fuchsia blossoms. He parked behind her, then broke off a flower on his way to her door.

Roses. He should've brought roses. Frank sighed. There was no time.

He straightened his jacket and rang the bell.

A few seconds later, Angeli, her housekeeper, pulled open the door. "Mr. Frank. Please come in."

Frank stepped into the foyer. "Is—"

"Frank!" Rosalita stood at the top of the staircase. "Why are you here?"

A smile escaped his lips and he ran up the stairs two at a time. "Come." He took her hand and led her to her bedroom, pulling the door after him.

"Frank, what are you—"

"Sit. Please sit."

Rosalita sat in the overstuffed chair with a rose brocade.

Frank fell onto his knees next to her. "I know this is fast and I know we haven't talked about it, but my job here is done and I'm returning back to the States and I don't want to go alone." He handed her the hibiscus he'd gripped.

"Frank, what—"

"Rosalita, I've loved you since the day I met you. I want you to be my wife. Will you marry me?"

While the words hung heavy in the air, he fumbled for the ring. The box was taped, and he groped to remove it. Finally, he freed the solitaire and pushed it under her nose. "Will you?"

Rosalita stared at the ring, then at Frank. "I, I, don't know."

Daggers thrust through Frank's heart.

She grabbed his face between her soft hands and pulled him closer. She kissed his forehead, then his nose. "You sweet man. You know I love you."

Hope chased out the daggers. "Then you'll marry me?"

"Frank. Dear, sweet Frank. Why are you asking me this so suddenly? Why can't we talk about it?"

"Rosalita, I am returning to the States, and I want you to come with me. As my wife." His shoulders sagged. "My job here is done and I'm flying home tomorrow. Please, come with me."

"Tomorrow? Have you lost your marbles?" Rosalita stood, knocking Frank back on his haunches. "You know I can't leave my mother for more than a few weeks."

"Bring her with us. Please."

"She isn't well. You know that." Rosalita shook her head. "No, Frank. I can't marry you. Not right now."

"But—"

"I can't leave the Philippines. This is my home. My country."

"But I love you."

Rosalita shook her head again, her dark curls flopping. "I love you, Frank, but I can't marry you. Not now."

The bedroom door opened. "Lita?" An older woman leaned into the room.

Rosalita jumped up. "Mama. I'll be right there."

"I heard voices. Is that colonel here again?"

"No, Mama. It's Frank."

"Oh." She turned and ambled down the hall, leaving the door ajar.

"Colonel?" Frank tried to quell the flame rising from his gut.

Rosalita shook her head, her curls bouncing. "She means Florentino Villacrusis."

"Villacrusis?" The flame erupted.

"It's nothing, really." Rosalita put her hands on Frank's shoulders, but he shook them away. "Frank, honest, it's nothing. Florentino has had a crush on me for years. Sometimes he comes over and brings me flowers."

"Villacrusis?"

"Frank! Stop it!" She held down his hands to quiet them, then lowered her voice. "Of course he hasn't touched me, and of course I want nothing to do with him. Stop acting like a jealous lover."

"That's all I'll ever be to you, isn't it? A jealous lover." Frank picked up the box the ring had come in, put the ring back in it, and shoved it in his pocket.

"Frank." Rosalita grabbed his biceps and pulled him closer to her. "I do love you. And yes, maybe someday, we can marry. But right now, I can't leave Mama. I can't leave the Philippines. There's no one I love more than you." She leaned in to kiss him, but he turned his head.

"I'm going back to the States," he said. "I won't be back this time."

Tears puddled in Rosalita's olive eyes. "Oh, Frank. I wish I could go with you. I do."

Frank shrugged. "Have a good life." He turned and hurried from the room.

⊁

Chapter 38

September 9, 1975
Atlanta, Georgia

Frank parked in the rear of the dojo and walked around. Landscaping had been added to the front entrance, and the windows were so clean they sparkled. He pushed open the door. The lobby was quiet, so he went on through the next set of doors. Activity bustled. New signs announced the dressing rooms and the classrooms. A juice bar had been added in a corner.

"May I help you?" a young man asked.

"No. Thanks." Frank continued to look around. He opened a door. A class was in progress. In the front, Lucky demonstrated a reverse spinning wheel kick, then turned. "Okay, let's do it." He glanced toward Frank and a grin erupted. "Bro!" He dashed to him and slapped his shoulder. "I thought you were half a world away. When did you get in?"

"You mean you didn't know?"

Lucky laughed. "No. Was someone supposed to tell me?"

"Seems like you always know what I'm doing."

Confusion flickered over Lucky's face. "Let me get Louie to take over here and we'll go talk."

"I'll wait upstairs."

Five minutes later, Lucky entered the living room of the apartment. "So what's going on?"

Frank opened his mouth to speak, then closed it.

"Frank? What's going on?"

"I thought you were my friend."

Lucky filled his lungs with air, then released it slowly. "I am your friend." He moved toward the sofa. "But it sounds like we need to talk. Sit down."

"I want to stand."

"Okay." Lucky leaned against the wall. "Can you tell me what's going on?"

Frank grunted. "I think it's you who needs to tell me what's going on."

"About what, Frank? You're being way too cryptic here."

"You know about what. About being with the CIA. About watching my every move. About pretending all these years to be my friend when you were really just keeping tabs on me."

"Uh-huh. No. You've got it all wrong."

"Then tell me what the hell is going on!"

Lucky took a deep breath. "Sit down, okay? It's a long story."

Frank shrugged and straddled a footstool.

Lucky dropped onto the sofa. He leaned forward, his elbows on his knees. "Your dad—your real dad—Danilo Quezon—and my dad—were both OSS. That was the international intelligence—"

"I know what it was."

"Okay. They were both OSS and they were very close friends. They had always promised each other that if anything happened, they would keep an eye on the other's kid. I knew nothing about that, of course, until it was time for me to go to college. Dad had kept his promise and knew that you were going to Duke, so he insisted I go there as well. I didn't know why he was so insistent, but I didn't have anywhere else that I particularly wanted to go, so I agreed. Dad arranged for us to be roommates."

"So our friendship was a farce right from the get-to."

"No! I had no idea that Dad had done anything. I didn't even know at that point that Dad was in the CIA. I thought he was a businessman who traveled a lot."

"So when did you find out? When did you start spying on me?"

"I never *spied* on you!"

"You told your dad things about me."

Lucky hung his head. "Yes. Only because your life was at stake." He shook his head. "Dad was furious when he found out Nixon had confiscated your passport and forced you into becoming an operative. He was in Vietnam at that time and didn't find out about it until you were already in the Philippines. He actually threw his ID at Bill Colby and walked out. Quit. I've never seen Dad lose his temper, but he told me he did that day. I was in Durham then, and he came to see me, and that's when he told me everything. He was worried sick about you and didn't know what to do about it, and he wanted my help in protecting you."

Frank drew in a deep breath. He had so much to think about. "So your dad is no longer CIA?"

"Yeah, he is. His spat with Colby didn't last long." Lucky stretched out his leg, then looked up and met Frank's eyes. "And you have no reason to be angry with me for withholding information."

"I sure as hell do."

"No. You don't." Lucky's dark eyes clouded. "You out and out lied to me about why you were in the Philippines."

Frank stared at his friend. "Yes, but I had to. I had no choice."

"Ditto, my friend. Ditto."

Frank stood and walked around the apartment. He stopped at the window and stared out at the traffic bustling up and down Roswell Road. He didn't have many friends. Life and circumstance had prevented him from getting close to many people. In fact, three days ago, there were only two people on the earth he counted as friends. Rosalita and Lucky. Now, there was only one. One who had stood by him and protected him, as only a true friend would.

Frank turned.

Lucky stood a few steps behind him, also looking out the window.

"I'm sorry," Frank said. "I shouldn't have doubted you."

Lucky's grin covered his face. "Hey, man, I'm just glad we could finally have this talk. I've waited for years to tell you."

Frank offered his hand and they shook, then Frank slapped Lucky's shoulder. "You got work to do, or can we go grab a drink?"

Lucky chuckled. "I think Louie can handle it. There's a new place just two doors down."

For the first time in a long time, Frank felt lighter. Free. Relaxed.

It was time to live his life dreams.

Chapter 39

November 20, 1976
Manila, The Philippines

Rosalita twirled her hair into a French twist and secured it with a comb.

"You aren't fooling me. You're going to call him, aren't you?" Imelda clicked her tongue. "Rosalita, dear, it isn't becoming to chase a man, even in America. Frank has made his position clear. He doesn't want to live in the Philippines, and you won't live in America, so why are you wasting your time? It's been well over a year, Sweetness. Come on. Go to Mass with me. You'll feel better."

Rosalita sighed and forced a smile. "You said I'd feel better after our shopping trip. Then you said I'd feel better after watching you sign the documents for your new hotel." She shook her head. "I don't think Mass is going to work, either."

"Nonsense. The sooner you stop mourning your relationship with Frank, the sooner you can move on with your life." She raised her hands in the air. "Go buy a big piece of property like I did. It will make you feel powerful and strong again."

"It doesn't work that way, Imelda."

"Sure it does. Why do you think I didn't put Ferdinand's name on the deed to the hotel? Having it in my name gives me power." She opened a tube of lipstick. "If you're going to be an old maid, Rosalita, the least you can do is be a powerful old maid." Imelda laughed and admired herself in the mirror as she freshened her make-up.

"But the hotel isn't in your name alone."

"Sure it is. I made General Gatan a limited partner, but he has no real ownership. The Webster Hotel in New York belongs solely to me."

"May I ask, if you don't mind, why you made him a partner? Wait. You don't have to answer that. I'm sorry. It's none of my business."

Imelda laughed. "I will answer. I've told you, wealth is power. Ferdinand is a powerful man, but I am a very powerful woman. What if something happened to my dear husband, God forbid? I could quickly be knocked from my pedestal, and then where would our poor Filipino people be? They need me to remain in power.

"General Romeo Gatan is a powerful man in his own political right. I told him that I awarded him with limited partnership for arresting Ninoy Aquino when Ferdinand declared martial law. Now General Gatan will feel beholden to me. If I exercise control over him in the business world, I can also easily control him in the political arena. He will be used to my power, and he will feel it his duty to support me in whatever I do, because I have honored him with this partnership."

Rosalita shivered. Sometimes Imelda frightened her. She thought of what might have happened if she'd turned over to her the photos she'd developed from Frank's camera all those years ago, like she'd been tempted to do. She'd promised Imelda she'd watch Frank, after all. Rosalita knew that Frank had no idea who he was messing with. She'd destroyed the photos, and she'd tried to stay away from Frank, excusing herself with busy work at the Cultural Center. But the longer she stayed away, the more she realized she loved him. Like now.

"That's why I encourage you to build your own wealth and assert your own power, Rosalita. Then if you want to marry a man, he will come to you on your terms. And if he cheats on you . . ." Imelda waved her hand as if shooing a pesky insect.

Rosalita nodded, although she wondered what Frank might be doing at this exact moment.

"Marriage is wonderful. But, understand, marriage is like the relationship between a ruler and his country. Sometimes she stays for love, sometimes she stays for money. Always, though, she knows all is never as it seems."

Imelda's voice brought Rosalita back to the present. "I understand." She smiled at her friend. "Go ahead to the church without me. I think I'm going to take a nap and perhaps I'll feel better. Wake me when you return, and we'll go out somewhere special for dinner tonight, okay?"

Imelda smiled. "Okay, then. Dinner it is." She pulled out her rosary—not the rosary she normally carried, but one with sparkling diamonds and large star sapphires—and started to tuck it into her purse.

"I've never seen that rosary before."

"This?" Imelda held up the strand of blue star sapphires, its brilliant diamond-studded cross swinging through the air. "It's lovely, isn't it?" She held it out to Rosalita. "I had it appraised at Van Cleef. They valued it a little over a quarter of a million dollars. It's something, isn't it?"

Rosalita lightly ran her fingertips over the chain of glowing star sapphires, over the diamonds embedded into the gold cross. "Yes, it is. Where did you find such an exquisite piece?"

Imelda reached for her treasure, then gave Rosalita a sly grin. "Let's just say I got it from Father Diaz many years ago."

"And you've had it all these years?"

"Yes, all these years. It's nice to have something to remember him by." Imelda stepped to the door. "See you in a bit, my friend."

Rosalita waited for Imelda to leave, then stretched across her bed. She had been wrong to turn down Frank's proposal. Wrong, wrong, wrong. But how could she fix things now?

CHAPTER 40

November 22, 1976
Roswell, Georgia

Thirty-seven years old. Frank shook his head. Hard to believe. He'd expected that by the time he was this old, he'd be married and have a couple of kids. But at least he and Lucky had the dojo, and that was one dream that made getting out of bed every morning a joy.

The waiter stopped at the table. "We must have cake," Mary Catherine said. She waved toward Frank and Lucky. "Everyone. It's Frankie's birthday."

"I don't want cake," Frank insisted.

Lucky shook his head as well, but said nothing.

"We will have cake." Mary Catherine looked at the waiter. "I'll have that death by chocolate one. Frank will have carrot cake. And Lucky—oh, that's right. White. Just plain white." She wrinkled her nose.

Frank threw his hands in the air. Trying to tell his mother anything was as productive as talking to a door.

A firm hand clamped down on Frank's shoulder from behind.

"Why, General!" Mary Catherine's face became animated. "Thank you for coming!"

Frank turned to see a stocky man wearing a dark, three-piece suit. The man extended his hand to Frank. "You know your mother is one special lady!"

Frank stood and shook the man's hand. Though he tried, he couldn't remember ever seeing him before, much less meeting him. "Thank you, sir."

"Erle Cocke."

"General Cocke was a friend of your father's, Frank," Mary Catherine said.

Frank immediately thought of Danilo, and wondered how the two knew each other.

"Yes, I was a firm backer of your father when he ran for mayor. Would have loved to see him in a higher office, God rest his soul."

He meant Richard, not Danilo. Frank's smile felt tight.

"Mary Catherine, my dear, you look beautiful." Cocke rounded the table and kissed her on both cheeks.

"General, this is Frank's friend and college roommate, Lucky."

Lucky stood and shook hands with the general. "Pleased to meet you, sir."

"I'll let you all enjoy your dinner." Cocke motioned toward Frank. "Frank, if you have a moment, I'd like a word before you leave."

"Of course, sir." Frank waited until General Cocke had walked away, then sat back down. Lucky did the same.

Mary Catherine's eyes grew round. "Oooh, I wonder what he wants? Maybe he'd like to help you get started in your father's footsteps. He's a very powerful man, Frankie. He was a big help to your father."

Richard was not *my father.* Frank took a deep breath and forced a smile.

After the waiter brought out the dessert tray, Frank excused himself and found General Cocke sitting on a corner bar stool.

"Get you a drink, Frank?" He turned to the bartender. "Whatever he's drinking, make it a double." The general pushed out the stool next to his with his foot.

"Thank you, sir." Frank nodded to the bartender, then turned to the General. "You wanted to see me, sir?"

The man leveled his hardened eyes at Frank. "I don't play around, Franklin Young, so I'm going to lay it out for you. I had a lot of respect for your father, which is why I'm coming to you. I understand you've worked with Lansdale and Casey."

Frank remained silent and watched Cocke's eyes.

"Doesn't matter how I know. I'm a General. I have a right to know things. What I also know is that you've worked in the Philippines on a gold recovery assignment for the CIA." He stared at Frank, his eyes steel.

Frank didn't blink.

"I don't want to know the particulars. I don't give a damn about the particulars. What I want is for some of that money from the gold to be stashed in my bank. I've got a Nugen Hand branch in D.C. I know Marcos wants his own branch of Nugen Hand in Manila. We are not going to let that happen, despite what he says or thinks. He's getting a little big for his britches, and he's about to find out who is really running things. He's sending gold to Switzerland, Australia, all over the damn planet. You're an American, boy. You were raised in this country. Now I don't care who your real pappy was, Richard raised you. Your loyalty lies here."

He took a huge gulp from his drink, then turned on his stool and leaned his face close to Frank's. "I'd die for this country in a heartbeat. I got the bullet holes in my body to prove that, but I'm not asking that of you. I'm just asking you to do what you can to make sure some of that gold ends up in my bank. Understand?"

Frank kept his face placid. "I understand. If I have an opportunity to do that, I will. But you must understand, sir, that I no longer work in the Philippines. I'm in the States. To stay. My partner Lucky and I have a dojo."

The General's eyes narrowed and his face darkened.

Frank clenched his jaw. He'd had enough. He couldn't get away from the cursed gold and the danger that surrounded it, no matter where he went. "General, I still have contacts in the Philippines. I'll make a few phone calls, recommend your bank. I'm sure you can help them with the paperwork, yes?"

The General eased back on his stool and smiled. "Of course. You can tell your friends their transactions will be clean as a whistle." Cocke extended his hand.

Frank looked at the man's hand, turned, and walked away.

CHAPTER 41

January 23, 1977
Atlanta, Georgia

"Hey, Frank!"

Frank gave the washer one more turn, then climbed out from underneath the sink, wiping the sweat from his eyes. "Yeah?"

"You got a phone call."

Frank sighed. "Okay. Put it through to the office." He washed his hands, dried them, then went around the corner to the office he shared with Lucky.

Lucky sat at the desk, writing out checks. Frank grabbed the phone and plopped onto the corner of the desk. "Frank Young."

"Hold one minute for Stansfield Turner, please."

"Oh, shit!"

Lucky looked up. "Mary Cat okay?"

"Yeah. I'm holding for the Director of the CIA." His stomach knotted. Absolutely not. He refused to return to the Philippines, no matter what they tried to tell him.

"Mr. Young?" The distinguished voice of Stansfield Turner came clearly across the line.

Frank stood. "Yes, sir?"

"I wanted to thank you for your service to the United States of America."

"You're welcome, sir."

"I don't think you're aware of how much you've actually done. But suffice to say, because of your work, we can all rest a bit more secure at night."

"Thank you, sir."

"I do have a question for you."

"Yes, sir?"

"You reported four locations where recovered gold was stored. The two palaces, the mansion, and the bunker behind the palace, right?"

"Yes, sir."

"You reported there were one hundred seventy-five burial sites filled with gold, and that maps of those burial sites were held by a Mr. Gary Morgan of Nevada."

"Yes, sir. Mr. Morgan told me he destroyed the maps."

"And then you concluded that your job there was finished?"

Frank's stomach somersaulted. For more than four years, he'd enjoyed being in the States. Enjoyed working with Lucky. Enjoyed finally running his own dojo. "Yes, sir."

"Mr. Young, Fabian Ver continues to lead successful gold recovery teams, and he's getting the information on where to dig from someone. I need you to go back to the Philippines and do one simple thing."

Every fiber of Frank's being screamed *just say no*. But instead, "What's that, sir?" dropped out of his mouth.

"Watch Fabian Ver. From a distance, of course. Just watch him and report where he is digging. Could you do that for me?"

Frank's stomach rumbled and he feared he'd be sick.

"Say *no*," Lucky whispered.

"I'm sorry, sir," Frank said. "I can't return to the Philippines. I'm sorry."

"We will make it worth your while."

"No. I cannot go."

"I understand. Thank you for your prior service." The phone clicked in his hand.

Frank finally exhaled. "Holy crap."

Lucky chuckled. "Once the government gets a hold of you, they never let you go."

"I said *no*. You heard me. I said *no*."

"I heard you. The question is, did Mr. Turner?"

Chapter 42

March 2, 1976
Atlanta, Georgia

"Ah, Frankie, we need to talk." Lucky dropped down into the visitor's chair of their shared office.

Frank looked up. "I was just going over the books. Looks like we had another record month." His smile froze before it formed. Lucky's normal grin was supplanted by worry wrinkles across his brow.

"It is going great."

"But . . . ?"

"Dad wants me to go with him on a humanitarian mission to Vietnam. Now that things are finally settling down over there, help them rebuild."

Frank studied his friend. He was full-bloodied Vietnamese, even though he'd been born in the Philippines and was an American citizen. "I can see that. How long will you be gone?"

"That's the thing."

"Yeah?"

"I may be there a while."

"Like a month? Two months? What are we talking about?"

"A year. Maybe longer." Lucky played with the stapler. "Probably longer."

"Oh, Lucky!"

"I'll be back once in a while to visit. I promise."

Frank nodded. There was no one in the world he felt closer to than Lucky. No one. No one he trusted more. He swallowed hard. "Sounds like we'd better go out check out that new disco down the road."

Lucky smiled. "Yeah. We better. Who know? By the time I get back, disco might be history."

Frank bit his lip. Sometimes, he wished he could control history—control time. Slow it down. Savor it more. Enjoy the good things when they happened. Because the good times rarely lasted long enough.

Chapter 43

June 12, 1980
Manila, The Philippines

"Rosalita?"

Rosalita's breath caught. It was Frank. She'd know his voice anywhere. She held the telephone closer to her ear. "Frank? What's the matter?"

"Mother." His voice rasped with pain. "Mom just died."

Rosalita sank on a nearby chair, her legs too weak to hold her upright. "Oh, Frank. I'm so sorry. When?"

"Just now. It just happened. I came downstairs and found her here, in her chair. I thought she was sleeping." Confusion and incredulity were evident in his voice. At least, to someone who knew him so well.

Rivulets coursed down Rosalita's cheeks. "What can I do?"

"I've already called an ambulance. And Lucky. I tried to call Lucky. I haven't been able to get through." Frank's thick voice broke Rosalita's heart.

"I'll be there right away."

"You don't have to do that." Frank sniffed.

"I know, but I want to. I need to be there for you, Frank."

"I probably shouldn't have called. I just didn't . . . I couldn't get Lucky . . . there was no one to call."

"Then I'll come. I'll leave right away." Rosalita wiped her cheeks, straightened her spine. "That is, unless you don't want me there." The long pause on the other end of the line caused fresh rivulets to course down her face.

"If it's not too much trouble . . . ."

▲

The next evening, Rosalita held Frank as his body collapsed into her arms. When she'd calmed him enough to talk, he explained that Mary Catherine had been well until the night before her death, when she said she felt too tired to climb the stairs to bed. She wanted to rest in her chair and watch television. Frank acquiesced, then found her the next morning.

"I could use your help with her things." Frank swallowed hard. "Ladies things, you know. Can you pick out an outfit for her to wear in the . . . for the . . . to her funeral?"

"Of course, Frank." Rosalita forced a smile and rubbed her thumb across his cheek, wiping away the moisture there. "I think Mary Catherine and I could both agree that your taste in ladies' clothing is questionable at best."

A relieved laugh broke from Frank's chest and he smiled. "Thank you, Rosalita. I'm sure Mom would appreciate your help."

"Run along then. You still have a few phone calls to make. I'll be up here if you need me." She kissed Frank on the cheek, but he turned and pulled her into his arms. He kissed her deeply on the mouth with all the passion and need his grief demanded.

She held him until he finally straightened. He said nothing. He simply turned and walked out.

She understood. There was nothing words could convey.

Rosalita sighed. She opened Mary Catherine's closet and pulled a leather tote from the rack. She pulled out several dresses, holding them up in front of the mirror. Mary Catherine looked smashing in emerald green. Even at her age, her auburn hair remained dyed to its youthful shade. Her eyes, once a sparkling green, had aged to a mellower but even more intriguing turquoise color.

The only choice was the satin emerald dress.

She placed the dress on the bed. And there, lying casually draped across the mirrored tray on the nightstand, was a rosary. A sapphire rosary.

Rosalita scooped it from the tray, carried it to the window and opened the shade. The jewels were real. It looked so familiar to her. Had she seen Mary

Catherine with it? She admired the artisanship, turning it over in her hand. There, on the back of the cross, was an inscription. Rosalita held the cross up to the window, peering closely at the curly words inscribed into the gold. The words were miniscule. She'd need a magnifying glass.

Rosalita peered out into the hallway and listened carefully until she heard Frank's muffled voice on the phone below. She returned to Mary Catherine's room and rummaged through the drawers of her bedside. Surely a woman of Mary Catherine's age used a magnifying glass sometimes, right?

No such luck.

Rosalita pawed through the drawer, her fingers finally latching onto a pair of reading glasses. They'd have to do. She snatched up the eyeglasses and returned to the window. Rosalita hovered the eyeglasses lens about an inch over the cross's inscription, raising and lowering them until the miniscule words came into focus. *"From Father My Old Man."*

Rosalita shook her head. What did that mean? She examined the rosary more carefully. All the beads were the same—star sapphires—except for one gold bead that joined the circle and led to the chain that ended with the cross. She examined the gold bead. Inscribed on it was the Greek letter symbolizing *Alpha.*

And then she realized where she'd seen it before. Imelda. Imelda had an identical rosary. What were the odds of that? Especially a rosary so unique— and so expensive.

Where would Mary Catherine have gotten such a rosary? Imelda said she'd gotten hers from Father Diaz.

She looked again at the words engraved. Did Imelda's cross hold a similar inscription? There certainly couldn't be too many rosaries like this floating around.

Rosalita's hands dropped by her side, then she quickly looked at the inscription again. There was no way around it; she'd have to compare the two rosaries. She dropped the rosary into her pocket.

Rosalita scurried down the hallway to the guest bedroom and opened her own travel case, hid the rosary in a pair of stockings, and closed the lid.

Frank opened his mother's nightstand drawer and again searched through the contents. The rosary wasn't there. He turned in a full circle. What had he missed? Could there be a false bottom in a dresser drawer? A short back? He opened each drawer, ran his hand over silky undergarments. Nothing.

"What are you looking for?" Rosalita stood in the doorway.

"Mother's rosary. Did you see it when you were selecting her dress?"

Rosalita pursed her lips as though thinking. "I don't think so. What did it look like?"

"The one she always carried. It had star sapphires and a gold cross with diamonds."

Frank's brow furrowed. "I can't find it."

Rosalita put her arms around him. "We'll find it."

"I just hope no one stole it." He pulled back from her and searched her eyes. "Rosalita, I must find that rosary."

"Maybe it was insured?"

Frank shrugged. "There's no way it could be insured for what it was worth."

Rosalita's eyes widened. "What was it worth?"

"I don't know. I just know I must find it."

Rosalita squeezed his arm. "It will show up." She leaned forward and kissed his cheek. "I'm sure of it."

Chapter 44

Frank took the phone from his ear, stared at it as if it were a foreign object, then held the receiver to his head again. "Tao, you know I don't want back in this again. I've made it perfectly clear, as long as Ferdinand Marcos is in power, I have absolutely no desire to return to the Philippines."

"Please, Frank. Just hear me out."

Frank sighed. "I'll listen, but I'm not going to change my mind."

"I'd never ask you to do this, except—"

"Except what?"

"It's Lucky."

"Lucky? What about him? What's he got to do with me coming to Washington or going to the Philippines?"

A long pause answered Frank. Finally, Tao spoke. "I think he's in trouble."

Broken shards of ice coursed through Frank's veins. "What kind of trouble?"

"I'm not certain." Tao heaved a long sigh. "When you didn't want to go back to the Philippines, Lucky asked to go."

"What? He said he was working with a humanitarian organization in Vietnam."

"That's what he wanted you to think. The truth is, we needed someone inside the Philippines Someone reporting directly to us. We set him up in a role to simply monitor Ver's digging operations."

"So Lucky went to the Philippines in my place? Because I wouldn't go?"

"Exactly."

"Damn it, Tao! Why did you let him do that? You know what it's like over there. Marcos's men are ruthless killers. I've seen them murder."

"We knew the danger of the operation. That's why we only had him monitoring Ver. Anyway, Lucky is due to land in Washington shortly. But he wants to meet with you and me and President Reagan and William Casey. And no one else. What he has to tell us can't be shared with anyone else."

And you're telling me this over the phone? But surely he was no longer being watched.

Frank chewed his lip. The last thing he wanted was to get involved in the gold saga again. But Lucky was his best friend. He'd watched his back for decades. Even when Frank had been blissfully unaware. And now, Lucky had gone to the Philippines because he wouldn't go. *Damn him.*

Frank sucked in his breath. "When do I need to leave?"

"There's a plane waiting on you at DeKalb. The sooner you can get there, the sooner you can get here."

Frank checked his watch. "I can be at the airport in less than two hours. Will that work?"

"It has to. But please, hurry."

Frank threw a change of clothes in the satchel Rosalita had given him for Christmas one year. Though the two of them talked on a regular basis now, his reluctance to return to the Philippines still stood like a stone wall between them. She refused to move to the States. He refused to go there. *That might be changing.* A rock settled in the pit of his stomach.

Frank notified Caretta, his mother's housekeeper, that he'd be gone for a few days, but he'd call her as soon as he knew his plans for certain.

As he stood by the door waiting for his cab, the phone rang again. Thinking it might be Tao calling back, he grabbed it.

"Frank? Lucky."

"Lucky, what the hell have you done? Your father just called and—"

"Not now, Frank. I think I'm being tailed."

"What? But you just landed, right?"

"I flew commercial. Stupid, I know, but I had to get out of there as quickly as possible. Listen, I need you to meet me before we go to the White House. I have something important I need to tell you. Something the others can't hear involving the CIA."

Frank gritted his teeth. "Where?"

"How about Bob and Edith's Diner in Arlington? It's on the way in from National."

"I know that place. Used to be a donut shop. But, Lucky, I'm flying out of DeKalb. I'm sure they'll have a car waiting for me in D.C."

"I've already talked with Dad. He'll arrange for a private car for you. This won't take long; then we'll each arrive separately for the meeting. There's no other way."

⚔

Frank arrived in D.C. to find a car waiting as promised. He took the keys from the officer's hand and drove off the lot. With only an hour before his meeting at the White House, Frank squealed tires as he turned corners at breakneck speed in the pouring rain. He arrived at the diner, parked, and entered.

As Lucky had instructed, he found a back booth away from the windows. Frank slid in, and the waitress appeared with a menu. Frank waved it away and ordered a cup of coffee. Fifteen minutes or so later when she came to offer a refill, Frank checked his watch. *Where is Lucky?* He should have arrived ten minutes earlier. At this rate, he wouldn't have time to utter more than a sentence before they'd have to race off to the White House. *Five more minutes, then I'm out of here.*

Lucky didn't show. Maybe he really was being followed, Frank reasoned, so he decided to go straight to the White House where he'd have more protection.

At the White House, Frank was ushered by Secret Service past the hallway to the Oval Office toward the President's own private living area. "No recorders allowed in this wing," the agent explained. The man led him to a door, knocked twice, and another agent opened it from the other side. He waved Frank inside, then stepped out and closed the door behind him.

He stood face-to-face with Tao. Tao stuck out his hand offering a warm handshake. Even though this was the first time Frank remembered seeing Tao, his face seemed somewhat familiar. And it wasn't only because of the resemblance to Lucky.

"Mr. President," Tao said, looking at Reagan. "I'd like you to meet Franklin Young. He's done a fine job for us in the Philippines for many years."

The President leaned across his wide desk, offering his hand. Frank met him half way, and was soon surprised at the firmness of the President's shake. "Good to meet you, son." Reagan nodded toward the other stranger in the room. "I don't think you've met our new CIA Director, William Casey."

"Thank you for coming, Mr. Young. I know this is short notice, but I believe this is an urgent matter," Colby said.

President Reagan motioned toward a comfortable-looking arrangement of overstuffed chairs. "Have a seat."

Frank glanced around the room, then settled into a chair and propped his foot on his knee. He'd long since grown past hero-worship of world leaders. These men were no better than he, and he no longer allowed himself to feel nervous around them.

"I understand you earned the trust of President Marcos, which isn't an easy task." Reagan chuckled. "I would know. Ferdinand and I have come to be good friends, though that wasn't always the case. Even so, I realize the man must be treated with kid gloves. He is determined to be the most powerful man in the world, and I sincerely believe he will stop at nothing to reach that goal."

Frank scowled. "No doubt in my mind."

Reagan scanned Frank up and down as if to appraise his net worth. Then, he looked at Casey and raised his eyebrows. "That's why we need him over there, Bill. That's why Frank is the man for the job."

Frank's stomach somersaulted. "And what job is that?" His fists tightened. "Everyone knows Marcos has found the gold. He's been funneling it into CIA coffers for a decade or more. He's stuffed it into American banks, where it's laundered and washed as clean as white linen. Hell, he's padded the pockets of a few American presidents with it." He leveled his gaze at Reagan. "No offense to you in particular, sir."

Reagan smiled. "None taken. What you've said is true. American democracy would fly out the window without money from the Filipino digs being funneled into the CIA. Unfortunately, when Jimmy Carter and Stansfield Turner took the reins, they cut back on our manpower and set up a bunch of spy satellites out there in space. But unfortunately, satellites don't have any common sense and they don't know when to follow a lead." He turned his direct glare back onto Frank. "We need someone like you over there to keep an eye on which digs are opened, so we can make sure we're getting our share of that gold. We want Marcos to store as much of it as possible here in the U.S. If it's in Australia or Great Britain or the Caribbean or wherever, we have no control over whose hands it falls into. That gold is the only way we can fund the cold war and support star wars."

Frank wondered if he should nod or respond, but since no one else did, he didn't either.

"You think getting those hostages out of Iran came without a price tag? That kind of thing costs money, Frank. Carter wasn't willing to spend it, but I am. If Ferdinand has all the money, then he pulls all the strings."

Frank mulled over the man's words. "But if you're good friends with him, why can't you simply request that he send us the money he owes? You trust him, right?"

Reagan laughed an easy laugh; he'd brought his movie-star personality with him to the White House. "I'll level with you, Frank, because I believe the only way you can go back in there is if you know what you're playing for."

"And what, exactly, am I playing for, Mr. President?"

Reagan looked at Tao, then at Casey. "I want Ferdinand Marcos out of the Philippines."

Frank's mind drifted. Where was Lucky? He should have been there a long time ago. Frank snapped back in focus and felt his jaw grow slack, and he wondered if he'd heard the man correctly. "You want Marcos out?"

Reagan smiled. "Not hardly the thing you expected to hear, is it?"

"No, sir, it isn't. So, you want me to coerce him to step down, is that it? Surely you don't think—"

"Marcos could never be coerced into stepping down. Not even by force; that's how men get killed. That's why he instituted martial law. No, that won't work with Ferdinand." He leaned back in his chair and stared into Frank's eyes, his face animated. "But we have something he wants here in America. Something the Philippines can never offer him."

Frank raised an eyebrow.

"Freedom. He wants freedom. After all he's done, many of his own people hate him. Coercion, after all, merely captures a man. Freedom captivates him."

Frank pursed his lips. It was true. Marcos couldn't walk out his door without a small army of guards, and neither could Imelda. But here in the U.S., the two walked the streets of New York City with merely one or two plainclothes bodyguards. Rosalita said Imelda reveled in it.

"How do you plan to offer him this freedom, sir?"

Reagan smiled. "Oh, we can't just offer it to him. He has to ask us for it." His smile turned into an old-fashioned grin. "This can't be an overnight operation, you see. Marcos has set himself up to go to the grave a century from now as president of the Philippines. He's too powerful to be ousted right now. If he could, Aquino would have already done it." He held out a palm. "Besides, we need to make sure we get as much of that gold as possible out of the country *before* Marcos steps down. He has the means to recover it; the next president may not."

Frank nodded. It made sense.

"That's where you come in. We want you to find out how much is left, and where it's located. We believe Marcos has cleaned out at least a dozen of those sites. Maybe more. We still don't know for sure if Marcos holds any of the maps or if that Morgan really did burn them. But if we know where all the gold is, the maps become less significant." He shrugged. "No matter what happened to the maps."

"Gary Morgan told me he burnt them, but there are photos of them."

A knock at the door interrupted them. Reagan nodded to Tao. "That must be your son."

Tao opened the door. A Secret Service agent entered and crossed to Reagan, who held up a finger to Frank. "Excuse me, please." He turned his head and the man whispered in his ear. Reagan grimaced and pulled back. "You're certain?"

The man whispered again, then looked at Tao, then Frank, nodded respectfully and left the room.

President Reagan stood and walked over to Tao. "Sir, please step out into the hallway with me."

After a moment, Reagan returned to the room without Tao. His ruddy face was redder than normal and seemed to crumble as he spoke. "There's been an accident. Mr. Nguyen's son has been killed."

Chapter 45

February 14, 1981
Manila, The Philippines

Frank hadn't expected the limousine that awaited him when he landed in Manila, but he didn't turn it down, especially in this chilly weather. The driver opened the back door and Frank slid inside. Rosalita was seductively arranged across the U-shaped seat, her body swathed in a sea of red silk.

"Happy Valentine's Day, Frankie." She smiled, and her ruby lips begged for his kiss without uttering a word. "Surprised?"

He was. Too surprised for words. After his mother's funeral, they'd had another heart-to-heart with the same impasse—she refused to live in the States and he refused to—nevermind. He was here. He leaned over and kissed her forehead, but she grabbed him and kissed him full on his lips. The limo grew uncomfortably warm.

If it affected Rosalita the same way, she kept it hidden. "Champagne?" She lifted a bottle from a bucket of ice.

"What are we celebrating?"

She tilted her head to one side. "Your return to Manila, of course." She smiled. "I've only been begging you to come for ages." She traced a finger down his arm. "I guess this means you missed me?"

Hoping to convey the sincerity of his words, Frank locked eyes with Rosalita. "With every breath I've taken." He slid his hand into her hair, pulled her toward him and kissed her tenderly at first, then with more fervor. "You know," he said when he finally pulled away, "you could have come to me in the States just as easily."

Rosalita smiled. "I know."

"There's something—I have some bad news, Rosalita."

"What is it? Oh, don't tell me you're not going to stay this time. Tell me this isn't a whirlwind trip, please."

Frank shook his head. "No, that's not it. I'll be here for a while. At least for as long as Triangle Tobacco will keep me here."

"Even then you can find other work here in the Philippines. Ferdinand could put you in charge of his tobacco importing. He likes you, Frank."

Frank prayed that was true, but he knew in his heart that Marcos trusted no one. And for good reason.

"What is it? What's the bad news?"

"My best friend was killed."

Rosalita's mouth formed a perfect O. "When? What happened? Oh, Frank. I'm so sorry. I wish you'd called me."

Frank shook his head and stared at the bubbles escaping the confines of the champagne. "His family only held a small ceremony. He was killed in an automobile accident. Ran off the road and into a concrete wall."

"How did that happen? Please tell me he wasn't drinking."

Frank jerked up his head. "Of course not." He realized he'd snapped, and gingerly touched Rosalita's hand. "It was raining. It happened near nightfall. He probably just lost control of his vehicle." *With a little help from the people chasing him.*

Frank wanted so much to confide in Rosalita. He wanted to tell her he thought General Ver had been behind Lucky's death. He wanted to tell her everything. He wanted to ask her if she'd taken his notes and the film from his camera. He wanted to ask her how much money she'd given Villacrusis. He wanted to know whose side she was on.

"I'm sorry, baby." Frank looked up, surprised to see Rosalita's eyes welling. God, how he'd missed her. Frank grabbed a breath and held it. His mother was dead. And now Lucky.

He swept her into his arms and buried his face in her luscious hair. Trustworthy or not, she was all he had.

Chapter 46

May 10, 1982
Mariveles, The Philippines

Frank stood on the deck of Marcos's presidential yacht, remembering the last time he'd been there. He squinted into the morning sun and pushed the thought aside.

"I wonder what's keeping him?" President Marcos checked the gold Rolex on his wrist. He smiled at Frank. "Just like the CIA to be late, yes?"

Frank returned the smile and offered Marcos a cigarette. "I think you're wise to do this, Ferdinand. This will go a long way toward proving your dedication to democracy."

Marcos took a long drag from the cigarette, then blew smoke over his shoulder. "Ronnie Reagan and his wife have been our friends for many, many years. I have nothing to prove to him." He looked again into the horizon. "I'm doing this to make sure the CIA trusts their president. I'm doing this for Ronnie." He stabbed the air with his cigarette as he talked. "The U.S. Government is nothing like the Philippine Government. The CIA gained too much control when Nixon was in office. They believe they run the show, and in some ways, they do. Ronnie will take back some of that control. Showing the CIA I have the gold Ronnie says I have will prove his trust in me is warranted. It will earn their respect."

Frank nodded, tried not to frown.

Marcos turned as Ver's car pulled up. "Here they are. Finally." He walked toward the ramp, and Frank followed.

A man emerged from the passenger side of Ver's car and turned to face them with a smile. Frank's mouth flew open, but he quickly closed it. *Tao!*

Tao had come to the site with the man who was likely responsible for the death of his son. *How could he contain his emotions?* "Frank," Marcos said, "I'd like you to meet my friend from the American CIA, Nguyen Tao." He turned to Tao. "This is my associate, Frank Young. Mr. Young keeps a residence in the U.S., in Georgia, as well."

Tao handled the introduction without any sign of recognition, and the men boarded the yacht and headed to sea. When they reached the summer palace, Marcos didn't invite them inside as he had the last time. Instead, he had a car waiting, and Ver drove them around back of the palace, where a small villa had been erected since Frank's last visit.

Inside, the vestibule reminded Frank of an entrance to a church sanctuary, complete with red carpeting, huge flower arrangements and gold candelabras. To the right were elevator doors. Marcos inserted a key and the doors opened. "Gentlemen." Tao and Frank stepped inside.

There were no floor numbers, but Frank counted the scraping sound the elevator made as it passed a floor and guessed they'd dropped four floors underground. When the doors opened, they were in a short hall similar to the one at ground level; same carpeting, same floral décor, but minus the candles. Across the way was a set of steel doors. Marcos unlocked these doors as well. They stood in the hallway and looked in. *Gold.* Gold everywhere. Floor to ceiling, left to right. A chill raced across Frank's scalp as he stared at the tunnel that seemingly had no end. For as far as he could see, larger than what he'd seen in either of the palaces, were stacks of gold bars. The ends of the bars nearest Frank were stamped with the letters *AAA*. Others in the stacks across from those bore Chinese symbols.

Tao clasped his hands behind his back. "How much is here?" The man's calm demeanor was as impressive as the quantity of gold.

Marcos smiled. "That's hard to say. My secretary has inventoried the contents of this tunnel, but since this is not the only storage of gold, I don't recall the amount this particular facility holds."

Still, Tao didn't appear overwhelmed.

"This tunnel is *huge*," Frank said. "How long is it? I can barely see the end."

Finally, Marcos had the praise he wanted, and he grinned. "Ninety meters long."

"Ninety meters! That's about a hundred and twenty yards. More than the length of a football field."

"That is correct." Marcos turned to Tao. "So you see, I have possession of what I have claimed. You can now report back to Director Casey and President Reagan that I am an honest man."

Tao nodded. "Of course, Mr. President. I will assure them you are a man of your word."

Frank noticed that Tao didn't agree that Marcos was honest. Tao likely believed, as he did, that Marcos, through Ver, had ordered the death of his son. *And yet he stands here smiling. How in God's name does he do it?*

At that moment, Frank felt more than respect for Tao. The man had truly given his all for his country. So much love and admiration filled Frank's heart that tears sprang to his eyes. He quickly turned his head and faked a sneeze. "Excuse me," he said. "My apologies."

"God bless you," Tao said.

No, God bless you. Frank wiped his eyes and smiled at Tao. "Thank you, sir."

⅄

Back in Manila that night, Frank accompanied Marcos to the palace, while Villacrusis, instead of Ver, drove Tao back to the airport. Frank thought it a small blessing and knew Tao must have been relieved.

Frank cleared his throat. His job this trip was not only to get an estimate of the gold and see where it was actively being retrieved, but, more importantly, find out where Marcos was hiding his wealth. CIA Director William Casey insisted that Marcos would be the kind of man who would keep accurate records of his wealth. So, Frank's job was to fish around to see if ledgers existed—and then try to get copies of those ledgers.

He forced a smile and turned to Marcos. "Mr. President, you mentioned you have a secretary who tallies the gold bullion. Are you referring to Villacrusis? He's a good man, isn't he?"

Marcos smiled. "Yes, Villacrusis is trustworthy. He has been with me many years. But no, he isn't my secretary." He fell quiet for a moment, then eyed Frank from the corner of his eyes. "Would you like to meet her? She should be working in my office right now."

She? "Yes, of course. It would be my honor."

Marcos chuckled. "Yes, it would, because few know of her." He waved his hand in the air. "She's not a secret, really. She just works late of the evenings, because she cares for her children during the day. I call her 'the Midnight Lady,' because she is often working long after I've retired. Very diligent."

If she's handling your gold and bank accounts, I guess she'd better be, if she values her life.

They entered Marcos's office. A tidy, middle-aged woman sat in a chair pulled up to one side of Marcos's massive desk. Her fingers flew over the keypad of a ten-key calculator, and she didn't pause to look up until she'd finished entering her figures. When she did, she smiled at Marcos, stood and bowed. "Good evening, Mr. President."

"Hello, Mary. I'd like you to meet Frank Young. Frank, this is Mary Gosilatar, my Midnight Lady."

Mary smiled at the mention of her nickname, and a rosy flush colored her ample cheeks. "Pleased to meet you, sir." Without hesitation, she resumed her seat and turned her attention back to the books.

"Likewise, Mrs. Gosilatar. It is my pleasure," Frank said.

She didn't look up.

"I told you she was diligent," Marcos whispered.

Frank's eyes roved Marcos's desk, where tally sheets, gold certificates, a huge stack of deposit slips and another of bank statements were neatly organized into piles. The stack of certificates alone must have been an inch or more thick. He tried not to ogle, but he did notice the logo of the Central Bank at Intramuros. Frank glanced around the room nonchalantly, then feigned a stifled yawn. "Forgive me, Mr. President. The sea always tires me."

"One drink before you go?"

"Of course, sir. Thank you."

Marcos poured their drinks, not offering one to Mary. Frank cut his eyes toward the woman.

"Mary doesn't drink alcohol." Marcos smiled. "It's best, anyway. One of us needs to keep a clear head." His smile faded and he stared down at the floor. "My memory isn't what is used to be." He tapped his forehead with a finger. "Too much up here, I suppose."

Too much alcohol in there. Frank stared at the man's glass. Since his mother's death, he'd become acutely aware of the alcohol intake of those around him. He took a polite sip from his own glass, then set it on the table. This time his yawn was real, and it seemed to come from every cell in his body. "Excuse me, sir. I'm so sorry."

Marcos laughed. "Forgive me, Frankie. You said you were tired. I shouldn't keep you." He clapped his hand on Frank's shoulder and extended his hand. "Rest well, my friend."

Frank shook Marcos's hand and bowed slightly. "And you, sir. Have a wonderful night."

On the drive home, Frank wondered about all those deposit slips and gold certificates. Marcos's wealth must be stashed all over the world. How could he convince the man to consolidate it all in one place—that place being the U.S.?

General Erle Cocke came to mind. His bank was in Washington, D.C.

Frank yawned again and rubbed his chin. In the morning, he would make a call to Reagan.

Chapter 46

September 18, 1984
Manila, The Philippines

Imelda held her husband's hand and smoothed a wisp of hair from his forehead. "How are you feeling, my love?"

"I'm fine, Imelda. Don't worry. I am taking care of things." Marcos smiled.

She pulled the chair closer to the hospital bed placed in Ferdinand's bedroom for his weekly dialysis. "That's part of the problem. You are always taking care of things, even when you should be resting."

Ferdinand patted her hand. "You are right. Always, you are right."

"Then why won't you listen to me?"

His eyes roved the room for a moment, then he shifted slightly in the bed, turning to face her. "I have listened. That's why I'm making some changes."

"What do you mean? What kind of changes?" Ferdinand had been forgetting small details lately, making silly mistakes he'd never made before; misremembering names of people he'd known for years, losing track of which banks held his accounts. He was sick and in no shape to make decisions affecting change.

"I've had Fernando draw up some documents for me. He's been working with Mary Gosilatar to prepare ledgers of each of our assets and accounts; those in our names, those in our aliases, and those owned through foundations and other means."

"Fernando Edralin? Your cousin? Is he qualified to do that?"

Ferdinand nodded. "He's a good attorney, Imelda. I realize you think he's still a child, but he's been practicing law for several years now. I trust him."

Imelda nodded. "What's the purpose of these documents?"

Ferdinand reached for her hand, and she slid it into his grip. He stared at her for a moment, his face serious. "I want to appoint a team of trustees to handle my accounts, in case I am ill or . . . incapacitated for any length of time."

"Oh, Ferdinand! Don't talk like that." Imelda's throat stiffened.

"Imelda, I would be a fool not to prepare for an emergency. Look at me." He held up a hand, the intravenous tubing draping from his wrist. "I want to make certain you are taken care of, and that business continues as usual if I am too sick to handle my affairs for a few days. That's all."

Imelda nodded. She didn't speak for fear of crying.

"I've been thinking for a few months now about who has strong business sense and enough knowledge of international banking to handle the gold affairs. It also must be those who have experience with the treasure hunt and can assist with moving the bullion. Above all," he held up a finger, "they must be trustworthy."

"Yes," Imelda managed.

"I'm considering General Fabian Ver, Tony Sandaga, Rudy Villanueva, Major Rolando Miranda, Tony Sagun, Major Angel Miguel and Frank Young. What do you think?"

Imelda let go of her husband's hand, stood and paced the length of his bedroom. "Why so many? Why would you give so many men access to your wealth? Wealth is power, Ferdinand."

"Listen to me, Imelda. Here, sit."

When she'd seated herself, she sat ramrod straight, hands folded in her lap, voicing her displeasure even in silence.

"My cousin Fernando suggested it, with good reason. Any transactions that occur will require my signature alone, or the signature of three of these men. They will keep each other in check this way, and the responsibility for any mistakes will be shared with dire consequences."

Imelda softened. None of these men would want to be responsible for another's misdoings. The idea had merit. "I don't believe you should make Frank Young one of the trustees, Ferdinand. I cannot give him my trust."

Ferdinand touched her arm. "Why? Rosalita has monitored him for years. He has worked hard to help us locate the gold. He helped me establish the tobacco firm, and he's brought many donations to my political fund from Triangle Tobacco. He's been a good friend, and he's an excellent engineer. Very smart. Very, very smart, Imelda."

Imelda shook her head. "I don't trust him. Why would he disappear for years at a time? He has done this twice. Rosalita is beautiful and has many suitors. Why would he not marry her? I think he is a coward. You need a brave man to be your trustee, Ferdinand. Not someone who will run away."

Lines creased Ferdinand's brow. "He is not a coward. Many men tremble when Fabian walks in the room. Many won't speak with him. Frank looks in his eyes and speaks with confidence." Ferdinand shook his head. "He may be many things, but he is not a coward."

Silence fell between the two for a moment, and Imelda listened to the dialysis equipment hum. She didn't want to upset her husband, especially not while he lay ill in bed.

"Besides," Ferdinand finally said, "Frank Young left the Philippines to care for his ailing mother. She died. And now he has returned."

"Forgive me, my dear husband, but I don't believe all that is true. He has left twice with little notice. Perhaps all isn't as it seems." She squeezed Ferdinand's hand. "Please. For me. Don't make Frank Young a trustee. At least not yet."

"Not yet?"

"Have Rosalita watch him and report to you. Give him a test, perhaps. See if he is as honest as you think, before you entrust your wealth to him."

Ferdinand scowled. "Rosalita? Rosalita has supposedly watched him for years now, and what good has she been? She's found nothing. Perhaps that means there is nothing to find, which means I am correct. Or perhaps it means she is smitten by Frank and can't see the truth of him."

Imelda smiled. "Perhaps she simply needs encouragement. A reward."

"What do you mean, 'a reward'?"

"You know Rosalita has invested in Florentino Villacrusis's treasure hunts. Money motivates her, just like anyone else. Give her a reward for information she finds. Make an offer in writing, so she will be encouraged to report to you. Then, if she reports nothing while money is at stake, you will know you can trust Frank with your finances." She shrugged.

Ferdinand studied her face for a long time. "I will do as you ask." He smiled. "When Rosalita comes for tea tomorrow, please send her to speak with me."

The next afternoon, Rosalita walked into Marcos's office on Imelda's arm. Marcos was prepared. "Forgive me for not standing, Rosalita, dear. I'm afraid I'm still a bit weak."

"Don't you dare get up, Ferdinand." Rosalita came behind his desk and kissed his cheek. "I hope you're feeling better."

He smiled and, over Rosalita's shoulder, winked at his wife. Imelda backed out of the room and closed the door behind her. "I am getting stronger by the minute. By tomorrow, I'll be my old self."

"That's good to hear." She clasped his hand in both of hers, then released him and sat in the chair across the desk from him. "Imelda said you wanted to speak with me?"

"Yes, my dear. I have a proposal for you." He opened the file folder Edralin had prepared for him earlier that morning, turned it around to face Rosalita and pushed it toward her.

Rosalita leaned forward and read the document, her eyes growing larger with each word. "Fifteen million U.S. dollars? In an account in Liechtenstein? In my name?" She looked at Ferdinand. "What's this about?"

Marcos smiled, feeling like a doting father. "I need your help, Rosalita. It's a simple request, really, but I want you to know that I don't ask for favors lightly. I don't want to use you, so I wish to compensate you for any trouble I may cause."

"What? What kind of trouble? I don't understand."

"I need you to bring information to me."

Rosalita again glanced at the bank account statement. "What kind of information?" She ran her finger across her name, then underneath the dollar amount.

"Information about Frank Young."

Rosalita's hand dropped to her lap. "I have watched Franklin for years, just as Imelda has asked. He has done nothing wrong. Why do you insist on doubting him? He's a good man, Ferdinand."

Marcos smiled. "I want to believe you, Rosalita. But much is at stake here. I must be certain I can trust him." He pursed his lips toward the account statement. "You have nothing to lose, and everything to gain."

Rosalita looked at the statement again, then licked her lips. "What, exactly, am I looking for? I mean, since I've yet to see anything, I don't know what I'm supposed to find."

Marcos leaned forward. "You know Frank has seen things and knows things that could endanger both my position and our family's wealth." He fixed Rosalita in his stare. "His many trips to America, often without notice . . . they make one wonder. Don't you agree?"

Rosalita blinked, but didn't answer.

Marcos straightened and placed his hands flat on the desk. "Bring me anything in his possession related to the gold. Whatever you find. He and Gary Morgan worked together, so it's possible Frank has copies of the missing maps. He may have photographed them, so look for photos or film canisters."

Rosalita shifted in her seat, then crossed and uncrossed her legs. "Anything else?"

"Watch everything he does carefully. Check his belongings, especially his papers. Look for bank deposits that would indicate he may have stolen from me. He's been inside those digs. It's possible he could have slipped out with a pocket full of diamonds or a few gold biscuits. It may not seem like much, but a small betrayal will lead to a large betrayal."

Again, Rosalita shifted.

Marcos smiled. "I realize this makes you uncomfortable, Rosalita. But if you scour his documents and find nothing, then we will both feel at peace, for we will know that Franklin Young is an honorable man."

Rosalita fingered the bank statement, picked it up, closely examined it. "How long do I need to do this?"

"How long? I don't know. If you find information right away, the money is yours. If not, let's give it two years. Not every snake reveals its stripes in the light of day. Some wait until darkness. If after two years Frank proves himself truthful, you can have the money. In the meantime, it is there in the Liechtenstein account, though the account will remain frozen until I contact them on your behalf."

Rosalita glanced from the statement to Ferdinand and back again. "Why Liechtenstein?"

"Liechtenstein is a small country with good banking laws that respect one's privacy. It is a tax haven." He smiled. "When you get your money, Rosalita, you will get all of it, plus interest, tax free." He closed the folder and laid it in front of him, out of Rosalita's reach.

She stared at him a moment, then a strained smile crossed her lips. "I will do it, Ferdinand. For you, for Imelda and for the Philippines." She stood and kissed his hand. "I will also do it for Frank, because he deserves to have his loyalty proven."

⁂

Rosalita walked down the hallway toward the Grand Staircase. She thought again of the bank statement that bore her name. She also thought of the green pages from Frank's ledger tucked in her dresser drawer, and of the photos of the treasure maps she'd stolen from Frank's camera. Frank was a good man—but what reason did he have to take those photos?

Fifteen million U.S. dollars. That kind of money could buy her any kind of life she wanted. She thought of Imelda's words. *Wealth is power.*

As she walked outside the palace door, yells from protesters in the streets nearly a block away reached her. Her lovely city, now a place of upheaval and unrest. She held her head high and walked toward the sound, leaving her driver Tony standing beside the door of her car.

"Miss Laurel?" he said.

Rosalita held up her hand and continued toward the noise from the demonstrators. Their outward objection and dissention seemed a welcome respite from the warring turmoil inside her head.

Wealth is power. If she had that kind of power, perhaps she could convince Ferdinand to let her inside his inner circle to invest in the gold recoveries. Of course, if that were to happen, fifteen million dollars would look like a pittance.

Wealth is power. She could quash much of the poverty in the Philippines and help restore the country to what it once was.

Wealth is power.

Chapter 47

March 3, 1985
Malacañang Palace, Manila, The Philippines

Rosalita picked absentmindedly at the cuff on her blouse. These political teas no longer seemed to accomplish anything. Marcos was more hated than ever, and though she still believed he had the best interest of the Philippines at heart, she also believed he could solve many of the country's problems if only he'd spread some of his personal wealth around. How much money did one man need, anyway?

"I will see you next week, Imelda. Thank you again for having us." Julieta kissed Imelda's hand, while Rosalita forced a smile in the wealthy matron's direction.

When they'd left, Rosalita picked up her purse and stood.

"Rosalita, can you stay a moment, dear?" Imelda's question sounded more like an order. "I'd like to speak with you in private. Join me in my office for a cigarette?"

Rosalita nodded and tucked her purse under her arm. She followed Imelda down the hallway, dreading another inquisition. *Today I'll give it to her.* She'd carried the green sheet of paper for weeks, undecided about sharing it with the Marcoses. She'd examined it a thousand times since she'd first found it in Frank's hotel room all those years ago, and from what she could tell, it was nothing more than map symbols. She'd studied it to see if perhaps it could have been taken from a particular treasure map, but it appeared to be copied from a book. Frank was a consummate student, always reading thick textbooks in a plethora of languages. She'd once called him her walking encyclopedia, but he joked that his was a head full of useless knowledge.

Imelda shut the door behind them and rounded her desk.

Always she sits behind the desk, as if she's the teacher and I'm her student. More and more, the woman irritated her, but Rosalita loved the respect and social status she garnered from being Imelda's closest friend.

"Cigarette, dear?" Imelda opened the slim gold case bearing her initials and proffered it to Rosalita.

Rosalita accepted, though she'd sworn again this morning to cut back. "Thank you." She took a deep pull and held in the smoke until the pressure in her head subsided. "What's going on? Is Ferdinand ill again?"

Imelda smiled, and Rosalita felt impressed anew with the woman's charm.

"No, dear. Thank you for asking. He's well." She lit her own cigarette and took a delicate puff. "I wonder if you have any news of Franklin. Have you found nothing at all?"

Rosalita hesitated, then reached inside her purse and produced the sheet from the engineering pad. "I found this."

Imelda's eyebrows rose. "Really?" She snatched it from Rosalita's hand, opened the page and devoured it with greedy eyes. After a moment, she held it up. "We must show this to Ferdinand." Imelda buzzed his office, then motioned for Rosalita to follow her.

When they entered Ferdinand's office, he dismissed the men who were with him. Imelda crossed to his desk and held out the green paper. "Rosalita found this in Frank's belongings."

Marcos put on his eyeglasses and peered at the paper. He smiled and laid it on his desk. "This is nothing. These are map symbols. Frank made a list for interpretation of the maps as he reverse-engineered the drawings." He smiled. "It's merely a reference tool."

Rosalita did her best to appear enormously relieved. "Oh, good!" She waved her hand in front of her face to create a breeze. "I was so worried that he'd done something treacherous. I feel a *fool* for doubting him." She pierced

Imelda with her gaze. "I should have known it would be nothing." She sighed and smiled. "What a relief."

"Thank you, Rosalita," Ferdinand said. "I know it took courage to bring this to my attention. Like you, I'm relieved to know it's nothing of conse-quence. You did the right thing." His smooth face softened. "Please continue to bring anything you find to our attention."

Imelda turned to usher Rosalita from Ferdinand's office, an obvious look of disappointment on her face.

She wants to see him go down. My dearest friend, and she wants the man I love torn apart.

Chapter 48

Malacañang Palace, Manila, The Philippines

Ferdinand Marcos looked around his office—at his life-sized portrait, the presidential seal, the exquisite furnishings. His glance finally landed on General Fabian Ver. "They've turned against me."

Ver walked to the window and stared out.

"Everyone. All my people." Marcos shook his head. The citizens should have gone along with his pronouncement that he'd defeated Cory Aquino, but they hadn't. It'd been over two weeks, and still angry protesters assaulted the palace.

"I can put down this rebellion." Ver's eyebrow twitched. "And quickly. But it will come at a price."

"What? With the CIA and the U.S. State Department watching my every move?" Marcos walked to the safe and tapped it with his fist. "We have so much more gold to recover."

Shouts and chants from the street became louder, drawing his attention to the open window. He peered off into the distance. "What's going on down at Camp Aguinaldo?"

Ver growled. "Aquino has her people in the street. Cardinal Sin is behind her. Sin is more of a communist than he is a Catholic." Ver's eyes narrowed. "We have our people on Camp Crame, so if the rebellion moves into Epifanio de los Santos Avenue, we'll squash it."

Marcos slammed the window shut. "And after all we've done for them, too." He went to his desk and slumped into his chair. "So much gold left to extract," he said, his voice barely audible. "Don't you think Reagan will let me come back when this settles down? What would it hurt?"

"Mr. President, what do you want me to do?"

Marcos leaned back in his chair. "I want you to go down to Camp Aguinaldo, get some men together, and have them take out all the rebel radio stations. Have the palace guards shut down the palace. We need to pack, and I don't want anyone getting in."

Ver stood. "Yes, Mr. President."

Marcos waited for the General to leave, then pulled out the account ledgers. He opened them to the latest entries and studied his situation.

⅄

Flanked by armed members of the Philippine Army, Frank was hustled into the palace amid shouts and hateful epithets. He'd seen on the news that the protesters had grown in number. If they weren't soon controlled, they'd torch the palace.

Inside, Imelda stood before him with mascara-smudged eyes and a stuffy, red nose. "It has come to this, Franklin," she said, waving her handkerchief across the room.

Crates were stacked along one side of the Grand Entrance Hall. The household staff worked furiously, packing the Marcos's belongings into boxes for shipping.

"What's happening? What is going on?"

Imelda's shoulders sagged and fresh rivulets coursed down her cheeks. "President Reagan is coming for us. Ferdinand believes we are no longer safe here. The people we have worked so long to save and protect have turned against us. They've bought Corazon Aquino's lies, and now they want us out. We won the election fair and square. You were there. You saw it." She sniffed and dabbed at her puffy eyes. "This is a mutiny. An outrage!"

"Where are you going? When are you leaving?"

She shook her head. "I cannot say, but I believe it is soon. We, even our poor children, none of us are safe here. Ferdinand has bargained with Ronnie, and he is going to give us asylum in America until we can prove the election belongs to Ferdinand and again restore peace here in the Philippines." Imelda held up her hand. "Do you hear that?"

Muffled chants came through an open window somewhere.

"Aquino." Imelda choked back a sob. "This is what she has done. Our country has never been in this kind of turmoil. She is of Satan!"

"How is the president? Rosalita told me—" Frank stopped himself. Imelda may not like that Rosalita said Marcos was depressed. "I just wanted to stop and say hello. I never dreamed this was happening here. May I see him? Perhaps I can help in some small way."

Imelda shrugged and held out her hands. "What can anyone do? No, he is not well, but he is doing what he can to see his family through this. Ferdinand is a good man. *A good man!*" She pursed her lips toward the stairs. "Go. Perhaps it will do him good to know you still support him."

⚔

Frank took the stairs two at a time. He couldn't believe Reagan or Colby hadn't told him this was happening. Since Bozeman had stepped down under Colby's direction, Frank had felt largely ignored.

"Mr. President?" Frank headed toward the office. He peered inside, but the room was empty. He backed out into the hallway. "Mr. President? Sir?" Frank re-entered Marcos's office, amazed to see it strewn with strings of shredded paper. Tentatively, he approached the desk. Piles of manila folders and a stack of ledger books cluttered the top, while cardboard file boxes taped shut were stacked nearby. The door of the safe that once held the maps stood ajar.

Frank peered into the hallway again. It was empty. He rushed to the desk and shuffled through the files. Political paperwork. Real estate deeds. Personnel files. Insurance certificates.

Frank moved to the ledger books and opened one of the ledgers. In it was a list of bank accounts, organized, as best Frank could tell, by country. The names on the accounts were those of Marcos and his aliases.

Frank ran his finger down each page, turning them quickly, seeing more and more accounts, each with balances in the hundreds of thousands and millions. *Why was this sitting out? Where was Marcos? Where was the Midnight Lady?*

This was the kind of information Reagan needed. Frank jerked out his pocket camera, tossed the lens cover onto the desk, and snapped photos of each page. This could be his ticket out, for once and for all. He turned page after page, snapping photos. Names and astronomical figures flew by: Jimmy De Vyra, Ferdinand Marcos, Charlie De Veyra, Rosalita Laurel.

Rosalita?

Frank placed his fingertip below Rosalita's name and traced it over to the amount. Fifteen million dollars U.S. He flipped back a page to see the country listed at the top. Liechtenstein.

The world imploded around Frank; roaring white noise filled his ears. He stared unblinking at Rosalita's name and the dollar figure next to it until his eyes watered. Fifteen million dollars. Marcos had bought her, too.

Frank finished the last photo, then slid back to the door and looked down the hallway. All clear. He bolted down the hallway, down the Grand Staircase, and out the door to his car.

Rosalita Laurel. Fifteen million dollars U.S.

The words burned into Frank's brain. He desperately needed to find her. Find out why Marcos had given her that kind of money. He thought of the missing papers in his hotel room. Of the film stolen from his camera. What else had she taken from him without his knowledge? Had she been selling those things to Marcos? If so, who had she told the president she'd gotten them from? If she'd implicated him, Ver would've killed him by now.

Frank whipped his car around the corner, turned again at the next intersection, and backtracked to Rosalita's villa. He would get answers.

When he neared her house, he pulled his car off the street and drove it through her neighbor's yard into a bank of leafless azaleas. He quickly switched out the license plates and plastered a U.S. Air Force sticker on the back end of the car.

With the stealth of a jungle cat, Frank made his way around the back of Rosalita's house. He tapped lightly on the back door. He framed his eyes and peered through the door's window.

Adriana, Rosalita's maid, looked back at him from the other side of the glass. She jumped, her hand covering her mouth.

"It's me," Frank whispered loudly. "Frank."

Adriana opened the door. "You frightened me."

"Sorry." Frank squeezed through the door quickly, closed it, and locked it. "Where's Rosalita?"

"I'm right here. What's going on?"

"I need to talk to you. Privately."

Rosalita glanced at her watch, then turned to Adriana. "I know it's your daughter's birthday. Please take the rest of the evening off."

"Gracias, Señora." She ran down the hall, then returned within seconds with her handbag. She gave a slight bow to Rosalita. "Gracias, Señora Rosalita." They watched her leave. As soon as she was out of sight, Rosalita led him to the sitting room, where they sat in adjacent over-stuffed chairs. Frank looked into her jade eyes. "I'm going to ask you something, and I want the truth."

Her face blanched and her lower lip trembled, leaving Frank with no doubt of her guilt. But of what?

"Why did Marcos give you fifteen million dollars?"

Her eyes filled and she dropped her head. She pulled her hands away, wringing them as though they were full of water and desperate to be dried. "I, I can explain. I didn't tell him . . . he never saw . . . I burned them. The photos, I mean."

"Why? Why would you do that? I love—I *loved* you, Rosalita. You deceived me."

Sparks flew from Rosalita's eyes and she jerked away from his grasp. "No, Frank. *You* deceived *me*. You've used me to get to Ferdinand. That's why you ran away every time things got hot between us." Realization flitted across her face. "Things didn't get hot between *us*, did they, Frank? They got hot around *you*. You almost got caught, and when you did, you ran away." She shook her head and her lips turned downward in a sneer. "You have used me since you met me. This whole relationship has been a lie."

"That's not true, Rosalita, and you know it."

"Then how did you find out about the money? How did you know Marcos gave it to me to keep an eye on you?"

Frank opened his mouth, but disgust clogged his throat and he couldn't speak. He turned away from her. "How dare you accuse me of using you, when the whole time we've been together you've been spying on me? You stole the film from my camera. You also stole pages from my notebook, didn't you?"

"I've been protecting you, Frank. From the inside. You have to believe me. Imelda didn't trust you and Ver wanted to kill you. I told them I'd keep an eye on you, but really I was protecting you."

"Why did you steal the notes and the film, then?"

Rosalita blinked rapidly. "I gave Ferdinand the notes just a few months ago. I knew they were just map symbols, but I pretended I thought they were something secret." She gave a slight shrug. "Ferdinand thought I was doing a good job of watching you and reporting to him, and he realized the papers meant nothing, so he trusted you more."

"And the film?"

"I had the pictures developed. I thought I'd surprise you with them, but when I saw they were photos of the treasure maps, I burned them." She touched Frank's arm. "Frank, you don't know who you're dealing with. Had Ver known you had those photos, he'd have killed you. You can't trust him, Frank. He's jealous of your relationship with Ferdinand—and your relationship—what's left of it—with me. He wants you dead."

Frank stared at her for a moment. "I'll never stop loving you." He turned and walked out the door.

CHAPTER 49

February 25, 1986-Tuesday
Washington DC - White House, Morning Briefing

Ronald Reagan looked again at the clock.

"Something must be up," Vice President George Bush said. "Casey wouldn't be late otherwise."

NSA Director General William Odom shrugged. "I have the report on the situation in the Philippines. Looks like if we don't get Marcos out of there quickly, we're going to have a full-blown riot."

Reagan nodded. "Maybe that's what's keeping Casey. He should be getting them out right now."

The door opened slightly and CIA Director Casey peeked into the room. "Sorry I'm late."

"Get in here," Reagan said.

Casey strode across the room and took his seat. "I was on the phone with our Ambassador in the Philippines."

"Marcos out?" Reagan asked.

"Not yet." Casey's face erupted into a grin. "But I have something you'll want to see."

Reagan guffawed. "Yeah?"

"Frank Young dropped off film of Marcos' ledger books."

The room was quiet.

Finally, Reagan spoke. "How soon can they get it developed?"

Casey's smile broadened. "It's done. Our operatives in Europe have already verified some of the accounts."

"How many accounts are there?"

"Dozens. Billions of dollars' worth."

Reagan gave a low whistle.

"If the accounts are good," Bush said, "we can assume everything else is good—like the amount of gold Tao reported a while back."

Reagan leaned back. "We've got to get him out of there."

"We've got planes at Clark right now," Casey advised. "Looks like we can get them out within twenty-four hours."

"I mean Young. We need to get Young out of there before Ver and his gang figure out what happened."

Casey pulled out a notepad and jotted a note. "Okay. We'll take him through Clark, as well."

General Odom sat with his hands together, his brow drawn. "I'm not sure I understand what's going on."

Reagan laughed. "We've just hit the jackpot, my friend." He leaned back. "We've got Marcos right where we want him—in the palm of our hand. If he doesn't do what we want, we can freeze his accounts. Hit 'im where it hurts."

Casey looked at the General. "And we can get our fair share of the gold now."

Bush laughed. "And then some."

CHAPTER 50

February 26, 1986-Wednesday
Malacañang Palace, Manila, The Philippines

Imelda moved a piece of pineapple around her breakfast plate. She looked up at her husband. "That Frank Young is such a nice young man. I suppose I should trust him more."

Ferdinand picked at a slice of cheese. "I'd like to see him before we leave."

"He was just here yesterday."

"Yesterday? I didn't see him."

Imelda dropped her fork. "He was in the palace yesterday afternoon. I sent him to see you."

Ferdinand's eyes narrowed. "He wasn't in my office, was he?"

"Why, yes. I'm sure he was. He was upstairs. I didn't see him come down."

Ferdinand dropped his fork. "My ledgers." He looked into the distance. "That *anak ka nang puta!*" He jumped up and ran to his office. As soon as he opened the door, he relaxed. It was still there. His ledger was on his desk.

He blinked. But it was open now, and he'd left it closed. He was sure of it. And Mary hadn't been in the night before—it was her day off. He stood there and considered. Surely Frank wouldn't . . . .

Something caught his eye. Ferdinand picked it up. It was a protective cap for a camera lens, the word *Nikon* engraved in the center. Marcos kicked the desk. Frank had a Nikon camera; he'd had it out when they were on the yacht.

Marcos picked up his phone and punched in a couple of numbers. He waited until General Ver answered. "Come to my office. Now. We have a flea to exterminate."

人.

General Fabian Ver gripped his pistol and leaned against the side of Frank Young's bungalow. He exchanged glances with the two men with him. "Kill on sight."

Colonel Lachica stepped back, took a three-step run, and threw his weight onto the door. It collapsed.

Lachica and Major Olivas lunged inside, guns drawn. The men disappeared around opposite corners as Ver looked around the tiny living room.

Lachica returned with Olivas on his heels. "He's not here."

"Tear the place apart. Find anything that can tell us where he has gone." Ver re-holstered his gun and plundered through a stack of green engineer's pads on which Frank had drawn some reverse-engineered maps. Ver growled. "He's been making copies." He flung the pad aside, then repeated the action with the next, and the next. Nothing. He slapped everything off the desk. Nothing. He jerked open the side desk drawers and pilfered through papers and miscellaneous office supplies. Nothing. Then the center drawer. Nothing.

Ver stared at the center drawer. It was shallow, not as deep as the desk. Why wouldn't it be? He reached to the back of the drawer. The back was loose. He pulled and prodded, and finally, when he pushed it back, it folded open. In the hidden recess was a waxed paper.

Ver pulled it out with uncharacteristic gentleness. His instinct told him what it was before he unfolded the paper. And his instinct was right. It was a treasure map. Like one of the Japanese maps, but this one was different. He carried the map to the window for better lighting. His eyes roved over the document; he stared hard at the block printing that looked similar to Frank's neat handwriting. But the map appeared much too old to have been drawn by Frank Young.

It was a map Ver had never seen. He turned the map to view it from different angles, then realized it depicted a site at the top of the mountain above Montalban Gorge. Young had a treasure map even Marcos didn't know existed.

Something caught Ver's eye. The name at the top. *Quezon*. Ver's mind processed the information. *Quezon*. He knew that name. His mind scanned its memory until he retrieved the needed information: Danilo Quezon. A Filipino who had known too much about the gold and where it was located. His memory brought up Danilo's face. Yes. Almost identical to Frank Young's. Perhaps the son was sent to finish the father's job? Ver's eyes narrowed. The son would suffer the same fate as the father. "Lachica! Olivas! Let's go!"

When the men rounded the corner, Ver grinned. "Lachica, contact Villacrusis and get an excavation crew at the top of Montalban Gorge. Tell them I'll be there soon to show them where to start the recovery." He turned to Olivas. "Take me to Miss Rosalita Laurel's residence. And hurry."

✦

Rosalita moved leadenly through her house. She hated that Franklin didn't trust her. After so many years together, how could he think those horrible things of her?

The phone rang. Hoping it was Frank, Rosalita grabbed it up.

"Rosalita, darling?" Imelda's voice, smooth as butter, dripped over the line.

"Imelda? Yes?"

"Are you alone, dear?"

"Yes." Something was wrong. Imelda never placed calls herself. She always had one of her attendants do that for her. "What's the matter?"

"Darling, you know about the protestors, right?"

"Yes. Are you okay? Is Ferdinand?"

"We're fine, but it doesn't look like things are going to get better any time soon. Ronnie just called, and he's sending a plane for us and is offering asylum in Hawaii."

"Ronnie?" As soon as the words left her mouth, she realized Imelda spoke of Ronald Reagan.

"Ronnie Reagan. He talked to Ferdinand, and it looks like we have little choice. We need to get away for a while."

"Oh, Imelda. I'm so sorry." Rosalita dropped onto the divan. "I will miss you so."

"You'll be coming with us, dear."

Rosalita sat up straight. "I can't, Imelda. This is my home."

"I said, you'll be coming with us."

"No. Mother needs me. You know that."

"Ferdinand has already sent someone to get her."

Rosalita's heart stopped. "Get her? What do you mean?"

"She's coming, too."

"What are you talking about?"

"Ferdinand and I discussed it, and we knew you'd probably not agree to come, so we sent someone for your mother. She's coming too."

"Imelda, I will not stand—"

"There's no other way. We need you. We've given you a lot of money. You're coming with us."

"I will not!"

"You most certainly will."

"Imelda—"

"I'm sorry, Rosalita. This isn't a time when we have choices. Someone will be after you soon. Get packed." The call disconnected.

Rosalita stared at the phone. Her mother would never agree to leave the Philippines. This was her home. And it was Rosalita's home. She grabbed the phone and dialed her mother's number. It rang several times, but there was no answer.

⚓

Ver didn't bother knocking. He kicked open the door with more force than necessary. It slammed into the wall and bounced from its hinges.

Rosalita jumped up from the velvet divan where she'd been sitting, her eyes red and swollen, tissues in her hand.

"Where is he?" Ver growled.

Rosalita's eyes widened. "Where is *who?*"

In two long strides, Ver closed the distance between them. His eyes narrow, he drew back his fist. "This isn't the time to play games, little girl."

"I don't know what who you're talking about."

His fist slammed into her cheek.

Rosalita reeled backwards and fell into a crumpled heap.

Ver yanked her into a sitting position. "Where is Franklin Young?"

Rosalita covered her face with her arms. "I don't know."

Ver jerked her arm down and smacked her with the palm of his hand on the other side of her face.

"Stop it! Leave me alone!"

Ver grabbed her by the throat and lifted her, then threw her back onto the settee. He turned to Olivas. "We'll take her with us. If we don't find him . . . " He glared at Rosalita. ". . . we've got bait to make him come to us."

Chapter 51

February 26 – 11:30 p.m.
On the outskirts of Manila, The Philippines

Frank stopped at a pay phone and dialed the emergency number Nguyen Tao had given him. His hands trembled and he found it difficult to control his voice. "It's time," he said. "Get me out of here."

"Thank God you're okay," Tao said. "Ver's after you."

"But why—"

"Marcos put a bounty on your head."

"Oh, shit."

"We're getting you out, but you can't delay. Get to Clark Air Base by 2:30 a.m."

"Then why—"

"I'm in Vietnam. I'll meet you there in two hours." Tao's voice was firm. "Go to Clark right now. The mission is over."

"But—"

"The plane will leave with or without you."

"But—"

"You must get out *now.*"

✦

Frank checked his watch. Eleven-thirty. He had three hours. That gave him time to get to his bungalow and pack a few things, then go see Rosalita one last time. His heart sank as he thought of her. He did love her, and he wanted things to be right between them. More than that, he wanted her to go with him.

He drove to his bungalow. As he neared, he cut the lights. He parked a good distance from it, pulling his car out of sight of the road. He didn't want to be a sitting target for Ver and his men. Before leaving the vehicle, he opened the glove box, took out the gun he kept there and tucked it into his belt. As he walked toward his home, he realized the door had been knocked off its hinges. Ver had already been there.

Or was he still there, waiting for him to return?

The son-of-a-bitch. Frank clenched his fists, then shook his head to clear it. There would be time for emotion later. For now, he needed to take care of the matter at hand. Evaluate the situation.

Frank crept around the perimeter of the bungalow. Nothing appeared disturbed; no sign anyone was still there. He palmed the gun and approached the door, making sure he made no sound. He slipped up to the open door, peered inside as best he could, then ducked and flattened against the siding, awaiting an attack. But no one was there. No one he could see, anyway.

Frank stepped through the open door, staying close to the wall with his gun in hand. The place had been ransacked. He looked at his research strewn around the room, his desk drawers open. *His map.* Heart pounding, he took a quick look through each room until he was sure no one was there. He hurried back to his desk and checked the secret compartment in the center drawer. Empty. His heart dived into his stomach. Ver had his map.

Anger boiled through his veins. No way was he going to let Ver steal anything else from him. Enough was enough. He ran outside and jumped into his car. He drove as fast as he could to Rosalita's home. Her car was still in the garage; hopefully, that meant it wasn't too late. Still, undoubtedly, Ver would be watching her house in hopes of finding him. He parked behind the garage and, after turning off the automatic door lights, grabbed his gun. Staying close to the side of the house in the shadows, he sneaked around the house, peeking in windows. The back of the house was dark, but lights were on in the front. From the windows, he could see nothing, nor did he hear anything.

After going all the way around the house, he returned to the back door. It was locked. This time, he couldn't afford to knock. Frank looked around one more time, then tucked the gun in his belt, took out his lock-picking kit and went to work. In seconds, the door was open.

Quietly, he stepped in, and quietly, he closed the door behind him. Where was she? He was afraid to call her name, so he went from room to room, looking. She wasn't there. In the last room, the sitting room at the front of the house, he saw it. The front door swung loose on the hinges that had been kicked in. Vomit churned in his stomach. Ver had beat him there.

He paused for a moment to think, then again toured the house, looking to see if maybe she was tied up somewhere or hiding in a closet. When he got to her bedroom, he noticed something that made his blood ice: her purse. She went nowhere without it. At least, nowhere willingly.

Frank's heart dipped to his stomach. Was she all right? Had they hurt her? Killed her? Surely they knew she wasn't involved with his assignment. Surely they did. His breath left him and he grabbed a wall to keep his balance. *Breathe, Frank. Breathe.* It was him they wanted. They wouldn't kill Rosalita. They needed her to get to him.

Now, the next question: where would they have taken her? The palace? No. Protestors were on the verge of overtaking the palace. Where? *Think, think.*

And then he knew. They had taken his map. They knew about his gold. They certainly knew he'd be trying to escape the country. And, they would assume he'd want to take some gold with him.

Be at Clark by 2:30. Frank recalled the urgency in Tao's voice. He checked his watch. It was 12:30. It would take him at least twenty minutes to drive to Montalban Gorge. Another twenty-five to return to Manila. And then a little over an hour to get to the air base. Frank sprinted to his car. He hoped he could find Rosalita quickly. He tossed his gun on the seat and threw the car into reverse.

Twenty minutes later, Frank drove up the mountain as fast as his car would go. Ver had the map; Ver had Rosalita. No doubt, the General was already at the tunnel taking what else didn't belong to him. As always. Well, he wasn't going to get away with it this time. And he wasn't going to hurt Rosalita. Every muscle in Frank's body tensed.

The overgrown pass that led to the underground cave of gold was so dark he had to drive with headlights, but as soon as he neared the top of the mountain, he turned them off. The full moon lit the mountaintop well enough for Frank to see without additional light. He drove past the turn-off, pulled his car as far as it would go into the scrub pines and palmetto bushes, and shut off the engine. He picked his gun off the seat and quietly crept through the woods toward the sound of heavy machinery.

Tire tracks in the weeds told him someone had already been there. Near the cave, two backhoes and a bulldozer worked in the glow of huge spotlights.

Frank stopped and surveyed the area. Just inside the tree line sat Ver's Mercedes. Frank hurried through the shadows to get a closer look. Ver paced around the car. Lachica sat behind the wheel. Someone—Olivas?—was in the back seat with a woman. Frank's heart pounded. He crept closer, but he already knew. *Rosalita.*

Frank's stomach clenched. Even with darkness on his side, if he rushed them from here, both he and Rosalita would be dead before he reached the car. Not sure how to handle the situation, Frank silently moved closer to the car.

Ver's two-way radio sputtered. "I'm on site," he said into the radio. "I expect Young will come to rescue his fair maiden."

"What?" Marcos' voice crackled over the airwaves. "You have Rosalita?"

"Affirmative."

"Bring her here. Now. She's leaving the Philippines with me."

Frank didn't know whether to laugh or cry. If Ver did as Marcos asked, Rosalita would be safe. But why was Marcos under the impression she was leaving the Philippines with him? He had to see her before she got on that plane.

Ver snapped off his radio and slapped the driver's door. "Marcos says to take her to Clark Air Base. So go on. I want to keep an eye on things here." He glanced around. "Young will show up yet. I know he will." Ver lowered his voice and spoke to Olivas. "Come back for me."

Frank strained to hear more, but couldn't.

Ver walked around the Mercedes and opened the trunk. He removed a rifle, loaded it, and popped off the safety. He slammed the trunk closed and the car sped off.

Frank hesitated. There wasn't anything he could do about the gold. Not at this moment. Not by himself. But he could do something about Rosalita. He had to get to the air base before she did. Certainly, she would go with him instead of with the Marcoses.

Frank moved deeper into the shadows and strode back towards his car. As he emerged from the tree line, a metallic snap sounded. Ver's rifle. He must've spotted Frank's car as it approached the site. But where was he now?

Frank's muscles tensed. Could Ver be watching him now? Some sound, some instinct, caused his body to react before his brain processed the information. He dived to the ground; his gun flew out of his hand. As he fell, a sound boomed near him and a blazing ember burned into his right shoulder, knocking him back. He'd been shot.

Another blast, and dirt exploded near his head. He grabbed his shoulder and rolled behind a tree. He frantically looked around for his gun. There it lay—out of reach. Warm, sticky fluid filled his hand. *Don't panic.* He swallowed his pain. More shots landed around him. His head spun. *Don't pass out.* He forced his concentration. *Focus your chi.* No fear, no pain. Just training. Frank took a deep breath and closed his eyes. Shutting out all the noise and dread that surrounded him, he counted the rhythm of his inhales and exhales, concentrating on the chi that surrounded him, feeling it circulate through his body, feeling it awaken and empower his body and mind. He was ready. His eyes snapped open. Frank sprung to his feet and landed in a basic stance, body at the ready, hidden behind a tree.

Silence. Frank struggled to hear. *Where had Ver gone?* The beating of his heart boomed in his ears. Frank remembered his breathing and refocused his mind on his surroundings. A twig snapped. Ver was close.

Frank pressed his body against the bark, allowing himself to feel the tree's life force, allowing himself to become one with his surroundings. The next rustle was from his left. Frank inched to the right. *Now or never.*

Frank jumped from behind the tree.

Ver spun around, but Frank was faster. As Ver swung the rifle toward him, Frank hammer-fisted Ver's wrist at the joint. The rifle flew through the air and landed in the clearing, six feet away.

But now Ver had the advantage. Frank's right arm was useless from his wound, leaving his right side unprotected, and the hammer-fist had opened him up. Ver slammed his fist into Frank's jaw.

Frank fell back, his head ringing from the force.

Ver leapt for the rifle.

Frank caught his balance.

Focus.

He took a two-step leap into a flying tackle, knocking Ver to the ground only inches from the rifle. Frank pounded his fist into the back of Ver's head. But Ver was heavier than Frank—and stronger. He bucked Frank off to the side and grabbed for the rifle.

Frank sprang to his feet and landed a hard kick to Ver's ribs, knocking him back. Then he side-sweep kicked the rifle farther from reach.

Ver grabbed Frank's leg and twisted, bringing Frank to the ground, hard on his shoulder. The world blazed white. Blackness chewed on the fringes.

Focus.

Ver's fist crashed into Frank's nose.

Red lights danced in Frank's vision. He filled his burning lungs with oxygen.

Focus.

Ver's fingers gouged into Frank's gunshot wound. New waves of pain drenched his body. Vomit climbed his esophagus.

Focus.

Still, the blackness crept closer. No! Ver would not win. Red darts of rage flitted around the perimeter of the abyss. *Focus this energy.* With every ounce of resolve he could muster, Frank forced out the blackness. This was life and death, and it wasn't going to be he who died. He squinted.

Ver crawled toward the rifle. His large hand gripped it.

Focus.

Despite his useless right arm, Frank rocketed to his feet and pounced on Ver's back, landing his right knee into the center of Ver's back. He wrapped his left arm under Ver's neck and used his knee to push him farther into the choke-hold. Ver struggled to release Frank's hold, but Frank pulled harder.

Again, Ver's superior strength helped him escape the choke-hold and roll out from under Frank. Frank jumped back up into his stance. Ver stood and aimed the rifle at Frank.

Rosalita. Frank kicked as hard as he could. The shot exploded as the rifle soared through the air. Frank spun around and brought his elbow into Ver's nose. Ver's head lowered and his arms instinctively raised to protect his face. Frank spun again and side-kicked Ver under the chin. Ver's body left the ground, then fell hard to the earth. He was unconscious before he landed.

Gasping for breath, Frank stood over the general's body. Ver was breathing. He was alive. Frank's hand automatically went to his bleeding shoulder while his eyes scanned the scene. Ver's rifle lay off to one side; Frank's pistol to another. He recovered his pistol, and for a moment, a long moment, pointed it at Ver. It would be so easy to do him in. Just pull the trigger. But he wasn't a cold-blooded killer.

Frank shoved the pistol into his waistband beneath his shirt, then took Ver's radio and rifle, balancing them in his left hand, and hurried to his car. He had less than an hour to make it to the air base. *To Rosalita.*

The world shifted for a moment as Frank reached behind the front seat to grab his gym bag. His surroundings spun and he grabbed the steering wheel with his left hand to steady himself. He'd lost too much blood. Frank jerked open his bag and grabbed a towel. He shrugged off his shirt and did his best to evaluate his wound. He needed medical attention, but there wasn't time. *Just stop the bleeding.* Without the ability to move his shoulder or use his right arm, wrapping his shoulder tightly enough to stop the bleeding wasn't happening.

Think, Frank. You don't have much time. It wouldn't have to be wrapped tightly. If he could wad it around the wound and put his shirt back on, the pressure from the shirt should be enough to stop the bleeding. *Focus. Focus your chi.*

Gritting his teeth, Frank went through the motions. *Hang in there. You can't pass out now. Rosalita needs you.*

He wrestled with the towel and the shirt until he staunched the flow of blood. He slid into the driver's seat. The car started immediately and Frank headed down the mountain, toward Manila, driving like a one-armed, angry demon.

Chapter 52

February 27, 1986, 2:18 a.m.
Clark Air Force Base – The Philippines

Frank nudged the gearshift into neutral and slammed the brakes, sliding to a stop just before the guard at the airbase leveled his rifle. "Sorry," Frank shouted through the open window. He flashed his identification to the guard at the air base gates, squinting against the glare of the airman's flashlight. The man hopped back and motioned him through.

Frank drove to the second checkpoint, where a uniformed officer held up a hand to stop him. Again Frank struggled to simultaneously shift, steer, and hold out his ID with only his left hand.

The whomp-whomp-whomp of helicopter blades grew louder. Frank glanced up. A large military helicopter swooped low over him, paused for several seconds, and then veered off toward the tarmac.

"Mr. Young." The officer pointed over the hood of Frank's car. "Go through that gate and turn left. Drive directly onto the runway. Your plane is waiting for you."

Frank made the turn and checked his watch. Not a second to spare. Ahead of him, two jets sat on runways two hundred feet apart. The helicopter landed between the planes. Frank slowed and watched. Farther to his right, Tao waved frantically at him. Frank parked the car on the tarmac. He hoisted his bag onto his good shoulder. Although he was aware of Tao's frenzied movements to his right, he watched the helicopter on his left. The blades were still rotating, but no one was getting off.

Tao ran to Frank. "Come on! We must go!"

"Not until I get Rosalita."

Tao reached for Frank's shoulder. Frank dodged him, grabbing his shoulder.

Tao stepped back. "You hurt?"

"I'm okay."

"Then please, come on. We must get on the plane."

"No. I won't go until I see Rosalita."

"There's a bounty on your head. Move it, now. "

The helicopter door opened. A man in a uniform stood by the door and helped Imelda, four children, and an elderly woman step off.

Where was Rosalita?

The women and children, flanked by two bodyguards, hurried to the plane and climbed aboard.

A Mercedes—Ver's Mercedes that had been on the mountain—squealed across the tarmac and screeched to a stop between the Marcos plane and the helicopter. Motion near the helicopter caught Frank's eye. Another person hobbled off Marcos' helicopter. The air around Frank suddenly cooled, and splinters of ice penetrated his spine. General Ver had arrived.

Frank glared at him. Evidently they had rescued him by helicopter.

Tao stepped around Frank to his good shoulder. "We must go." He pushed Frank toward the plane on the right.

Marcos waved toward Frank, saying something that was drowned out by roaring engines. Ver nodded, and Marcos and Ver appeared to argue briefly, their hands animated. Together, they walked to the Mercedes.

Ver opened the back door. Rosalita majestically stepped out of the car, straightening her form-fitting pencil sheath as she did. She tossed the ends of a pashmina scarf behind her shoulder. Large, dark sunglasses covered her eyes.

Frank's heart skipped a beat. She was gorgeous—and she was safe, and soon they'd be leaving the Philippines together, perhaps for the last time.

Relief started at the top of his head and flowed through his body. He felt like he smiled with his whole body.

But why was she wearing sunglasses in the middle of the night?

Marcos took her hand.

"Frank, get on your plane," Tao said tersely.

"No. Not until I see Rosalita." He strode toward Rosalita.

Tao jumped in front of Frank. "No! You can't! Get on your plane!"

Frank shoved him out of the way and continued toward the car.

Rosalita pulled away from Marcos. Ver put his arm around her shoulders and directed her toward the Marcos' plane.

Frank broke into a jog. Rosalita jerked loose from Ver and turned toward Frank. As they ran toward each other, Ver hurried Marcos onto his plane, swung around, and then, as if in slow motion, pulled around the machine gun strung over his shoulder. He lifted it and aimed it at Frank.

"No!" Tao screamed.

Frank, almost to Rosalita, wiggled his gun free from his belt, cocked it, and, ignoring the hot flashes of white pain searing through his shoulder, aimed it at Ver.

"Stop!" Tao ran between Frank and Ver.

Rosalita, within a few feet of Frank and directly between Frank and Ver, froze.

Frank, his gun still pointed toward Ver, ran to Rosalita, then rotated her so his body protected her from Ver's machine gun.

Tao, between Ver and Frank, raised both arms with his fingers extended to the sky. "Both of you," he shouted to be heard above the engines, "Put down your guns."

Rosalita, behind Frank's injured shoulder, jumped around to again be in front of Frank.

"Get behind me!" Frank shouted.

"No. Ver won't shoot me."

"I can't shoot him with you between us."

"There won't be any shooting," Tao said.

Frank held out his left arm to hug her, gun still in hand, but she stepped back. "What happened to you?"

"I'm okay. I'll tell you all about it on the plane."

Rosalita's face twitched. He wished he could see her eyes. He reached for her sunglasses, but she pulled back out of his reach. "I'm not going with you, Frank. I have . . . I need to . . . I'm going with Imelda and Ferdinand."

Frank shook his head. "What?"

"I'm going to Honolulu with the Marcoses. It's the only way."

Frank dropped his arm. "The only way for *what?*" He stepped forward and this time removed the dark glasses. Her face was bruised and marred by a cut above her eye. "Oh, Rosalita. What has he done to you?" He gently touched her face and spoke softly. "I love you. I have always loved you." He stroked her chin with his finger. "You must come with me."

Rosalita dropped her head, then looked up, tears in her eyes, yet she half smiled, speaking barely above a whisper. "I love you, Frank, but wealth is power." The roaring engines nearly covered her words. "Things aren't always as they seem. I must go with them. Perhaps someday you will understand."

Frank shook his head as his throat clogged with emotion.

Rosalita slid against him, wrapped her arms around him, and dropped something weighty into his pants pocket. "For later," she whispered. "When you're on the plane." She kissed him on the cheek, then turned and regally strolled directly toward Ver's machine gun.

When she was even with Ver, she slapped the gun. Before Ver could react, she turned and strutted up the plane's stairs, disappearing into the belly of the noisy beast.

Ver repositioned his machine gun and glared at Frank, the airport spotlights making his eyes glow like embers of fire.

Frank remained in his stance, his gun still aimed at his nemesis.

Tao turned to face Frank and walked toward him. "Enough, Frank. Get on that plane."

"Get out of the way, Tao," Frank said.

Tao reached Frank. He grabbed Frank's arm and yanked it upward.

Frank sucked in a deep breath. He tried to twist away, nearly striking Tao with an elbow.

Tao's eyes glittered with something fresh, something vile and angry. Something Frank had never seen in the man before. "You don't want to do that," Tao said, his words staccato. The look—*was it hate?*—disappeared, quickly replaced with steely calm. "You are on a U.S. Air Force Base. Let it go."

Frank hesitated.

"C'mon." Tao's words were kinder now. "Let's get you out of here. Get some help for that shoulder." Tao continued to position himself between Ver and Frank until Frank was safely onboard.

Frank fell heavily into a window seat that allowed a full view of Marcos' plane—Rosalita's plane. Ver strode to Marcos' plane and saluted, then walked to his Mercedes. The engine on Marcos' jet screamed into high speed and the plane taxied down the runway and then lifted into the air. Rosalita was gone. Frank continued to watch the plane's lights as it gained altitude and slowly disappeared. She was gone.

Within moments, Frank's jet rolled down the runway and lifted into pre-dawn sky. Everything below shrank—the hangar, the airbase lights, people on the ground—and Ver. Frank watched until Ver became a pinprick.

Frank ran his left hand over his hair and continued staring out the window. All was still dark, except for a few lights flickering here and there.

A section of one mountain was fully lit with spotlights, and as they traveled over it, Frank realized it was the recovery operation at Montalban Gorge. *His gold.*

He sank back into his seat. He had lost everything. His gold. His true love. His legacy. Everything.

Tao gently touched Frank's arm. "You okay?" he asked quietly.

Frank nodded.

"Let me look at that shoulder." Tao set a first aid kit on the seat next to Frank.

Frank stood and unbuttoned his shirt the best he could.

"Let me get that." Tao helped with the final button, then eased Frank's arms out of the sleeves. He removed the blood-soaked towel. "You lost a lot of blood."

I lost my entire heart.

"I'll radio ahead and have an ambulance waiting for us as soon as we land in the good ol' U.S. of A."

"I'll be fine."

"It looks like the bullet just grazed your shoulder. I can't tell for sure, but it doesn't look like the bone was hit." Tao dabbed alcohol over the wound.

Frank sucked in his breath.

"Sorry." Tao turned toward the front of the plane and hollered to the flight attendant, "Get some whiskey for this man." As Tao's surprisingly gentle fingers continued to clean the wound, he spoke softly. "Your papa would be so proud of you." He covered the wound with gauze. "You completed your mission, and your country is better for it. Like Danilo's mission, few will ever know what you have done." He completed the bandage, then helped Frank into a clean shirt.

Finished with his task, Tao took the bloody shirt and towel to the back of the plane.

Frank stepped back to the window seat. As he did, he felt the weight of something in his pants pocket. He slipped his hand inside, wrapped his fingers around something cold, serpentine, and pulled it out. It took him a moment to recognize the thing once so familiar to him. A slight smile crept across Frank's face as he fingered his mother's sapphire rosary. He eased into the seat.

"Here you go, sir." The attendant handed Frank a tall glass filled to the brim with amber liquid.

Frank took a long drink.

Tao returned and slid into the seat next to Frank. "It's easy to dwell on what was lost on this mission," he said. "But trust me; much more was won than lost."

"How well did you know my father?"

Tao leaned back into the seat. "Well. Very well." He smiled. "There was a time he was the only person in this world I trusted. The only person."

Frank sipped his drink and looked out the window. The first hint of a new day glowed orange on the horizon. More relaxed than he'd been in years, Frank reclined his seat. He glanced at the Vietnamese man next to him. "Tao," he said, "tell me about my papa."

www.ingramcontent.com/pod-product-compliance
Lightning Source LLC
Chambersburg PA
CBHW062129170626
46813CB00002B/628